The
Fernández Case

The
Fernández Case

RICHARD WALTER

THE FERNÁNDEZ CASE

iUniverse books may be ordered through booksellers or by contacting:

iUniverse
1663 Liberty Drive
Bloomington, IN 47403
www.iuniverse.com
844-349-9409

ISBN: 978-1-6632-0854-5 (sc)
ISBN: 978-1-6632-0855-2 (e)

Print information available on the last page.

iUniverse rev. date: 09/30/2020

For Alexis, Dave, Monica, and Pat

One

I woke up just before the alarm sounded. Stripping off my pajamas, I quickly dressed in gray sweatpants and a burgundy and gold Washington Redskins jersey with Sammy Baugh's number thirty-three on it. Noting the time, 6:23 a.m., I hustled out of my apartment on P Street near DuPont Circle and walked briskly towards Connecticut Avenue. Vehicular traffic was already picking up for the morning rush hour, but the sidewalk was relatively free of pedestrians. It was Monday April 2, 1973 and dawn was breaking cool and crisp.

After about a minute of warm up exercises, I started jogging slowly down Connecticut towards Lafayette Square. Once there, I made my way past the White House and the Treasury Department on the Fifteenth Street side and then down to Constitution Avenue. I was stopped briefly by the light and I jogged in place for about thirty seconds. Once the light changed, I crossed Constitution onto the grounds of the Washington Monument and continued towards the Tidal Basin, which I planned to circle enough times to work up a good sweat. There I joined a scattered crowd of fellow joggers. Many were regulars and we exchanged grunts and nods as we passed one another. It was still a bit too early for the cherry blossoms, but I could see the buds about to bloom. With the steady thump of my sneakers providing the background, and with Thomas Jefferson looking on stoically, I took the opportunity, as I often did, to reflect on where I had been and where I was going.

Washington, D.C. is my hometown. I had been born and raised there. My father, Frank Corbett, Sr., also D.C.-born and bred, had been a lawyer for the State Department for most of his adult life. While he traveled abroad occasionally on department business, most of his work was in the

1

District. My mother, who was from Ohio, came to Washington during World War II as a secretary. Assigned to State, she met my father, who was just starting his career there after graduating with his law degree from the University of Virginia. They fell in love, got married and nine months later gave birth to their first child – me, Frank Corbett, Jr. Two siblings followed over the next several years; my younger brother, Henry, and a sister, Catherine.

My parents had a small three-bedroom house in the Northwest part of the District where they raised the three of us and where they still lived. My brother Henry was now in Philadelphia, finishing up his Masters in Business Administration at the Wharton School after graduating from Princeton *summa cum laude*. My sister Catherine was in her third year at Johns Hopkins, doing exceptionally well in their demanding pre-med program and a cinch to be admitted to Medical School. Both are hard-working, responsible, and well-embarked on successful career paths.

Me? I'm different. I was never a particularly serious student, either in high school or college. But I did do pretty well on the basketball court where I averaged twenty points a game for my high school team, won all-District honors, and managed to earn an athletic scholarship to George Washington University despite my mediocre grades. At GW, I spent most of my time playing basketball and trying to avoid a serious commitment to the classroom. I majored in history, but by now have forgotten most of what little I did learn. I did manage to graduate but if they had a category of "without honors," that would have fit me perfectly.

At loose ends after graduation, I decided to give law school a try. Following my father's footsteps, I somehow gained admission to the University of Virginia. I tried it for a year and actually did reasonably well. But my heart wasn't in it and, during the summer after my first year, decided not to return – much to my parents' disappointment.

When I made my decision not to go back to Charlottesville, it was the early nineteen sixties and we were beginning to ramp up our involvement in Vietnam. If I had stayed in law school I would have earned a student deferment. But I was now classified "1-A" and was a prime candidate to be drafted. I decided to beat my draft board to the punch and instead enlisted in the Army. Thanks to my college degree, no matter how undistinguished, I was eligible for Officers Candidate School. I did pretty well and earned my lieutenant's stripes before being sent off to Saigon. And, even though I had only completed one year of law school, the Army, in its infinite wisdom, determined that I should work in the Criminal Investigation Division. So instead of fighting the Viet Cong, I ended up policing our own soldiers.

Most of the work was routine. One case, however, involved a particularly nasty racket dreamed up by a rouge captain. He convinced a number of soldiers under his command to marry Vietnamese girls, mostly teenagers who were desperate for the chance to escape their war-ravaged country. The soldiers then sold their "wives" into prostitution with the proceeds divided among themselves and the captain. After several months of gathering evidence, we broke up the ring and sent the captain and his men to long terms in Leavenworth.

Exposing that racket and bringing the perpetrators to justice helped ease somewhat my growing disenchantment with the war. Even though I didn't get out of Saigon much, I knew that we were bombing the hell out of the country, both North and South, and carrying out atrocities like the My Lai massacre on a regular basis. I got my discharge at about the same time that story broke. When I returned to the States, I seriously debated joining the anti-war movement. But when I saw the excesses of the protestors – and particularly their demonization of the men with whom I had served – I decided that was a route I could not follow even though I agreed with many of their criticisms of what we were doing in Southeast Asia.

My military experience left me with a dislike for chains of command, paper work, and the stifling of individual initiative. It did, however, provide me with a good grasp of investigative techniques. I enjoyed ferreting out clues and tracking down the guilty. A career in law enforcement seemed attractive, but I was reluctant to commit myself, not sure that I would always agree with the laws and law makers. A career in the police, the FBI, or the CIA seemed too close to the things that I had disliked about the Army.

At loose ends after my discharge, I used what little pay I had accumulated to hit the road in what might be called "a journey of self-discovery." After bumming around the United States for a while, I wandered into Mexico, where I picked up a smattering of Spanish. Re-entering into Texas I worked for a while as a farm hand and then in the oil fields. Europe was next.

I shipped over as a merchant seaman. I used my pay from that to spend several months getting to know as much as I could about the various countries I visited. I did a lot of reading, hiking, and talking with people from all walks of life. In Germany I met up with a group of university students who were on their way to South America for volunteer work in Peru. I still had enough money left to purchase an airfare to Lima and went along with them on what promised to be a trip that combined adventure with doing good. We ended up in a small village in the Andes where we pitched in by helping to build schools, plant gardens, and improve sanitation. It was rewarding work and my Spanish improved to near native fluency. But after nine months, I felt that I had done as much as I could and it was time to return home.

Back in D.C., I ended up living with my parents while I still tried to figure out what to do with my life. My parents were supportive, but I knew they were concerned about their eldest son's seemingly aimless path in life. I found a job in construction that paid reasonably well and lost myself for a while in the physical routine or pouring concrete, carrying bricks, and hammering nails. One night, I went out with some GW buddies and as we drank our beers one of them suggested – almost as a joke – that maybe I should think about becoming a private detective like the ones you saw in movies or on television. "That would really be cool," he said.

At the moment, I didn't think much about it. But later that night, back at home in bed, I thought *What the hell. Why not give it a try?* It would allow me to do what I had enjoyed doing in the Army without being caught up with all the rules and regulations of a large bureaucratic institution. In the morning, before I left for the construction site, I called an old family friend, Fred Matthews, who had been an FBI agent for as long as my father had been at State. I told him what I was thinking about career-wise and he suggested we meet for lunch to discuss it further.

I met Fred around noon at Bassins, a friendly neighborhood bar and grill on Connecticut. Fred looked exactly like Central Casting's idea of one of Mister Hoover's agents: Clean-shaven, short-brown hair carefully combed and parted on the right, white shirt, narrow black tie, dark suit, black shoes polished so that you could see your face in them, trim build, and a firm, no-nonsense handshake. After we both ordered hamburgers and fries, I began to ask him for advice as to how I might become a private investigator. He was not encouraging.

"It's a lousy business Frank – dull, routine work for people who should be seeing a psychiatrist rather than an investigator." The look of scorn on his usually expressionless face showed clearly what he thought of my would-be profession. "But listen son, if you want a career in law enforcement, what about the Bureau? You have a year of law school and military experience. Try to finish up your degree and I'll see what I can do…."

I waved away the suggestion. "Thanks Fred, but I had enough of wearing a uniform and following the rules in the Army. I want to be on my own."

Fred shrugged and realized that it was no sense arguing further. Sighing deeply, he said "Well, if that's the way you want it Frank, I'll do what I can to help. I can get you in touch with some former agents who have gone out on their own. They might even be able to send a few clients your way once you get established."

Fred finished his lunch and left in something of a rush, mumbling something about paper work he had to get back to. But he repeated his promise to give me a hand. I thanked him for his time and his kind offer.

Fred kept his promise. He put me in touch with several experienced private detectives, who helped me get into a crash course on criminal investigation and shepherded me through the necessary paperwork to get my PI license. Nine months after my lunch with Fred Mathews, I opened my own office on G Street on the third floor of a building next to the downtown YMCA. The lettering on the door, "Frank Corbett, Private Investigator," lacked the panache of "Spade and Archer," but it was a start for what I hoped would finally be a career path that would lead to some financial stability and an end to my lack of purpose in life.

With my travel and linguistic background, I planned to appeal to Washington's already sizable and growing foreign community – embassy personnel, people working for the World Bank and the International Monetary Fund, journalists, businessmen. Specialization, I had been told by my mentors, was now the way to go. Just like the family doctor, the detective who handled all kinds of cases was fast becoming an endangered species. My father, who clearly had his reservations about my career choice, nonetheless promised he would try to send work my way if any of his many contacts in the local diplomatic community were in need of my services.

My first weeks, as I had been warned, were pretty rough. I did get a few clients referred to me through Fred Matthews and his friends. But after interviewing them, I began to think that Fred and his pals were putting me through some sort of fraternity initiation to see if I had the right stuff to become a brother. My first potential client was a sixty-year old man who described himself as an "inventor" and who was convinced that an unnamed and mysterious "they" were out to steal his plans for an ultra-secret, ultra-potent weapon that would neutralize all threats to our national security. I politely showed him to the door, with the excuse that I was too inexperienced to take on such a "complicated" case.

My second would-be client was a timid middle-aged man who told me that his wife was planning to smother him with his own pillow while he slept. Perspiring into his handkerchief, which he held constantly at his forehead, he explained to me at great length and in great detail the many indignities his wife had heaped upon him in their twenty years of marriage. I told him that there was little I could do without something specific to work on. He seemed almost relieved and insisted on paying me a small retainer even though I hadn't done anything more than listen to him, take some notes, and nod sympathetically for about forty-five minutes. After he closed the door quietly behind him, I was beginning to think that Fred Matthews had been right about most clients needing a psychiatrist more than they needed an investigator. I pondered whether instead of the two chairs I had in front of my desk I should install a couch.

Three weeks after opening my office, I finally had a case that required some leg work and for which I received a decent fee. Fred knew a couple in Chevy Chase whose fifteen year old daughter had run away from home. They hadn't heard from her in several weeks and the local police had been unable – or unwilling – to track her down. Fred referred them to me, figuring I might be young enough to get information from teenagers. After talking with her high-school friends, I was able to locate the daughter. She had ended up in New York City, strung out on drugs and sharing a filthy pad with a group of would-be Hippies. After I identified myself, she told me she never wanted to see her parents again. She also accused me of being a pimp for the capitalist system representing that proto-typical bourgeois institution – the family.

Since my job was only to track her down, not bring her back against her will, I left New York and reported what I had found to her mother and father. They did not seem terribly surprised by the news. I expected them to ask me to return to New York and to bring their daughter back by force if necessary. But instead they said they would handle things from now on and that my assistance was no longer required. I didn't press the matter. I had done my job and the rest was up to them. While the father wrote a check that provided me with my first sizable fee, they had an argument so bitter and so acrimonious that I understood why their daughter had fled the home. I also wondered if they would bother to try to get their daughter to return – or simply abandon her to her fate. I figured it was probably fifty-fifty either way.

What I had earned on that case allowed me finally to move out of my parents' home and into my small apartment. It wasn't much, but like my office, it was mine.

Over the next few months I got more cases involving teenage runaways. I was able to locate most of them and began to get something of a reputation in that line of work. And it was, unfortunately for the larger society but fortunately for me, a growing field. Increasing numbers of young people from comfortable, middle-class families were leaving home and heading out on their own. Tracking them down did not often provide the kind of challenge and excitement that I had envisioned when I got my PI license, but it certainly helped pay the rent. Still, I hoped for more.

With these thoughts in mind I made my last lap around the Tidal Basin and headed back to my apartment. Weaving my way through the growing pedestrian traffic, I tried to keep a look of serious purpose on my face. Jogging had become quite respectable, engaged in by young and old, men and women. An awareness of the need to keep physically fit had become almost an obsession with many. Nevertheless, I always felt a bit conspicuous as I shuffled past the Brooks-Brothers crowd on their way to deal with the serious business of managing the nation's and the world's affairs. They were usually too engrossed in the upcoming problems of the day to pay much attention to a tall, sneaker-clad young man loping along to the beat of his own drummer.

Two

I got back to my apartment around seven thirty. After I shaved and took a quick shower. I fixed my usual breakfast of two eggs over easy, three slices of bacon, toast, orange juice and coffee. What to wear to the office had originally been something of a dilemma. I would have preferred a sweatshirt, jeans, and sneakers. But my mentors had informed me that appearances were important and recommended a sober business suit, white shirt, and tie – and maybe even a fedora to give me that Bogart look. But that sounded too much like the unofficial uniform of the FBI for my tastes. Instead, I compromised on pressed khakis, black loafers, a button-down Oxford blue dress shirt, and a charcoal gray blazer – no tie.

Thus attired, I arrived at my office just before nine. I had no appointments, but made it a practice to stick to a nine-to-five routine. I opened the door and found some fliers, brochures, and a few bills at my feet, the residue of the Saturday delivery. I picked up the assorted mail and shuffled through it hoping for an envelope from my most recent client with the promised check for services rendered. This had been a case where I had not only located the wayward teenager but actually convinced her to return to her parents. I had hoped their gratitude would produce a little extra in appreciation, but so far there was no envelope with their return address.

When I opened up for business, my buddies had kidded me that my first move should be to hire a curvaceous secretary I could call "sweetheart" and who would cater to my every need. That certainly had its appeal and I often daydreamed about the possibility. Maybe in the future but right now it was out of the question. I would have to take care of all the menial office chores – answering correspondence, paying the bills, maintaining the case files – myself. These chores also included keeping a large coffee pot going throughout the day, mostly for myself but also to offer to any clients who passed through the door. There was also the question of where a secretary might sit – aside from on my lap of course. My office was only one room, and not a very large one at that. I suppose that if the time came, I could have a partition put up to divide the room in two. On the other hand, by the time I had the funds to hire a secretary I might be able to afford larger accommodations. Perhaps even a suite of offices. It didn't hurt to dream.

I put the mail on my desk and opened one of the two windows that looked out onto G Street. The day was starting to warm, the temperature forecast to hit the seventies so I let the incipient spring breezes make their way in.

Strapped for money, I hadn't been able to spend much on office furniture. Most of it was bought from government surplus. My aged desk was solid oak, although when purchased it was covered with enough varnish to sink a battleship. It probably dated from the Johnson administration – Andrew, not Lyndon. I spent some laborious days stripping and staining it and was pleased with the result. The rich texture of the natural wood was fully restored and added some luster to the place. On the top of the desk I had placed "In" and "Out" boxes, both of which were currently empty. The two wooden chairs for clients in front of the desk had received the same restoration treatment and I had bought new padding for them to provide some comfort. Against the wall to my right as I sat behind the desk were two standard issue drab green four-drawer metal filing cabinets. At the moment, only one of the top drawers was partially filled with case files. Against the wall to my left was a cherry-wood side table that my mother had rescued from the basement of our house and had donated to the cause. It, too, had undergone some cleaning and was quite presentable. On it rested my twelve-cup coffee maker nestled among a few of the trophies I had been awarded for my exploits on the basketball court. I had been hesitant to display them, but one of my mentors argued that my jock background could be an attraction for clients and I acceded. So far, they hadn't done me much good. They were about the only adornments in the room other than a framed copy of my college diploma and an enlarged copy of my PI license.

I followed my usual morning office routine. I poured water that I kept in a covered pitcher on the side table into my coffee maker, filling it to the twelve-cup limit. I then opened a fresh can of *Folgers* and took a moment to appreciate the aroma before putting a generous portion into the brew basket and plugging in the machine. The red light went on and I was immediately rewarded with some satisfying gurgling noises that told me the maker was hard at work. Soon the smell of freshly-brewed coffee filled the room. As soon as the amber light went on informing me that the brewing process was complete, I grabbed my GW mug and filled it to the brim. No cream and sugar for me, although I did have some of those awful packets of fake cream available for any client desperate enough to need them along with some sugar cubes that I had purloined from the drugstore on the ground floor. Clutching my mug I sat down behind my desk and took my first sips, savoring the fresh brew.

I had economized on all the furnishings in my office except for the chair behind the desk. I figured I would be spending a lot of time sitting in it and I needed something that could accommodate my six feet three inches and provide me with the required support and comfort. So I spared no expense in purchasing a spanking new large-sized high-back swivel chair padded in brown leather. It was on casters that allowed me to move smoothly back and forth and reclined so that I could lean back and place my feet on the desk for reading.

That was the position I now assumed. The coffee mug rested on my desk blotter so as not to mar the surface I had restored with such painstaking care and within easy reach of my left hand. In my right hand I held a copy of *The Washington Post* purchased from the newsstand in the building lobby on my way up to my office. Before I put my feet on the desk, I removed my loafers so as not to leave any scuff marks.

I unfolded the *Post* and began to read it, gradually draining my coffee mug as I did so. *This isn't so bad*, I thought to myself, *a nice way to pass the early morning hours.* For a second I wondered how Fred Matthews was spending his morning and that brought a quick grin. But it faded quickly when I realized that Fred and his fellow agents were receiving a steady salary no matter what the work load might be. I, on the other hand, was more like a salesman working on commission and perhaps I should do more to try to rustle up some clients.

I pushed that thought away for the moment, refilled my mug, and returned to the *Post*. Most of the news coverage had to do with the evolving

Watergate scandal, which the *Post* had played a major role in uncovering. A local judge, John Sirica, was trying to get White House aides to testify and from what I could tell a complicated legal tug of war was ensuing with neither side currently enjoying the advantage.

Engrossed in the details of the latest developments in the unfolding scandal, I almost didn't hear the faint sound of knocking on my door. *Could it actually be a client?* Those who had come to my office before had always called first. Maybe it was a mistake. Maybe they had the wrong door. Maybe my ears and my imagination were playing tricks on me. But no, there was the knocking again and through the frosted glass that formed the top half of the door I could see the outlines of a human shape which appeared to be female.

I thought about crying out "Come on in" but then remembered that the door had an automatic lock that I had forgotten to reset. Hurriedly, I put down my coffee cup, folded my newspaper, and struggled into my loafers. "Just a minute," I called out. "I'm coming." This was an occasion where a secretary would have come in handy.

When I opened the door standing before me was a spectacularly beautiful young woman. I had a momentary flash to all those mystery novels I had read and movies I had seen where the detective was hired by a lovely female. Now, it seemed, was my turn. For a second I reminded myself that in many of those stories the beautiful client turned out to be guilty herself of some horrendous crime. But it was far too early to make any judgments of that sort.

"Mr. Corbett?" she asked with an inquisitive look on her face. Even though I was reasonably presentable, perhaps I wasn't quite what she expected.

I tried to think of something witty to say, just like Sam Spade or Philip Marlowe, but the best I could come up with was "Yes. That's me. And you are…?"

She gave me a shy smile and extended her hand. "Elena. Elena Fernández."

I took her hand in mine and felt a tingle go through my body. "Won't you please come in," I said, standing to one side as she passed through, catching a whiff of her perfume as she did. While her back was to me momentarily, I ran my fingers through my unruly brown hair, hoping to straighten out the tangled mess that I usually paid little attention to. The current fashion among men of my age was plenty of hair, both on top and in front. I, however, remained clean-shaven and kept my hair off my shoulders. My choices had little to do with appearance and more with what I found easiest to maintain.

I pulled out one of the chairs for Miss – at least I hoped it was Miss – Fernández and waited for her to sit down before I returned to my own spot behind the desk.

Once we were both seated, I got the ball rolling by asking her if she would like a cup of coffee. "That's most kind of you Mister Corbett," she said, "But I am not a big coffee drinker. Perhaps if you have some tea....?

"I'm afraid not," I said apologetically, and made a mental note to stock up on some tea bags for future use. As I did so, I took a closer look at my would-be client. She had wavy dark hair, parted in the middle and falling in waves down to her shoulders, large dark eyes, clear olive skin, sparkling white teeth, full luscious lips, and, from what I could tell, curves in all the right places. As she had passed me on the way to her chair, I had guessed that she was about five and a half feet tall. She was dressed soberly in a gray suit, cream-colored blouse, and shiny black shoes with medium heels. She had on only enough makeup to accentuate rather than detract from her beauty. I took all this in as quickly as I could. After all, I was a trained investigator and cataloguing details was an essential part of the job.

"Well Miss...." I raised a quizzical eyebrow and she nodded affirmatively at the unspoken question. I suppressed a satisfied smile. "*Miss* Fernández. How can I be of assistance?"

A serious look crossed her face. "It's about my brother Manuel. He has been missing now for almost three weeks and Fred Matthews suggested that you might be able to find out what has happened to him. He said that you had some experience in tracking down missing young people." *Good old Fred*, I thought to myself. "And," she continued, "as you might have noticed, I am a foreigner – from Argentina – and Mister Matthews said you spoke Spanish and knew something about South America...."

I *had* noticed. Her name, her looks, and her accented speech were all telltale clues. I also noticed that there was tension in her voice and in her posture and tears were beginning to form at the corner of her beautiful eyes. To set her at ease, and to prove my bona fides, I suggested that we switch to Spanish and encouraged her to continue with her story.

She gave me a warm smile and I could see her shoulders relax a bit. "Thank you Mister Corbett." Then, wrinkling her brow in concentration, she said, "My brother is – was – studying medicine at Duke University." I was impressed; maybe not Johns Hopkins, but still one of the best medical schools in the country.

"When did you last hear from your brother?"

"It was about a month ago. I called him to see if he would be coming to Washington during his spring break. But he told me that he was involved in a special research project and couldn't spare the time." She briefly looked down into her lap and bit her lower lip before returning her gaze to me. "Manuel is always honest with me. But this time, I knew that he was lying. It wasn't any 'special project' that was keeping him from visiting. He just didn't want to spend a week with our father."

At this point, I was tempted to interrupt but I resisted and let her continue the story. "That was the last time I heard from him. When I called again later in the week to see if I could change his mind there was no answer. I didn't think much of it at the time. I knew that Manuel often had to stay on campus well into the night. But then a few days later Manuel's roommate called to ask me if *I* knew where Manuel was. He had been away from their apartment visiting his parents and when he got back there was no sign of my brother." She choked back a sob. "That's when I really got worried. I called the Dean of the Medical School to ask him if he might know where Manuel was and he told me he was just about to call my parents himself. Manuel had not been to class for a week, had not called in sick, and was, apparently, nowhere to be found. This is all totally out of character for him."

I took a handkerchief out of a pocket in my blazer and handed it over the desk as tears made their way down Elena's cheeks. I gave her a moment to compose herself. Then I asked the logical question. "Did you contact the local police?"

"Yes I did. I called both the University police and the Durham police. They said they carried out what they told me were thorough investigations but could find no trace of Manuel. It seemed as though he had simply vanished without telling anyone and no one had seen him leave. They told me they would continue to look into the matter, but they were not optimistic." She dabbed at her eyes with my handkerchief.

"So you contacted the FBI and Fred Matthews...."

She interrupted, putting up her right hand palm out. "Yes. And please let me explain," she said, putting my handkerchief in her lap. "I am a second-year law student at Georgetown." I raised my eyebrows. There are not yet that many women in law school, much less at one of the quality of Georgetown. This was a pretty impressive pair - Elena and her brother. But why train yourself in our legal system unless you were planning to stay in the U.S.? Reading my expression and my mind, she explained, "I have decided that I want to stay in the United States after I graduate and either practice law with a private firm or, more likely, work for the U.S. government after I become a citizen. And to see if government work might be my choice, I took an internship at the Department of Justice last summer..."

"And that's when you met Fred Matthews."

"Yes. I helped him and his team with some of their investigations."

"So when your brother went missing...."

"Yes. After the police in North Carolina told me they could find no trace of Manuel, I got in touch with Mister Matthews." She wrinkled her brow and again chewed briefly on her luscious lower lip. I was doing my best to concentrate on her story, but was finding it difficult to ignore her beauty and keeping thoughts that had little to do with what had happened to her brother from intruding. "He was very sympathetic and said he would look into it but that there was little he could do until some evidence appeared that showed Manuel might have been kidnapped, making it a federal crime." Again, she anticipated my question, "And if he has been kidnapped, so far there has been no contact from the kidnappers, so...."

"So at the moment it's a missing persons' case outside of the FBI's jurisdiction."

"Yes. Exactly. And that's why Mister Matthews recommended that I come to see you Mister Corbett. He said that you had experience in locating runaways and he thought you might be able to help me."

I took a minute to digest what she had told me. "You said some tension had developed between your brother and your father. Do you think that has anything to do with Manuel's disappearance?"

She considered for a moment. "I don't really think so…"

'What was the cause of the tension? Would it have been sufficient for your brother to give up his studies and take off without a word?"

She shook her head. "No. No. Let me explain." She leaned forward. "My father is a professional diplomat. He currently is the *chargé d'affaires* at the Argentine Embassy. He has been working here in Washington for the past several years after serving in various other posts around the world. Our embassy in Washington is considered the most important posting in our foreign service. So for my father, this is a very significant and prestigious assignment. When he got the post, Manuel was enrolled in the Faculty of Medicine – or as you would say – the Medical School of the University of Buenos Aires and was just finishing up his second year."

She paused for a minute and I asked her if she would like some water. She said yes and I poured her some from the pitcher. She took a couple of sips and continued her story. "The universities in Argentina are very – how should I put it? – *active* politically. Manuel was not openly involved in politics himself. He was sensitive to the fact that if he were to join a student political organization or take a leadership role it would reflect badly on our father. But Manuel did have friends who were active in leftist groups and was not totally unsympathetic to their ideas - although he did not approve of their methods. But my father was afraid that somehow Manuel would become 'infected' by the leftist ideas and movements that were predominant in the school and arranged instead for him to transfer to Duke. That took a bit of doing," she explained. "Manuel did not have the normal undergraduate degree and all the usual pre-med requirements. But my father argued that the elite high school he had attended in Buenos Aires was the equivalent of the first two years of college here and that the two years of medical training he already received made up the other two. Plus, Manuel had excellent grades and scored in the top percentile in the standard entrance exams. Whether those arguments carried the day, or my father was able 'to pull a few strings,' Manuel was admitted to Duke as a third year student.

My father was very happy with this solution and so, at first, was Manuel. While my brother missed Argentina and his friends, he was initially very appreciative of the opportunity to study at a first-class medical school - and one that was free from the kind of political turmoil that often interrupted his studies at home. But it didn't take long for him to become disillusioned."

Elena caught my puzzled expression. "Let me explain. Manuel is not like most medical students here, who plan to follow a career path that will make them financially comfortable – even rich. He believes that medicine should serve all the people not just the well-to-do. And he also believes in dealing directly with the kinds of illness that affect the majority of the poor in our country and in the rest of Latin America – many of which are rooted in things like inadequate housing, poor nutrition, and illiteracy – and that those social and economic conditions must be addressed as well."

"So at Duke," I interrupted, "he mixed with wealthy kids who were thinking more of what their profession could do for them than what they could do for others. And that probably strengthened his leftist sympathies. Just the opposite result of what your father had hoped."

Elena smiled. "Yes indeed Mister Corbett. You have it exactly. Manuel continued to value the training he received and the professors with whom he worked. But he became increasingly – how do you say it? – *turned off* – by the attitudes of his fellow students."

A random thought dredged out of the back of mind suddenly hit me. "If I recall correctly, wasn't Che Guevara a doctor from Argentina?"

She seemed a little surprised by my knowledge. "Yes. That's true. And Manuel often speaks of Che with some admiration, although I don't think…."

"You don't think your brother would go so far as to drop out of medical school and join a revolutionary group in the hills somewhere?"

My question seemed to give her food for thought. After about ten seconds, she shook her head. "No. That does not sound like Manuel. As much as he wants to see fundamental change occur, he firmly believes that it should take place without violence. We have seen – and are still seeing – too much violence in our country. No. I cannot imagine Manuel taking up a gun and becoming a *guerrillero*. I am sure that he is still devoted to using his training as a physician to improve conditions in our country in a peaceful manner."

While she said this with some confidence, I could see the worry in her eyes. I didn't want to push the issue, but perhaps she had her own doubts. Maybe something she didn't know about had pushed her brother over the edge and, even as we were speaking he was camping out with his fellow revolutionaries in some God-forsaken part of Argentina.

"I'm sorry Señorita Fernández…."

"Please call me Elena Mister Corbett."

I grinned. "Okay Elena. And please call me Frank." She smiled and nodded. "I'm afraid that I interrupted you Elena. You were telling me about the tension between your brother and your father."

"Yes – uh – Frank. During the Christmas vacation they had a terrible row. Manuel revealed his political sentiments and the discussion became extremely heated. They had had some arguments before, but nothing like this. My brother berated my father for his 'bourgeois' background and chastised him for working on behalf of a military government which served only the interests of the privileged and for the past seven years has ruled Argentina in a brutal and authoritarian manner. Manuel went even further, claiming that the military regimes had engaged in torture and assassination. At one point he said that my father's own hands were stained with blood."

There was a look of pain and sadness on Elena's face as she spoke. "My father was enraged. I've never seen him so angry. He defended himself as a professional diplomat who served whatever government was in power, democratic or non-democratic. His job was to represent the best interests of our country regardless of the nature of the regime. He also pointed out that our 'bourgeois' background was what allowed Manuel to study medicine at a premier private university. That only seemed to anger my brother more, and he lashed out, calling my father a 'lackey' of global capitalism – and worse. And my father rejoined with some epithets of his own, calling my brother a "Communist dupe" and an ingrate. Really Frank, I think if my mother and I had not been present, they would have come to blows."

Except for some of the details, it seemed a familiar story. Most of the runaways I had tracked down had left home after a violent family argument. I began to wonder if Manuel's disappearance might be something of a delayed reaction to the falling out he had had with his father.

"We all calmed down after that explosion," Elena continued. "But the breach wasn't healed. Manuel went back to Durham the next day with the excuse that he had some experiments that he needed to monitor – but we all knew that wasn't true. Since then, he and my father have had no communications that I know of and I've already told you about Manuel's refusal to visit us over his spring break."

"You must have informed your parents about Manuel's disappearance," I said.

"Yes. Of course. And my mother is terribly worried."

"And your father?"

I thought she was going to let the tears flow again, but she held them back. "I can't really tell. He claims that Manuel is engaged in some kind of childish game just to spite him and that he will turn up eventually. He also has refused to get involved in trying to find my brother. I suppose it's because of the possible consequences that involvement might have for his own position at the embassy where he is next in line to be the ambassador." She did little to hide her disapproval as she said this. "But underneath, I am sure that he is as concerned as my mother and I. He is a professional diplomat, trained not to show emotion; something that often carries over to his family. But even though he tries to hide it, I've seen some signs of real strain under the surface. And he has been unusually abrupt with me and my mother."

I nodded with what I hoped was a look of sympathy. Then I asked, "Do you think your father might be right? That Manuel is just trying to exact some revenge for the argument they had?"

This time there was no hesitation. "No," she said with conviction. "I know my brother well enough to know that he would never do such a thing, no matter what my father might say. Some kind of elaborate hoax! No. Never. It has to be something else although I have to admit I cannot think of what it might be."

"I presume that the reason *you* are here rather than your parents is because of what you have just told me. That at this point your father doesn't want to get involved." I then explained how in all my previous cases it had been the parents who had initiated the search for the missing child.

"Yes Frank. That is why I am here to ask your help instead of my mother and father. In fact," she added, "my father has expressly told me *not* to pursue the matter. He has no idea that I am here talking to you. And if he did know…" She shook her head from side to side as though she could hardly believe the words that came out of her mouth.

I again nodded sympathetically, but found the actions of the elder Fernández strange to say the least. No matter what the political disagreements and generational tensions I couldn't buy the idea that a father would be so unconcerned as to write off his son's mysterious disappearance as some kind of a prank. But, I reminded myself, in my short career as an investigator I had run into plenty of parental behavior that was hard to fathom. The days of *Ozzie and Harriet* and *Leave it to Beaver* were long gone.

Taking a legal pad from my top drawer, I held up my hand palm out and asked Elena, "Could you give me a few moments to make some notes? We've covered a lot of ground and I want to make sure I don't forget anything important."

"Certainly Frank," she replied with a smile. "Does that mean you will take the case?"

I smiled back. "As it happens, I'm available. So yes, I'll do what I can to find out what happened to your brother. But we need to go over some details. First, there is the matter of..."

"Of your fees," she interrupted.

"Yes. I need a two hundred dollar retainer and I charge fifty dollars a day plus expenses."

"That will not be a problem," she assured me, taking out a check book.

Before she could begin writing, I held up my hand again to stop her. "I meant to ask you. Has anyone in Argentina seen your brother? Could it be that he has gone back there for some reason?" Again I was thinking of the guerrilla-fighter-in-the-hills scenario.

Elena shook her head. "No. I have called every friend of ours I could think of and nobody has seen him."

"The reason I asked is that if I cannot locate your brother here in the States, the next logical place to look would be Argentina. That is, unless you wanted to hire a local investigator there. If I went, it would add considerably to your expenses."

She didn't hesitate. "No. I agree. You may have to go to Argentina. And that is why, when Fred Matthews recommended you, I was pleased to learn that you knew Spanish and had lived in South America. Plus I don't really know any private investigators in Argentina and would have to go there myself to interview them. All of which would take more time and money. So," she said with a smile, "If you are willing to take the case, I am willing to cover all the expenses, no matter where it may take you."

I wasn't going to argue. And I wasn't about to inquire where the money she would pay me would come from. I hoped that somehow it came out of her father's accounts and not hers. But as my mentors had advised me, sometimes it's best not to ask too many questions. While I was attracted enough to Elena to have undertaken the assignment free of charge – buckling up my armor, grabbing my sword and shield, and mounting my trusty steed – I simply couldn't afford the grand gesture. Now if I were a highly successful PI with the suite and the secretary I envisioned, maybe I could take on a case like this *pro bono*. But I wasn't. I needed the money and couldn't let my heart rule my head.

While Elena wrote out her check, I extracted two copies of a standard contract form from my desk drawer and filled in the blanks. When she turned over the check, I gave her the copies to sign and told her to keep one and return the other to me.

Once we had gotten that paperwork out of the way, I asked Elena to suggest people at Duke – fellow students, friends, and professors – who might have some clues as to her brother's whereabouts. She gave me the names and phone numbers of Manuel's roommate and the Medical School Dean along with a few others and I added them to my note pad. She also gave me her own phone number and told me to call her at any time if I had more questions. I smiled and nodded, enjoying the prospect of keeping in touch with her.

Glancing at my watch, I saw that it was almost eleven. "Listen Elena," I said. "I'm going to leave for Durham as soon as I can. If all goes well and I am able to meet with the people whose names you have given me, I'll try to report back to you sometime tomorrow evening. How does that sound?"

"That sounds fine Frank. I'll expect your call."

She stood to leave, straightening her skirt and grabbing her purse. She extended her hand across the desk and I again took it in mine, this time giving it what I hoped was a reassuring squeeze and holding on to it a beat or two longer than necessary. She didn't seem to mind and gave me a smile in return. I thought about giving her some verbal reassurances as well but didn't want to raise any false hopes. While my brain was thinking of logical scenarios as to what had happened to her brother, my gut was telling me that this was not going to be a simple case. I shared Elena's fears that something serious had happened to her brother and that it was going to take a lot of digging – and a lot of luck – to find out what it was.

I stood up and went around the desk to escort Elena out of the office. Opening the door for her, I decided to forget my reservations and offer a few upbeat words. "Listen Elena," I said with what I hoped was a comforting smile, "I've had quite a few cases that have been similar to yours and in every instance I've been able to locate the missing person. I'm glad you came to me and I promise I'll do everything I can to find your brother." A bit exaggerated perhaps, but close to the truth. Of the dozen or so runaways I had been hired to track down, only one had eluded me.

"Thank you Frank. I'm sure that you will. Please do call me tomorrow evening," she said. Then, with a serious look, she added, "no matter what the news might be."

"Sure thing Elena. *Hasta mañana.*"

"*Hasta mañana,*" she replied with a smile. As she turned and made her way down the hallway I spent a few seconds to take in the view of her swaying hips. Once she had turned the corner and was out of sight, I closed the office door behind me and went back to my desk to go over the notes I had made and to plan my next moves. After a couple of minutes, it suddenly occurred to me that my new client had not returned my handkerchief. She probably had forgotten, caught up in the emotion of telling me her story. Whatever the reason, I was not displeased. If she kept the handkerchief, it was no great loss. I had plenty more. On the other hand, if I wanted to remind her of it, that would offer another chance for a face-to-face meeting – and perhaps an opportunity to move beyond the investigator-client relationship to something more personal.

As I added details to my legal pad, I made a note to call Fred Matthews and thank him for the referral. This case, I thought to myself, had the potential of being far from routine and closer to the kind of investigation that I had envisioned when I got into this business. I owed Fred one. Almost perversely, I hoped that my trip to Durham would not be successful and that Manuel Fernández's mysterious disappearance would remain just that – mysterious. That would mean a chance to travel to Argentina to see if I could pick up any clues there. That was a prospect I found immensely appealing.

Three

Before heading to North Carolina, I decided to try to find out more about the Fernández family – especially the father. I called an old GW friend at the State Department, Dwight Whalen, who was on the Latin American Desk and might be able to give me some background information. His secretary answered and after I identified myself she put me through to Dwight. I told him about the case and asked if I could see him as soon as possible. To my surprise, he agreed to meet within the hour, asking me to come down to Foggy Bottom as soon as I could. I had expected some excuse about his being swamped with work or having some important lunch date he couldn't break. Instead, I thought I detected a tone of interest and even some concern in his voice. Later on I would berate myself for not picking up on the clue his response offered.

I had known Dwight during our four years together at George Washington. We were not what I would call "best friends" but we had forged something of a bond by being on the same basketball team, first the freshmen squad and then the varsity. Outside of the basketball court, we didn't have much contact. Dwight lived in a nice furnished apartment close to campus while I lived at home. It didn't take long for Dwight to tell me that he came from a wealthy family and had attended an elite prep school. I never could understand why - with his credentials and his wealth - he hadn't gone to an Ivy League school. He had the grades for it. But for some reason he had chosen George Washington. Although he never admitted it, I think the choice of a "lesser" school was a show of minor rebellion against his father, who was a successful banker and who had expected Dwight to follow in his footsteps. Dwight, however, had determined early on that he wanted a career in the Foreign Service and GW, being in the nation's capital, made sense in that regard. When I first met Dwight and told him my father worked at State, I saw his eyes light up although he never openly pushed me to put in a good word for him with my dad. He was determined to make it on his own.

If Dwight did rebel against his father, it was the only trace of non-conformist behavior from him I ever saw. At GW he took all the right courses, made all the right grades, wore all the right clothes, and dated all the right girls. Playing guard on our basketball team where I was a forward, Dwight rarely made a bad pass and took only the uncontested shot. He didn't score a lot but in each of his four years he had the highest percentage of made baskets and free throws on the team. He practiced hard and played hard but never lost his cool. He didn't celebrate much if we won and didn't get down if we lost. He never got in a fight, something I could not claim, and rarely hit the floor in a scramble for a loose ball or rebound. He was so methodical and unemotional that we kidded him that he didn't even need to shower after a game. While the rest of us were usually drenched in sweat Dwight's uniform was often as dry at the end of the game as it had been at the beginning. I wondered if by force of will he kept himself aloof from normal bodily functions.

Ultimately, Dwight's disciplined life earned rewards. He graduated at the top of our class with a double major in political science and economics. He went on to get a Masters Degree in International Relations from Georgetown and earned a perfect score on the demanding Foreign Service Entrance Exam. He was assigned to U.S. embassies in Asia, Africa, and Latin America and gradually and inexorably made his way up the ranks to become one of the chief honchos on the Latin American Desk. Over the years we had kept in desultory touch and from time to time would go out for a beer to catch up and to reminisce over old times.

While it was never explicit – and Dwight was very hard to read – I always got the sense that he harbored some resentment towards me. I couldn't quite put my finger on why. Maybe it went back to our days playing basketball where I had been the flamboyant star, taking – and often making – impossible shots and getting the majority of the glory when we won and excused when we lost while Dwight's solid, workmanlike play was rarely the stuff of headlines.

In the real adult world, however, it was clear that Dwight had far outpaced me. His career path was steady and increasingly successful while mine was full of ups and downs and so far characterized more by aimlessness than any real sense of purpose. At our last meeting a few months ago, I filled him in on my plans to begin work as a private investigator. He nodded and said "That sounds like an interesting career Frank," but in his deep blue eyes I could see a flicker of disdain. Behind the mask I imagined him thinking: *Just another crazy choice. When is this guy finally going to grow up?* Maybe I was projecting my own thoughts onto Dwight. He, of course, in addition to the well-ingrained reserve that he had shown from the time we met was now too much the diplomat to blurt out what he might be thinking. Besides, I was certain, not too far at the back of his mind was the fact that my father was still a pretty influential guy at the office where he worked and where he was ambitious to move up the ladder – perhaps even to the very top: Dwight Whalen, U.S. Secretary of State. A long shot perhaps, but from what I knew of Dwight's drive, self-discipline, and intelligence, not totally out of the question.

I got to the main entrance of the "New State Department Extension" at eleven forty five. As America's role in the world had grown so too had the bureaucracy designed to handle foreign affairs. This meant a bigger building for the diplomatic corps and support staff. The new structure had been completed in the early 1960s. It was of modern design and impressive in size, but to my unpracticed eye it lacked any charm or distinction. I had often heard my father grumble in recent years that the growth in staff and building size was in inverse proportion to the department's real influence in the making of foreign policy – which under President Nixon had shifted rather decidedly to the White House.

I had visited the building to see my father and friends like Dwight on numerous occasions and knew my way around. Showing my identification at the reception desk, I passed to the elevator and pressed the button with the up arrow. It opened immediately and took me noiselessly to the fourth floor. Exiting the elevator, I turned right and headed directly for Dwight's office. Knocking firmly on the outer door I heard his secretary say "Please come in Mister Corbett." Clearly I was expected.

Dwight's secretary was a pretty young brunette in her late twenties. I doubted Dwight called her "sweetheart" but who knew?

"Please have a seat Mister Corbett," she said with a smile. "Mister Whalen is on the phone," she explained, "but he is expecting you and should be right out." She pointed in the direction of a black leather couch and I took a seat. After less than a minute had passed, Dwight came out of his office and into the reception area to greet me.

"Frank, my old friend," he said with a grin, extending his right hand for me to shake and pounding me on the shoulder with his left. "Great to see you again." Then, grabbing me by the elbow, he escorted me into his office and motioned for me to take a chair while he returned to his seat behind his desk, which, as I expected, was neat as a pin. Also as expected, he was dressed in a well-tailored dark suit, a white dress shirt with a starched collar, and a crimson necktie with a Windsor knot. His wavy blond hair was carefully combed and when he smiled his teeth shone like those of a model in a *Colgate* commercial. He bore some resemblance to the movie star Tab Hunter and we used to kid him about it. But he made it clear he didn't appreciate the reference and after a while we dropped it, although once in a while, just to get a rise from him, I would call him "Tab."

Physically, he seemed little changed. He stood about five foot eleven, had a trim build, and looked to be in excellent physical shape. While he was of average height and weight, he had long fingers and very strong hands, which made him an excellent ball handler. Rarely could anyone strip the ball from him.

Before he took his seat, he removed his jacket and placed it carefully on a coat rack in the corner. My guess was that he had been in shirtsleeves when I had arrived but had put on the jacket to greet me. Now it was time to remove it again. But I was sure that there would be no loosening of the tie.

Dwight was still single. He made sure to remind me every time we met that he had *plenty* of girlfriends, but had yet to find the "right" one. Besides, he added with an air of self-importance, his job required working nights and weekends, leaving little time for social life. There were no family pictures adorning the walls of his office. Instead there were about a dozen photos of Dwight in the company of various high-ranking government officials, including a prominently displayed one that showed Dwight standing next to National Security Advisor Henry Kissinger,

who many considered one of the two most powerful men in the country –
and with the unfolding Watergate scandal weakening President Nixon –
perhaps even *the* most powerful. There were a few pictures of Dwight in
his basketball uniform but these were, I noticed, solo shots. There was not
one of him with the rest of the team.

Settling into his seat and leaning forward over his desk, Dwight said,
"So Frank you have a case that involves Manuel Fernández."

"That's right Dwight. His sister came to see me this morning...."

Dwight interrupted. "His sister, Elena right? Quite a looker," he said
with a grin.

I nodded. Dwight seemed pretty well informed about the Fernández
family, just as I had hoped. I nodded. "Yes indeed. I had some difficulty
staying focused on what she was trying to tell me. But it seems that Manuel
has rather mysteriously dropped out of sight and she has hired me to try
to find him. Before I head down to Durham where Manuel is studying
medicine at Duke and where he was last seen, I thought I'd check with
you for some background on the family."

Dwight paused for a moment, looking over my shoulder into a far
corner. At the same time, he unobtrusively put his hand under the desk
and the noise level in the room underwent a subtle change. Had Dwight
activated a tape recorder? Maybe I was letting my imagination and the
Oval Office taping system revealed by the Watergate hearings get to me.
It certainly piqued my curiosity, but I decided not to say anything. If
Dwight wanted to record our conversation, that was okay with me. I had
nothing to hide.

"Well, before I get to what I know about the Fernández family Frank,
let me paint the bigger picture." Uh oh, I thought. Dwight was in one of
his lecturing moods. I half expected him to pull out a map and a pointer.
"Overall, the political situation in Latin America is pretty favorable right
now." I assumed that Dwight meant "favorable" for the United States, not
necessarily for the Latin Americans. "We have a good partner in Brazil,
which is under firm military control, and even though Mexico often takes
an anti-Yankee stance in public, in private they do more or less what we
want them to. The Caribbean and Central America, except for Cuba, of
course, are solidly on our side, as are Venezuela and Colombia. We've had
a dust-up with Ecuador over fishing rights, but nothing serious."

As Dwight spoke, I simply nodded. So far, he wasn't telling me anything that I didn't know. While I was no news junkie I did read the *Post* every day and kept up with most current events. Living in D.C. it was almost impossible not to.

Dwight locked his face in his most serious look. It reminded me of those times when he was concentrating on making the perfect pass to set up a sure basket. "But southern South America is an area of real concern. There is a military government in Peru we cannot figure out. It claims to be anti-communist, but it has carried out an aggressive agrarian reform, nationalized U.S. companies, and established ties with the Soviet Union and Cuba. As for its southern neighbor, thanks to the election of Salvador Allende, a Marxist, we've been having quite a tussle with Chile. Allende has been a disaster, especially in terms of the economy, but his coalition won enough votes in recent congressional elections to stave off the possibility of impeachment. So he probably has three more years in his term – unless something unforeseen should occur." Dwight seemed to be biting his tongue. My guess was that he knew more about what that "something unforeseen" might be – most likely some sort of military coup – and was dying to tell me what it was just to show off his "insider" status but knew he shouldn't reveal anything, especially if a tape recorder was running.

"We think the *Tupamaros* in Uruguay – you do know about them don't you…" I nodded yes. "We think they are pretty much done as a serious threat." By "pretty much done" I knew Dwight meant that most of the Uruguayan revolutionaries had been killed, imprisoned, or forced into exile.

"So that leaves…."

"So that leaves Argentina."

"Exactly Frank. Exactly. That leaves Argentina. It's our biggest headache right now. I don't know how much you know…."

"Just what I read in the *Post*. They've recently elected a new civilian president after seven or eight years of military rule. It seems the new guy they just elected – what's his name?"

"Cámpora. Héctor Cámpora."

"Right. Cámpora. Cámpora, as I recall, is just a stalking horse for the old dictator, Juan Perón, who plans to return to Argentina and take over at some time not too far down the road."

Dwight gave me a tight, almost patronizing smile, like a professor rewarding a student who had gotten the right answer in an oral exam. "That's right Frank. We expect Cámpora to call for new elections fairly soon and for Perón to win them easily."

"So what's the problem? As I recall, wasn't Perón some kind of fascist?" I added an unnecessary dig. "Isn't that just the kind of guy we love to cozy up to?" I flashed back to my Vietnam experience where the U.S. allied itself with a series of unsavory local leaders.

Dwight didn't appreciate the insinuation and his jaw clenched for a half second. But instead of an angry defense, he simply shrugged as if to say that I wasn't too far off the mark. "You have a fair point there Frank. But I'm afraid that Perón's more complicated and slippery than the fascist label would suggest. He still has a devoted following among the working classes who benefited the most from his previous government. And now he's added much of the middle class as well, especially among the youth, who have only a hazy recollection of his first regime. They seem to regard him as some sort of reincarnation – no, make that pre-incarnation of Fidel Castro. And he has done little to dissuade them from that belief, spouting a lot of nonsense about socialist revolution. We don't think he really believes it and is simply adopting the rhetoric for political purposes. But combined with some other facts on the ground his avowed leftism and the likelihood he will soon be president has us very worried. And there are some other complications as well…"

Dwight paused for a few seconds to gather his thoughts. "What do you know about the *Montoneros* and the *Ejército Revolucionario del Pueblo?*" he asked.

"Not a whole lot. Aren't they like the *Tupamaros* - urban revolutionary groups that carry out a lot of violent actions? As I recall, a few years back didn't the *Montoneros* kidnap and kill an ex-president of Argentina?"

Dwight inclined his head to show that I was on target. "Yes. They've been very active the past several years, causing all kinds of chaos. We've had to double the security at our embassy in Buenos Aires and a lot of American businesses have pulled out of the country after these groups kidnapped and held for ransom some high-ranking executives. They've been somewhat restrained lately, waiting to see how things play out with Perón. But these are well-armed organizations with committed followers and a growing base of sympathizers. If things fall apart in Argentina, we could see another Cuba." If possible, Dwight's expression had become even more serious and somber.

"That's very interesting and informative Dwight," I said with a tinge of sarcasm "But what does all this have to do with the mysterious disappearance of Manuel Fernández?"

"That's simple. We think that Manuel Fernández has left for Argentina to join one of the guerrilla groups, most likely the ERP," Dwight said, using the acronym for the *Ejército Revolucionario del Pueblo* – The Peoples' Revolutionary Army. "We know that he has friends in both the ERP and the *Montoneros* and that he was active in politics when he was a university student in Argentina. Apparently, he became tired of being on the sidelines and has decided to join the cause."

I tried to keep a poker face. I had had my suspicions from what Elena had told me that what Dwight said was on the money. But I also had fresh in my mind her rather definitive denial that her brother would follow the radical path of violent revolution.

"According to his sister," I said, "their father believes that his son is engaged in some sort of elaborate charade that stems from a falling out they had over Christmas. At any rate, he has not raised any alarms."

Dwight gave me a quick smile. "No. I'm not surprised. Fernández Senior is next in line to be Argentina's ambassador to the United States. And his chances for that promotion would be pretty slim if it was to be found out that his one and only son was fighting with the guerrillas against the very government he is assigned to represent."

There was something about this that I found troubling. I still couldn't buy the fact that a father would simply write off his son in that manner, no matter how bad the blood between them had become. And if Manuel had indeed joined a group like the ERP, I assumed that fact would become known - if not widely - at least among Argentine government circles. And that would doom the father's chances for any advancement. In fact, he probably would be removed from his post altogether. For the moment, I decided to keep these thoughts to myself.

"Well Dwight," I said. "You seem to know a lot more about this case than I do. I presume that State has been involved in trying to locate Manuel?" Dwight inclined his head slightly to indicate that this was so, but didn't offer any details. Trying to draw him out, I asked, "Anything else you can tell me?"

Dwight pondered my request for a moment before he said, "We've known about Manuel's disappearance from Duke for some time now." I raised an eyebrow. "Given his previous affiliations and his father's prominence," Dwight explained, "we've been keeping a close eye on him." I didn't ask who was providing the "eye" but assumed that it was the FBI. If so, I wonder if good old Fred Matthews was aware of the surveillance. And if that were the case, why hadn't he informed Elena of that fact when she contacted him? I made a mental note to get in touch with Fred once I returned from Durham.

"We did a little snooping around at Duke but came up empty. And there is no official record of Fernández having left the country. But we are still pretty confident that he somehow made it back to Argentina undetected and has gone underground with the guerrillas. We have our people in Buenos Aires working hard to try to confirm all this but so far they have no leads."

"That sounds like Manuel's possible defection is a pretty high priority," I said.

For just a second I saw a flicker of discomfort pass over Dwight's baby blues. But then it was gone. "Well, to tell you the truth Frank…" I automatically put my mental guard up. When someone uses the phrase "to tell you the truth" you wonder what that means about everything else he has told you. "…we would like to see if we can resolve this matter so it doesn't cause the elder Fernández any undue embarrassment. We are hoping that if we can contact the son, we can somehow convince him to come to his senses and abandon any hare-brained thoughts of being a revolutionary."

That sounded pretty unlikely to me. If what Dwight said was true – that Manuel had given up the idea of practicing medicine and had gone to the extreme of joining the revolutionaries – then no amount of persuasion from the U.S. government would sway him from the course he had chosen. But then again, I knew from my experience in Vietnam, we could employ a lot of tools – some of them not sanctioned by the Geneva Convention – to convince people to do what we wanted them to do.

Again, I kept these thoughts to myself. Instead, I said "And of course the future ambassador, Fernández Senior, would be much in your debt if that were to happen."

Dwight gave me a grin. "That's it exactly Frank. You catch on fast."

Well, I thought to myself, it didn't take a Sherlock Holmes to figure out that particular quid pro quo. And while it seemed a logical explanation, I suspected that there was more to the story than Dwight was letting on.

I sat silently for a while, trying to digest all that Dwight had told me. He interrupted my thoughts. Looking at his watch, he asked, "Anything else Frank? I do have another appointment in a few minutes…."

"No. No Dwight. That's all. You've been a big help."

"What are you going to do now?"

"I'm still planning to go to Durham and poke around. Maybe I can find out something that the police might have missed."

"And if you come up empty?"

"Then the next trip will be to Argentina."

Dwight nodded, a slight smile playing on his face. Reaching into his drawer, he pulled out a business card and scribbled something on the back. Stretching out his hand to give me the card, he said, "Here's the name and contact information of someone in Buenos Aires who has been helping us look for Manuel Fernández. If you go there, be sure to look him up. He knows the guerrilla groups as well as any American and I'm sure would be of great assistance to you."

Taking the card, which had Dwight's name, title, and the State Department seal on one side, I saw the name "Roy Smallwood" along with an address and a phone number on the back. I slid it into my shirt pocket. "Does this Roy Smallwood work for State?" I asked, knowing in advance what the answer would be.

"Not *for* State," Dwight said. "At least not officially. Let's say he works *with* State."

I gave Dwight a wink as I got up to leave. "I understand buddy. And thanks again. You've been a big help."

Dwight rose from his chair and rounded his desk to escort me out of the office. "Not at all Frank. Glad to be of assistance. After all, what are friends for, right? And who knows? Maybe you'll have better luck finding Manuel Fernández than we have had." The tone of his voice, however, had

31

a clear undercurrent of doubt – and again maybe some discomfort. "And if you do, don't forget us. You know, I scratch your back, you scratch mine."

"Okay Dwight," I said. "I'll keep that in mind – returning the favor so to speak. But *you* also have to remember that my first responsibility is to my client. It's Manuel's sister who has hired me and if I do find him, I report to her first. Then it's up to her to decide what to do next."

I could see that my commitment to PI ethics didn't sit too well with Dwight, but he simply nodded and said, "Sure Frank. Sure. Absolutely. Whatever the two of you decide."

Dwight opened the door for me and extended his hand for a farewell shake. I extended mine and we performed the ritual that we had performed countless times. "Good luck to you Frank," he said as he began to close the door. "And do keep in touch."

"I will Dwight. And thanks again." He gave me a final wave and shut the door. I turned and made my way through the reception area, giving Dwight's beautiful secretary what I hoped was my most dazzling smile. I took the stairs down to street level and exited the building, walking briskly in the direction of my apartment. I wanted to leave for Durham as soon as I could and by the time I reached DuPont Circle I was almost jogging. Along the way, I tried to recall has much as I could of my conversation with Dwight Whalen. Preoccupied with these thoughts, it wasn't until I had reached my apartment door and was inserting my key that an image made its way into my brain. When I had taken Dwight's hand for the final shake, the grip had been firm but the palm had been moist. Trying to recapture my picture of him as we said our goodbyes, I could also swear that there had been pronounced circles of sweat under his armpits. I shook my head as if to clear the image from my brain but it stuck. Maybe I was reading too much into it, but those memories only reinforced my strong suspicion that my old friend and teammate knew a lot more about the Fernández case than he was letting on.

Four

Back in my apartment, I quickly fixed and ate a ham on rye sandwich which I washed down with a coca cola. Packing an overnight bag with a few essentials that included my licensed Smith and Wesson .38 I headed down to the basement garage.

For the first few months after returning to D.C. from my foreign travels, I had tried to get along without a car. But I finally tired of asking friends and family for the loan of their vehicles and decided to buy one of my own. I scanned the *Post* for used cars and was lucky to find a low-mileage forest green MG-B. I really enjoyed driving it, although it could often be temperamental. Removing the canvas top was always an adventure and putting it back on even more so. I invariably ended up with skinned knuckles as nothing seemed to fit right. In cold weather it was often hard to start and the gear box was clumsy. I had more than my share of breakdowns. Fortunately, I had an army buddy who had opened up an auto repair shop only a few blocks away and he managed to keep my MG in reasonably good shape without charging me an arm and a leg.

The day was warm and sunny so I decided to remove the top for the trip to North Carolina. After the usual struggle, I stowed the top away and started up, encouraged by the steady hum of the engine. Crossing over the Memorial Bridge, I headed south towards Richmond and beyond, following a new Interstate Highway that made the driving easy but also monotonous. I tried to break the monotony by listing to WGMS, Washington's classical music station, for as long as I could. But the signal faded by the time I got to Richmond. I fiddled with the dial but couldn't find anything I liked so I turned the radio off.

By the time I had passed Petersburg, it was beginning to get dark and I was getting hungry. Pulling off the Interstate, I followed a sign that indicated gas and food a few miles ahead. Sure enough, after a few minutes I spotted a country diner off to my right with a parking lot that was already nearly full. I pulled into one of the last remaining spaces, my MG dwarfed by a collection of campers, trailers, trucks, and large sedans. Most of the license plates were out-of-state so I presumed that the clientele was primarily composed of tourists, more than likely northerners on their way to the warmer climes of the south. A few stickers from Disneyworld and Cypress Gardens suggested that some had already accomplished their mission and were returning – probably reluctantly – to the north.

Before entering the diner, I put the canvas top back on my car. It was already getting chilly and would be even colder once I resumed my journey. Luckily the procedure went quickly and without me incurring any substantial injury. Inside it was crowded but I found a place at the counter. The diner was a good choice, the waitress working behind the counter taking my order in less than a minute. She was a plump redhead in her forties. Her name tag said "Thelma" and her hairdo and her accent told me that I was indeed now in the southern part of the country. She had a nice smile and when I ordered baked ham, hash browns, peas, and hush puppies, she nodded in approval. The food came quickly and was surprisingly good. My clean plate earned me another smile from Thelma as did my request for apple pie and coffee. Polishing these off, I asked Thelma for the bill, left her a generous tip, and paid the cashier.

After a brief stop in the bathroom, I left the diner and headed to the car. I felt refreshed, re-energized and looked forward to hitting the road again. As I unlocked the car door and prepared to slide in butt first, as is advised when somebody of my height tries to fold himself into a small sports car, something caught my eye. Across the parking lot I saw a gray sedan that for some reason looked familiar. *Had I seen it before on the highway?* It was parked so that whoever was in front had a full view of the entrance to the diner. I could make out two men, shapeless and featureless from a distance, sharing the front seat. I saw the glow of a cigarette from the passenger side. Maybe they had already eaten and were just relaxing before continuing their journey. But I hadn't noticed two men alone in the crowd composed mostly of families at the diner. Instead, it seemed that they were on some kind of stakeout, keeping an eye on whoever entered or left. For a second, a shiver went up my spine. *Were they watching me?*

Taking a deep breath, I closed the door and started up the engine. Engaging the gears, I made my way slowly out the lot, passing by the gray sedan. Full darkness had now descended and there was not much in the way of illumination to let me see who was inside. As I passed by, all I could make out were the same indistinct outlines and the glowing ember of a cigarette. Accelerating onto the access road to the Interstate, I kept a close watch in my rear-view mirror to see if I was being followed. But as I gradually picked up speed I caught no sign of any lights behind me. I sat back in my seat and loosened the tight grip I had on the steering wheel. Back on the Interstate, I put the pedal down and joined the flow of traffic.

By the time I had crossed into North Carolina, I had almost convinced myself that I had let my imagination get the better of me in suspecting that somehow the men in the gray sedan were on my tail. It was probably too much coffee plus the excitement of being involved in what promised to be a challenging and interesting case. And there were a hundred different logical explanations of why two men might be sitting in the parking lot of a diner. Nevertheless, there was still a small seed of suspicion in the back of my mind that I couldn't quite root out. I vowed to keep an eye out for any sign of that gray sedan once again appearing in my vicinity. What I would do if it did I hadn't yet decided upon, but if somebody was following me I was determined to find out who and why – and who had ordered them to do it.

I got to Durham at about nine o'clock and checked into the Washington Duke Hotel in the downtown area. I had been to Durham once before when Duke took a look at me for a possible basketball scholarship and put me and another recruit up in the same hotel. While I was impressed by the campus and the attention, I ultimately decided to stick closer to home. Frankly, I was worried that while I might do okay on the court I wasn't sure I could cut it in the classroom of what I perceived to be a high-powered academic institution.

Settling into my comfortable and quiet room, I unpacked my overnight bag and kicked off my shoes. Then I placed calls to the Medical School Dean and to Manuel Fernández's roommate, whose names and numbers Elena had provided. I was able to reach both and arranged to meet them the following day. Using the stationery provided by the hotel, I wrote down a few reminders to myself and a list of questions to cover in tomorrow's interviews. There was a TV in the room and I switched it on just in time to catch the local news. There was nothing of interest to me; no reports of missing students – or worse – unidentified bodies found in the woods. I switched the set off and hopped into bed. It had been a long day and it didn't take me long to drift off to sleep.

Five

My internal alarm clock woke me up at six thirty. I shaved, showered, put on a fresh dress shirt to go with my blazer and khakis and went down to the hotel coffee shop for breakfast. I ordered my usual bacon, eggs, toast, juice, and coffee. The waitress asked me if I wanted hominy grits as well, another sign that I was in the South. I said sure, why not? About ten minutes later, everything arrived as ordered and I polished it off.

Fully fueled for the day ahead, I decided to take a quick stroll around the downtown area. It wouldn't provide the exercise of my usual jog but at least it would be something. I stepped outside into a pleasant sunny morning, somewhat warmer than in Washington. As I walked, I observed that nothing much had changed in the downtown area from the time of my other visit. Durham was dominated by tobacco and textiles and the city had all the earmarks of any other factory town. Not much in the way of southern charm that I could see. The odor of tobacco permeated the air. As I passed by the local Woolworths, I didn't see much that was different on the outside. But I presumed that inside there were no longer the signs that separated black from white. Some change had come to the South in recent years, but I frequently wondered how much. My walk also took me by the local ballpark, home to the minor league Durham Bulls and I saw some fresh paint that indicated they were getting ready for the start of the season. I felt a twinge of envy. In D.C. we didn't even have a minor league team to root for. As I walked I kept an eye out for the gray sedan I had spotted but saw no signs of it – or of anybody following me.

Returning to the hotel, I freshened up and then left for my appointment with the Medical School Dean. I had parked my MG in the lot adjacent to the hotel. Before getting in, I took a look around to see if there were any gray sedans parked anywhere in the vicinity. There were none. Exiting the lot, I headed for the Duke Medical School.

The Duke campus adjoins the city of Durham on the western edge. Actually, there are two campuses. The "East Campus" is for women and is closest to the city. The architecture is mostly southern colonial and Georgian. A mile-long avenue connects the "East Campus" with the main "West Campus," which is for men and which is dominated by College Gothic architecture. When I visited, I thought it was a rather peculiar arrangement – but it seemed to work.

Unlike the city of Durham, both campuses had plenty of charm. Trees and bushes were already in full bloom and with the top down on my MG the sweet natural smells of spring almost – *almost* – overcame those of factory smoke and tobacco.

The Medical School sat at the northern end of the West Campus. I followed the road around to the parking lot in the rear and, since it was relatively early, found one of the few slots allocated to visitors. Figuring that college campuses are usually safe places, and not having anything of importance to steal, I decided to leave the top down and trust to luck that nothing happened to spoil my optimism.

The Dean's office was on the second floor. I knocked on his door precisely at eight thirty, the time we had agreed on for our appointment. A female voice with a deep southern accent invited me to enter. Opening the door, a woman of about forty with brown hair, thick glasses, and a no-nonsense appearance rose from behind her desk to greet me.

"Mister Corbett?" she asked.

"Yes. I am here for an eight-thirty…."

She cut me off. "To see Dean Baker. Please have a seat," she said, pointing to a black wooden chair with the University's seal on the back. "I'll tell Dean Baker you are here."

As I sat, she knocked gently on the door that led to the Dean's office. "Dean Baker. Your eight-thirty appointment is here."

No more than ten seconds later, the Dean emerged and I got up from my chair, extending my hand in greeting. He took it in his and I felt his strong and confident grip. Probably a surgeon, I said to myself.

"Mister Corbett. I'm Roger Baker, Dean of the Medical School. Quite punctual I see," he said with a slight smile. "Please do come in."

He showed me into his well-appointed office, the walls covered with various diplomas, awards, and photographs. I took a seat in a comfortable leather chair as he settled in behind his desk. "Before we begin Mister Corbett, I'm afraid I have to see some sort of identification." The tone was mildly apologetic but his eyes were serious. I dug out my PI license and handed it over. He took his time to check it while I took my time sizing him up.

Except for the name and the accent, he was about what I expected. Probably in his early fifties, he was almost as tall as I was and a little bit heavier. He had a full head of hair, mostly dark but showing signs of gray. He wore the kind of tweed jacket with elbow patches that I automatically associated with academics, charcoal gray pants, a white dress shirt and a dark blue tie.

Reaching across the desk to return my license to me, apparently satisfied that I was legit, he asked, "So Mister Corbett, how may I be of assistance? You said over the phone that you were investigating the disappearance of one of our students, Manuel Fernández?"

"Yes. That's right Dean Baker. I've been hired to locate him and I wanted to try to pick up the trail with a fresh perspective. I presume you have already spoken with the local police?" He inclined his head to signal yes. "I was hoping that I could go beyond the routine questions they might have asked to get some insights into Manuel's personality and behavior. Anything to provide some clue as to why he has dropped out of sight."

Baker looked skeptical. Before responding he extracted a pack of *Camels* from his shirt pocket and offered me one. I declined. I had never smoked and didn't plan to start. The Dean took out a lighter, spun the wheel, admired the flame, lit the end, and took a deep drag. Not the best example for a doctor to set, I thought to myself, but perhaps not surprising given the pressures of his job and the fact that he worked for a university founded by a tobacco king.

"I'm not sure that I can add much more to what I've already told the police and some government officials…"

"Government officials?"

"Yes. They came to see me about a week after I had spoken with the police."

"Do you know what agency they were from?"

Baker paused for a minute. "You know, that's a good question. They showed me their credentials and badges and I more or less assumed they were FBI men. But now that you mention it, I'm not so sure. I'm afraid that I just focused on the badges and not the specific agency. Why do you ask?"

I waved my hand in the air. "Just curious. It's not all that important. Now about Manuel Fernández...."

Baker had a puzzled look on his face, probably still mulling over my question about the two "agents." "I didn't have a lot of direct contact with Mister Fernández. As Dean, I don't do a lot of teaching. It's mostly administration," he said with a frown, "And what teaching I do is mostly with those students who plan to be surgeons." My deduction from his handshake proved to be correct. "Mister Fernández was planning to specialize in primary health care, nutrition, and epidemic diseases. We have a very strong program in those areas," Baker explained with a tone of pride.

"As Dean," he continued, "I naturally keep track of all our students, depending mostly on their primary instructors to tell me how they are progressing. All the reports that I received concerning Mister Fernández were extremely positive," Baker said, pointing to a file folder on his desk. "They praised his performance and claimed that he was one of the most dedicated, hard-working, and accomplished of our students. Given the quality of our program, that was high praise indeed. He was even working on a special research project outside of the curriculum, gathering information on the impact of the federally-funded school meal program on children from low-income families. One of his instructors told me he was planning to write up his findings and send them on to the Ministry of Health in his home country."

There were no surprises yet in what Baker was telling me. It simply confirmed what Elena had said. "What was your impression of him personally?" I asked. "Did he seem to have any problems adjusting? Was he happy here in school?"

Baker looked a bit surprised, then thoughtful. I presumed that these were not questions he had been asked before. "Well, from what I could tell, he was neither happy nor unhappy. Medical School is a demanding grind for all our students, no matter how talented. They don't have much time for a social life and most of them are pretty serious." He wrinkled his brow. "And for the few foreign students we have, like Fernández, the demands can sometimes be even greater as they need to adapt to a different culture and environment."

Baker took another drag on his cigarette, tilting his head back and waving the smoke away with his free hand. "When Fernández arrived, I called him into my office right after orientation and asked him how things were going. As I recall, his father is some kind of diplomat…." I nodded that this was the case "…and he told me that he was used to moving about and living in different countries. His English, by the way, is excellent. Hardly any accent at all. In my subsequent meetings with him, I never got any hint that he was having any personal difficulties in adapting to life at Duke and Durham. In fact, from all I could tell, he was thoroughly enjoying the opportunity to study medicine here."

"Was he active politically?"

My question brought a chuckle. "We had our years of campus turmoil during the height of the Vietnam War but by the time Fernández got here things were pretty quiet. Besides, only a handful of medical school students ever got involved in campus politics. They are much too busy with their studies to engage in demonstrations. Besides, most of them tend to be pretty conservative politically."

"I've heard that Manuel was uncomfortable with what he perceived to be the narrow career focus of his fellow students and their lack of concern with such things as health care for the less privileged. Any indications of that in your reports?" I asked, pointing to the file on his desk.

The question seemed to catch Baker by surprise. He held up a finger for me to wait while he took a closer look at the file. After thumbing through it, he looked up. "No Mister Corbett. Nothing in the file – and nothing I have heard. Of course, there are the usual tensions among our students. This is a very demanding and competitive school and personality conflicts are not uncommon. We have our share of shouting matches and even a few fistfights break out from time to time. But there is no indication," he said firmly, again pointing to the file, "that Fernández was ever involved in any kind of dustup. Of course, he might well have been keeping the feelings you describe to himself. Even though we maintain a close watch on all our students, we certainly don't know *everything* they are thinking or feeling."

Baker suddenly snapped his fingers. "I'd almost forgotten, since it's been a few years. But your question about Fernández triggered a memory. When I spoke with him during orientation, he made a point of telling me how much he appreciated being at an American university where he could focus on studying medicine without politics intruding. He said that in his own country the level of political activity is so high that it often takes twice as long to get a degree worth half as much. Of course, that was at the beginning of his studies. It's always possible that he could have become more political – and more disillusioned – as time progressed. But, to repeat, there are no signs of that in his record."

I didn't see any sense in pursuing this line further. "What about his social life? Did he have a girlfriend? Did he go to a lot of parties? Any problems with alcohol?"

By this time, Baker's cigarette, which he had placed in an ashtray while he spoke, had dwindled to a long gray ash. He took a moment to pull another from his pack and light up. After the first puff, he said. "We don't get too involved with that part of the student's life, unless, of course, we think it is beginning to affect his – or her – performance."

He read the look on my face. "Yes. We do have some female students." He kept his face and the tone of his voice neutral, but I gathered from his body language that the breaking of the gender barrier in what had been up till then an all-boys club did not meet with his approval.

"Again, as far as I know – and as far as his instructors' reports say – Fernández had no such problems."

Up to now, my interview hadn't produced much. Everything Baker had told me simply confirmed what I already knew. "That pretty well exhausts all my questions. Do you have any thoughts of your own as to what might have happened to Manuel?"

He took another deep drag and let the smoke out slowly. Putting the cigarette down, he folded his hands in front of him, leaned forward over the desk, and gave me a serious look. "Can I count on your discretion Mister Corbett?"

I felt my heart beat a little faster. Maybe I was about to get a break. "Certainly. Whatever you have to tell me will just be between the two of us." Of course, that was probably a rash promise to make. If he gave me a solid lead, I might have to reveal my source somewhere down the road.

But I figured that if I didn't make it, he would clam up and I would get nothing. I didn't feel totally comfortable about entering this ethical gray area but consoled myself with the thought that my first priority was to look after the best interests of my client.

"What I'm about to tell you isn't exactly a deep dark secret, but it's also something we don't want to be widely known." Baker lowered his voice and I moved my chair closer to his desk. "As I said, this is a *very* competitive and demanding medical school. We screen our candidates carefully, looking not only at academic achievement and potential but also at such things as character and personality. We expect a lot of our students and society expects a lot from doctors. They have to be competent, compassionate, and well-grounded psychologically. We do our best to make sure they are as well prepared as possible to be the kind of doctors of whom we can all be proud. And to achieve that we... well to be frank, we put them through hell – tough classes, long hours, high expectations."

What he was telling me did not come as much of a surprise and I thought I could predict what he would tell me next. "It's rare, but it happens – maybe two or three cases a year. Students crack under the pressure. Sometimes we can see it coming, but sometimes we can't. A student will seem to be doing well – good performance on exams, great work in the labs, a positive attitude – and then *bam*," Baker clapped his hands together, "out of the blue they just drop out. Here one day, gone the next. Usually they let us know, either at the time or soon thereafter. But there are some we never hear from again. I presume they are so embarrassed they just want to forget the whole thing." Baker closed his eyes for a minute. "And then there are the extreme cases...."

"You mean suicide," I interjected.

"Yes," Baker said, moving his head mournfully from side to side. "Yes. I'm afraid so. Sometimes right here in the hospital, usually by hanging. But they do it off campus as well. As with the dropouts, it's rare, but sadly it does happen."

"And that's what you think might have happened to Manuel Fernández? He cracked under the pressure and dropped out – or..."

"Or took an even more drastic course. Although I presume that if Manuel *had* done away with himself there would be some sign of it." I nodded in agreement.

I wasn't about to discount the Dean's explanation out of hand. But neither scenario seemed all that plausible. While Manuel was under some stress from the fight he had had with his father, his medical studies did not seem to have suffered as a result. And, from what Elena had said, he was determined to get his degree and embark on his career.

"When do these incidents usually occur?" I asked Baker.

"You mean at what point in a student's studies?"

"Yes."

"It's most common in the first year, when the pressure is the greatest. But we've had instances of it occurring in later years as well. There is no hard and fast rule."

I decided not to pursue it further. I had asked Baker for his opinion and he had provided me with what he thought might be an explanation. I didn't want to turn the conversation into an extended back and forth.

By now, the Dean had let his second cigarette turn to ash and I saw him take a look at his watch. "Now, is there anything else Mister Corbett?" he asked in a tone that suggested the time he had set aside for me had expired.

"No. Nothing that I can think of," I said, rising from my chair. "Thank you for your time Dean Baker. I know that you have a crowded schedule and I appreciate the fact that you fit me in on such short notice."

Baker came around from behind his desk and extended his hand. I grasped it in mine and we shook. He escorted me to the door and as he opened it, said, "I do hope you locate Manuel. Everybody at the school who knows him is mystified by his disappearance and praying for the best. We all hope that there is some reasonable explanation for this mystery and that he can return to finish his studies."

While I thought Baker was sincere, the look on his face said that if he were a betting man, the odds of such a happy outcome were long indeed. I thanked him again for his time and said that if anything turned up, I would be sure to let him know. He nodded and closed the door behind me.

Heading back to the parking lot, I pictured Baker returning to his desk, lighting another cigarette, putting Manuel Fernández's file back in its place, and turning to the next item on his agenda. Minus the cigarette and the file folder, I planned to do the same.

Six

My next appointment was with Manuel's roommate, Steve Kowalski. He had given me directions to the apartment he shared with Manuel and we agreed to meet around ten.

I found my car as I left it. Looking around I saw no sign of a gray sedan. It might be paranoia on my part, but it didn't hurt to keep checking.

I exited the parking lot and followed secondary roads until I got to the main highway that connected Durham and the Duke Campus to Chapel Hill, home of the University of North Carolina. Heading west, I went a couple of miles until I spotted the Casa Grande apartment complex on my right, just beyond a small shopping center. I turned off the highway and entered a well-landscaped area with two and three-story apartment buildings constructed in a faux Mediterranean style with white stucco walls and red-tiled roofs more appropriate for Southern California than central North Carolina. Following Kowalski's directions, I located Mariposa Lane which led me to Hacienda Circle and the apartment he shared with Manuel Fernández at number 114.

I wondered if Manuel had been attracted to – or offended by – the pretentiousness of the make-believe "Spanish" style of the streets and buildings. I parked in a space for visitors and followed the path to 114. There was a hand-lettered sign that read "Kowalski-Fernández" inserted in a slot at the top of the mailbox. I was at the right place. I pushed the buzzer and heard the bell chime twice on the other side of the door followed by heavy footsteps.

The guy I presumed was Kowalski opened the door. "Mister Corbett?"

"That's me," I replied, extending my hand.

He gave me a grin as he took my hand. "Steve Kowalski. Please come on in."

When Kowalski took my hand I braced myself for a crushing grip. The guy was about my height but outweighed me by fifty pounds. From the look of it, mostly muscle. He had dark curly hair, coal black eyes, and a nose that looked as though it had been broken more than once. One of his front teeth was chipped. He seemed more like a football player or a boxer than a medical student. But his grip was surprisingly gentle. He had a deep soft voice and there was little about him that seemed threatening. He was dressed casually in jeans, a sweatshirt, and tennis shoes

I followed him through the door and into the living room, where he pointed to a chair opposite a couch. "Please have a seat Mister Corbett. Would you like some coffee? I always have a pot ready. A necessity for medical school I'm afraid."

A man after my own heart. "I'd love one thanks. Just black please— no cream or sugar."

"Coming right up," he said turning towards a kitchen in the back.

While Manuel's roommate attended to the coffee, I took a look around. It was about what I expected of a student apartment. It was sparsely furnished with second-hand stuff probably passed down by previous occupants. There was, however, an expensive stereo set-up with multiple speakers in the corner and I could hear it softly emitting some of Dave Brubeck's *Take Five* album in the background.

Kowalski returned from the kitchen with two mugs of steaming coffee and handed one over to me. I noticed that the lip of the mug was not as clean as it might be, another sign this was a student apartment, but I ignored it and took my first sip. It was a little too hot but surprisingly good. I put it down on a coffee table that separated my chair from the couch which Kowalski had occupied to let it cool.

I looked over at him and saw him brace as he waited for my questions as though preparing for some kind of blow. I thought about how best to put him more at ease. "How did you and Manuel Fernández end up as roommates?" I asked.

Not exactly original, but it seemed to do the trick. A slight smile played on his lips and his shoulders seemed to loosen. "We met during orientation and found that we had a lot in common despite our different backgrounds.

We both had names that people had trouble pronouncing," he said with a quick grin. "And we both were interested in the same medical issues."

Kowalski picked up his coffee cup and drank deeply. "I come from Western Pennsylvania. Coal country. I was lucky to get out and receive a good education at Penn State…."

"Let me guess," I said. "On a football scholarship."

"Right," he said with a note of pride, "Starting outside linebacker for three years. Even some All-American mention and a chance to go to the pros."

Being the sports fan that I was, I wondered why I couldn't place his name. Penn State was well-known for its linebackers. But then I figured Kowalski probably played while I was out of the country and not able to keep up with the sports news in my regular obsessive fashion when I was home.

"But you decided to go to medical school instead."

He nodded. "Yeah. My grades were okay and I thought I could do more good by being a doctor than playing for money on Sunday. And, just so you don't think I'm too noble, I tore my knee up pretty seriously my senior year – and that kind of made the decision for me."

I wasn't about to pass judgment. Whatever the reason for his choice, he had a pretty impressive résumé. I could see how he and Manuel Fernández might hit it off.

"Where I come from," Kowalski explained, "there is a lot of poverty and all the health problems associated with lack of education, poor living and working conditions, and malnutrition. I told Manny when we first met that my goal was to go back to my hometown and set up a practice that would help the folks who were suffering from these conditions. I thought he might find that naïve or even stupid but instead his eyes lit up and he told me that was exactly what he planned to do, even though it wouldn't be in his hometown. He wanted to go to the poorer areas of Argentina and do the same kind of work that I planned – and still plan – to do in Western Pennsylvania."

Two pretty admirable guys, I thought to myself.

"It didn't take long for us to decide to room together and the next day we found this place," he said, waving his right hand in a circle, "and moved in. We've been together ever since." A pained expression crossed his face. "Or at least we were until Manny disappeared a few weeks ago."

"What happened, exactly?" I asked.

He shifted a bit uneasily on the couch. "Well, like I told his sister – and the police – I went home for a long weekend at the beginning of March. And when I got back, Manny wasn't here. I didn't think much of it at first, figuring he was on campus and maybe pulling an all-nighter. But when he didn't show up the next day I got worried. I checked with the neighbors, but nobody had seen him for a couple of days. When I got to campus, I asked around and got the same answer. That's when I called his sister and she called the police."

As Kowalski spoke, he held his two massive hands together with the fingers interlaced and I could see the white of his knuckles. The tension that I had noticed earlier was back in full force.

"Did he say anything to you before you left for the weekend? Any indication that he was in trouble of any kind?"

"No. Nothing at all. Everything seemed normal. He was working hard, as always." I heard a catch in his voice as he said this.

"Did he ever say anything about the problems he was having with his father?"

"He did kind of mention it to me when he got back from Christmas vacation, but didn't make a big deal out of it." Kowalski paused for a moment. "But you know, thinking back on it, I guess it probably bothered him more than he let on. I got the sense that it might be gnawing at him even though he never said anything more about it."

"Did he ever tell you what the disagreement was about?"

"No. Not really. And I didn't want to pry." He paused for a moment and then asked me, "Why? Do you think it has something to do with Manny's disappearance?"

I hedged. "I really can't say. At this point, I'm just trying to gather information."

I took a minute to finish my coffee. Kowalski offered me another cup, but I declined. "I've spoken to Dean Baker about Manuel and from what he tells me, he was a gifted and serious student who didn't do much partying. No girlfriends. No alcohol. Is that correct? You know sometimes academic administrators don't have the full picture and…."

Kowalski interrupted. "No. Dean Baker had it right. Look, Manny *was*...." he blanched for a moment and took a deep breath "...Manny *is* a very good-looking guy. Sort of the Latin lover type, but in a wholesome way if you know what I mean. Lots of girls here were interested in him and he dated on what I guess you would call a fairly regular basis. Usually we went out together or with a group of friends when we could. Medical School doesn't really allow for much of a social life. Manny never had problems finding a girl to go out with him, but he never had a steady girlfriend or a serious relationship. He once told me that he was too wrapped up in his studies to get too deeply involved with anyone until he graduated. I also got the impression that if he married he would prefer that it be with someone from his own country – an Argentine."

"Did he have a girlfriend back home? In Argentina?"

"If he did, he never mentioned her to me."

"So no girl in the picture. And alcohol...?"

Kowalski shook his head back and forth. "No. In fact, Manny hardly did any drinking. Every once in a while I talked him into having a beer after an exam, but he usually kept it to one glass – and he seemed to be doing it more out of obligation than enjoyment." Kowalski paused for a few seconds, searching his memory. "He once told me that one of the things he admired about Che Guevara was the fact that he didn't touch alcohol."

That led naturally to the next question on my list. "Was he political? Engage in any protests? That sort of thing?"

Kowalski chuckled. "You know Mister Corbett..."

"Frank."

"You know Frank, funny you should ask. I got the same question from the two government agents who came to see me about a week after Manny disappeared and...."

I interrupted. "Do you know what agency they were from?"

He rubbed his forehead for a few seconds trying to recall. "Now that you mention it" he said, with a rueful look on his face, "they came by pretty early in the morning and woke me up before I had my coffee. I was still kind of groggy. They flashed their badges but I didn't take the time to look more carefully at their credentials. I guess I should have. At any rate, I presumed they were from the FBI. At least they looked like the kind of

FBI agents you see on TV. You know, dark suits, white shirts, black ties, crew-cuts."

I nodded. It was beginning to be a familiar story. "And they asked you about Manuel's politics?"

"Yeah. Right. I had to laugh. Most medical students are about as apolitical as you can get. They've got too much going on to get involved in protests. Besides, most of them are pretty conservative and if you took a poll I think you would find the majority supported the Vietnam War and probably voted for Nixon both times."

"And Manuel?"

"He was never involved in any political activity that I knew about. Every once in a while we'd chew over what was going on at home and abroad. I guess you could say we were exceptions to the rule of medical student conservatism. We differed on the war. I generally supported what we were doing while Manny was opposed. But we agreed on the need for government spending on things like health care and education. And that was because of the kind of medicine we wanted to practice. But we really didn't spend a whole lot of time on that kind of stuff."

"Did he ever mention the political situation at home?"

"You mean in Argentina?" He repeated the hand-on-the forehead gesture. It seemed to be working. "Not a whole lot. I know he kept up with the news from Argentina, going over to the library whenever he had some free time to read the newspapers. Once or twice he talked about - what's his name? - the former dictator."

"Juan Perón?"

Snapping his fingers, he said, "That's it. Juan Perón. He told me this guy Perón was planning to return to Argentina and take over."

"How did he feel about that?"

"He didn't say much. As I told you, we rarely talked about politics. But I do remember him saying once that if this guy Perón did come back, he hoped that he could restore some peace to the country. He said that there was too much violence in Argentina and that was one reason he was glad to be here, away from all that."

I nodded. So far, everything Manuel's roommate told me seemed to jibe with what I had heard from Dean Baker. "Steve, when I spoke with Dean Baker he suggested that Manuel might have dropped out of school without telling anyone because of the pressure of his studies. He said that it was rare but that it did happen. What do you think?"

This time he didn't laugh. He wrinkled his brow and again brought his massive hands together with his fingers interlaced, almost as though he were praying. With a solemn expression on his face and in a somber tone in his voice he said, "I don't really think that Manny would do that. Why should he? He was one of the top students in our class. He worked hard but he was handling it okay. It just doesn't make any sense." He paused, looking uncomfortable, "But….

"But….?"

"I've known a few of the guys who flamed out. Sometimes you could see the signs. They were so up-tight and so tense that you just knew they were going to break. But there were others who never gave a clue. Everything appeared normal. They seemed to be sailing along and then – all of a sudden – they were gone. Some you heard from later, but others, it was like they dropped off the face of the earth."

Again, Kowalski was reconfirming what the Dean had told me. "And Manuel…?"

Kowalski took a deep breath and slowly let it out, his cheeks puffed. "I still don't think so. But even though he was my roommate, I sure didn't know everything about him. He kept a lot of things to himself. He could be a very private person. 'Still waters run deep' and all that."

"So maybe the fight he had with his father finally got to him and he snapped. Something like that?"

Kowalski nodded. "Yeah. But I still don't believe Manny dropped out – or maybe I don't *want* to believe it. I can't swear to you that it didn't happen."

We both knew that "dropping out" could mean more than simply leaving med school. But Kowalski already looked miserable enough so I didn't bring it up.

"I presume the police have already been over this, but were there any clues here in the apartment as to what might have happened? Any signs of a struggle?" I saw the quizzical look on Kowalski's face. "We don't think he's been kidnapped since there's been no ransom demand and he's been missing for several weeks now. But it could have been a kidnapping attempt that went bad and.....” I let the implication hang in the air. It wasn't a pretty thought.

Again Kowalski shook his head vigorously from side to side. “No. I sure didn't see anything like that. Everything was completely normal when I got back from my visit home. No signs of forced entry, nothing missing or out of place. In fact, all of Manny's stuff still seems to be here and where it should be. If he took off on his own, he didn't pack much.”

“Do you mind if I take a look at his room? Maybe the cops missed something.”

“Sure thing,” he said. Getting up from the couch, he waved for me to follow. He headed down a corridor that connected the living room with the kitchen. The bedrooms were on the right with a bathroom in between. Stopping at the first door, he took a key from his pocket and inserted it into the lock. “We didn't usually lock our doors,” he said with a quick grin, “unless we were entertaining and didn't want any sudden interruptions.” I returned the grin. “But this is Manny's room and I've made it a habit to keep it locked since he disappeared.” He turned the handle and opened the door for me to enter. “The police went over everything pretty thoroughly and I tried to put everything back the way it was before they came.”

“Thanks Steve,” I told him. “I'll make sure to leave everything in its place.”

He hung his head for a minute and when he raised it I could see tears glistening in his eyes. In a voice choked with emotion, he said “I want everything to be the same for Manny when he comes back - just like he never left.”

I reached over and patted him on the shoulder. I thought it unlikely that his hopes would be realized. But I was touched by his obvious affection for his roommate. He was a very decent guy. “I understand Steve. I promise I'll leave everything as I find it.”

He rubbed his eyes and struggled to regain control. “Well,” he said, his voice steadying, “I'll leave you to it. I have to get ready for classes this afternoon. If there's anything you need, just give a holler.”

I thanked him again. He nodded and headed for his own room, leaving the door ajar. I left it that way and turned around to begin my search.

It was an uncommonly neat room. Against the wall to my right was a bed that was made up to military precision standards. I was tempted to take out a quarter and bounce it off the blanket. Just beyond the bed was a closet. I opened the door and saw shirts, pants, and sport coats hanging neatly and in perfect order. There were several pairs of shoes on the floor of the closet, all polished to a mirror finish and with shoe trees to maintain the proper shape.

Next to the closet was a chest of drawers that had seen better days but was still serviceable. I opened each drawer to see the same kind of ordered neatness; socks and underwear carefully folded and sweaters neatly placed in plastic bags.

I went through each drawer methodically, looking for anything that might be out of place and came up empty. I made sure that everything went back exactly as I found them.

There was only one window in the room, looking out onto a nicely landscaped courtyard. Under the window was a "desk" crafted in the typical student fashion. A door placed over two filing cabinets at either end. I sat down in a wooden chair that had seen better days. On the top of the desk were note paper, pens, pencils, and paper clips, all neatly arranged. Nestled at the side of one of the filing cabinets was a brown case that contained a *Royal* portable typewriter. I assumed Manuel used it as needed and then stored it out of the way.

I opened the file drawer to my right and began the laborious process of going through each file of manila folders one by one. It didn't take as long as I had expected. An initial look told me that they were almost all class notes, organized, like everything else, in perfect order. I did find one file containing some financial material, but like the class notes, it provided no real clues as to what might have happened to Manuel Fernández. I presumed that he received personal correspondence, but if so there were no letters in the file. If I hoped to find written evidence of some dark secret – a mysterious girlfriend, coded messages from underground guerrilla groups – those hopes were dashed. No hints here. There was the possibility, of course, that either the police or the mysterious government duo had removed one or more of the files, looking for the same clues. I would ask Kowalski if they had taken anything once I had finished my own search.

Closing the file drawer, I turned to the wall opposite the bed. There was only one piece of furniture – if you could call it that – a bookcase crafted by placing flat boards between cinder blocks. Maybe there were some clues to be found there. I got up from behind the desk and prepared to continue my investigation when I came face-to-face with Che Guevara. I don't know how I had missed him, but there he was staring at me with those hypnotic eyes, sketched in black against a red background.

I didn't make much of it. His sister had told me – and his roommate had confirmed – that Manuel had a certain admiration for Che. But so did millions of other young people. And what college student no matter his or her political affiliations didn't have a poster of Che on the wall? Along with James Dean, Marilyn Monroe, and other pop culture icons. Still, there seemed to be some interesting crossovers between the young Argentine medical student I was looking for and the martyred Argentine doctor tracked down and killed by the CIA in Bolivia.

You often can tell a lot about a person by the books he reads. In Manuel's case, there were few surprises. The majority were medical text books with a heavy emphasis on diet, nutrition, and epidemic diseases. I thumbed through a couple of well-worn volumes. Unlike many students, including yours truly, Manuel did not mark up his book with marginal notes and underlining. Instead there were slips of paper every few pages noting items of importance. The notes he made to himself were in Spanish and in a neat-hand. If he hoped to be a successful doctor, I thought with a smile, he would have to work at making his handwriting less legible.

The medical books occupied most of the shelf space. There were, however, a few volumes of literature and politics. I quickly scanned the titles. From what I could tell, Manuel did have a predilection for leftist writers. His collection included C. Wright Mills' *Listen Yankee!*, Regis Debray's *Revolution within the Revolution*, and Gabriel García Márquez's *One Hundred Years of Solitude* in Spanish. Next to García Márquez was Che Guevara's *Reminiscences of the Cuban Revolutionary War*. I pulled it out and leafed through to see if Manuel had underlined anything or had even added his slips of paper. While the spine indicated the book had been read, there were no marks in it. No marginal notes that showed approval of a particular strategy or sympathy for a particular political statement.

Like the poster of Che, I didn't make too much of the collection. These titles, I'm sure, could be found in thousands of student rooms throughout the world and didn't by themselves prove any specific political direction.

Besides, there were other tomes – Dante's *Inferno*, Shakespear's *Collected Works*, Faulkner's *The Sound and the Fury*, Salinger's *The Catcher in the Rye* – that had nothing to do with politics.

I stood in the middle of the room and took a last look around. If only the walls could speak, I thought to myself, I might get some hint of what had happened to Manuel Fernández. But they were silent. Everything I had seen in his room seemed to confirm what I already knew about him – hard-working, serious, and well-organized. And despite what Dwight Whalen had told me, I saw little evidence that he had become a romantic revolutionary who had forsaken his family and his career to enter into the guerrilla struggle in Argentina. It was still a possibility, of course, but from all I could tell a rather remote one.

Closing the door behind me, I called out to Kowalski to tell him I was finished. Coming out of his own room with an expectant look on his face, he asked if I had found anything useful.

"I'm afraid not Steve." His face sank. "I guess the only surprise is that everything is so neat and orderly. Not what my own room was like when I was in college," I said with a grin.

He grinned back. "Not like mine either. I'd be embarrassed to show it to you. But," he added, "That was Manny. Neat as a pin."

"You told me that the room was *exactly* as you found it when you got back from your weekend trip."

"Yes. I haven't touched a thing," Kowalski said a bit defensively.

"What about the police? Or the government guys? Did they remove anything during their search?"

Kowalski shook his head vigorously from side to side. "No. No way. Not at all."

"How can you be so sure?"

"Because I was in the room with them the whole time to make sure that they put everything back the way they found it. If they had tried to take anything, I would have seen them do it."

So no missing clues, I thought to myself. "So why didn't you keep a close watch on me Steve?"

He shrugged. "I don't know. You seemed more trustworthy somehow. You know, being hired by Manuel's sister and all." Then his eyes narrowed. "You didn't take anything did you?"

I opened my coat and held my arms out. "You're free to search me."

He waved his hand dismissively, a little insulted. "No. No. That's okay."

There wasn't much more to say. Kowalski gave me the names and addresses of four other med students who lived in the complex and who knew Manny. The police had already spoken to them but apparently not the government agents, if that's who they were. I didn't expect to get much from them but thanked Kowalski for his help and promised to get in touch with him when I found out what had happened to his roommate. I didn't say *if* I found him at this point, wanting to keep up his confidence and mine. But the look on his face as we shook hands said that he knew as well as I did that there was a better than even chance he would never see Manuel Fernández again.

Seven

I walked to the nearby apartments to talk to the other med students. Two were out and the two I spoke with didn't have anything to add to what I already knew. They confirmed the fact that Manuel was serious and hard-working but also likable and easy to get along with. They had no idea what had happened to him and like his roommate were worried about his mysterious disappearance, which seemed to them totally out of character. I thanked them for their time and told them I would let Kowalski know whatever I found out.

My next stop was the Durham police station. On the way I stopped for a quick hamburger and a cup of coffee at a local eatery called Baily's near the east campus. From there, I drove to the station house located a few blocks from the Washington Duke hotel. I found a parking spot a block away and entered through the main doors a little after one thirty. At the desk, I showed the sergeant on duty my PI credentials, told him I had been hired to try to track down a missing Duke med student, Manuel Fernández, and asked if I could speak to the officer in charge of the investigation.

He gave me a look that I suppose all policemen reserve for private detectives, something akin to acute indigestion. For a moment I thought he was going to tell me to get lost. But after a few seconds of the silent treatment, he reluctantly picked up the phone and put a call through. Once the connection had been made, he provided the basic information in a bored voice to whoever was on the other end, casting unfriendly glances in my direction as he did so. I was pleasantly surprised when he nodded his head, hung up the phone, and told me that the officer in charge of the investigation would see me. He pointed me down the corridor to my right, second door on the left. I thanked him and hurried down the hall.

The lettering on the door said "Detective Lyle Merriweather." I knocked and heard a deep southern voice say, "Come on in."

I opened the door to find Detective Merriweather sitting at his desk, a sheaf of papers in front of him and a cup of coffee in his left hand. Without getting up, he waved me to a chair in front of the desk while he put his coffee cup down, pushed the papers in front of him to one side, and gave me a steely stare. No handshake, no introduction, no preliminaries. While the look on his face wasn't quite as hostile as that of the desk sergeant, it wasn't exactly warm and welcoming either.

Merriweather was somewhere in his mid-forties. He had curly reddish-brown hair, beginning to recede a bit, light skin with freckles, gray-green eyes, thin lips, a pointed chin, and a nose that, like Steve Kowalski's, had been broken more than once. He wore a white dress shirt with the sleeves rolled up and his tie loosened. Since he was sitting, I couldn't tell how tall he was, but I estimated probably about five ten or eleven. He looked wiry and tough. I noticed a tattoo of a black shield with the left profile of an eagle and the word "airborne" on his right forearm. I used that as a way to break the ice.

"I see that you were in the Army: The 101st airborne, The 'Screaming Eagles.'" I said, pointing to the tattoo and hoping to impress him with my acute powers of observation.

"Yeah. What of it?" he responded, the ice still frozen.

"Well, so was I. I did a couple of tours in Vietnam, working for the Adjutant General in Saigon. Criminal Investigation Division."

I could sense some melting. "Hmm. Is that so? We might have overlapped." Glancing at his arm and the tattoo, he added, "Actually, I got this when I was still in training. After a few jumps I decided the paratroops were not for me and became an MP instead. I was in Saigon in the mid-sixties."

I gave him a grin and we began to trade war stories. After about fifteen minutes, the ice had melted into a warm puddle and we got down to business.

"So you're here trying to find out what happened to Manuel Fernández?"

"Yeah. I spoke with the Dean over at the Duke Medical School this morning and he speculated that maybe Fernández dropped out because the pressure of his studies finally got to him. When I talked to his roommate later he more or less dismissed that explanation – but didn't have any alternative theories." As I spoke, Merriwether started tapping a pencil eraser rhythmically on his desk but kept his face expressionless.

"I know that you looked into the matter and wondered if you found anything that wasn't in the official report. You know, some piece of information that might not be worth noting down but that might help me get a handle on his disappearance."

Merriweather frowned and I could see him searching his memory. Finally, he shook his head. "No. Nothing I can think of." Leaning forward, he looked me straight on. "You know, we get maybe two or three calls every month from parents of kids at Duke who haven't heard from them in a while and want us to try to track them down. In most of these cases it's just a matter of the kid forgetting to write or call home. We can usually locate them on campus and tell them their parents are worried and to get in touch right away. We usually stay around to make sure they call."

I didn't have much trouble reading the look on Merriweather's face. For the cops, this must be a pain in the butt. He saw my expression. "Yeah. Not exactly challenging police work." But then he got more serious. "Sometimes, though, the kid really has taken a powder. The most harmless cases are when they go on some kind of crazy road trip. They cut classes and take off for New Orleans and Mardi Gras – something like that. Naturally, they don't want to let their parents know what they're up to and they eventually return. But we also have others who drop totally out of sight and never come back. In those cases we can't do much more than snoop around and then notify the State Police and the FBI. Once they've flown the coop and are beyond our jurisdiction, it's out of our hands."

"And that seems to have been the case with Manuel Fernández?"

He wrinkled his brow. "Yeah. That *seems* to have been the case."

"But you're not convinced?"

He put both hands on his cheeks and rubbed them vigorously, then put them flat down on the desk. "His case fits the general pattern – just like the Dean said. But nine times out of ten, the kid who takes off leaves plenty of evidence. Usually, there is a history of trouble – drinking, missing classes, and more and more these days, signs of drug use. And, when we search their rooms – like we did with Fernández – we find some written evidence; a diary maybe, or letters. But with Fernández…."

"Nothing. Nothing that fit the pattern."

"Right. From all we could tell, he was a good student who expected to graduate. And there was absolutely no physical evidence to indicate why he had left – or indeed, except for the fact that he was no longer around, that he had left at all. There was nothing missing or out of order in his apartment and no witnesses who had seen anything suspicious. It was though he had vanished by magic. Here one moment and gone the next. Poof! Just like that." He punctuated this last remark, as had Dean Baker, with a clap of his hands.

"You ever have a case like that before?"

"Never. And it still bugs me." He took a breath. "I guess it's no secret that the Duke kids don't always get along with us. Most of them are okay, but we spend a lot of time making sure they don't get out of hand and cleaning up their messes when they do. And there's always been some 'town-gown' tension, what with most of the students coming from pretty well-to-do backgrounds and often acting like spoiled brats. Many of us," he said, waving his right hand in a circle above his head to indicate the rest of the force, "served in Vietnam. And we weren't wild about all that campus anti-war stuff. When some of the more radical students took over the administration building several years ago, a few of us were ready to take action and bust heads. But the administration kept us at arm's-length and finally resolved matters without our intervention." The look on his face seemed to indicate that he thought this was too bad and that he would have enjoyed roughing up some of the rebellious students.

I wasn't sure where Merriweather was going with this, but I could guess. "So these days," I said, "when a student goes missing, it may be that the investigation isn't as thorough as it might be."

He shrugged and his face flushed. "Yeah. I'm afraid so. My partner and I were assigned to the Fernández case and we *did* conduct a thorough investigation. *But*," he added, lowering his voice, "our chief pulled us off it after a few days. He told us we had other, more important cases to deal with than another missing Duke student, who would probably show up eventually."

"Was that standard operating procedure for your chief?"

Merriweather looked decidedly uncomfortable. I could see he was engaged in some mental gymnastics as he wrestled over how to respond. He glanced over my shoulder to assure himself that the door was closed and then beckoned me closer to his desk. Again in a low voice, he said, "Listen. What I'm about to tell you has to stay *strictly* confidential. I could be in big trouble if you blab a word of this. Understood?"

"Sure Lyle." I figured it was now safe to be on a first-name basis. "You have my word on it."

He let out a breath. "Okay. Here's the deal. We hadn't been on the case for more than twenty-four hours when the chief had a visit from two guys from the government and…"

I interrupted. "Any idea which agency?"

'We weren't introduced. They only spoke to the chief and I only saw them briefly in the hallway. I presumed they were from the FBI. They were the standard government issue. You know the type. Mid-thirties, dark suit, crew cut."

I nodded. "At any rate," he continued, "after their visit, the chief called us into his office and told us we should wrap up our investigation as quickly as possible and move on to other cases. While he didn't give us any details, he said Fernández's disappearance had to do with some complicated and sensitive 'diplomatic matters' and we weren't to stick our noses into it. Just drop it."

"Just like that?"

"Just like that."

"And that's why it still bugs you?"

Merriweather nodded and shrugged his shoulders as if to say, "Yeah. But what can I do?"

This was a new wrinkle. But there was little I could do at the moment to follow up on it. After promising Merriweather I would keep this information confidential I couldn't very well go to the chief and ask him what was going on. Even if I did, he would most likely stone wall me. But once I got back to Washington I could sniff around and see if either Fred Matthews or Dwight Whalen could shed some light on what these somewhat mysterious "government officials" had been up to – and just what were the "diplomatic matters" that necessitated curtailing the investigation into Manuel Fernández's disappearance.

"So what do you think happened to Fernández?" I asked Merriweather.

Again, he rubbed his face and shrugged his shoulders. "Damned if I know. Given the way he just vanished, if I had to bet I'd say it was some kind of kidnapping. Whoever did it probably waylaid him someplace where nobody could spot what they were up to and took him away by force. If they'd done it at his apartment there would have been some clues. But..."

"But it's been several weeks and no ransom demand" I interjected.

He inclined his head in agreement. "Right. If he was kidnapped, why no word from the kidnappers?"

Suddenly, a dark thought hit me. "What if somebody just wanted to get rid of him?"

Merriweather looked skeptical. "You mean somebody with a serious grudge?"

"Yeah. Or maybe someone who had a bone to pick with the family. Manuel's father is an important figure in the Argentine diplomatic service. Maybe he rubbed somebody the wrong way at some point in his career and this is their way of exacting revenge."

As I spun this theory, I had some difficulty in believing it myself. As things turned out, I was closer to the truth than I knew.

"From all we know," Merriweather said, "the kid was well-liked and nothing came up in our investigation to indicate he had any enemies out there; certainly nobody on our radar who would go to the extreme of murdering him. As for the father, who knows? That's something you would have to look into." He paused for a minute. "You know, come to think of it, we never did hear from the kid's parents, only from his sister. I didn't think much of it at the time, but now that you mention him it strikes me as pretty strange. It's always the parents who call us when a kid goes missing."

I then explained the recent falling out between father and son and what Elena had told me about Fernández senior's explanation for why Manuel had dropped out of sight.

Merriweather again looked skeptical. But then, with a sigh, said, "I've been at this business for a while and learned not to dismiss any possible motive for what might seem strange or abnormal human behavior. From what I was able to gather about the kid's character, I can't imagine him dropping out just to spite his old man." He shrugged again. "But who knows?"

We probably could have kicked around a few more theories but by this time I figured I had discovered all that I was going to find out in Durham and that it was time to head back to Washington. I thanked Merriweather for his assistance and as we shook hands he wished me luck and asked me to keep him posted. As I had with Steve Kowalski, I promised that I would, whatever the final result. And also as with Kowalski, I couldn't shake the feeling that the news I would provide him would not be good.

Eight

The drive back to Washington was uneventful. I stopped at the same diner where I had eaten on the way down. The parking lot again was full with a mix of in-and out-of-state licenses. I found a space next to a big truck at the far corner of the lot and as I walked to the diner scanned each vehicle for the gray sedan. I came up empty.

I took a stool at the counter and picked up the menu. Thelma was again working and gave me a conspiratorial wink as I ordered fried chicken with all the fixings. The quality of the food had not declined in twenty-four hours and I once more polished things off with pie and coffee.

Exiting the diner I again scanned the lot for the gray sedan and again didn't spot it. Of course, if someone was pursuing me, they could be hiding at any number of places along the access road and pick me up as I headed for the highway. I didn't notice anything as I got back on the interstate, but still couldn't shake the feeling I was being tailed.

Purring along at a smooth sixty miles per hour, I found WMAL on the radio and tuned in Felix Grant's jazz show, one of my favorites. With the Modern Jazz Quartet, Charlie Byrd, and Charlie Parker in the background, I tried to put my thoughts in order.

What had happened to Manuel Fernández? His father believed Manuel had disappeared because of their falling out. From what I had been able to gather, the chances of that having happened were pretty slim. Dean Baker suggested that the pressure might have gotten to Manuel and he had dropped out. But his roommate was almost a hundred percent positive that had not been the case. His disappearance had all the earmarks of a kidnapping. But there had been no ransom demand. Then there was the possibility that someone had decided to kill him and hide the body.

Unlikely – and gruesome – but still a possibility. I wasn't sure, however, that it was one that I wanted to share with his sister until every other avenue had been pursued.

And then, of course, there was Dwight Whalen's belief that Manuel had decided to join Argentina's revolutionaries. From what everyone in Durham had told me that also seemed unlikely. Manuel had not been overtly political and despite his generally leftist sympathies his sister had been emphatic that he was opposed to violent actions. Still, as Lyle Merriweather had reminded me, human behavior could often be unpredictable and the most unlikely explanation often turned out to be the one that was correct, Occam's Razor notwithstanding.

At this point I didn't have enough hard evidence to discount any of these theories. And after about thirty minutes of mulling them over, I decided to give my mind a rest and simply listen to the music and enjoy the ride.

Making good time, I crossed over Memorial Bridge a little after nine. I headed up Constitution Avenue to Sixteenth Street, where I turned left towards DuPont Circle and my apartment. Rush hour was long over and there was little in the way of traffic. At this time of night, the District was virtually deserted, most of the federal workers having departed for their homes in the suburbs. D.C. night life in places like Georgetown had picked up in recent years but nobody would mistake downtown Washington for Times Square.

I pulled into my basement garage at nine-fifteen on the dot. Locking up, I decided to exit out onto the street rather than take the interior stairs to my second-floor apartment. I carried my overnight bag in my left hand just in case I needed my right hand free. Out on the street, well-lit by lamps, I saw the usual line of cars parked bumper-to-bumper all along the block. So far as I could tell, there were no gray sedans and all the cars looked empty. Nonetheless, I still had that creepy feeling between my shoulder blades that someone was watching me.

After scoping out the cars, I headed upstairs. Unlocking the door to my apartment, I saw that everything had been as I had left it. I'd gotten into the habit of laying out little traps to determine if anybody had broken in during my absence and so far as I could tell no one had.

Putting my bag down on the floor I headed for the phone and dialed the number Elena Fernández had given me. After several rings, an older female voice with a decidedly Spanish accent picked up at the other end. I guessed it was probably a servant and in Spanish identified myself and asked if I could speak with Señorita Fernández. "*Un momento señor*," she replied, and after a brief interval Elena's voice came over the phone.

"Hello Mister Cor...Frank" Then, in a rush, "Do you have any news? Did you find out anything about what happened to Manuel?"

I began to have some second thoughts about having called her. On the one hand, I *had* promised to get in touch as soon as I returned from Durham and knew that she was expecting my call. Not to have contacted her would only have added to her anxiety. On the other hand, at that point all I had to tell her was mostly speculative and too complicated for a telephone conversation. I preferred for various reasons to discuss what I had found out – and not found out – face-to-face.

"Well, I did gather some useful information," I finally replied. "But it's a little too complex to discuss over the phone. Besides, I'm pretty tired and would like the opportunity to sleep on some thoughts before I lay them out for you. Can you meet me for breakfast tomorrow? Say eight o'clock in the coffee shop at the Mayflower Hotel?"

I could sense that she was not happy with the postponement. I could hear the disappointment in her voice when she said, "Well yes. Yes Frank. That would be fine. I'll see you at the Mayflower tomorrow." Then she added in a warmer tone, "Thank you for calling. I know that you must have had a tiring day and I appreciate your getting in touch with me."

After exchanging *hasta mañanas* she hung up the receiver. I pressed the button for a new dial tone and immediately called Dwight Whalen at his home number to see if he knew anything about the mysterious G-men who had showed up in Durham. But after about twenty rings and getting no answer I hung up. Dwight was probably at some embassy reception, spreading the charm.

I then called Fred Matthews, who was at home and picked up right away. First, I thanked him for sending Elena Fernández my way. Then I filled him in on my trip to Durham and asked him if he knew about any FBI surveillance on Manuel Fernández or if he had any clue to the identity of the two government agents who had met with the Durham chief of police.

There was a lengthy pause before he answered. "I'll need to check on it Frank," he said. "But so far as I know, the Bureau has not been involved in keeping tabs on Manuel Fernández, either recently or in the past. When his sister asked me to look into what had happened to him, nothing came up on our radar. But," he repeated, "I'll look into it first thing in the morning and get back to you."

I decided to push him a little. "Listen Fred. I spoke with a buddy of mine at State who thinks Manuel has dropped out of school – and out of sight – to join some revolutionary movement in Argentina. And since it's well–known that the FBI kept close tabs on radical antiwar students, I just wondered if maybe somehow Manuel was brought to the Bureau's attention and…."

Matthews interrupted, sounding annoyed. "Yeah. Yeah. We did do that. It's hardly a secret. But since things have quieted down on most campuses, we've lowered our profile. So I'd be pretty surprised if we were still keeping watch on Fernández – that is, if we ever did in the first place. Was he active in the antiwar movement?"

"Not from what people at Duke told me. He had political beliefs that I guess you could label left of center, but didn't participate in any protests. All the reports I got indicated he was a serious and dedicated med student, aiming to finish his degree and not prone to making any waves."

"Hmmm," Matthews mused. "That's curious. Did your State Department source indicate where he got his information that Fernández was off to fight the revolution?"

"No. Not really. And I'm not sure he has any hard evidence to back it up. It seemed more like 'informed speculation' on his part."

"Well Frank. It seems you have quite a mystery to unravel. Not your simple case of a runaway teenager is it?"

"No Fred. Not at all. But thanks again for sending the case my way. It's intriguing in a variety of ways."

I could hear him chuckle over the phone. "Not the least of those ways being Elena Fernández, right?"

I laughed back. "Busted."

Fred said he would call me tomorrow as soon as he checked on the possibility of any FBI surveillance on Manuel Fernández. After a few parting remarks we broke the connection.

What I had told Elena about being tired from the trip was not an exaggeration. But my mind was also racing, trying to digest all that I had absorbed during the day. I decided that before hitting the sack I would write down as much of what I could recall from my various conversations over the past two days before I let something slip from my memory. Perhaps it would be some vital clue that would unlock the entire mystery. I grabbed some lined notebook paper and began to scribble down everything I could recall from the time of my meeting with Elena Fernández to my conversation with Lyle Merriweather.

After about an hour of non-stop writing I had filled almost ten pages. It was now past eleven and I could feel my eyelids hanging heavy. Putting down my pen, I decided that I had reached the point of diminishing returns and needed to get some sleep. Undressing quickly, I slipped into my pajamas and after brushing my teeth and using the toilet, dropped gratefully onto my bed and pulled the covers up. Even though my brain was still percolating, physical fatigue took over and I was soon fast asleep.

Nine

I awoke with a start when my alarm went off at six thirty. Rubbing the sleep from my eyes I jumped into my jogging gear. I wanted to get in my daily run before my scheduled eight o'clock breakfast with Elena Fernández.

Outside, our warm and sunny spring weather had been replaced with a chilly drizzle. I could feel my muscles complaining as I did a few warm-up exercises, paying the penalty for missing my run the day before and my twelve hours or so cramped into my MG. But once I started jogging down Connecticut Avenue, I was able to pick up the pace and establish a good rhythm. I made good time and managed to get in a few extra laps around the Tidal Basin that helped compensate for missing out the previous day.

I was back in my apartment by seven thirty. I shaved, showered, brushed my teeth, and dressed quickly in my office outfit. I made it to the Mayflower coffee shop at a little before eight but Elena was already there ahead of me. I knew she must be anxious to find out the results of my trip.

The coffee shop was bustling, full of the national – and international – movers and shakers who were either temporary guests or who lived at the hotel full-time. The Mayflower was the best-known hotel in the city, a favorite of politicians, lobbyists, and journalists. As I made my way to the corner table where Elena was sitting I could hear a background hum of "significant" conversations, most of which, so far as I could determine, were dominated by the potential implications of the Watergate Scandal. I thought I even heard the word "impeachment" uttered a few times as I navigated the room.

Elena rose to greet me, extending her hand, which I took in mine and gave a gentle squeeze. Some color rose in her cheeks as I did so. We took our seats. I gave her what I hoped was a confidence-building smile as we exchanged pleasantries and placed our orders – the full complement of bacon, eggs, hash browns, and orange juice for me, looking to replenish after my morning exercise, and only a fruit cup and a Danish for Elena. The waitress left us with a carafe of coffee and I poured a healthy cup for myself. Elena already had a cup of tea in front of her along with a pot of hot water.

She was dressed casually in black slacks, a white blouse, and a cream-collared sweater. On the back of her seat was a tan raincoat. Her face was still beautiful but there were dark shadows under her eyes as though she had not gotten much sleep. I kicked myself mentally realizing that my ambiguous phone call and postponing my report had undoubtedly been the cause. I could also see a slight tremor in her hand as she added sugar and cream to her tea and took a tentative sip. Putting her cup down, she folded her hands tightly in front of her and her shoulders stiffened as though bracing for the worst.

"Well Frank," she asked with a note of trepidation and somber look, "What were you able to find out?"

I couldn't think of any way to sugarcoat what I had to say. "I'm afraid not a whole lot – not much more than you already knew." I could see the look of dismay on her face as I went over my conversations with Dean Baker, Steve Kowalski, and Lyle Merriweather. I left out for the time being any mention of the mysterious government agents who I suspected had followed me to Durham and who may have been the same team that had showed up soon after Manuel went missing. I also didn't raise the possibility that Manuel might have been the victim of foul play and was now buried somewhere deep in the North Carolina woods. There was no evidence that was the case and I didn't want to upset her any more than she already was. And, while Manuel's disappearance had all the characteristics of a kidnapping, she already knew that there had been no word from the kidnappers, if that is indeed what happened.

I did tell her about the Dean's speculation that Manuel might have snapped under the pressure and had dropped out, but she immediately shook her head firmly back and forth. "No. No Frank. Finishing school and becoming a practicing physician was all that Manuel wanted. And he was doing well. No. It's inconceivable that he would just quit like that."

I didn't argue. I thought she was probably right. Before I could continue laying out my other possibility our waitress brought our food and Elena urged me to dig into my breakfast before it got cold. I felt a bit awkward about the interruption, especially as Elena barely touched what she had in front of her, so I cleaned my plate as quickly as I could.

Once I had finished, I leaned forward and encouraged her to do the same. I didn't think anybody was paying us much attention amid the hubbub of the room, but I thought it best to keep what I had to say next between the two of us. "Well Elena," I began, "I really didn't get many answers in Durham to the mystery of your brother's disappearance. But before I left, I checked in with a friend of mine at the State Department who works on the Latin American Desk and who knows your father and is familiar with you and your brother."

Elena's eyes got wider and I could see her trying to sift through her memory as to who my friend might be. At this point, I thought it best not to reveal Dwight's identity to Elena and maybe get him in trouble with Fernández senior. While I didn't want to put Dwight's career ambitions above the interests of my client, I also didn't want to do any unnecessary damage to his reputation if I could avoid it.

"And what he told me was that your brother had dropped out of medical school – and out of sight – to join a revolutionary group in Argentina. He said it was most likely the *Ejército Revolucionario del Pueblo* and..."

She again shook her head decidedly from side to side. "No. No. Your friend must be mistaken. You did ask me about that during our first meeting. It's just not possible. Manuel abhors violence," she said in a firm voice. But then, with a reflective look on her face and at a lower pitch, she added, "It just doesn't make any sense. I can't imagine Manuel doing such a thing..."

I could sense some doubt in her tone and her look, as I had before when we discussed this possibility. This time I decided to pursue the issue. "Look Elena, I know from my own experience that sometimes things happen to people that lead them to make rash decisions based more on emotion than common sense. It can come as a total surprise. And it can happen to people we think we know well. Everything seems normal and then they do something we never expected. Could that have happened to Manuel? Could something – some event that maybe you weren't aware of – have touched him off? We know that his political sympathies were on the left. Maybe he decided that the course he had set for himself – being a doctor and treating the poor – would take too long to accomplish what he hoped to achieve. Maybe he decided that more direct action was called for. Maybe…"

She waved for me to stop the bombardment. I was beginning to sound like a prosecuting attorney trying to convict someone of a crime. Her hands were tightly clenched in front of her and her eyes were moist. I reached over the table and put my hands over hers and gave them a soft squeeze. "I'm sorry Elena. I didn't mean to upset you. I just want to explore all possibilities…"

She gave me a smile as I removed my hands. "No. Frank. It's all right. I understand. You are just doing your job."

I breathed a sigh of relief and returned her smile. She took a deep breath to compose herself and then paused a moment to gather her thoughts. "Despite what your friend has told you, I still can't believe that Manuel would give up his studies and his career to join a revolutionary group like the People's Revolutionary Army. But I've also got to admit that it is an explanation that would fit the facts – the falling out with my father over politics and his disappearance without telling anyone. As much as I hate to admit it, looking at everything objectively, it seems perhaps the most logical and likely reason for why he dropped out of sight so mysteriously."

I didn't want to complicate matters, but I thought of a point that might undermine the theory. "Do you think he would have taken this step without talking to you about it? You said the two of you were very close."

She chewed on that for a few seconds. "That's difficult to say. We always confided in one another and didn't keep any secrets between us. But maybe Manuel was afraid that if he did tell me of his plans I would try to talk him out of it…"

"And maybe he was afraid that you would succeed?"

"Yes. And there is something else. You said that perhaps something happened – some event – that might have caused Manuel to make a rash decision based more on emotions than on common sense."

I nodded, encouraging her to continue. "Well last fall we got word that one of Manuel's best friends – Gregorio Robles – had been found dead in a shallow grave just outside of Buenos Aires. He had been tortured and then executed with a bullet to the back of the head. It was horrible. Manuel was very upset. He had known Gregorio since childhood. They had gone to the same schools from elementary through high school. Like Manuel, Gregorio planned to be a doctor who would serve the poor. When Manuel went to Duke, Gregorio stayed on at the medical school of the University of Buenos Aires, where he became a leader of the main Marxist group there. Manuel and he would still hang out together whenever my brother returned to Buenos Aires, just like they always had. But politics had begun to strain their friendship."

Elena paused for a minute to take a drink of water. I could see that the memories of what she was describing were painful ones. "Gregorio was becoming increasingly radical in his thinking. He and Manuel had some pretty bitter arguments. Gregorio accused Manuel of being insufficiently committed to fundamental change in our country – as they say here – 'part of the problem, not of the solution.' He also said that Manuel was no better than his father, serving a military regime that protected the rich and exploited the poor and…."

I held up a hand to interrupt. "Do you think that might have been behind your brother's confrontation with your father?"

She thought for a moment. "Yes. Probably so. I hadn't made the connection before. It was only a week or so before Manuel came home for Christmas that he heard Gregorio had been killed."

"I'm sorry for the interruption," I said, asking her to continue.

"The thing is, when Manuel returned from Buenos Aires at the end of last summer he told me – in the strictest confidence – that Gregorio was an active member of the People's Revolutionary Army. While Gregorio continued his studies during the daytime, he helped rob banks, plant bombs, and kidnap politicians and foreign executives at night."

She paused for another sip of water. Putting down the glass, she continued. "When Manuel told me this, I was not totally surprised. Gregorio had always been very opinionated, very sure of his beliefs – and impulsive. When I made it clear that I totally disapproved of the course Gregorio had taken, Manuel seemed to agree with me. I remember him nodding his head when I condemned Gregorio's actions. But now that I think back on our conversation, I also remember a look that seemed to be one of unspoken admiration on Manuel's face. And maybe even a bit of guilt that his best friend had made a commitment that he himself could not." Then, with a wave of her hand, she added, "But maybe my memory is playing tricks on me. I still can't believe that Manuel would do what your friend suggests. I just can't." Tears formed at the corners of her eyes. "Or maybe I just don't *want* to believe it."

I thought about moving to Elena's side of the table and taking her in my arms, providing what comfort I could. But that would be unprofessional – plus I didn't know how she would react. Instead I said, keeping my voice soft, "I can understand your doubts Elena. But from what you have just told me we cannot rule out the possibility either. And, at the moment, I really don't have any other leads to follow here. So, if you want me to stay on the case, it looks as though my next move would be to go to Buenos Aires, snoop around and see if I can find out anything about your brother. But, as I said before, that will add considerably to your expenses."

She shrugged and then gave me a quick smile. "Don't worry Frank. Money is not a problem. I just want you to find my brother, no matter what it costs. And no matter what you might find out. I need to know."

The thought hit me then that if Manuel had indeed returned to Argentina to join the revolution that was a more encouraging possibility than some of the others. At least he might still be alive although I guess from what happened to his friend Gregorio joining the People's Revolutionary Army carried considerable risk. But I decided now was not the moment to express these thoughts to Elena. She was already carrying enough of a burden.

Ten

Trying to put Elena at ease, I shifted our conversation to less pressing matters. We spent about forty-five minutes telling one another about our respective backgrounds and experiences. I was even able to elicit a chuckle or two from her with some of my more outlandish anecdotes. By the time we finished and I paid the bill, her body language suggested that she was less tense than when I had first seen her. But I could still see the worry in her eyes.

Before we left our table, Elena took a sheet of paper from her purse and jotted down the names and numbers of a few people in Buenos Aires who might be helpful in my search for Manuel. I folded up the paper and put it in my inside jacket pocket. I told her that I had an old friend from my days in Saigon who lived in Buenos Aires and knew his way around.

We left the Mayflower a little after nine. The drizzle had stopped and the sun had come out, promising another warm and sunny spring day. Outside the hotel we turned left towards K Street. When we reached the intersection with Connecticut, we walked a few blocks west on K to a branch of the Riggs Bank where Elena had her account. She withdrew three thousand dollars and then handed the envelope with the cash over to me. I put it in the same pocket as her list of names, giving it a pat and putting a look on my face that I hoped said *"It's safe with me."*

Exiting the bank we continued on K to the nearest bus stop. Elena was headed for Georgetown to do a bit of studying in the library before her first class at eleven. I waited with her until her bus arrived. As it was pulling up, we prepared to say our goodbyes. Her eyes still had that worried look but she mustered a smile. "Well Frank," she said, "Best of luck to you in Buenos Aires. And *please* do let me know as soon as you can what you find out."

"I will Elena. As soon as I can," I assured her.

As the bus doors opened she extended her hand and I took it in mine. Then, impulsively, I leaned forward and gave her a kiss on the cheek. Very unprofessional I know, but it somehow seemed the right thing to do. Elena looked surprised but thankfully not displeased. She blushed a bit and before she turned to board the bus gave me a warm smile and a friendly wave.

"*Hasta la vista* Frank," she said as she climbed the steps, looking back at me over her shoulder with a look that under other circumstances I would describe as almost coquettish.

"*Hasta la vista* Elena," I replied as the doors closed and the bus carried her off to Georgetown.

I stood still for a moment, stupidly watching the bus make its smoky, noisy way down K Street. I must have looked like a character from some sappy romantic movie, standing on the pier as the boat carrying the woman he loved drifted out of sight.

After a few seconds of immobility, I shook my head and wiped the goofy grin from my face. It was time to get down to business.

I retraced my steps along K Street and headed to my office. Along the way, I stopped at a travel agency I had used in the past and purchased a ticket on Pan American for my trip to Buenos Aires. Luckily, there was room on tonight's flight out of Kennedy, arriving in Buenos Aires early the next afternoon. I paid in cash for a round trip ticket, leaving the return date open. That took up eight hundred of the three thousand Elena had given me. I kept two hundred in cash and transferred the rest to traveler's checks.

By the time I got to my office it was ten thirty. After locking my plane ticket, the traveler's checks, and the cash in my office safe, I called Dwight Whalen at the State Department. When I got through to his office, his secretary told me that he had been called out of the country on a "special assignment" and was not expected back for several weeks. When I asked for details, she gave me the "confidential" line and hung up rather abruptly. I immediately wondered if Dwight's taking off had anything to do with my visit and our conversation about Manuel Fernández, a conversation that had clearly made him uncomfortable despite his best efforts to hide it. Maybe I was being overly-suspicious. There could be a host of reasons why Dwight had been called overseas – any number of crises to manage.

There was one way to put my suspicions to rest. I had an excellent source at State – my father. I dialed his number and when his secretary picked up she recognized my voice immediately. "Frank," she said. "How good to hear from you. It's been a while."

There was a bit of a tease in her tone, and perhaps a bit of admonishment as well. My father's secretary, Betsy Clark, an attractive redhead about my age, and I had dated for a while a year or so ago. We initially hit it off, but over time decided that we were not meant for a long-term relationship and parted company with few recriminations. But from what my father let slip from time to time, Betsy had not yet found a suitable replacement and was still carrying a bit of a torch for me.

"Yes Betsy," I replied, offering up a lame excuse. "Actually, I've been pretty busy with my new job. It's kept me hopping and out of town for a good part of the past several months."

Even though it was true, it sounded hollow even to me. Betsy had been skeptical about my career choice and it was one of the main reasons that we had stopped seeing each other. I suppose I was trying to let her know that I had made the right decision and that things were working out well for me. But just why I felt I had to justify myself to her I couldn't say.

"I suppose you want to speak to your father," she said. I thought I detected a tone of disappointment but maybe that was just my imagination. When I said that I did, she put me right through.

When my dad picked up, I asked him if he might be free for lunch. He was and we agreed to meet at twelve thirty at one of our favorite spots – Duke Zeibert's on Connecticut Avenue.

Almost as soon as I hung up, the phone rang. I picked it up immediately. "Frank?" It was Fred Matthews.

"Yes Fred. How are you?"

"Fine. Fine. Listen. I contacted everybody I could think of this morning to see if we had been running any surveillance on Manuel Fernández and came up empty. If there was any government agency keeping tabs on him it wasn't the Bureau."

The thought crossed my mind that if the FBI had been involved in some hush-hush operation to spy on Manuel, Fred would be under constraint not to reveal that fact to me no matter his long-time friendship with our family. But from the tone of his voice, I thought he was telling me the truth.

"Thanks a lot for looking into the matter for me," I said. "I really appreciate it."

"Sure Frank. Sure. No problem."

"Any ideas as to who the mysterious G-men who showed up in Durham might be?"

There was a brief pause and then he said, "When you called last night, I began to think over other possibilities if it turned out that it wasn't the Bureau that was keeping an eye on Manuel Fernández. And the first thought that came to me was that it might be our friends across the Potomac." By that he meant the CIA in Langley. "As you know, they are prohibited from operating domestically, which is supposed to be our domain. But they've crossed that line on more than one occasion. So I figured, given that it involved foreign nationals, the Agency might consider Fernández fair game."

I didn't interrupt, but I had been entertaining the same thought.

"So after you phoned me, I called a friend of mine at Langley to see if he knew about any surveillance on Manuel. He said that as a favor to me he would look into it. I could tell, understandably, that he wasn't very enthusiastic about it. But I just heard from him before I called you and he swears that the CIA has not been running any covert action that involves Manuel Fernández – or any member of his family. I have my doubts. There was something in his voice – I guess the way that he so definitively denied any Agency involvement that didn't ring true. I can't prove it of course, but if I had to bet, I'd bet that it was Agency spooks that showed up in Durham after Fernández disappeared."

Although I didn't express them, I immediately had my own doubts about Fred's suspicions. The bad blood between the FBI and the CIA was an open secret and the two agencies seemed to spend as much time fighting each other over turf battles as dealing with their respective enemies. And I didn't think Fred was immune from the consequences of that rivalry. Besides any number of other government agencies might conceivably have sent agents to Durham – the Pentagon, the National Security Agency, maybe even the Secret Service, thinking that Manuel, because of his leftist sympathies, might even prove to be a threat to the President. In the current climate of paranoia stirred up by the Watergate Scandal, I could imagine any number of scenarios to explain the presence of the men in the gray sedan.

I decided that trying to unsnarl the bureaucratic tangle at this stage would not be productive. Instead, I thanked Fred again for his efforts and told him that my next step was to go to Argentina and see if I could find any leads there. He gave me the names of a couple of people he knew in the U.S. Embassy who might be able to lend me a hand. He wished me luck.

After I hung up, I pulled a legal pad out of my desk drawer and wrote down the names that Fred had given me as well as those that Elena had provided. I took out the card from my wallet that had the name of the contact Dwight Whalen had suggested and added it to the list. They might prove helpful but they were all strangers. I needed someone I knew and trusted in Buenos Aires. Luckily, I had just that person.

I had met Alfredo Billinghurst in Saigon where he was covering the war for an Argentine magazine and we had hit it off immediately. We had left Vietnam at about the same time, Alfredo returning to Argentina and me to the States. We kept in touch by dropping each other a line every two or three months. In his most recent letter, Alfredo had informed me that after being assigned to various Latin American countries as a foreign correspondent for his magazine, he was now back in Buenos Aires covering local news. He encouraged me to get in touch with him if I ever decided to visit Argentina and promised to put me up in the guest bedroom of his new apartment.

Now was the perfect opportunity to take advantage of that offer. I drafted a telegram informing Alfredo that I would be arriving in Buenos Aires the next day, adding the flight number and the time of arrival. Despite the short notice. I hoped he could meet me at the airport. I did not add any details about just why I was finally showing up in Argentina, but Alfredo knew about my new career and being no slouch in the deduction department could probably put two and two together to guess that the reason for my visit was business, not pleasure. I knew that if anyone in Argentina had the contacts and the knowledge to help me track down Manuel Fernández, he was the one. As it turned out, my confidence in him was not misplaced.

Eleven

I left my office at about noon and headed for Duke Zeibert's. Along the way, I stopped at Western Union and sent my telegram to Alfredo. When I arrived at Duke Zeibert's a little after twelve thirty, my father was already at our favorite table in the corner. Like the coffee shop at the Mayflower, Duke's was a Washington landmark and a favorite hangout for politicians and other power brokers. In fact, as I made my way to our table I recognized some of the same faces I had seen earlier at breakfast. I wondered if they had even made it to Capitol Hill in the interim. Maybe they just hopped from one watering hole to another.

My father rose to greet me, as he always did, with a grin and a firm handshake. To the casual onlooker, it was apparent that in my case, at least physically, the apple had not fallen far from the tree. My father, at six four, was an inch taller than I was. He had the curly brown hair I had inherited from him and a trim figure. Now in his mid sixties, he still had the build and bearing of the athlete he had been in college. When time and weather permitted, we often played a pretty fierce game of one-on-one basketball in the improvised court we had set up in our driveway. We'd been doing it ever since I was big enough to compete and over the years I had finally gained the edge and now won most of our match-ups. But even so my dad could put up a pretty tough fight and was not above throwing the stray elbow in my direction if it gave him an advantage.

Despite – or maybe even because – of our competition, Dad and I had always gotten along. He had been a constant and supportive presence, encouraging me to follow my own path in life. From time to time, my mother had made clear her exasperation with my apparent aimlessness, especially in comparison with my more serious and more goal-oriented siblings. But my father had always taken my side in those discussions. While he never said so, I always suspected that having followed a rather conventional career path himself, he secretly admired – and was perhaps even a bit envious – of the semi-rebellious route I had followed.

Not all was sweetness and light between us. We had some pretty strong arguments over politics and policies, particularly over the Vietnam War. He had been a strong supporter of our intervention from the get-go and even after all that had gone wrong, still believed it was the right thing to have done. When I got back from my tour, I had made clear my own disillusionment. I had come to believe that the whole thing had been a mistake from the beginning and the best thing to do was to get out and cut our losses. We often went round and round, never shaking the other from his established position. It helped that we respected each other's opinions and appreciated the shades of gray that colored any complicated issue. I suppose that our ability to disagree – even on some fundamental issues – without being disagreeable made it difficult for me to understand the violent break that had occurred between Manuel Fernández and his father. But then didn't somebody say that each family is unhappy in its own way? And while I regretted repeating the stereotype, even if only to myself, perhaps the Latin temperament made it more difficult for either of two proud Fernández men to admit that the other might be right.

Putting these thoughts aside, I took my seat opposite my father, who had already made his way through his traditional pre-lunch martini. He invariably limited himself to only one, but it was an important part of his luncheon ritual. He pointed at his glass and raised an inquisitive eyebrow, asking with the gesture if I wanted a martini as well. I didn't and I shook my head from side to side.

There were menus on the table but they really weren't necessary. We always ordered the same thing; grilled rockfish for my father, crab cakes for me.

After the waiter took our order, I filled my dad in on what I was now calling "The Fernández Case." He listened intently, nodding his head from time to time. About halfway through my narration, a couple of congressmen dropped by to shake my father's hand and to thank him for some favor he had provided. He responded politely, smiled, and managed to hide the annoyance I knew he felt at the interruption. After they left,

I finished up my story just as our food arrived. We changed the topic to personal matters while we enjoyed the always superb food.

After we finished and were on our second cups of coffee, we picked up where I had left off. Putting his cup down, my dad asked, "So Fred Matthews thought the two 'government agents' sniffing around Durham might be CIA?" There was an undercurrent of skepticism in his voice. The State Department also had a touchy relationship with the Agency, but had to work with it in a more cooperative manner than did the Bureau. Agents were assigned to our embassies around the globe and while propinquity might have bred some contempt among their Foreign Service brethren, their covers had to be maintained for the common good of pursuing and protecting national interests.

"Yes," I replied. "But he could only speculate – no hard proof. Do you have any ideas? Does State have some kind of surveillance operation of its own?"

My father shook his head in the negative. "Not that I'm aware of. Usually we work with the Bureau on such matters. And, like the Agency, we are forbidden from doing any domestic spying. But," he added with a look of distaste, "As we're finding out with this Watergate business, there's an awful lot of illegal stuff going on behind the scenes. So who knows? If you had suggested a year ago that anybody at State was involved in that kind of activity, I would have dismissed it out of hand. Now...." He let it hang in the air, but the implication was clear. Nothing could be ruled out.

I shifted the conversation. "What's your take on Dwight Whalen? He seems convinced that Manuel Fernández dropped out of sight to join the guerrillas in Argentina. He may be right. But from the information I have gathered so far, there are plenty of reasons to question that assumption."

I paused for a minute, thinking of how best to phrase what I was going to say next, wrestling with some ideas that were not yet fully formed. Thinking back on my conversation with Dwight, I continued, "He seemed a little too anxious to sell me that particular explanation. Maybe I'm reading too much into it, but behind his usual smooth surface, I sensed that my presence and my questions had made him jumpy. When I called him this morning, his secretary told me he was out of the country on some sort of 'special assignment.' Maybe just a coincidence, but I wonder.... do you know anything about what might be up with him?"

My question made my father uncomfortable and for a moment I regretted putting him on the spot. He shifted uncomfortably in his chair and I could see him consider carefully what he would say next. "We're stepping onto some slippery ground here. You know that I'm bound by strict confidentiality rules and there are some things I cannot reveal – even to you."

I nodded. "Look Dad, I…"

He waved it away. Then, leaning forward, he lowered his voice. "What I can tell you is this; these so-called 'special assignments' are not uncommon. Emergencies do occur suddenly and without warning and desk officers are called to travel abroad at a moment's notice to try to help put out some sort of diplomatic fire. But…" he paused again and lowered his voice to the point where I had to lean over the table to hear him, "in every instance the assignment is cleared through the legal division before the officer leaves the States. And…."

I finished the sentence for him: "And Dwight's 'assignment' did not come through your office."

My father's face remained expressionless. But I had an image of him testifying before a congressional committee, which he did often, and responding to a touchy question with the standard, "I can neither confirm nor deny…"

Very interesting I thought to myself. My curiosity about Dwight's behavior increased. He was the last person I would have suspected of doing something "off the books." Was he somehow involved in the mystery surrounding Manuel Fernández's disappearance? And if so, what was the connection? I decided to pump my father for more information.

Before I could pose my next question my father held up a hand. "You asked me for my 'take' on Dwight." He was still keeping his voice low. "Even though we are in different offices and don't have much in the way of personal contact, I've been keeping an eye on him ever since he entered the service, seeing as how he was your friend and teammate for four years. And…" An uncomfortable look passed over his face.

"And?"

"Well son, to tell you the truth, there are some things about him I find worrisome. Things I wouldn't have brought up except in circumstances like the present."

"I understand Dad. What kind of *things?*"

"As you know, Dwight showed his ambition from the start. He wanted to move up the career ladder – and he wasn't about to waste any time in doing so. As is true, I should add, with many of our younger officers. There is no doubt that he has done exceedingly well, both in his overseas assignments and back here at Foggy Bottom. To have such a high position on the Latin American desk at such a young age is quite an accomplishment. And I hear talk that he has even greater aspirations."

I nodded in agreement.

"And that's all to the good. There's nothing wrong with ambition. But I've also heard tidbits here and there about the way he has gone about his, what should I call it? – his *career management* - that I find off putting to say the least."

He stopped for a moment to take a sip of water. Then he continued. "Some of it, of course, comes with the territory. If you want to rise in the ranks, you need to please and impress your superiors. To do that you need to stand out among other junior officers who are striving to make the same impression. But from what I have heard, Dwight has too often gone beyond the acceptable lines in furthering his own career."

My father could see the quizzical look on my face, begging for more details. "He's been known to take credit for things that were actually accomplished either by his co-workers or his subordinates. He is known for treating his peers as decidedly his inferiors. From what I can tell, while the people on the top floor have a very good opinion of Dwight, those at his level or below...." There was another pause. "I'm looking for the right word. Well, frankly son, they *despise* him. I've heard him described as totally ruthless, running over anyone who gets in his way. And, while I hate to say it, some of those who have worked closely with him are convinced that he would put his own interests above those of the Department – and the country – without blinking an eye." Then, as if to soften the blow, he added: "Of course, this is just what I've heard from others. Whenever I see Dwight in the halls or a meeting, he goes out of his way to greet me in a most affable manner and to ask about you."

I took a moment to digest what my father had told me. I must admit that it did not come as a total surprise. Although Dwight had been a good teammate, willing to sacrifice his own chance to score points to make the extra pass or to take on the unenviable task of trying to guard the other team's best player, there was always something cold and calculating about him. I always had the impression that while he was willing to play the role assigned to him, he didn't take much pleasure in it. And while he was often quick to congratulate me when I had a particularly good scoring night, I always detected an undertone of insincerity in his praise. Nothing I could put a finger on, but it was there. He always exhibited preternatural self-control, never letting his hair down, even when we went out to celebrate after an important victory. While the rest of us whooped it up over numerous pitchers of beer, Dwight would sit more or less silently at the table, observing us, I always thought, with some disapproval.

So the fact that he "kissed up and kicked down" did not come as a great shock. What I did find jarring was his apparent flouting of the rules by taking off on a "special assignment" without going through the proper procedures. Of course there might be some logical explanation for it. Maybe the "assignment" was so special and so secret that he had gotten permission from someone higher up in the Department to bypass the legal office. Or maybe he thought he had enough justification to take off on his own and was confident he could explain his actions when he returned.

I ran these alternative scenarios by my father. With a shrug of his shoulders and a skeptical look on his face he said, "Well, it would be highly unusual. But I guess not totally out of the question."

I decided not to push him any further. I had already forced him out of his comfort zone and he probably was beginning to regret that he had revealed as much as he had. While what he had told me about Dwight gave me some insight into why my former teammate seemed to be upset by my visit to his office to ask about the Fernández family, I still couldn't see any real connection between his unease and Manuel's disappearance.

When our waiter, who knew us well, saw us sit back in our chairs, he took that as a signal to bring the bill. Ordinarily, given my chronic lack of funds, my father paid for lunch. This time I insisted on treating him, using some of the cash I had gotten from Elena Fernández. I guess I wanted to impress him with the fact that my own career – while perhaps not as stellar as that of Dwight Whalen's – was also on an upward trajectory. He gave me a grin as I won the tussle over grabbing the check. As we waited for my change, he took out a business card and wrote down on the back of it the names and numbers of two men he knew in Buenos Aires who might be of assistance to me. I put the card in my wallet along with my change – minus a generous tip – planning to add those names to what was becoming a rather lengthy list of potential contacts.

Outside, my father and I headed to K Street. At the corner with Connecticut Avenue we prepared to go our separate ways. By now my father was used to me taking off for exotic – and potentially dangerous – locales. Nonetheless, I could see concern in his eyes as we shook hands and he squeezed my shoulder in the strongest physical show of affection he allowed himself. I said I would get in touch with him as soon as I got back from Argentina, figuring it wouldn't be a long visit, and thanked him again for his help. As usual, he reminded me to call my mother before I left and as usual I promised him I would. I had never once failed to do so, but his reminder had become something of a ritual between us.

I made my way east on K Street. As I turned to cross over at Sixteenth Street, planning to return to my office by way of Lafayette Square, I looked back over my shoulder to see if I could catch a last glimpse of my father. He was already out of sight, but out of the corner of my eye I saw two men dressed in identical dark suits suddenly stop in their tracks and simultaneously turn to look into a nearby shop window.

It didn't stretch my deductive powers to guess that they were following me. Perhaps they were the same two from the gray sedan but I couldn't make out their features at this distance. I thought about confronting them, but more than likely they would simply deny being on my trail. And if they were government agents, there was probably a never-ending supply of others to replace them once they had been burned. For the moment, I decided, the best thing to do was to continue my preparations and try to keep an eye out for anybody on my tail.

Walking at a normal pace, I got back to my office in about ten minutes. Along the way I made a few sudden stops and turns, but could see no sign of my pursuers. Either they had given up the hunt or had turned the assignment over to others I could not spot.

Once in my office, I looked out the window onto the street. I didn't see anything suspicious. There was nobody loitering around on the sidewalk reading a newspaper, for example. There was just the normal stream of pedestrian traffic.

I tried to put the possible surveillance out of my mind. I had other things to focus on. I added the names my father had given me to my list of contacts in Buenos Aires and removed the checks, cash, and passport from my office safe, putting them into an old beat-up briefcase I had had since college. There was also the .38 caliber Smith and Wesson in my safe and I debated taking it with me. I had purchased the gun along with a permit when I got my PI license. So far I had never really needed it. But this case was shaping up to be of a significantly different order of magnitude than tracking down missing teenagers. I knew I couldn't carry it onto the plane, but I could put it in my luggage. But then I would have to go through customs and if they checked my bag carefully, I would have a lot of explaining to do. In the end I decided to leave it in the safe. As I closed the door to the safe and twirled the dial, I hoped that I had made the right decision. As it turned out, I don't think it made much of a difference.

Twelve

Later that afternoon, I took the hourly Eastern shuttle from National to LaGuardia. From there I took a taxi to Kennedy Airport, arriving a little after seven for my eight o'clock flight to Buenos Aires.

Earlier, back in my apartment, I had dutifully called my mother to tell her about my trip and, as part of the ritual, told her not to worry, knowing that was a useless gesture. Even though, like my father, she was now accustomed to my departures, she did little to hide her concern. I did my best to reassure her, but probably with little luck.

After hanging up, I turned to the chore of packing. I knew that in the southern hemisphere the seasons were reversed and as we in the States were heading into spring, in Argentina it was the beginning of fall. I figured the weather would be about the same and packed accordingly. My father recommended that in addition to my usual blazer and slacks I take a business suit with me. Since I only had one, a leftover from my college days and slightly out of style, I didn't have to agonize over which suit to take. Fortunately it still fit and was in reasonably good shape. I packed it on top of my other clothes, hoping it wouldn't get too wrinkled on the flight down. I also made sure to include my jogging gear, hoping I could keep up my routine.

At the Pan Am desk I checked in for the flight. My suitcase was well under the weight limit. I kept my briefcase along with a small carry-on bag in my possession as I boarded the Jumbo 747, finding my seat about half way down the length of the plane on the right-hand side next to a window that looked out onto the wing.

Once the plane was in the air and the seat-belt sign turned off, we were served a pretty good dinner. In my experience, meals on international flights were a cut above those on domestic. Sipping an after-dinner Scotch, I took out a guidebook to Argentina that I had picked up at my travel agent's office and began to thumb through it. As I read about the country I would soon be visiting, my thoughts turned to my first encounter with the man who would be there to greet me when I landed:

It was one of those miserable, almost unbearably hot and steamy days that marked the summers in Southeast Asia. Even though I had had the "advantage" of growing up in the malarial swamp that was Washington, D.C. in July and August, I still found the heat and humidity in Saigon particularly oppressive. I had spent a frustrating afternoon trying to track down a suspect who supposedly had some information for me about a heroin-smuggling operation allegedly involving some of our guys. I was hot, sweaty, and frustrated and decided to cool off in a downtown bar that was only a few blocks from the local hotel where I had been billeted.

It was crowded, noisy, and filled with cigarette smoke. I found an empty stool at the bar and ordered a cold beer. Sitting to my right was a guy about my own age, staring gloomily into the distance, an empty beer bottle in front of him. Hearing me order, he signaled to the bartender for another bottle and turned in my direction, extending a beefy hand. "Alfredo Billinghurst," he said, flashing a grin that revealed sparkling white teeth under a thick black moustache.

I returned the grin and grasped his hand: "Frank Corbett. Pleased to meet you."

For a few seconds, we took each other's measure. I judged Alfredo to be about my height, but weighing some twenty to thirty pounds more, He was hefty through the shoulders and upper chest, but it was mostly muscle, not fat. I was not surprised to learn later that he had played rugby and done a lot of rowing growing up. He had shiny black hair, swept back from a high forehead and ending in curls that formed a line over his shirt collar. There were flecks of gray beginning to show on the sides. By the time we parted company a year later, these flecks had become more prominent. He was dressed casually in a white short-sleeved shirt and tan linen slacks, standing out among the mostly uniformed crowd.

Alfredo was very easy to talk to, hardly surprising given his profession. He had been working as a foreign correspondent on an Argentine newsmagazine for three years. Cultivating contacts was his business.

Asking me right off what my duties were, he was intrigued to learn that I was working in the criminal investigation division and sensed immediately that I might be able to give him leads into major stories; "Nothing like uncovering corruption among the 'occupiers' to sell magazines." His eyes twinkled when he said this, but I could see a more serious purpose behind the comment.

I didn't take offense. I was committed to doing my part to expose and bring to justice any of our Army brethren who were engaged in criminal activities. If some of the cases I worked on led to adverse publicity in the international press, then so be it. Perhaps it would serve to deter others from trying the same thing. While I was not much concerned with "selling magazines," as my friendship with Alfredo developed, neither was I averse to dropping a hint or two that gave him leads into stories that revealed the seamier aspects of how some of our service-men comported themselves in Vietnam.

At that first meeting, after we had nailed down what each of us was doing in Saigon, I asked him about his name. I didn't know much about Argentina, but Alfredo Billinghurst seemed to me to be a strange combination – Spanish and English. Not at all, he assured me. Argentina, like the U.S., was basically a country of immigrants, albeit mostly from Southern Europe. In his case, he was the by-product of an Englishman who had come to Argentina in the 1930s to work for a branch of Barclay's Bank, planning to stay only a few years. But he met an Argentine woman, fell in love, married, sired Alfredo and a younger sister, and took up permanent residence. A not unusual story he assured me.

Alfredo had grown up in a small town just outside of Buenos Aires – Hurlingham – which he described as a near replica of an English village. He went to private schools where the predominant language was English. But his mother and the Argentine governess who helped raise him made sure he learned to speak Spanish like a native. Thanks to his father's wealth – and connections – he was accepted at Oxford where he studied history and politics. At Oxford he was bitten by the journalism bug and decided it would be his life's career. Returning to Argentina, his stellar academic credentials got him a job as a beat reporter for an English-language newspaper, *The Buenos Aires Herald*.

After a couple of years covering local news, he yearned to expand his horizons. Not many Argentine publications had foreign correspondents. They depended instead on wire services for most of their international news. Moreover, most of the mainstream Argentine papers and magazines were generally conservative – both politically and journalistically. In the late sixties, a group of younger reporters, recent graduates of the local state university, determined to found a magazine that would break with traditions and chart a new course for Argentine journalism - a magazine that would appeal especially to the younger generation. Alfredo was good friends with several of the organizers and they asked him to join in the new effort, promising him the possibility of foreign assignments. He was a little hesitant at first not wanting to give up steady employment with an established publication for a risky venture that might fail. But after some soul-searching he decided to take the plunge and signed on.

For the most part the staff of the proposed publication got along well and thought along the same lines. But they had a major tussle over what to name their new magazine. Most of them had been inspired and impressed by the success of *Ramparts* in the States, the counter-cultural magazine that had become required reading for the rebellious youth and their sympathizers and which also did well commercially. *Ramparts* provided a model for the Argentines to follow and some even suggested that they simply translate the title into Spanish for their own magazine. The majority argued that it would be too derivative and that the translation would be awkward. Others proposed *Adelante, Revolución, Nueva Era* and even *Aquarius*. Finally, they settled on *Chispa*, or *Spark*.

Getting financial backers was easier than they had feared. There was already a saturated periodical market in Argentina and trying to crack it would be no easy chore. But they were able to sell the argument that *Chispa* would be a real cutting-edge effort that would immediately gain traction among the younger generation. It also helped that most of the founders were from well-to-do families and were able to get parents and other relatives to pony up. Alfredo told me that he had even convinced his father, whose political beliefs made Barry Goldwater seem a socialist, to kick in. His father probably had second thoughts when he saw the front cover of the inaugural issue. It featured the classic red and black photo of Che Guevara.

Whatever the misgivings of the original backers they soon dissipated. From its first issue *Chispa* became a publishing sensation. As its founders had predicted, it was particularly popular among the younger generation – especially the middle-class youth who were increasingly leftist in their political orientation. They were hungry to be part of what they saw as a global youth culture in rebellion against their elders and the "establishment." Advertisers, including many multi-nationals willing to be identified with a publication that was directly critical of them, fought to buy space in *Chispa*. Weekly sales and subscriptions skyrocketed. By the end of its first year it had nearly double the circulation of the next most-popular magazine in the country.

One of the major enticements *Chispa's* creators had dangled in front of Alfredo was the opportunity to be their main foreign correspondent. He was perfect for the job. Not only was he bi-lingual in English and Spanish he also could converse without difficulty in French, German, and Italian. He was first posted to Europe, where he covered Cold War politics and picked up a rudimentary knowledge of Russian. He spent nine months as *Chispa's* correspondent in San Francisco, reporting on the growing student unrest in the Bay Area. After that, it seemed logical for him to cover the U.S. intervention in Vietnam, the main source of the domestic turmoil he had witnessed in the States.

He had been in Saigon for more than a year, covering the war in both the capital and the countryside. He had arrived in Vietnam a skeptic of the U.S. effort, influenced by his sympathy with the arguments made by protestors on American campuses. Engaged in a little rebellion of his own, he confessed, in Argentina he had come to believe that many of the political and economic problems of his homeland had been caused by the overwhelming influence of Great Britain in that country. Therefore, the anti-imperialist rhetoric of the radical youth struck a responsive chord with him. But his time on the ground had tempered his views. Things weren't so simple. So far as he could see, there was no direct economic motivation for the U.S. to be involved in Vietnam. If the classic Marxist explanation for imperialism – that it was driven by a scramble for resources and profit – were true, then the U.S. had gravely miscalculated. In fact, the war was costing the U.S. its own precious resources – both material and human – and was distorting the domestic economy.

Alfredo had reported in detail on the effects of the B-52 strikes on the North, the extensive use of napalm and Agent Orange in the South, and the corruption and ineffectiveness of the South Vietnamese government. But when he went into the field, he also saw plenty of evidence of the brutal atrocities committed by the Vietcong. He had come to admire the courage and dedication of many of the American fighting men he saw in action. While his overall view was still critical – and he thought the best course was for the U.S. to withdraw – he had come to appreciate, as I had, that neither the Hawks nor the Doves had a monopoly on the truth or that there was any easy solution to the conflict.

Of course we didn't discuss all of this at our first meeting. Instead, we got to know, like, and respect one another over the course of several months. We made it a practice to meet at the same bar on a weekly basis, schedules permitting. On occasion we went out to dinner on a double date. Alfredo had a French girlfriend who was a fellow correspondent and I had been seeing an Army nurse I had met on one of my investigations. Neither female relationship turned out to be serious or lasting, more a happenstance of being in a war zone at the same time than anything else. But Alfredo and I stayed close and I considered him one of my best friends. The thought of seeing him again brought a smile to my lips and I let out a low chuckle as I remembered some of our adventures together.

Finishing my drink, I turned off the overhead light and covered myself with the blanket Pan Am had provided. Pushing my seat back, I stretched out my lanky frame and closed my eyes. Despite the discomfort, the effects of a long day soon caught up with me and in a few minutes, the drone of the engine in my ears, I was soon fast asleep.

Thirteen

I was already awake when the cabin lights came on and the crew began to serve breakfast. Raising my window shade, I looked out and saw a green landscape below that seemed to extend forever. Just then, the captain came on the intercom and told us that in a few minutes we would be passing directly over Brasilia, the futuristic new capital carved out of the Brazilian wilderness. When it came into view, few details were discernible but it was still startling to see the outlines of a modern metropolis amid the vast expanse of Amazonian forests.

About an hour later we began our descent into Rio de Janeiro. We had made previous stops in Miami and Belén at the mouth of the Amazon. Rio was our final stop before Buenos Aires.

As the jet glided down to the Rio airport, I had a spectacular view of Guanabara Bay and Sugar Loaf Mountain. The plane landed smoothly and taxied to the gate. The doors opened and about half the passengers disembarked. Thirty minutes later, they were replaced by a new batch headed, as I was, for Buenos Aires. But instead of taking off immediately, the captain informed us that there was a slight mechanical problem that needed attention and we would be on the ground for another hour while it was being worked on. Fortunately, the problem was resolved within the announced time frame, but it meant a delay in our arrival to Buenos Aires and I hoped that it would not cause Alfredo any undue inconvenience.

Once we were in the air, the captain apologized for the delay and said he would do his best to try to make up for some of the lost time. Despite his efforts, we were still about an hour and half past our scheduled arrival time when he announced that we were beginning our descent into the Ezeiza Airport of Buenos Aires. I looked out the window and saw what appeared to be the American Midwest unfolding below me in regular geometric patterns that delineated cultivated fields. Soon we were over the broad and brown Rio de la Plata estuary and I caught a glimpse of the skyscrapers of downtown Buenos Aires.

My guidebook had told me that Argentina's capital and its surrounding suburbs contained eight million inhabitants, making it one of the largest urban areas in the world. Like many Latin American capital cities, it dominated the country. One in three Argentines lived in Buenos Aires. In comparative terms, it was as though seventy million Americans lived in Washington. Sometimes when I was stuck in rush hour traffic, I thought to myself, it seemed that was the case.

As we flew over Buenos Aires and its outskirts towards the airport, which was about fifteen miles from the city center, I could appreciate the scope of the metropolitan area. It extended out into the distant plains – the *pampas* – as far as the eye could see. It reminded me a bit of Los Angeles in terms of its spread – or maybe Chicago, with its tall buildings on the lake and then spreading out onto the flat prairie of Illinois.

We made another smooth landing and the passengers applauded as the plane came to a full stop in front of the terminal. As I descended the stairs, the early afternoon sun shone in my face and I felt a cool breeze that hinted of fall. Looking up, there were scores of people waving from the observation deck of the terminal, shouting out names of friends and relatives. I looked for Alfredo, but if he was there I couldn't make him out in the crowd. Some of my fellow passengers had better luck, waving and shouting in joyous greeting.

I showed my passport to the immigration inspector, who, like his brethren throughout the world, seemed to have a perpetually bored expression on his face. He asked me the purpose of my visit and I told him, fibbing slightly, that it was a combination of business and pleasure. He gave me a skeptical look but didn't ask for details and stamped my passport with a ninety-day tourist visa. I then proceeded to the baggage claim area where there was a mad scramble going on as passengers from several flights that had landed within a few minutes of each other fought to get their luggage.

Fortunately it only took about five minutes of discreet maneuvering to extricate my suitcase from the crowd and make my way to customs. When

I reached the custom's desk, there was an agent in a light blue uniform who could have been a carbon copy of the one who stamped my passport, right down to the bored expression. He ordered me to open my suitcase, my carry-on, and my briefcase for inspection. He seemed to take an inordinate amount of time going through my meager possessions, taking some delight, I thought, in rumpling up the suit I had carefully packed on top to reduce wrinkles. That hope was now dashed.

As he dawdled, I could hear grumbling from the people behind me, chafing at the delay. I began to wonder if the slowdown meant that the agent expected some financial incentive to speed things along. Not sure of the protocol, I kept my hands off my wallet. Finally, with something of a sneer, he gestured for me to close up my bags, scribbled his initials on the customs form, and waved me through.

Outside the customs area there was a mob scene. Behind a barrier that didn't look particularly formidable, people were waving, shouting out names, and jumping up and down to gain a glimpse of those passengers still waiting to go through customs. It reminded me of a crowd at a sporting event during a particularly exciting sequence. Through the din, I heard a familiar voice shout out my name. "Frank. Frank. Frank old friend. Over here. Over here."

Swiveling my head in the direction of that voice, I saw Alfredo, who had muscled his way to the front of the throng and was waving both hands over his head as if he were doing jumping jacks without leaving the floor. I made my way through the barrier, signaling I would meet him on the far side of the crowd. He nodded his understanding and, after pushing my way through, using my bags almost as weapons, we finally met up in a cleared space.

I knew what was coming next. Putting my bags down, I opened my arms and prepared to welcome Alfredo's enthusiastic *abrazo*. It had taken me a while to get used to this Latin custom, worrying at first that it was a little less than manly to embrace another man. But after a while I had let my reservations slip away and had come to enjoy the ritual.

"*Francisco. Tanto tiempo. Qué tal? Como te va?*" Alfredo said in Spanish, thumping me on the back and practically squeezing the breath out of me.

"Just fine my friend," I replied, giving him a few hearty thumps of my own. "It's great to see you again after all these years."

We stood apart for a moment, giving each other the once over. My Argentine friend seemed to have put on a little weight since Saigon and there was a bit of a bulge over his belt. His hair now was more gray than black. He was decked out in a blue blazer, a white shirt with a black tie, and gray pants, in contrast to his usual informal garb in Vietnam. Otherwise, he still had his infectious grin and I guessed that despite the paunch, he still had strength and stamina to spare.

He insisted on carrying my suitcase, leaving me with the carry-on and the briefcase. Outside the terminal, he put my bag down on the curb, raised his right arm and waved it back and forth. In less than thirty seconds, a late-model black Mercedes drew up in front of us. A young man in his twenties dressed in sweater and slacks was behind the wheel. He turned off the motor, got out of the car, and quickly went round to open the trunk. Before I had time to react, he scooped up my suitcase and my carryall, placing them in the trunk and closing the lid. I held on to my briefcase. He then turned the keys over to Alfredo, who in turn clapped the young man on the shoulder and shoved a couple of bills into his hand. The young man thanked him and headed off towards the terminal.

"Come on Frank," Alfredo said, pointing towards the door on the passenger's side of the front door. "Get in."

I followed instructions and found myself settling into the soft leather seats of the luxury sedan. Alfredo was already at the wheel. He started the engine, which purred like a kitten, released the hand brake, engaged the gear, and pulled away from the curb with a squeal of rubber like a bank robber leaving the scene of the crime. I was forced back against the seat and then jolted forward. Without any hesitation I put on my seat belt. Glancing sideways, I saw that Alfredo had not attached his own and apparently had no intention of doing so. I could see a wicked grin on his face as he took delight in my discomfort.

"So," he said as he accelerated onto the modern four-lane highway that my guidebook told me connected the airport to downtown and which, like the terminal I had just passed through, was a legacy of the presidency of Juan Perón, "Welcome to Argentina my friend. Tell me, what brings you down our way? Hungry for a good steak? Anxious to learn the tango? Or just missing an old pal?" The tone was jocular, but I knew that there was more than just idle curiosity behind the questions.

"All of the above," I said, momentarily going along with the light tone, "Plus, I'm afraid, more serious business." As we sped along the highway I filled him in on the details of Manuel Fernández's disappearance. For the most part he kept his eyes on the road, weaving in and out of slower traffic. I recalled his admiration for the legendary Argentine race driver Juan Fangio and wondered if he was using the trip to hone his skills for more competitive conditions. Every once in a while he would glance in my direction when I mentioned something that seemed to catch him by surprise. When I told him that Dwight Whalen suspected Manuel had joined the People's Revolutionary Army he almost left the road, jerking the wheel back just in time.

When I had finished my recitation, he absent-mindedly banged the steering wheel repeatedly with his right hand while he digested what I had told him.

"Manuel Fernández," he mused. "I know the old man. I interviewed him once or twice when he was posted to Europe. A bit stuffy and full of himself, but also a well-regarded professional diplomat. I think I met the son briefly here in Argentina but I have no clear picture of him in my mind."

Aside from being a journalist, Alfredo came from a family that was well-established in the Argentine elite – as were the Fernándezes. The elite were like a large extended family. In Saigon, Alfredo had told me that everyone in the Argentine elite knew everyone else. They went to the same schools, belonged to the same exclusive clubs, attended the same social functions, and usually married within the same circle. When they got together, tongues invariably wagged about their comings and goings, their marriages and their scandals.

After another pause, while he overtook a lumbering truck that was taking up more than its half of the road and that we passed with what looked to be only an inch to spare, Alfredo turned towards me and exclaimed, "Ah ah. Now I remember the daughter. Elena, right?" I nodded yes. "Quite a dish as I recall. Quite a dish indeed. You sure this pursuit of her missing brother is strictly business *amigo*?"

"Oh. You think she's good looking? Frankly, I hadn't noticed..."

He turned to look at me again. Worried that he might continue to keep his eyes off the road, I quickly confessed. "Yes. Quite the looker. No doubt about it. And smart too. And after the case is closed, one way or the other, I wouldn't mind getting to know her better. But until then, it is all strictly business."

"Okay Frank. Okay. How can I help you?"

"Well, first you could slow down. I won't be of much use to Elena Fernández or anybody else if I end up in the crumpled wreckage of an expensive car."

I was only half-joking. There was moisture on my palms and a knot in my stomach from the wild ride.

Alfredo did not take offense and let up on the accelerator. I saw the needle dip below the one hundred kilometer an hour mark and settle to a more reasonable eighty. "Sorry Frank," Alfredo said. "The thing is that I was not expecting your flight to be delayed and I have set up some rather important appointments for this afternoon." Looking at his watch he added, "And I'm already late for my first."

"Sorry my friend," I said. "I didn't mean to inconvenience you. You should have left a message for me at the airport. I could have managed on my own."

He lifted his right hand momentarily from the wheel and waved away my apology. "No way *amigo*. It's taken too many years to get you to Buenos Aires. Besides, we aren't as compulsive as you *Yanquís* about being punctual. I'm sure I can still see all the people I need to. No problem. Don't worry about it."

"If you say so."

"I do."

"Speaking of your job," I said in a teasing tone, "you must be doing pretty well to be driving a Mercedes. I guess *Chispa* is still a big hit in the publishing world."

Alfredo chuckled. "Yes, we are doing okay. But we've got some new competition. A few years ago a guy named Jacobo Timmerman started publishing a local newspaper, *La Opinión*, which is modeled after *Le Monde*. It has become essential reading for the same audience we appeal to. Fortunately, being a weekly magazine, most of our readers have remained loyal, finding features in *Chispa* they cannot find in *La Opinión*. However, some of our advertisers have backed out recently and our circulation has been more or less flat over the past several months."

"So the Mercedes…?"

I could see the back of his neck and his cheeks begin to turn red. "Let's just say it's kind of a gift and leave it at that."

I didn't pry but I had my suspicions that somehow a woman was involved.

"So as I was saying *amigo* now that I've slowed down, how can I help you?"

"As I told you, my State Department contact, Dwight Whalen, believes that Manuel has joined the People's Revolutionary Army. So I was hoping that somehow you could get me in touch with them so I could check it out and…"

Alfredo's hands tightened on the wheel as he looked over at me, deep concern on his face. "I don't know Frank. Are you sure? Do you know what you're getting into? These guys are not exactly Boy Scouts. They may have noble purposes but their actions are often vicious. They, along with the *Montoneros* – you've heard of them, right?" I nodded yes. "They remind me of the Vietcong. They have no qualms about killing anyone they consider the 'enemy' – and their 'enemies' can be pretty broadly defined. And North Americans are not exempt. In fact, they are sometimes specific targets …"

I interrupted. "But mostly diplomats, businessmen, people connected with the military right? Not someone like me."

Alfredo shook his head. "I'm afraid not Frank. They would more than likely figure you for some kind of spook. They see the CIA lurking behind every bush. To tell you the truth," he said with a shrug, "I can't really blame them. The military regime that is still holding the reins here, has been trying for years to infiltrate and eliminate the ERP leadership. And while we – meaning local journalists – have not found any hard evidence of the U.S. aiding in their effort, we have pretty strong suspicions. Most of the military men here are devoutly anti-communist and have had at least some training in the U.S. The U.S. supplies most of the military aid and equipment. We know for sure that U.S. advisors were helping the Uruguayan government fight the *Tupamaros*. You've heard of Dan Mitrione haven't you?"

"You mean the 'public safety' advisor allegedly in the employ of the Agency for International Development who was kidnapped and executed by the *Tupamaros* a couple of years ago?"

Alfredo gave me a somber glance. "Exactly. While there were all kinds of official denials, it seems clear that Mitrione was providing expert advice to the Uruguayan police and military on interrogation techniques to extract information from captured guerrillas."

I was silent for a moment. We both knew that similar tactics –techniques that went way beyond the line of what was permitted by the Geneva Convention - had been employed by the U.S. in Vietnam. I remembered that Alfredo, at considerable personal risk, had written several exposés about such practices for *Chispa*.

What my Argentine friend was telling me about the likely reaction of the local revolutionaries to my attempts to contact them did not come as any great surprise. It was a hurdle that I had been aware of from the beginning. But it was one that I was determined to try to surmount.

"Listen Alfredo," I said. "I know that there are risks involved. But they are risks that I am willing to take."

I could see he was about to interrupt. Reading his mind, I said, "And it's not just because I find Elena Fernández attractive. I'm not on some sort of quixotic quest to find her brother and win her heart." Although I had to admit to myself that maybe there was a bit of that in the mix. Alfredo used to tease me about what he called my "Sir Lancelot" complex whenever a case I was on in Saigon involved women, especially young women.

Alfredo seemed to accept my denial. But I thought he deserved more of an explanation. "I guess it's a little complicated," I began. "You know I've been kind of drifting through life since I got home from Vietnam." He nodded silently. "Bumming around Latin America and Europe, working odd jobs, not really sure what I wanted to do with myself. And then I decided that being a private investigator was what I wanted. And up to now it's been what I would label 'sporadically satisfying.' I've been tracking down troubled kids and returning them to their parents. My success rate has been pretty darn good. That's one of the reasons Elena Fernández hired me to try to locate Manuel. But most of the cases I've worked on have been cut and dried. Not much of a challenge. They all follow the same pattern and I think any reasonably competent investigator could have produced the same result. But this case is obviously different and it means a lot to me. If I have to put my life on the line to find out what happened to Manuel Fernández," I concluded somewhat melodramatically, "then so be it."

Alfredo gave me a look that seemed to mix skepticism with sympathy and gave a deep sigh. "Okay *amigo*. Okay. I think I know – *cómo se dice?* – 'where you are coming from.' I have some contacts that might be able to put you in touch with members of the ERP. I'll do my best to try to convince them that you are who you say you are. But…."

"I know. I know. No guarantees."

"That's right *amigo*. No guarantees." I could hear the concern in his voice.

We had both turned somber and we let some time pass in silence. The traffic had begun to thicken and Alfredo had been forced to slow down even more. When we crossed over a broad multi-lane highway called the Avenida General Paz, Alfredo informed me that we were now in the city of Buenos Aires – the federal district – proper. He also told me that most *porteños,* those who lived in the port city, claimed that we were now in the "real Argentina," with the rest of the country simply providing a backdrop to the capital. That attitude, I assumed, did not exactly endear the city's inhabitants to those many Argentines not privileged enough to reside within its limits.

After about twenty minutes of wandering through city streets, with Alfredo making heavy use of his horn, banging on the steering wheel in frustration, and shouting curses at drivers he thought were blocking our progress, he finally pulled up to the curb outside the ten-story building which housed his apartment. We were, he informed me, at the corner of Malabia and Arenales. As I got out of the car I could see a lush green park on the other side of the street. The park, Alfredo told me, contained the city's Botanical Gardens, making this a prime location within what was called the Barrio Norte, Buenos Aires's elite neighborhood.

A doorman called a *portero* was waiting for us at the entrance. He and Alfredo exchanged big smiles, handshakes, and greetings of *buenas tardes* as we entered. Alfredo introduced me to the *portero* whose name was Ernesto. As I shook hands with Ernesto, Alfredo explained that I would be staying with him for a few days.

Ernesto looked to be in his sixties. He had soft brown eyes, thinning gray hair, a wrinkled face, and an obsequious aura. He insisted on carrying my suitcase to the elevator that would lift us up to Alfredo's seventh-floor apartment despite my assurances that I could handle it on my own. Alfredo gave me a look that said "Don't argue," so I didn't.

When the elevator arrived, Alfredo held the door open while Ernesto placed my suitcase inside. Then the *portero* stepped aside so we could enter. There was not a lot of space, barely room for both of us and my luggage. So there was no room for Ernesto, who offered to walk up to the seventh floor to lend further assistance. Alfredo assured him that it would not be necessary. Somewhat reluctantly, after looking me carefully up and down, the *portero* closed the elevator door and disappeared from view. Alfredo pushed number seven and after a few seconds we began to ascend.

"Your *portero* seems awfully anxious to please."

Alfredo gave me a look that I couldn't quite read but there was a glint in his eye "Yes indeed."

I could tell from Alfredo's tone that there was more to it. "In fact," he continued, "I'm pretty sure he has been hired – or coerced – by someone in the government to keep tabs on me."

I raised my eyebrows in surprise. "It has become a fairly common experience for journalists and others who might be critics of the regime," Alfredo explained. "Every building in Buenos Aires has at least one *portero*. There is nobody better placed to report on the comings and goings of its residents."

"So much for freedom of the press," I said.

"Yes. We've always had to fight censorship and intimidation here. It's become even more of a struggle lately," Alfredo said, a look of seriousness on his face. "To be fair, the government has been facing a major threat with the appearance and growth of the Montoneros, the ERP, and various others. Since most of their leaders and members live here in Buenos Aires, it makes sense that the authorities try to do everything they can to get information on people who might be involved in revolutionary activity. Unfortunately they often paint with a broad brush and the innocent get swept up along with the guilty."

"I see," I said, although I wasn't sure I did. "To get back to your *portero*, the two of you seemed to be quite friendly what with the handshakes and the smiles."

"All part of the game Frank. All part of the game. He knows that I know he is reporting about me – and those who visit me - to higher ups."

As he said this about 'those who visit me,' he nodded in my direction, indicating that I was undoubtedly one of the visitors upon whom Ernesto would be reporting. Indeed, that was probably why he was so keen to follow us up to the seventh floor, hoping that I might reveal more about myself. I suddenly had a mental image of Ernesto picking up the phone while we were in the elevator, telling his superiors that I had arrived, providing a detailed description. This image produced a hollow feeling in the pit of my stomach. I had only been in Buenos Aires a few hours and already was the target of curiosity for the authorities!

Alfredo saw my discomfort and tried to put me at ease. "Don't worry too much Frank. Ernesto and I have a kind of unspoken understanding. I make it a practice to give him generous 'bonuses' every month in return for, shall we say, a certain amount of discretion on his part. While I cannot offer any guarantees, my guess is that Ernesto does less than a thorough job in his reports about me."

I wasn't much comforted by Alfredo's assurances and began to wonder what kind of place I had landed in. It was clear that I had a lot to learn and not much time to learn it

Fourteen

Alfredo's apartment was modern, spacious, and to my surprise neat as a pin. I had presumed that he still stuck to his slovenly bachelor habits. When I remarked on this he informed me that he had a maid come in three times a week to do the housecleaning. The aroma of expensive perfume that hit my nostrils as soon as I stepped inside did not belong to any maid. I hoped I was not unduly inconveniencing my friend. I was about to ask him if that was the case when he excused himself for a quick trip to the bathroom before he rushed out to his already behind-schedule appointments. Before he left, he gave me a quick tour, showing me the kitchen, bathroom, and the guest bedroom and told me to make myself at home. He said he would be back shortly after eight when we could go out to dinner. I barely had time to thank him before he was out the door.

In the guest bedroom, I unpacked my suitcase. I hanged the suit I had brought in a closet with the hope, probably in vain, that the wrinkles would somehow disappear. If not I would need to visit a dry cleaner. I put the rest of my items in a dresser, hung my jacket up next to my suit, removed my tie and unbuttoned my shirt. After I had settled in, I debated what to do next.

Usually, upon arrival in a strange city, I like to walk around to get my bearings. Alfredo had pointed out a spare set of keys in a bowl on the coffee table in the living room. The keys would allow me to exit and enter both his apartment and the building. I was in the process of reaching for them when I began to feel the effects of my long flight and my lack of sleep. A walk could wait I decided. Instead I picked up some recent editions of *Chispa* from the coffee table. I figured they would help me get a fuller picture of just what was going on in Argentina.

Taking a seat on a comfortable couch in the living room, I began to leaf through the magazine. Alfredo's apartment faced the Botanical Gardens and large glass sliding doors led out to a balcony with a splendid view. I found my eyes wandering from the print to the view outdoors and could feel my lids getting heavy. Even though the articles in *Chispa* were interesting and written in a lively style, my head began to nod.

After about fifteen minutes of reading without absorbing much, I gave in and headed to my room. Stripping to my underwear, I slid between the fresh sheets, pulled a light blanket over me, and was soon fast asleep.

I was awakened by the sound of Alfredo opening the front door. I heard him call out my name and responded with a rasp in my voice, "In here Alfredo. I've been taking a *siesta*. I'll be out in a second." Rubbing the sleep from my eyes, still a bit groggy, I hurriedly put on my pants and shirt and padded barefoot out into the living room, where Alfredo was in the process of putting some pieces of paper into a wall safe hidden behind a painting.

"Can't be too careful *amigo*," he said with a wink as he shut the safe, spun the dial, and replaced the picture. "Wouldn't do to have my notes and tapes of confidential conversations falling into the wrong hands," he explained. "It's hard enough as it is to get people to open up these day. Just imagine the consequences for me and my sources if the powers that be got a look at this material!" He gave a slight shudder and although the tone was light the look on his face was not.

Rubbing his hands together he said, "Now that you are rested, how about something to eat? Want to try one of our famous steaks?"

It was almost eight thirty and I was starving. "Sure thing Alfredo. Just give me a minute to wash the sleep out of my eyes and put on a fresh shirt," I said, heading back to my room.

"Don't forget your shoes Frank. We're pretty formal around here."

I gave him a baleful look over my shoulder. "Thanks for reminding me. I certainly wouldn't want to embarrass you."

We kept up the teasing chatter as I got ready. When I deemed myself presentable we headed down to the street where Alfredo's car was parked. We got in and Alfredo pulled from the curb more sedately than he had with his exit from the airport. The restaurant we were going to wasn't far away and even though it was popular and usually crowded, Alfredo told me with a hint of pride that he could always get a table – a not too subtle hint of how well-connected he was.

As we made our way through the city's streets, I alternated between taking in the sights and listening to my friend describe what he had been up to while I had taken my nap. As he did so, I began to feel a bit guilty. I was refreshed and feeling full of beans, looking forward to what promised to be a memorable meal. Alfredo had told me that the restaurant we were going to, La Cabaña, was one of the best in the city. It had an international reputation as *the* place in Buenos Aires to get a great steak. But, as I looked at my friend, I could see the effects of what had been a long day. And, if the lingering perfume in his apartment was any indication, probably a long night the day before. His shoulders were slumped, there were hollows under his eyes, and he looked disheveled.

I knew that he was operating under pressure. My presence was an added complication in his life, one he obviously didn't need. When he was in the middle of describing a particularly tense interview, I broke in. "Listen my friend. If my showing up on your doorstep almost out of the blue is causing…"

He held up a hand and interrupted me in turn. "Hey Frank. Don't worry about it. I'm delighted to see you after all these years. Sure I'm busy these days, but what's new? Remember Saigon. Just relax. It's no burden to have you around. In fact, it's nice having somebody I can trust to talk to you. Just to show you the state we are in, I have to watch my tongue even with my closest friends. We all have been operating in a climate of fear and suspicion."

"Okay Alfredo. Just so you're sure. I mean I could always check into a hotel …"

Again he interrupted, taking his right hand off the wheel and giving my offer a dismissive wave. "Come on Frank. You can stay with me as long as you like. Really. No problem."

I thought about bringing up the possibility that my presence might also put a crimp in his personal life, but decided that I had said enough. Not sure that I bought his reasoning, I let the matter drop.

"Thanks a lot my friend," I said sincerely. "I appreciate it." After a pause, "So what's going on here that has everybody on edge? I only know what I've read in the *Washington Post*. What's happening behind the scenes?"

Before he had time to answer, we reached the restaurant. It was located about three blocks south of the Congress Building, which I had glimpsed briefly as we passed it. Alfredo informed me the building had been closed since the military had taken over seven years earlier. It was scheduled to re-open, however, after the installation of the new democratically-elected government on May 25. Alfredo found a parking spot directly across the street and after we had exited the car, he had made sure to lock it carefully. Dodging traffic, we crossed the street and entered the restaurant. The first thing I saw in the foyer was a stuffed steer, making it abundantly clear, if there was any doubt, that this was a serious steak house. There were several people standing in line, but Alfredo went straight to the maitre d', who greeted him with a broad grin and showed us immediately to a table for four. When I raised a quizzical eyebrow, Alfredo informed me that two of his colleagues from *Chispa* would be joining us later. From the conspiratorial wink he gave me I guessed that they were of the female persuasion.

A white-coated waiter came over to our table ten seconds after we had been seated. Alfredo asked him to bring us a bottle of champagne. As he scurried away to fetch the bottle, Alfredo gave me another wink: "Time to properly celebrate your arrival Frank." Before I could say a word, the waiter reappeared with the champagne, uncorked it ceremoniously, and poured us each a generous portion. After placing the bottle in an ice bucket, Alfredo told him that we were waiting for two guests to join us and that we would order our food once they arrived. The waiter gave an understanding nod and left us to serve other customers.

I was beginning to appreciate the clout Alfredo had. Here we were in one of the city's most popular restaurants, bypassing the crowd standing in line, leisurely enjoying our pre-dinner drinks while we waited for others to arrive. I could imagine the looks of envy – and perhaps annoyance – of those waiting to be seated while we raised our glasses. "Here's to you *amigo*," Alfredo said as he touched his glass to mine and uttered the traditional Spanish toast: "*Salúd, amor, y pesetas – y el tiempo para gozarlos*" "Health, love, and money – and the time to enjoy them."

Alfredo took a healthy swallow of the bubbly and I did the same. The drink seemed to perk up my friend. His shoulders straightened and I could see the habitual twinkle return to his eyes. It was only a momentary respite. As soon as I reminded him of his promise to fill me in on recent history, his look turned somber.

"Okay," he began, "here's the scoop. It's too complicated to sketch in all the details, so I'll just give you a quick overview. Over the past seven years, the military has been in charge. The coup that brought them to power was the fifth time they had overthrown a democratically-elected government since 1930. They promised this time things would be different. They really would end corruption, get the economy in order, and 'restore Argentine greatness,' whatever that meant. They got off to a good start in some ways – albeit violating more than a few individual rights and cracking a few heads along the way. But then a few years back – in May 1969 to be precise – it all fell apart. In that month there was a massive student-worker uprising in the interior city of Córdoba. They were protesting the economic and political policies of the government. The military leadership was forced to send extra forces to the city to put down the uprising, which we call the *Cordobazo*, a week of rioting that cost scores of lives and millions in property damage."

He paused to take a slug of champagne and then continued." Things haven't been the same since. The original head of the junta was ultimately forced to step aside to be replaced by a nondescript general named Levingston. He lasted only a few months until he was, in turn, replaced by the real strong man of the regime, General Alejandro Lanusse. Changes in leadership made no difference. Things got worse and worse. The economy tanked and the guerrilla groups began to make their presence felt. You know that a few years ago the *Montoneros* kidnapped and executed a former president, right?"

"Sure," I replied. "It was front-page news."

"Yeah. That was their most spectacular blow. But there have been plenty of others. The guerrillas have specialized in bank robberies to fund their operations, attacks on police and military installations, and kidnappings and assassinations. The toll keeps rising and the military seems almost powerless to do anything about it."

Alfredo paused again to polish off his glass of champagne. Reaching for the ice bucket, he pulled the bottle out, topped off my glass, and refilled his own. "This story goes best with something to drink," he said with a smile. Then he turned somber again. "So in the middle of all this, Lanusse decides to roll the dice. You've heard of Juan Perón, right?" I nodded yes. "Well he's been in exile ever since the military turned on him – one of their own – and kicked him out in 1955. Since then he's spent most of the time in exile in Spain. Gone but not forgotten to say the least. The workers who brought him to power and sustained him in return for significant benefits have never abandoned him. They've been demanding his return almost from the day he was forced to leave. All the regimes since – civilian and especially the military – have said no way, no how can Perón be allowed to return. But none of those regimes was able to match what Perón had done for the workers or to shake their loyalty to him. On top of that, many of the younger generation, especially middle class university students who have only a vague memory of some of the more unsavory aspects of Perón's rule, have latched on to him as a revolutionary hero. Sort of a pre-Castro Castro if you will. And they have begun to glorify his wife Evita, claiming that if she were alive today she would be a guerrilla."

I nodded. What he was telling me jibed with Dwight Whalen's lecture.

Alfredo shook his head as if he could not believe what he was saying. I was beginning to appreciate some of the complexities of the situation into which I had stepped.

"So, facing a growing clamor not only from the working classes but also from an increasingly vocal sector of the middle classes Lanusse decided to allow Perón to return. But certain conditions were imposed, the most important being that Perón could not run as a candidate in national elections. To get around this obstacle, his supporters put up a substitute – a hack politician and Perón loyalist named Héctor Cámpora. He ran on the slogan of 'Cámpora to office, Perón to power.' Not exactly subtle," Alfredo said sarcastically and I chuckled in agreement. "But it worked. Cámpora got almost fifty percent of the vote, twice as much as the next candidate, and was declared the winner. He'll be inaugurated at the end of May, but nobody expects him to stay in office for long. Probably his first move will be to call for new elections and to announce that Perón will be eligible to run."

I shook my head. "And I thought politics in the States were bizarre."

Alfredo shrugged as if to say, "That's the way things are. What are you going to do?"

"From what you tell me Alfredo," I said. "This guy Lanusse must have been pretty desperate to have allowed Perón to come back."

He gave me a little grin. "Yeah. It would seem so. But…"

"But what?"

"Look *amigo*. On the surface, it appears that Lanusse is on the side of the angels. He has more or less admitted that the military experiment has failed. He has tried to cut the Gordian knot of keeping the Peronists, who today represent at least half the electorate, out of the system altogether – which has more or less been the case for the past eighteen years. He has been trying to restore civilian democracy in a reasonable and responsible manner."

Alfredo paused and poured himself yet another glass of champagne. My glass was still mostly full and I covered it with my hand when he offered to add some more. I knew from past experience that Alfredo had a remarkable capacity for alcohol. He could drink me under the table with ease. I was already feeling a little light-headed from drinking on an empty stomach.

"However," he continued, after draining half his glass, "Here's what I think." Leaning forward and lowering his voice, he said, "It's all smoke and mirrors. Lanusse and his army buddies figure that Perón will inherit such a mess that he is bound to fail. After all, he's been out of power and out of the country for almost two decades. While no one doubts his political savvy, he hasn't really been tested like he will be once he takes over. Back in 1946, when he first assumed the presidency, the country was in great economic shape, enjoying a postwar boom and there were no guerrilla groups around. Peace and prosperity reigned. Now it's just the opposite. Add in the fact that despite getting 'rejuvenation therapy' from a quack in Romania, Perón is in his mid-seventies and not in the best of health. To top that off, my sources tell me that he is planning to name his third wife, Isabel, as his vice presidential candidate…"

When he saw the surprised look on my face at this bit of news, he let out a low chuckle and again shook his head as though he, too, was having a hard time believing what he was saying.

"Let me explain *amigo*. You know about Evita, actually his second wife, right?"

"Sure. Sure. You said something about her being a kind of icon for the revolutionary left."

"Yeah. Here's the connection. In the early fifties, when Perón was running for re-election, he proposed that Evita be his running mate. His supporters were all for it, but the military vetoed the idea and Perón had to change plans and have her candidacy withdrawn. As it turned out, she died of cancer the next year. So after Perón gets kicked out, he meets up with this Argentine dancer in Panama and soon after that they get married."

"That's Isabel?"

"Right. Well Isabel is no Evita so far as the masses are concerned. But she is *el líder's* wife and the heir to Evita's legacy. So Perón plans to fulfill the promise originally made more than a quarter of a century earlier. He wants to have his wife as his running mate. If elected, she would be his vice-president and next in line to be president if anything should happen to him. And that would truly be disastrous."

"How so?"

"First, Isabel is totally unqualified for the job. At least Evita had some smarts and experience, if little in the way of education. One could imagine Evita running the country – but Isabel, no way. Second, she and Perón are very much under the influence of a shadowy figure who wormed his way into their confidence while they were in exile in Madrid. His name is José López Rega, who claims to have special powers that allow him to see the future. He's been helping Perón and Isabel chart their personal and political course…"

"Kind of like Rasputin in Russia."

"Yes. There are some parallels. So when, as seems almost certain, Perón and Isabel become the president and vice president of this great country of ours, López Rega will likely be pulling the strings."

Alfredo had a half-smile on his face as he said this, but I also noted a tone of resignation and sadness. "So the way I see it, Lanusse and his pals have a good idea of how this scenario will play out and are more than happy to have it unfold. Perón will be incapable of governing the country successfully in this moment of crisis. Something might happen to him health-wise and Isabel – *and* López Rega - will take control and things will get progressively worse. Once everything has fallen apart, and Peronism has been thoroughly discredited – shattering the myths that had sustained it - the military will step in again and this time *really* impose an authoritarian regime. Farewell to democracy – and the free press – and maybe even worse. I've interviewed some military men who believe that the only solution for Argentina's problems is the total eradication of all 'Marxists' from society – even if that means killing thousands, if not more of their fellow countrymen."

Alfredo gave me a solemn look and I felt a chill run through my bones. After what we had both seen and experienced in Vietnam, we knew that such "solutions" were not as far-fetched as they seem at first glance.

"Sorry to dampen the mood Frank," Alfredo said as I handed him my now empty champagne glass for a refill. "But you wanted to know."

I just nodded.

We both were silent for a moment. Then Alfredo said, a rueful look on his face, "So here we are, somewhere between a comic opera and a Shakespearian tragedy. If I had to guess, we are more likely to end up with *Julius Caesar* or *Macbeth* than any happier outcome."

"It certainly sounds pretty grim. I had no idea that things were so bad."

"Yeah. We are in a kind of limbo, waiting for other shoe to fall. It's almost as though we are experiencing a kind of national lunacy. Nobody trusts anybody. It could be that your best friends are secretly allied with one side or the other and are afraid to reveal their true loyalties because they fear the consequences. I tell you Frank, if…."

At that moment we were interrupted when Alfredo's guests arrived. And a delightful interruption they were: two exceedingly attractive young women. Both of them had shoulder-length dark hair, fine features, and trim figures. They were dressed casually in dark sweaters and slacks. Alfredo spied them as they approached our table and stood to greet them. I quickly followed suit. He exchanged kisses on the cheek with both of them and then introduced me to them. One was Gloria and the other Raquel. Without hesitation, I followed Alfredo's lead and gave them cheek kisses as we told each other what a pleasure it was to meet.

These formalities out of the way, I held a chair for Gloria while Alfredo did the same for Raquel. Since they were physically so similar, I wondered if they might be sisters but quickly learned that they were not. Both worked at *Chispa* with Alfredo and he had invited them to join us, he said with a straight face, because he owed them a favor in return for things they had done for him at the office. I suspected, however, that there were other motives at play. Alfredo always had had an eye for the ladies and I presumed that he had some sort of romantic attachment – or hoped to have – with one or the other, or perhaps both of them. While it was difficult to pick up the odor of their perfumes amid the smell of broiled meat and cigarette smoke that permeated the restaurant, from what I could tell neither girl was wearing the scent I had noticed in Alfredo's apartment.

As soon as our waiter spotted our guests being seated, he came to take our orders. Alfredo called for another bottle of champagne to be followed by two bottles of red wine to accompany dinner. He insisted that I ask for the baby beef, which he said was extraordinary. The two girls nodded their head in agreement and we all asked for the same thing, along with fried potatoes and salad.

The waiter returned at once with the champagne and poured us all a glass. We toasted again, this time to my arrival in Buenos Aires which I answered, after taking a small sip, with my thanks and my pleasure at being in their company. Alfredo took his usual healthy swallow while the girls followed my example and took tiny sips.

Putting his glass down, Alfredo began to discuss something in a confidential tone with Raquel. From their expressions, I assumed that it was probably an important item of office business. That left me to converse with Gloria, sitting to my left.

We began with the usual "getting to know you" repartee. Gloria asked what brought me to Buenos Aires and I told her in vague terms that I was a private investigator following a lead on a case. That seemed to pique her interest and she started to press me for details. She did, after all, work for a magazine that specialized in investigative journalism and she might have thought there could be a story in what I was doing. I deflected the line of questioning she was about to embark on with one of my own: "So tell me Gloria - what is it that you do at *Chispa?*"

"I'm actually a photographer…"

"Isn't that rather unusual?" I interrupted. "I mean for a woman to be a professional photographer; especially in Latin America. From what I understand, it is men who…."

Now it was her turn to interrupt me. "Yes Frank, I suppose so. There are not too many of us here. But I do believe it is not so uncommon in the United States and in Europe. We are just a little bit behind the trend, that's all." She seemed a little annoyed by my question, although I was pretty sure it was not the first time she had been asked it.

Alfredo had overheard us and broke off his own conversation with Raquel to add, "And Frank, while Gloria is too modest to tell you, not only is she one of the few female photo-journalists in this benighted country, she is also one of the very best. You should see the list of prizes she has won."

Gloria blushed at the praise, but I could see a look of pride on her face. When Alfredo returned to his conversation with Raquel, I asked Gloria to tell me more about herself and her career choice. She told me that she had attended the local public university, where she, like many of her more radically-inclined peers, studied sociology. When it became clear to her that her job prospects were not very bright in that crowded field, she took some courses in journalism. She had always been interested in photography, having been given a camera of her own at a young age, and she determined to combine those two interests. When some of her classmates came together to create *Chispa*, they welcomed her on board. And, as they say, the rest was history.

While she was talking about her university days, the thought crossed my mind that she might have known Manuel Fernández and his friend who had joined the guerrillas. I thought about asking her, but decided that would reveal too much about why I was in Argentina. It wouldn't take her more than a few seconds to make the connection between that question and my case.

Our food arrived before Gloria could turn the tables and ask me how I had come to my career choice. All of us stopped talking and began eating. As advertised, the baby beef was spectacular – so tender I could almost cut it with a fork. I could only bob my head, my mouth full of meat, when Alfredo asked me "Isn't this the best steak you've ever had *amigo*?" Indeed it was.

After we had all finished the main course and were waiting for dessert, I asked the three Argentines why they were always calling each other Che. It seemed as though they uttered the word in every sentence. Did it have something to do with Che Guevara?

Raquel, who I had learned was actually one of the main editors of *Chispa* and in a sense Alfredo's boss, gave the explanation. "It's part of our language and our culture Frank, unique to Argentina. I'm not sure where it comes from, but we use it all the time, particularly among friends. I guess it would translate in English as something like 'friend,' or 'buddy' or – what's the other word in English Alfredo…?

"Pal," Alfredo offered.

"Yes. 'Pal.'"

"So when *Che* Guevara ended up fighting with a bunch of Cubans, and they knew he was from Argentina…." I said.

"Exactly," Raquel said. "Actually his first name, as you probably know, was Ernesto. But the Cubans gave him the nickname so strongly associated with our country, and it stuck. It actually became internationally famous. Who could have guessed?" she asked rhetorically, a smile of bemusement on her face.

Having filled me in on the use of Che, Raquel and Alfredo resumed their conversation, which, from their body language, was about some serious business that needed urgent attention.

Gloria confirmed my observation. "You'll have to excuse Raquel if she is being a little rude," she said. "We have something of a crisis at the office and it needs to be straightened out as soon as possible."

I was surprised Alfredo hadn't mentioned this crisis previously but assumed he didn't want to add to my discomfort about imposing on him.

I told Gloria I understood. At that moment, the waiter served our dessert. We had all ordered *flan con crema*, a traditional dessert from Spain that was made of eggs and butter molded into a kind of pudding and topped with whipped cream. Like everything else I had eaten that night, it was superb. I was beginning to understand how Alfredo, despite his obviously pressure-packed job, was putting on weight.

After I polished off my *flan*, I resumed my conversation with Gloria. When I asked her what sorts of stories she covered, she told me that they ran the gamut – from photographing well-known Argentine celebrities at chic social functions to the most grisly crimes in downtrodden neighborhoods. Not altogether innocently, I asked her if she had covered any of the violence associated with the local guerrilla groups, specifically the ERP. I saw a look of suspicion cross her face and recalled that Alfredo had warned me that many Argentines, upon learning that I was a private investigator, might assume that I was really some sort of CIA agent, particularly if I began to snoop into the activities of the revolutionary groups.

I saw Gloria turn towards Alfredo with her eyebrows raised, as if to ask *Is this guy on the up and up?* My friend, who had the gift of keeping track of two conversations at once, nodded to her with a look that said, *It's okay. You can trust him.* Her shoulders relaxed and she looked around to make sure that nobody nearby was listening in. Lowering her voice and leaning closer, she said, "Well yes I have. As a matter of fact, I've done numerous stories about them. Why do you ask?"

"Just curiosity," I lied. "I've heard a lot about them since they seem to have targeted North Americans and have caused my country's representatives here a fair amount of trouble."

"Indeed they have. Indeed they have. But it's not just North Americans. Their targets are pretty wide-ranging. They have been responsible for many more Argentines suffering than foreigners."

"What's your impression of them?"

She took a few moments to formulate her answer. "To be honest, that's a difficult question to answer. One of the first stories I did on them – in fact I was on an assignment with Alfredo – involved a policeman targeted by the ERP so as to intimidate others. They shot him to death while he was making a phone call from a public booth and left a message warning that this would be the fate of other 'defenders of the oligarchy' who didn't abandon their duties. They also left the policeman's widow with five children to raise on her own and only a meager pension with which to feed and clothe them."

A frown crossed her face as she recalled the story. "On the other hand, I've also seen the bodies of members of the ERP after the secret police have finished interrogating them. Believe me, it's not a pretty sight."

"I can imagine," I said, deciding not to mention that I had seen many of the same horrible results from "interrogations" in Vietnam.

"I can understand and sympathize with those who want to bring fundamental change to Argentina. After all, that's what we are trying to do with *Chispa*." She gave me an inquiring look, "I don't know how much you know about our recent history…"

"Alfredo gave me a quick course while we were waiting for you and Raquel."

She nodded. "Then you know that we have been in a rut ever since Perón was ousted – either repressive military regimes or ineffective civilian governments. No leader, no group has been able to break the vicious circle. More and more people – especially young people – are increasingly frustrated. That's why many are attracted to the ERP and the *Montoneros*. They promise something radically different: a genuine revolution along the lines of what happened in Cuba. And there is also a considerable amount of romanticism involved. Young people in particular are attracted to the image of a heroic revolutionary carrying a rifle and changing the course of history."

The way she said it indicated that she did not share that particular perspective. I suspected she saw it as naïve – and dangerous. What she said seemed to jibe with what others had told me. The Argentine Marxist revolutionaries, like their contemporaries elsewhere, seemed to be a mixed bag of starry-eyed idealists and cold-blooded killers.

"Do you think the recent elections and the return of Perón will undercut the revolutionaries' appeal?" I asked.

She considered my question carefully. "Who knows? There are some recent signs that that might already be happening. But I'm skeptical. I don't think Perón is nearly as radical as some of his younger supporters believe. Plus, I don't think he is surrounded by the kind of people who would let him go in that direction even if he were so inclined."

"So if he fails, that might offer an opening for the guerrillas to grow in strength. Maybe even take power?"

She shook her head. "I suppose anything is possible. But I can't see the military allowing that to happen." Her opinion seemed to coincide with Alfredo's and I wondered if it was more or less the consensus among the staff at *Chispa* - and, if so, how many others shared it.

I could have gone on talking with Gloria for hours. She was not only extremely attractive but also clearly very intelligent and accomplished. But Alfredo banged his hand on the table. "Sorry to break up the party Frank. But it's been a long day and we all have plenty to do tomorrow. I'm afraid it's time to call it a night and head for home."

Somehow, while I had been engrossed in my conversation with Gloria, the waiter had slipped the bill to Alfredo. When I saw my friend pull a fistful of cash from his pocket, I reached for my own wallet until I realized that I had not yet changed my dollars for Argentine *pesos*. Nonetheless, I pulled some twenties out and offered them to my friend, who waved them away dismissively. "No, no Frank," he said with a grin. "This is my treat. After all, you are my guest and this is a special occasion in your honor."

I knew him well enough not to make an issue of it and simply thanked him for his generosity, as did Gloria and Raquel.

Outside, Alfredo offered to drive the girls to their apartments, but they protested that they lived too far out of the way and would instead share a cab. Alfredo did not put up much of a fight, an indication that even his legendary stamina was beginning to fade and he was anxious to get home and go to sleep. Before we parted, I told Gloria how much I enjoyed talking with her and hoped I could see her again. She gave me a warm smile and said that she too enjoyed meeting me and suggested we meet up again sometime if our schedules permitted. Alfedo could let me know how to contact her.

By this time Raquel had flagged down a taxi and we went our separate ways. Heading back to his apartment, Alfredo told me more about our two companions and how much he admired them. "It's not easy to be a female journalist in this country. Usually they are relegated to the society pages or the arts and entertainment section. To cover politics the way Gloria does and for Raquel to be an assistant editor, that's highly unusual." Then, with a tone of feigned concern, he said, "I hope you didn't find their company an undue imposition."

I chuckled. "Well maybe if they had been fat, ugly, and boring, I would have. But they were just the opposite."

We both laughed as Alfredo sped through the now almost deserted streets of the city.

Fifteen

Despite the long nap and late meal, I slept like a baby. I had brought my jogging gear with me and before we went to bed, I told Alfredo I'd like to get a run in before breakfast. He gave me a look that said: *You must be kidding.* But when he saw I was serious suggested a route that wouldn't make me look either crazy or suspicious – or both. In case I hadn't noticed, he told me, there were heavily armed police and security forces everywhere, carrying serious automatic weapons and with itchy trigger fingers. Strange behavior like running through the city streets in sweatpants could produce a "shoot first, ask questions later" response.

I set my internal clock for six o'clock and managed to get dressed and out the door without waking Alfredo. In the lobby, the *portero* was in the process of mopping the floor. He gave me a startled look as I said *Buenos Días.* He recovered in time to open the door for me as I walked briskly out onto the sidewalk. If he indeed was reporting on my actions, I wondered if he would now rush to the phone to let his superiors know I was out and about at an unusual hour.

Dawn was beginning to break. It was a cool, crisp day with a hint of fall in the air. I crossed the street, at this hour free of traffic, and followed Alfredo's advice. Entering the Botanical Gardens, I noticed some of the leaves were beginning to turn. The trees in the gardens were a mixture of jacarandas, acacias, and what my guidebook had informed me were ombus, oak-like trees with a large base, twisted branches, and imposing crowns. There were also many palms, giving the city something of a tropical feel even though the climate seemed more like Washington than Miami. Along the way, dozens of stray cats scurried out of my path, casting suspicious glances my way as I disturbed their routine.

Exiting the gardens, I followed Avenida Sarmiento which ran along the west side of the city zoo until I reached the Avenida Libertador. This was a broad multi-lane avenue that, when I reached it, reminded me of Constitution Avenue back home. The traffic was still light but it was picking up so I was careful crossing over to the other side where the Parque Tres de Febrero was located. Alfredo told me that in the Parque I would find other joggers, a mixture of foreigners, more than likely including some of the Marine guards from the U.S. Embassy, as well as a few venturesome *porteños* who had taken up the fad. In this group, he said, I would not stand out. Nonetheless, he warned, everyone in Buenos Aires was on the lookout for anything out of the ordinary and some joggers might even be carrying weapons in self defense. "Sorry," he said with a shrug, "But that's our reality these days."

Once in the park, I found a nice, broad gravel path and picked up my pace. I could hear the pebbles crunch under my sneakers as I passed several well-tended lakes and ponds, enjoying the sounds of birds whose songs I was hearing for the first time. It wasn't the Tidal Basin, but it was pleasant enough.

There were a handful of other joggers, some of whom appeared to be fellow countrymen and with whom I exchanged nods and grunts as we passed going in opposite directions. About ten minutes into my run, I spied a couple of well-built guys with crew cuts who had the appearance of Marines, heading towards me. One of them was running with a back-pack that looked a little heavy. I figured he was probably carrying some kind of weapon in it. When we were abreast I gave them a wave and was tempted to shout out *Semper Fi* but thought better of it. Neither returned my greeting and the guy with the backpack give me a careful once-over. As they passed out of sight, I suddenly had a vision of the Marine who I presumed to be armed stopping in his tracks, taking aim, and shooting me in the back. What irony, I thought. Shot to death in a foreign country by one of our own. But it was all in my overactive imagination. No shots were fired. As I turned my head, the two Marines, if that was who they were, were almost out of sight around a bend in the path.

I chalked up my vision to the dire picture of present-day Argentina that Alfredo and Gloria had provided the night before. It couldn't be any worse than Saigon, I told myself, providing a small dollop of comfort and reassurance. At any rate, I made it back to Alfredo's apartment unscathed at seven thirty, feeling refreshed by my run and hoping that it had helped lose some of the calories I had accumulated the previous night.

I used Alfredo's keys to let myself into the apartment, trying to be as quiet as possible. I figured that after the long day, long night, and abundant quantities of alcohol my friend had downed, he would still be fast asleep and I didn't want to disturb his well-deserved rest. To my surprise, he was awake and dressed. He had coffee already prepared, along with juice, some fruit, and fresh rolls, called *medias lunas*, or half-moons, that were the Argentine version of the French croissant. He had them delivered daily from a bakery down the street. They were warm and delicious.

As we sat at the dining room table and ate, Alfredo looked remarkably alert. The fact that he had consumed enormous quantities of champagne and wine the night before seemed to have had no discernible effect. In fact, there was a gleam in his eyes and a schoolboy's eagerness in his voice when he told me why he was up so bright and early. *Chispa*, he told me, was planning a special cover story on the mysterious José López Rega, the man about whom so little was known and who had such influence over the Peróns. That was what Raquel and he had been discussing in hushed tones for much of the meal last night – how to proceed with what promised to be an explosive exposé of *the* man behind the scenes.

Alfredo had already done considerable digging into López Rega's past and had come up with material he thought would prove devastating to the presumed future president and his vice-president. He had a number of early interviews to add substance to his investigation and would be busy throughout the day working with *Chispa's* staff to put the story together. When I asked him about the dangers involved in publishing such revelations, he brushed them aside. But I could see a look of worry behind his confident gaze. Alfredo was experienced enough to know that journalism, especially investigative journalism, in countries like Argentina was not the kind of profession that encouraged life insurance companies to offer expensive coverage to its practitioners. Crossing the wrong people could bring threats and warnings, sometimes punctuated with a physical beating. At the worst it could lead to outright assassination. My friend knew these risks and accepted them. He always had and I knew he always would. I think that's why he could understand my willingness to put my life on the line to do my job and to try to find out what had happened to Manuel Fernández.

After breakfast Alfredo grabbed his briefcase and headed for the door while I went to clean up after my run. He wasn't sure when he would be back, but would try to make it before eight p.m. I promised I would be back by then unless something unforeseen came up. With that, he gave me a cheery wave and wished me luck. I reciprocated.

By the time I had shaved, showered, and put on my suit, it was after nine. I took out the list of names and numbers I had been given by Elena, my father, Fred Matthews, and Dwight Whalen and started dialing. I decided to begin with the contact provided by Dwight — a guy named Roy Smallwood who was ostensibly engaged in some kind of business in Buenos Aires. When I got through after several rings, a bored secretary told me to hold the line while she checked with Señor Smallwood as to his availability. When she returned to the line, she told me that her boss could fit me in later in the afternoon, say two thirty. I said that was fine with me but before I had time to ask for directions, she hung up. It seemed a strange way to treat someone who might be a perspective customer.

I shrugged and dialed the first name on Elena's list of Manuel's friends. This time I got a warmer reception. A young man by the name of Héctor Martínez answered and said he and others who knew Manuel were quite upset by his disappearance and would be delighted to meet with me. We set up a lunch at a downtown restaurant and Héctor offered to round up the others to join us.

Hanging up, I figured I had enough on my plate, deciding to hold off on calling anybody else on the list. With time to kill before lunch, I headed outside to explore the city. Since I already had gotten my exercise, I took the subway to downtown instead of walking. After a short ride on a train that was only moderately crowded, I exited at the Plaza de Mayo, the main square of the city dominated by the presidential palace, the Casa Rosada, or "Pink House," so named for its distinctive pale rose color. I spent an hour or so playing tourist, visiting the museum in the colonial *cabildo* that faced the Casa Rosada on the west side of the square and educating myself on some of the details of Argentina's struggle for independence. I then walked through the main cathedral on the north side of the plaza, where the remains of the country's great hero of the struggle against Spain, General José de San Martín, rested.

Leaving the cathedral, I headed east and then turned north at the next block onto Calle Reconquista. Alfredo had advised me to find a *casa de cambio*, or exchange house, rather than a bank, to change my dollars into pesos. Both banks and *casas de cambio* were thick on the ground along Reconquista, which cut through the heart of the city's financial district. Alfredo had recommended the *Casa Baires* and had instructed me that once there I should ask for a Señor Bordaberry. I was to tell him that Alfredo had recommended him.

Locating *Casa Baires* about two blocks down Reconquista on my left, I entered to find a long line. I took a number, preparing to wait my turn, which, from the look of things could be a while. But then a tall, slim man in his forties, dressed in a dark three-piece suit, approached and asked in impeccable English if I was Mister Corbett. I said that I was, surprised he knew my name. After introducing himself as Mario Bordaberry, he immediately cleared up the mystery. "Alfredo called to tell me you might be in this morning." Taking me politely by the elbow, he said, "Please come with me Mister Corbett" and led me through the crowd, a maneuver that produced some hostile stares from those who were waiting patiently to be served. Passing through a waist-high wooden gate, controlled by a buzzer and protected by two well-armed security guards, Bordaberry asked me to follow him to a private office along a corridor which extended behind the main desk where public transactions were taking place.

Bordaberry opened a door halfway down the corridor and ushered me in. The room was small and spare in the extreme: one metal desk with an adding machine, a telephone, a calendar, and a note pad on top; standard issue office chairs, one behind the desk for Bordaberry, and two on the other side for clients The walls were bare and there were no personal touches anywhere. I presumed that all the offices along the corridor were identical – and probably interchangeable. I speculated that there might be more luxurious accommodations elsewhere in the building for more "privileged" clients. Clearly, I didn't rate such treatment. Although lacking in any character, the space we were in did have the advantage of privacy. The door behind me was solid and even though I imagined there were clients doing business with the *casa* on either side of us I couldn't hear a thing other than my own breathing.

"So Mister Corbett," Bordaberry said with a smile, still speaking in English, "How can I be of assistance?" As he spoke, I saw him take a quick look at his watch. Given the crowd outside, I presumed that he didn't have time for small talk so I got right down to business.

"I need to change some dollars into *pesos* and Alfredo said you would be able to help me out."

Bordaberry gave me a quick smile and nodded. "How much would you like to change?"

I reached into my pocket and pulled out three hundred dollars in cash. Bordaberry watched without expression as I carefully counted out the bills and laid them on the table in front of him. Without touching the money, he held up a finger for me to wait and then picked up the phone. He turned his head to the side as whoever was on the other end answered. I could overhear him asking what the house was giving for the dollar at the moment. The currency must be pretty volatile, I thought to myself, if he had to check on it on what I presumed was almost a minute to minute basis. After fifteen seconds of listening, he placed the receiver back in its cradle and turned to me with a smile. "I can offer you one hundred and twenty pesos to the dollar. Is that going to be satisfactory?"

I noticed when I had come in off the street that there was a blackboard in the *Casa's* window that had exchange rates for major currencies listed in chalk. I presumed these were official figures and were in chalk because of frequent adjustments. On the board he dollar had been quoted at ninety *pesos*. What Bordaberry was offering was a healthy mark-up. I smiled at him, wondering if he was doing me a favor because of Alfredo.

"That seems very generous," I said, pushing my dollars in his direction. Without speaking he picked up my cash and not bothering to count it, took a key from a chain he extracted from his vest pocket and unlocked a right-hand drawer in the metal desk. Opening the drawer, he took out a lock-box and opened it with yet another key. He put the dollars inside and, at the same time, withdrew a wad of Argentine *pesos*. They were in large denominations of one hundred and one thousand, colored mostly in red and featuring patriotic figures from Argentina's past. He then used the adding machine, counting out the local currency bills as he punched in the numbers. He made some final calculations, ripped the paper out of the machine, placed most of the bills on the desk in front of me, and returned the rest to the lock box, which he placed back into the drawer. He showed me the paper from the machine with his calculations, using his finger to indicate the line that had the conversion from dollars to *pesos*. He then carefully counted out the full amount, which came to a grand total of thirty six thousand *pesos*. I noticed that there was no commission. I was getting the full amount. It had to be thanks to Alfredo that I was getting such special treatment.

As Bordaberry handed me the cash, I suddenly felt very wealthy. From three hundred dollars to thirty six thousand *pesos*! It was irrational of course. Over time, I knew, after I had paid a few bills, reality would sink in. But for the moment I enjoyed having so many thousands in my possession. At the same time, I also felt a little guilty.

"Excuse me Señor Bordaberry, but I…."

"Please. Call me Mario."

"Very well…Mario. I certainly appreciate the deal you have given me. But shouldn't you be charging me some kind of commission? I mean the rate you are providing seems almost too generous."

I began to put my hand back into my pocket to withdraw some bills to return to him. He saw my gesture and immediately put up his hand to stop me. There was a look of wry amusement on his face. "No. No Mister Corbett. No need. Don't worry. No problem."

He again looked at his watch and I presumed he wanted to get me on my way so he could get to the crowd waiting out in the lobby. Then he gave a slight shrug, leaned over the desk, motioning me closer and lowered his voice, even though I was sure nobody could hear us.

"You are recently arrived to Argentina Mister Corbett. Are you not?"

I nodded. "Well, you have arrived at a moment of great uncertainty – politically and economically. Unfortunately, that is not unusual here. We often do not have any idea what is going to happen from one day to the next. Perhaps we'll wake up tomorrow and find that the military has decided to rescind the recent elections and take full control."

He gave another shrug and held his hands out, palms up. "Who knows? These crazy things happen all the time. Or perhaps crops will be hit by a drought or a plague of locusts and the agricultural exports that are our lifeline will shrink and we'll go into a recession. Or, more to the point, the finance minister will decide to devalue the currency by twenty-five percent. So what can we do to protect ourselves under these circumstances?" he asked rhetorically. "We buy dollars and keep them locked away for the rainy day that might be just around the corner. While we cannot be sure of much in Argentina, we can be sure that dollars will remain sound and that our currency will continue to lose value. There have been some exceptions to that rule, but they have been rare."

He sat back and gave me a wry smile "Today I am giving you, as you say, a very 'generous' rate of exchange for your dollars, one third above the official rate. Of course, you provided cash. With travelers' checks it would have been somewhat less, but not by much. What matters most is for us – for me – to have dollars. This morning the official rate is ninety *pesos* to the dollar but tomorrow – or even this afternoon – it could be one hundred. And next week, *quién sabe?*, maybe one hundred and thirty. If that were to happen, you might come to see me and ask why you had gotten so little for your dollars, not why so much. Do you see Mister Corbett," he concluded, shaking his head as though he could hardly believe what he was saying. "It's all a kind of game. A game with some generally understood rules, of course, but with rules that could change at any moment. So please don't worry about my compensation. And if you have more dollars to change in the future, I do hope that you will return to see me. I promise that I shall treat you fairly."

I looked at him with bemusement. What he had said did not come as a total surprise. I had run into similar situations in other Latin American countries, where political and economic instability were chronic and the dollar offered one of the few sure refuges in a climate of crisis and uncertainty. I reached across the desk to shake his hand, thanking him for changing my dollars and for his explanation. I assured Mario that any future business I might have would come his way. He returned the thanks and escorted me to the lobby, where the crowd had grown thicker and, it seemed to me, more truculent and impatient. Before seeing me on my way, Mario whispered into my ear that I should keep a firm hand on my *pesos* as pickpockets abounded on the streets outside and would see a foreigner just emerging from a *casa de cambio* as easy prey. I thanked him for his advice, assuring him that I would keep a tight grip on my bills and my wits about me. He gave me a friendly pat on the shoulder as I passed through the security gate. As I opened the door to step out onto the street, I heard him call out the number of the next person in line.

Sixteen

I left the *Casa Baires* and proceeded north on Reconquista. Heeding Ernesto Bordaberry's advice, I kept my right hand in my pocket with a firm grip on my *pesos*. At the intersection with Calle Corrientes, about a block away, the crossing light had just turned red and I had to wait with a sizeable crowd before passing to the other side. I took the opportunity to glance around and saw two shady types behind me at the edge of the crowd. When I caught their eye, they immediately turned their heads to look in another direction, a sure tip-off that they were following me.

When the light changed, I hustled across to the other side. When I reached the sidewalk, I made a sharp turn to the left and looked behind me to determine if I was still being followed. I could no longer see the two shifty-eyed characters who probably had been discouraged when I had spotted them and who, I presumed, were now looking for other targets.

Still keeping my hand in my *peso*-laden pocket, I headed west on Corrientes, aiming for the intersection two blocks on with Calle Florida. Florida, my guidebook had informed me, was one of the most famous streets in the city – a pedestrian-only thoroughfare lined with fancy stores, restaurants, and cafés. Reaching the intersection, I turned right and continued heading north. I had arranged to meet with Héctor and Manuel's other friends at a restaurant called Ligure located on Juncal at the edge of the Barrio Norte, about ten blocks for where I was presently located. The restaurant, Héctor had informed me, was relatively small and quite popular. Therefore, we planned to meet at about twelve thirty, somewhat early for lunch, but a time that more or less guaranteed us a table.

I looked at my watch and saw it was a little after noon. Given that I was now on a pedestrian-only street, I figured I had plenty of time to get to Ligure by the appointed hour and slowed my pace to a leisurely stroll, taking some time to stop and glance into shop windows to admire the luxury items on sale. The street was crowded and I was occasionally jostled by serious-minded young men in business suits hurrying along with purposeful strides, reminding me of similar scenes in Washington.

My slower pace and a few wrong turns made me a few minutes late in arriving at Ligure. But knowing the Latin tendency to consider appointment times "flexible," I presumed I would still be the first to arrive. I was wrong. When I entered the restaurant I encountered a line of customers waiting for tables and mentally kicked myself for being late. But as soon as I made an appearance, a slim young man dressed in a sweater and slacks got up from a table about halfway to the rear of the restaurant and headed toward me. Giving me a smile and extending his hand, he said, "Señor Corbett I presume. I am Héctor Martínez. Please follow me. We have a table."

I shook his hand and accompanied him to the table he and his three friends had occupied. There were further handshakes and introductions as the others rose to greet me. The other male was Roberto and the two females were Marisol and Cristina. I asked all of them to call me Frank. While they were all in their mid-twenties and I had a few years on them, I didn't think the age difference or the circumstances required the formality of calling me Señor Corbett.

Once we were all seated I took a closer look. They still had smiles on their faces, but I could see curiosity and concern written there as well. All four were casually but well-dressed and were uniformly attractive. I guessed from their appearance and their clothing that they were likely of the same upper-class background as my friend Alfredo and the Fernández family.

Before we had a chance to discuss Manuel, the waiter came to take our orders. While the others placed theirs, I looked at the menu and saw some dishes that looked a bit exotic. I decided to try the rabbit in wine sauce. I figured that I would have plenty of opportunities to try the delicious Argentine steaks and the rabbit would be a nice change of pace. As I placed my order, I could see some eyebrows go up around the table along with nods of approval.

After the waiter left, we began to chat. Héctor assumed the role of spokesman for the group and told me that they were all good friends with Manuel, knew that he had gone missing, and would be happy to provide whatever help they could in the effort to find him.

I told them that I appreciated the offer and then gave them a brief summary of what I had discovered so far. They listened attentively and without interruption and I could see their faces grow more and more somber as I laid out the story – omitting some of the details and speculations. When I mentioned the possibility that Manuel might have joined the ERP, without naming my sources, I could see a collective shaking of heads. Roberto, who was sitting to my right, looked around the room carefully and then moved his chair closer to mine. Leaning towards me until our heads were only inches apart, he said in a low voice, "Listen Frank. I have known Manuel since we were in elementary school together. He would never – and I mean *never* – choose violence as a way to resolve anything. Even though he is plenty tough, from the time he was a kid he did everything he could to avoid a fight. The idea that he would join a murderous bunch like the ERP just doesn't make sense." I could see the others bob their heads in agreement.

I thought about bringing up some counter-arguments. They hadn't been in close contact with Manuel in recent years and perhaps they didn't have a good read on how his politics and his position might have changed. There was also the fact that his friend Gregorio Robles *had* joined the guerrillas and had been captured by the authorities, tortured, and murdered. This obviously had made a great impact on Manuel and might have influenced him to change course and to consider other, less-peaceful options to the kinds of social and political changes to which he was committed. But in the end I didn't see what good mentioning these things would do. It would only upset them further.

I asked them if they could offer any alternative answers to what might have happened to their friend and received only shrugs and shakes of the head. It was as much a mystery to them as it was to me. Taking another tack, I asked each of them to talk in general terms about what Manuel was like, hoping that there might be some clues in their collective recollections.

Beginning again with Héctor, they recounted stories that often brought the smiles of happy memories to their faces followed by looks of sadness as they began to consider the real possibility that they might never see Manuel again.

When our food arrived, we interrupted the discussion about Manuel and began to eat. My rabbit was cooked to perfection – so tender it fell off the bone and with an exquisite sauce. We had ordered wine, but I kept my consumption to one glass. I noticed that most of the others – with Roberto being an exception – did the same. While we ate, the conversation shifted to more general topics. I got some compliments on my Spanish and the two girls asked me about my family, my background, and my decision to become a private detective. Marisol observed that I wasn't quite what she expected. Her image of North American detectives was formed by movies and television and I didn't seem much like Humphrey Bogart or Howard Duff. I laughed and told her that I was just starting out in the business and perhaps after a few more years under my belt I would begin to look – and act – more like them. Over dessert and coffee we switched back to the subject of Manuel and his disappearance, but without achieving much in the way of new information or insights.

If the circumstances had been different, I would have enjoyed spending more time in their company. They were a very attractive and intelligent group. Héctor and Roberto were both finishing up their university studies in law and architecture respectively while Cristina and Marisol were already teaching history and literature in a local private high school. They were very well-informed about global events and the latest books and movies and seemed to genuinely enjoy each other's company. They were, from all I could tell, very nice kids. Maybe if the leadership of the country fell into hands like theirs, the future of Argentina might not be as grim as Alfredo seemed to think it was.

By the time we had finished our lunch, it was almost two o'clock. I told them that I had a two-thirty appointment and since I had gotten a little lost in locating the Ligure I had best be on my way. Marisol asked me the address I had to find – an office in the fifteen hundred block of Corrientes – and gave me directions. Then, with some color rising in her cheeks, she offered to accompany me to the office so that I wouldn't get lost. The prospect of spending more time with her was not at all an unpleasant one and I said that I would appreciate her company. She gave me a warm smile and I thought I saw a quick look of envy cross Cristina's face, but maybe I was imagining things. Both Héctor and Roberto, I noticed, were trying not very successfully to hide their grins

When the waiter brought the bill, I insisted on paying. The two men made some protestations and suggested a sharing of the costs, but I said rather firmly that the lunch was part of my investigation and would be covered by my expense account. They gave in pretty easily with shrugs, smiles, and thanks. I began to have second thoughts when I saw the total, six thousand *pesos*! But I soon realized that translated into fifty dollars – not bad for a lunch for five at a good restaurant. I lifted the wad of bills from my pocket and peeled off the requisite number along with a small tip. Alfredo had told me that tips were usually included as part of the bill, but I figured leaving a small token of appreciation was appropriate. The waiter had been attentive but unobtrusive and deserved something extra.

As we left Ligure, Héctor, Roberto, and Cristina looked for a taxi to share. They were all headed in the same direction, the Belgrano district to the north. I promised that I would contact them through Héctor as soon as I had anything to tell them about Manuel and thanked them again for their help and told them how much I had enjoyed meeting them. The men responded with *abrazos* and slaps on the back. Cristina offered her cheek for a kiss and I obliged.

They were able to find a taxi immediately and piled in, giving Marisol and me a wave of farewell as they took off. Marisol, smiling, took my arm and steered me to the right, saying that we would head for the Nueve de Julio. As we walked, she began to ask me more questions about my family, my background, and life in the United States. She had never been to the U.S. and was, like most I had met in Latin America, intensely curious about what was going on there. She seemed up-to-date on the Watergate scandal and began to pepper me with questions. I did my best to respond, sounding, I hoped, reasonably well-informed but confessing, as well, that there still remained much to be explained. It was pretty clear that she believed there was some sort of evil conspiracy behind the whole thing. While I had my doubts on that score, I didn't try to convince her otherwise.

After about ten minutes, we crossed the Nueve de Julio and turned left. Another ten minutes found us at the intersection with Corrientes, where we turned right. The building I was looking for was several blocks to the west and we reached it a little before my scheduled appointment time of two thirty. I realized by then that even the most obtuse stranger to the city could easily have followed directions from the Ligure to where we had arrived. But I was not at all displeased that Marisol had used the excuse of being my guide to accompany me. I also had noticed that she had attracted more than a few appreciative glances from males of all ages who had passed us in the opposite direction.

For a moment, I felt a pang of regret that I was in Buenos Aires on business rather than pleasure. Beginning with Gloria from last night and now Marisol standing there in front of me, there seemed abundant opportunities to enjoy pleasant female companionship in a city that clearly offered many ways to have a good time. But I *was* here on business and when Marisol asked me if we might meet later in the day, perhaps for a drink, she couldn't hide the look of disappointment when I told her that I was going to be occupied well into the night with my efforts to find out what had happened to Manuel Fernández.

A serious look crossed her face when I mentioned the main reason for my presence in Buenos Aires. "Of course Frank," she said. "I understand completely. And I do hope you can find out what has happened to him. But, if you need any help, please let me know." Then rummaging in her purse, she pulled out a pen and a piece of paper and began scribbling. Handing the paper to me, she said, "Here is my phone number. Please do not hesitate to call if you need my help."

I took the paper and tucked it into my coat pocket. "Thank you for your offer Marisol. I appreciate it. And let's hope that things turn out for the best and I can find Manuel." When I didn't say anything about contacting her, her face fell and I kicked myself mentally. "And whatever happens," I said, trying to recover, "I hope we have a chance to meet again. I would really enjoy that."

She perked up. "I would too Frank. Now you had better hurry or you will be late for your appointment."

We exchanged smiles and she inclined her head towards me for a kiss on the cheek. As I performed the ritual, she also gave me a warm hug, pressing her body against mine for a few delightful seconds. I was almost tempted to change my mind and arrange to meet her later, but my better judgment prevailed and we disentangled. I turned from her and entered the building. I could feel her eyes on me as I made my way through the door and when I looked back over my shoulder I could see her still standing where I had left her. She gave me a final smile and a wave and then headed up the street and out of sight.

Seventeen

The building I had entered had an impressive lobby, with marble floors, wood-paneled walls, and gleaming brass fixtures. At the back were two elevators and a guide to the offices. The one I was looking for, "Roy Smallwood, Exports and Imports," was on the fifth floor, number 510. I pressed the button for the elevator and saw the one to my right begin to descend. After about fifteen seconds, it came to a halt and an operator opened the door. I stepped in and asked him to take me to the fifth floor. He simply nodded, closed the door behind me, and turned the lever for us to ascend. When we got to the fifth floor and the operator opened the door for me, I looked at my watch and saw that it was two-thirty on the dot.

I asked the operator which way to office 510 and without uttering a word, he pointed to the left. I thanked him, receiving a grunt in return as he closed the door behind me. I strode down the hallway and found the office at the end on the left. There was a small sign next to the door that repeated the information on the guide below: "Roy Smallwood, Exporter and Importer." As I read it again, I chuckled under my breath and shook my head. How often had the CIA used that cover for one of its agents? By now, how could it fool anyone?

I knocked on the door and heard a female voice say, "Come in."

I turned the handle and entered into a reception area. Straight ahead was a desk, behind which sat a young woman who added to my impression that Buenos Aires was full of attractive females. She had the dark hair, dark eyes, and olive skin that were so common in this country of mostly Spanish and Italian immigrants. Although she was seated, from what I could see she had all the right curves in the all the right places. She had on a low-cut blouse that revealed an ample cleavage. The only thing missing from the other young *porteñas* I had met up to this point was a smile. Instead, she gave me a look that was on the border between boredom and hostility.

"Yes?" she said. Even though it was only one word, combined with her expression, it suggested that I was an unwelcome intruder, someone who had interrupted something vitally important – like manicuring her fingernails.

I tried to turn on the charm. I approached the desk and gave her my warmest smile, extending my hand as I did so. "I'm Frank Corbett," I said. "I called this morning. I have a two-thirty appointment with Mister Smallwood."

She ignored my hand and gave me a blank look. I withdrew my hand and began to wonder if I had wandered into the wrong office. Or maybe I was in some sort of Argentine version of the *Twilight Zone*. I had spoken to her in English, figuring that if she was Smallwood's secretary she had to be bilingual. But maybe not, so I tried again in Spanish. Still there was no response. She just continued to stare at me for another ten seconds. Then a light seemed to go off somewhere in her head and she reached into the center drawer of her desk and took out what appeared to be an appointment book. Opening it, she ran her finger vertically down a page and stopped about a third of the way down and ran it horizontally. "Hmm," she muttered, "Frank Corbett. Yes. Yes. Here it is. Yes, I see, two thirty," she said, more to herself than to me.

When she continued to look at the book as if she couldn't quite believe what it contained, I decided to try a prompt. "Could you please tell Mister Smallwood that I am here for my appointment?"

She looked up at me with that blank look still firmly in place. I was beginning to wonder if she was all that slow or that maybe her performance was some sort of an act the purpose of which I couldn't divine. Finally, she turned from me without a word and picked up the phone.

"Mister Smallwood," she said in English, "Your two-thirty appointment is here." She paused for a moment, casting a glance in my direction, and then I heard her say, "Yes. Mister Corbett. He called earlier today...." As she listened to whatever Smallwood had to say, she wrinkled her brow as if whatever it was required great concentration. "Yes sir," she said, "I'll tell him." With that she hung up the phone and swiveled around to face me. As she performed this maneuver, I saw that she was dressed in the shortest of skirts and had truly spectacular legs. From all I could tell, drawing on my well-trained skills as a P.I., she was employed by Smallwood more for her beauty than her brains.

"Mister Smallwood will see you now Mister Corbett," she said, pointing do the door behind her.

"Thank you very much… señorita?…."

If I was hoping for a name, I was disappointed. She simply repeated the gesture indicating that I should head for Smallwood's door. My charm offensive having failed miserably, I did as I was told and headed for the door. Before knocking, I turned my head briefly and caught the secretary stealing a speculative look in my direction. I thought I detected a small smile play along her lips, but perhaps it was my imagination.

Rapping on the door, I heard Smallwood on the other side ask me to come on in. I pushed the door open and entered. I took a quick look around. The office had all the right props: a standard-issue desk, two filing cabinets in a corner, a map of Latin America on the wall with red pins sticking out of various places, a coffee table strewn with business magazines, a couch, and a couple of office chairs for visitors. But it all had the look of impermanence. There were no family pictures, no diplomas, no commendations, nothing to say that this space belonged to its occupant. Smallwood could be out of it at a moment's notice and no one would ever know that he had been there. And that, I assumed, was just the way he wanted it. They don't call it a "front" for nothing.

I approached the desk where Smallwood was seated and held out my hand. "Mister Smallwood," I said with a smile, "I'm Frank Corbett. As I hope your secretary told you Dwight Whalen recommended that I look you up and…"

Smallwood stayed seated and ignored my outstretched hand. He gave me the same blank look as his secretary, although I did see his eyes narrow at the mention of Dwight's name. *What's going on here?* I asked myself. Was it some kind of office protocol to be purposely unfriendly? Or was it a routine that Smallwood and his secretary had worked out to put people off guard? It certainly didn't seem the best way to treat potential clients, only reaffirming my well-founded hunch that this was no business operation but rather a cover for whatever Agency operation Smallwood was involved in.

Without a word, Smallwood pointed to one of the client chairs and gestured for me to take a seat. We spent the next fifteen seconds staring at one another. Smallwood was, I guessed, in his fifties. He had thinning red hair, a freckled florid face, and a nose that, like Steve Kowalski's, looked as though it had been broken more than once. His suit coat hung on a rack in the corner and he had loosened the tie on his white dress shirt and had his sleeves rolled up, revealing well-muscled forearms. Strewn across his desk were file folders, newspapers, and various notepads. These, of course, all on the surface seemed to have to do with his alleged business operations, but I suspected that instead he was gathering data on political matters and preparing reports for his superiors, either at the embassy or directly to Langley. From my perspective, at least, he might as well have had CIA written on his forehead. I began to wonder what the connection was between him and Dwight.

He interrupted my musings: "So what do you want Corbett? What brings you to this lovely corner of the world?" He almost sneered.

I gave him the abbreviated version. "I'm a private investigator, looking for a missing person, an Argentine who was studying medicine in the States and who disappeared about a month ago. There are no real leads. Nobody saw him leave on his own and if he was kidnapped there has been no contact from the kidnappers. When I spoke with Dwight, he implied that my missing person might have returned to Argentina to fight with the local guerrillas. Those who know him, however, think that's pretty unlikely. But the person who hired me thought that I should come here and look around just in case. When I told Dwight I was traveling to Buenos Aires, he gave me your name and said you might be able to help. And that's why I'm here."

As I spoke, I could see a look of annoyance cross his features. I didn't know exactly what he was thinking, but I got the distinct impression he considered me a nuisance and that he was not about to offer much help.

"So how do you know Dwight?" he asked, his tone curt.

"We went to G.W. together and were on the basketball team. We've kept in touch over the years and when this case came up…"

He held up a hand to cut me off. "And what's the name of this missing person?"

"Manuel Fernández. He's the son of…."

He interrupted again. "The number two man in the Argentine embassy in Washington. And, as I understand it, the son is something of a trouble-maker and has some questionable friends here in Buenos Aires."

"Well, there seems to be some difference of opinion on that score."

There was a doubtful look on his face and I decided not to get into an extensive argument with him, figuring that wouldn't be productive. Besides, he might have some information about Manuel that I did not. The fact that he knew so much about the Fernández family only reconfirmed my suspicions that he was doing more than running a one-man business.

He gave me five more seconds of the "stare" and then asked, "So what do you want from me?"

"According to Dwight, Manuel disappeared so he could join the *Ejército Revolucionario del Pueblo*...I presume you've heard of it." I said with a touch of sarcasm. He simply nodded, but the look on his face said, *Of course I have you jerk. Who in this damned country hasn't?*

"Well, I need to get in touch with that outfit to see if what Dwight suspects is really true."

This time the look on his face said: *Who is this crazy idiot? Does he have some kind of death wish?* But instead he placed both his hands palm up on his desk, "And what makes you think I can be of any help?"

I was getting tired of his song and dance. It was time to cut to the chase. I leaned forward and said, "Look Smallwood – if that *is* your name – why don't you drop the routine. I know that you are no innocent businessman. You have the Agency written all over you – from the decorative secretary to the bare-bones office. And how many times are you guys going to use the import-export cover? You might as well advertise in the paper that you are CIA. Who do you think you are fooling? And why would Dwight Whalen give me your name as a contact unless he was pretty sure you would be plugged in enough to help me out?" As soon as those words left my mouth, I began to ask myself why Dwight hadn't told me that Smallwood was CIA? Maybe he thought I would figure it out on my own, but why the omission? It was something to try to puzzle out later. Right now I had to see what I could get out of Smallwood.

As I spoke, Smallwood did his best to retain his cool. Nonetheless, he couldn't resist balling his hands into fists. But he decided to hang tough. Once again, the silent treatment and the blank stare. I decided to turn up the pressure. "Listen *Roy*, I have a good friend here in Buenos Aires who happens to be a well-known investigative journalist. Maybe I should suggest that he take a look into your little operation here. Maybe he'd come with a photographer and do a feature story on you. Get your name and face splashed all over his magazine – maybe even on the cover. How about if…"

I'd gotten to him. His knuckles had turned white and the color had risen in his already florid cheeks. "Not much of a patriot, are you Corbett?" he spat out. "You're willing to put my life at risk so you can locate some nut-job who wants to overthrow a government that up to now has been pretty pro-U.S. and what's more…"

This time I cut him off. "Come on Roy. Let's not go over the top. And for your info, I spent three years in Vietnam and I figure my patriotic credentials are every bit as good as yours." Then, to turn things down a notch, I said, my hands extended palms up, "All I'm asking is for a little cooperation. Is that too much to ask?"

He took a deep breath and I could see him weighing his options. Finally, he said, "Okay Corbett. Listen carefully. You want to make contact with the ERP, right?" I nodded. "Well, we've been trying for years to get someone on the inside but have had absolutely no luck whatsoever. These guys are well-organized, well-armed, and extremely secretive." He paused for a moment. Then he leaned over the desk towards me. "What I'm about to tell you is strictly confidential. If you utter a word about it, I'll do everything in my power to make your life a living hell. Got me?" I nodded again. Taking another deep breath, he said, "Over the past couple of years we've recruited half a dozen locals to try to infiltrate the ERP. They were well-trained and dedicated, but each and every one of them got found out within a matter of weeks. They never got to report back and when we didn't hear from them, assumed the worst. We only found one body, and what had been done to it wasn't pretty. We presume the other five met the same fate and were disposed of in some unmarked grave." A look of resignation appeared on his face and he gave a slight shrug. "We've pretty much given up any sustained effort to get some of our people into their ranks. We have left it up to the Argentines to try to handle the ERP from now on."

I began to feel some sympathy for him. His frustration with his failures and his feelings for the fate of the men he had recruited seemed genuine.

"I'm sorry to hear that Smallwood. And don't worry; what you just told me will remain just between the two of us."

The atmosphere between us seemed to cool down. Smallwood unclenched his fists and I leaned back in my chair.

"Thanks Corbett," he said, "I just wanted you to know what kind of a group we're dealing with here. Not exactly the Boy Scouts."

I gave him a quick smile. "Yeah, I've heard those same words before. These guys are ruthless, dedicated, violent - and effective. Not too different from the Viet Cong. Don't worry, I'm under no illusions."

Smallwood sat back in his chair and used his right hand to scratch the back of his left. He paused, looking at me with less hostility. I figured he was weighing some options and waited for the result. After about fifteen seconds, he leaned forward with a serious look on his face. "Okay Corbett. If you want to hook up with the ERP, I'll see what I can do. I have some local contacts that might be able to help. But there are no guarantees. And if by some chance you do make contact, don't expect any help from me – or anybody else. You are strictly on your own. Understood?"

I gave him a serious look of my own. "Understood," I said. "And thanks Smallwood. I appreciate the effort."

He shot me a skeptical look. "Yeah. Well if this does work, you might not be so thankful." I could imagine him flashing back to the six local agents he had lost. "How do I get in touch with you Corbett? Where are you staying?"

I hesitated for a moment. After using the threat of my friendship with a "well-known investigative journalist," I was reluctant to mention Alfredo's name. I was sure that Smallwood would immediately recognize it. Even giving him Alfredo's phone number might involve my friend in complications he didn't need. I still had my doubts about Smallwood and I didn't want to put my friend at risk. So I said, "Listen. I'm kind of between places right now and don't have a fixed address or phone number. Why don't I call you tomorrow, say around ten o'clock, to see if you've been able to arrange anything?"

I could tell from the look on his face that he didn't buy my story, but he didn't press the matter. Instead, he nodded and said, "Okay Corbett. I'll see what I can do and expect your call tomorrow." Having said that, he stood up and leaned across his desk, extending his hand. I was a little surprised, but I took it and we exchanged shakes. He didn't say anything more. No "nice to have met you" or "good luck" or "if there is anything else I can do, don't hesitate to call." My guess was that he would be glad to see the last of me – and I didn't expect he would make much of an effort to gain me access to the ERP. I had put him on the spot with my threat to expose his cover and he had responded grudgingly to my request. And in the process, he had tried to dissuade me by telling me how dangerous the guerrilla group was. I figured that when I called tomorrow at ten, he would either be conveniently "unavailable" or tell me that he had struck out in his attempts to get me in touch with the ERP.

I thanked him again and he simply nodded, as if to say, *Sure – and it's your funeral.* As I turned to leave the office, I saw him pick up the phone. But he waited until I had closed the door before I could hear him dialing. I wondered who he was calling and was sorely tempted to try to hear what I could through the closed door. But his secretary was eyeing me from the moment I left Smallwood's office with the same unfriendly look she had bestowed on me from the beginning still firmly in place. As I headed to the outer door, I could feel her eyes on my back, monitoring my every step. Reaching the door, I turned back and gave her my best smile. She was staring straight at me with the same hostile expression.

I tried one last time to get a rise out of her. "Thank you señorita. It's been a real pleasure to have made your acquaintance." Still no response just the empty stare. I shrugged and closed the office door firmly behind me.

Once out on the street, I decided to walk back to Alfredo's apartment. Taking the small map that had come with my guidebook out of my pocket, I traced the route. From Corrientes to the Botanical Garden looked to be about thirty blocks. Even though I had jogged in the morning, I figured that some additional exercise, especially after a heavier-than-usual lunch, would do me no harm. Besides, it would give me time to think.

My meeting with Smallwood had raised more questions than answers. Why had Dwight given me his name without revealing that he was a spook? Why hide that fact when he must have known I would immediately figure it out? And what, *precisely*, was the relationship between the two men? And, had Dwight told Smallwood that I might be showing up on his doorstep? And if so, why had Smallwood initially been so hostile and off-putting? What was going on here?

Maybe in the future, I could figure out the answers. But for the moment, I could only speculate, and nothing that I could come up with was very satisfactory. So I decided to put these questions out of my mind for the moment and enjoy my stroll through the city, taking in the sights, sounds, and smells.

By now, it was almost four o'clock and the sidewalks were crowded with fellow pedestrians. There was much more foot traffic than I was used to in D.C. and I thought Buenos Aires more like New York or Chicago in that regard. People of both sexes were well dressed and looked much healthier than the average for much of Latin America. But I saw few smiles on their faces. Maybe Smallwood's secretary, I thought to myself, was the norm and the others I had met the exceptions. But then I recalled what Alfredo had told me about the current situation, and I could appreciate the lack of light-heartedness. There was a lot of uncertainty – both political and economic – and I suppose that put many on edge. Moreover, despite the abundant police presence – there seemed to be two or three uniformed men carrying automatic weapons on every corner, carefully eyeing everyone who passed – there was also a still-present threat of violence from the various revolutionary organizations like the ERP. I thought to myself that if I was worried that a bomb could go off at any minute or a shoot-out occur without warning with me in the middle I wouldn't have much of a smile on my face either. I didn't think it was as bad as Saigon, but I sensed some of the same tension.

Lost in these musings, I suddenly felt a familiar tingling at the back of my neck that signaled somebody was following me. I tried a couple of tricks to see if I could spot anyone. I stopped suddenly to retie a shoelace, glancing back as I did so. Nobody that I could see made a sudden stop of their own behind me. A couple of blocks further on, I turned to stare into a shop window, looking quickly over my shoulder for the same telltale signs. But I didn't see anything or anyone who was acting suspiciously. I repeated the same maneuvers several blocks later, but with the same result.

By the time I reached Alfredo's building, I had almost convinced myself that my fears of being followed had been more imaginary than real. But those fears still lingered. Just because I hadn't seen anyone didn't mean they weren't there. It could be that they were awfully good at their job and that even someone like me, with my training and experience, couldn't spot them. The next question, of course, was: *If I were being followed, who was it?* There were numerous possibilities: The Argentine security forces, tipped off by the building *portero* that I was staying with Alfredo; CIA people, informed by Smallwood that I was on to him and sniffing around things I shouldn't be; or even members of the ERP who somehow had found out I was looking for Manuel Fernández and were keeping tabs on me.

There probably were other possibilities as well. But it didn't do me much good to obsess on them. My only choice was to continue on the course I had charted and to see where it led me – and to keep my eyes and ears open and be ready to react whenever the situation required it.

As I passed through the lobby on my way up to Alfredo's apartment, I gave the *portero*, who was sweeping the floor in a desultory fashion, a smile and a *buenas tardes*. He briefly stopped his sweeping and returned my greeting with what looked to be a forced smile. I saw him look at his watch and imagined that he would soon report to whomever he reported to that I had returned to the building at around four thirty.

Getting into the elevator, I grinned to myself. I was in a situation of mystery and danger in a city and a country about which I knew little. And trying to get in touch with the ERP, as everyone had warned me, was not only playing with fire but probably near-to suicidal as well. But, Lord help me, I was thoroughly enjoying every minute of it. For the first time since I had decided to become a private investigator, I was becoming convinced that I had made the right choice. This was what I was good at I told myself, and what I loved to do. And, perhaps foolishly, I hoped fervently that I would be able to contact the shadowy ERP and finally get some solid leads as to what had happened to Manuel Fernández. As it turned out, my hope would be realized sooner than I had expected.

Eighteen

I used the key Alfredo had given me to enter his apartment. As expected, it was empty. Presuming that my friend wouldn't be back until eight at the earliest, I got comfortable, taking off my coat and loosening my tie. Retrieving my briefcase from the bedroom, I withdrew my notes on the case and, sitting at the dining room table, began to jot down the pertinent details from my lunch with Manuel's friends and my strange visit with Smallwood.

It took about an hour for me to finish my note-taking. With some time to kill until Alfredo returned, I went back to reading the issues of *Chispa* that were on the coffee table. I found them intriguing and informative, written in a lively style and with wonderful photos, many of which had been taken by my companion at dinner last night. While I couldn't get all the subtleties, I also appreciated the artistry and humor of the editorial cartoons. I particularly enjoyed Alfredo's articles, written in his unique style.

By the time I had made my way through four issues, the sun had set and I had lost track of time. I was just looking at my watch, which said quarter after eight, when I heard the key in the lock, the door open, and Alfredo come in. He looked as though he had had a rough day. There was fatigue written all over his face. "Hey Frank," he said, as he shrugged off his jacket and flung it onto a nearby chair and let his briefcase fall with a heavy thump to the floor. Before I could ask him how his day had gone, he held up a hand and said in a tired voice, "I need a drink Frank. How about you?"

I really didn't need one, but was happy to keep him company. "Sure," I said. "But heavy on the ice and light on the Scotch please."

He gave me a look that I couldn't quite t read. He seemed more serious than usual and I assumed it had something to do with the pressure he was under in preparing the López Rega story. I was wrong. He headed for the trolley that held his liquor bottles and said over his shoulder, "You might change your mind after you hear what I have to tell you."

"What is it Alfredo? Were you able to…?"

"A drink first Frank. Then the news."

I kept a rein on my impatience as Alfredo poured the amber-colored imported Scotch – Johnny Walker Black – into two squat glasses. Two fingers for him, one for me. He added ice to my drink but kept his straight. Handing me my glass, he motioned for me to take a seat on the couch while he settled into a chair to my right. Leaning forward, he extended his glass towards mine and we touched them in a toast. Then he hoisted his glass and took a deep, satisfying swallow while I barely sipped mine. Putting his glass down on a side table, he gave me a somber look, deep concern in his eyes.

"Okay Frank," he said with a note or resignation in his voice, "I've managed to get you a meeting with members of the ERP." Then, in a barely audible tone, he added, "I hope we both don't come to regret it."

A smile lit up my face and I clapped my hand together. "That's fantastic Alfredo. How in the world did you manage…?"

He waved away the question. "Don't worry about that my friend. That, I'm afraid, is the least of your worries. Let's just focus on getting you through the night."

"You mean it's to be tonight?" I asked in surprise, with a bit of panic in my voice.

"Well, technically early in the morning tomorrow – very early."

Taking another pull on his drink, he explained the details. He would drive me to a park on the south side of the city and let me out at two a.m. precisely. He then had to drive away, leaving me alone to find my way to the statue of some historical figure in the center of the park, where I was to wait until two fifteen for my rendezvous with the ERP. If there was any deviation from the plan – if, for example, Alfredo should try to follow me or to wait for me in a nearby location, then the meeting would not take place and there would be no second chances. I was to be totally on my own, with no signs of any backup whatsoever. It was more or less what I expected but to hear Alfredo lay it out in such stark terms made my stomach churn.

"I did my best to vouch for you Frank, but this is a very suspicious bunch - and not without reason. They know that the U.S. government would like nothing better than to see them thoroughly destroyed. Their concern that you might somehow be involved in efforts to achieve that end is perfectly understandable. They have my word that you are who you say you are, but that might not be enough." Then he looked me squarely in the eye. "Are you *absolutely* sure you want to go through with this? You could just fail to show up and that would be that. How do you basketball players say, 'No harm, no foul.'"

I was beginning to think Alfredo had been right about the amount of whiskey in my glass. Instead of sipping, I took a healthy swallow of my own and felt the pleasant burn as it made its way down my throat. I looked straight at him, took a deep breath, and said, "No. No *amigo*. This is what I have to do if I'm going to have any chance of cracking this case. I'm going through with it, whatever the risks. And thanks again Alfredo. I know it couldn't have been easy to set this up."

Alfredo slumped in his chair and his expression suggested that he wanted to keep trying to dissuade me from meeting with the revolutionaries. But instead, he finished off his glass and set it down on the coffee table. Rousing himself, he stood up and said, "Well let's go out and have dinner. I don't know about you, but I'm starved. And you could probably use some nourishment as well." Although he didn't say it, I guessed that he was also thinking that if were to be my last meal, it might as well be a good one.

Nineteen

Alfredo took me to a restaurant only a few blocks from his apartment. It wasn't nearly as fancy as La Cabaña, but it had wonderful food and even on a week night at nine-thirty, was jammed pack. Once again, Alfredo worked his magic and we were escorted to a corner table, bypassing the line of waiting customers. As we dug into our steaks I asked my friend how the article on López Rega was going.

"We worked on it all day Frank. We had to double check many of our sources, some of whom seemed to be getting cold feet about the possibility of the quotes we use coming back to haunt them. But I think we have most of them reassured that their anonymity will be protected. Even if we do lose a few, I think we have enough for a good, tough story that should stir the pot."

"I presume it's not a story that is going to please this guy," I said.

"You presume correctly pal. He's not going to like it one bit," he said with a broad smile. Almost immediately, however, his face turned grim and he downed about half a glass of wine. Although I knew first-hand his enormous capacity for alcohol, I was beginning to worry that my friend was drinking more than he should. And as I watched him pour another glass while I had barely touched mine, I felt a sense of guilt. Alfredo was under considerable pressure and might well be in some danger when the story on the mysterious López Rega broke. And now I had come along and had involved him in arranging a meeting with one of the country's most vicious revolutionary groups, with the distinct possibility that things could go terribly wrong. Watching Alfredo gulp his wine, I had a moment where I considered scrapping the whole thing. But having gone this far, I decided,

I had to keep going. I rationalized my decision by reminding myself that Alfredo and I were both professionals, simply doing our respective jobs.

After finishing the meal and dessert, we ordered coffee and told the waiter to keep bringing it until we told him to stop. For my part, I was sufficiently wired with excitement and only needed a cup or two. But Alfredo, exhausted from a long and tense day and having drunk most of a bottle of wine, desperately needed the jolt of caffeine. As we drank, we purposely avoided talking about what the next few hours might bring and instead chatted about what we had been doing over the past few years after we had parted ways in Vietnam. By the time Alfredo had determined he had consumed enough coffee, we were the only patrons left in the restaurant. We could see the staff checking their watches, anxious for us to leave so they could close up. But they were either too polite – or too respectful of Alfredo's influence – to make any obvious gesture.

When Alfredo asked for the bill, the relief on our waiter's face was palpable. I offered to pay – or at least to split the cost – but Alfredo was insistent that this would be his treat. I wondered if he was thinking in the back of his mind that it might be his last opportunity to stake me to a meal.

We got back to Alfredo's apartment a little after midnight. Alfredo said he would try to get some sleep but to be sure to wake him in an hour so he could drive me to my rendezvous. I offered to take a cab, but he said absolutely not. He would drive me and that was that. I didn't see any sense in arguing with him, so I didn't.

I didn't know what the dress code was for meeting with members of the ERP, but decided that casual was probably appropriate. I had worn my suit to dinner, but back at the apartment changed into slacks, a shirt, and a sweater. It wasn't terribly cold, but I had brought along a light jacket and decided to carry it along as well. I debated leaving my passport with Alfredo, but decided I had better have it with me. The revolutionaries would more than likely want to verify that I was who I said I was. And I had a darker thought. It might help the police to identify my body. I pushed that thought aside, but I could feel my stomach churn again and my pulse beat a little faster as I considered the possibility.

Twenty

I woke Alfredo at one thirty. He had been able to sleep – don't ask me how – and bolted upright when I shook his shoulder. Rubbing his eyes, he gave me a baleful look and I thought he was going to ask me one more time if I was sure I wanted to go through with this. But seeing how I was dressed and, reading the look of determination on my face, he told me to wait for a moment while he splashed some water on his face and used the bathroom. Emerging five minutes later, he grabbed his car keys and we headed for the street where he had parked his Mercedes.

Getting into the car, Alfredo started the powerful engine and pulled slowly from the curb. At the corner, he turned left and headed down Avenida Santa Fe. As we did so, he and I both looked in all directions to see if anyone might be following us but saw nothing to indicate that anyone was on our tail.

Alfedo told me that our destination was the Parque Patricios in the neighborhood of the same name. It was located on the south side of the city in what was basically a working-class part of town, dotted with small-scale industries and older residential buildings.

At this time of night, there were few people on the streets and little in the way of vehicular traffic. I did see the occasional bus and we passed by some police cars parked at intersections. Alfredo told me that there were also unmarked cars – mostly Ford Falcons – that the police and the paramilitary forces used to round up suspected revolutionaries. I didn't see any during our drive, but he assured me that plenty were out and about.

We arrived at the Parque precisely at two a.m. From the car, Alfredo and I looked around. The entire area looked deserted. There was nobody in sight and there was no traffic to speak of. Alfredo turned towards me and gestured to the right. "The center of the park is that way, about fifty yards straight ahead. You can't miss it. You'll see some statues and a fountain. Just wait there until your contact – or contacts – arrive. *But*, if you spot anything suspicious, anything that seems out of place, hightail it out of there. I'll be waiting three blocks back on this street, Monteagudo."

I was about to protest. The instructions had been pretty clear. I was to come alone and if there were any indications that someone was following me, all bets were off. If whoever was meeting me saw Alfredo's car parked nearby, that might mess up everything. "But, didn't they say...?"

"It's not up for discussion Frank. I'm not about to leave you high and dry. I'll park in the shadows and keep the lights off. If you don't show up in forty-five minutes, I'll assume everything went as planned and head for home. Agreed?"

I had my doubts that Alfredo would keep his word. I was pretty sure that after he had waited a while, he would follow my path into the park, looking for me – or what was left of me. But it would be a waste of time to argue and the clock was ticking if I were to make it to my rendezvous on time.

I reached my hand out and we shook. "Thanks again my friend," I said with a catch in my voice. "See you soon."

He grabbed my hand in both of his. "*Suerte amigo. Hasta pronto.*"

I got out of the car and shut the door quietly behind me. Alfredo gave me a wave and drove off into the night.

Turning to my right, I followed the gravel path that led to the center of the park. It was chillier than I expected and I began to shiver, whether from the cold or from anticipation tinged with fear, I couldn't say. I put on my jacket, now thankful that I had thought to bring it, and as I hurried down the path, the shivering stopped.

I took in my surroundings. There was some ground mist and it gave the park, which seemed completely deserted, a spooky feel. There were lamps to light the way, but they were few and far between and there were plenty of shadows that would allow for total concealment. The air had a certain chemical odor and I thought I picked up the scent of rotten meat, but couldn't be sure. A few animals scurried away unseen, startled by my approaching footsteps. I wondered if this park had the same number of cats as the Botanical Garden, or if the noises I heard were of some other four-legged creature.

When I arrived at the center of the park, I checked my watch. It read 2:10, five minutes to the time set for my meeting. The fountain and statues that Alfredo had told me about were shrouded in mist and there was only one lamp that seemed to be working, casting a weak glow. I wondered if the other lamps had simply burned out or if they had been put out of operation on purpose.

There were several benches nearby and I debated whether to stand or sit. I preferred to stand, as that would give me some advantage if I needed to beat a hasty retreat. It would also make it easier – if I positioned myself correctly – to see anyone coming. But then I remembered that the purpose of this exercise was to make contact. And to do that, I had to make whoever was meeting me confident they could approach. If I looked too wary and uncomfortable, that might scare them off. So, against my instincts, I decided to take a seat on a nearby bench that was in front of some trees and bushes, and try to appear as relaxed as I could. Settling into the bench, I stretched my arms out on either side and hoped that my posture conveyed the message that I was not suddenly going to bolt.

After several minutes, I took another look at my watch. It was now 2:20, five minutes past the appointed meeting time. *Where were these guys? Had they had second thoughts? Had they spotted Alfredo and decided to call the meeting off?* My mind spun through several scenarios and despite my best efforts to control myself my right foot began to tap in impatience. I willed it to stop, took some deep breaths, and tried my best to relax. I decided to give them fifteen more minutes before giving up the ghost and heading back to where Alfredo was waiting for me.

Time seemed to drag on endlessly. It was eerie being alone in the park with only the occasional stirring of unseen animals keeping me company. I guessed that there was still some traffic in the nearby streets, but whatever sounds it made were muffled and indistinct.

Just as I was about to throw up my hands and get up from the bench, I felt the unmistakable outline and cold steel of a gun barrel pressed against the back of my neck. A voice behind me whispered in Spanish, "Don't move a muscle Señor Corbett – and do *exactly* as I say. If you deviate in any way, I won't hesitate to pull the trigger."

Instinctively I began to nod my head as a sign of agreement but stopped myself just in time. Instead, trying to keep my voice calm and steady, I said, "I understand. Whatever you say."

"That's good Señor Corbett. We wouldn't want any misunderstandings would we?"

Then, with the gun still firmly pressed against my neck, I felt another pair of hands slip a blindfold over my eyes while yet another tied my hands behind my back. So there were three of them. And they were very good. They had made their way through the foliage behind me and even though I had been expecting them and had been listening as carefully as I could, I hadn't heard a thing.

Once the blindfold was in place and my hands were secured, whoever held the gun removed it from my neck. He didn't say anything, but I was sure he still had it trained on me. I then felt hands grab me by my upper arms and begin to propel me forward. It was momentarily disorienting but whoever was guiding me kept a tight grip and while I stumbled from time to time, they kept me upright. So far as I could tell by the crunching of pebbles under my feet, we were sticking to the gravel path but I had no idea in which direction we were headed.

After several minutes on the path, we came to an abrupt halt. The only sound I could hear was the shallow breathing of my captors. Then one of them whispered in my ear. "You need to take a step up Señor Corbett." I did as I was told and immediately felt the texture of the ground change. Now I guessed we were on grassy terrain, off the regular path. And we began to take a less direct route as I was pulled one way and another every ten paces or so. I guessed that we were passing through a grove of trees and bushes, a guess that was confirmed as my head was suddenly forced downward, presumably to avoid hitting a low-lying branch.

After about five minutes of walking on the new surface, we again came to a halt. Two men on either side held me in a tight grip while I could hear another man, probably the one with a gun, walking away from us. Within seconds, I heard a car door open and I was hustled over what felt like a sidewalk and quickly bundled into the back seat of a waiting car. More doors opened and closed quietly as my captors piled in. As I heard them lock the doors, my excitement that I had made contact and would soon be a step closer to solving the mystery of why Manuel Fernández had disappeared mingled with the fear that I was now totally at the mercy of the men who held my fate in their hands.

Twenty One

Even though I couldn't see anything as I was bundled into the car, my sense of hearing and of smell was becoming more and more acute. I could tell that there were two men in front and one sitting next to me in the rear of the car. Whoever was driving started the engine and I could feel the vehicle accelerate slowly. As soon as that happened, I felt the barrel of the gun again on my neck and the whisper of the same man. "Don't get any ideas about trying to escape Señor Corbett."

"Don't worry. All I want is a chance to talk with you. That's all, I assure you."

He gave a non-committal grunt and removed the barrel from my neck. But I was sure he still held it in his hand, ready to use.

We spent the rest of the trip in silence. I did my best to keep track of the many turns we made but soon gave it up as hopeless. I was totally lost. After what I estimated to be about half an hour, I could feel the car slow and move from a smooth surface to a bumpier route that felt more like dirt than pavement. We bounced along for a few minutes and then came to a stop.

The doors in the front opened and I heard the driver and his companion get out. The man holding the gun stayed where he was and I had no doubt that his weapon was aimed squarely at me. The door on my side was opened and again two pairs of hands grabbed me by the upper arm and pulled me out of the vehicle. I could hear the man holding the gun following me out.

Underneath my feet, I could again feel grass. Wherever we were, there was almost complete silence aside from the noises made by insects. There was no sound of distant traffic and the air seemed fresher than downtown.

I guessed that we were probably out in the countryside somewhere, but, of course, had no idea where.

I was half-dragged over what seemed to be some kind of lawn and then brought to an abrupt halt. I could hear a key being inserted into a lock and a door opened. None too gently, a hand pushed me through the door. I was immediately assailed by a musty odor which suggested a place that had not been inhabited recently. I was led into what I guessed was some kind of living room and after about ten paces, was unceremoniously dumped into what felt like a rough wooden chair.

I bit back the temptation to ask any questions and just sat quietly. I could hear some shuffling of feet as my captors moved around and the sound of a match and then the smell of some kind of fuel that I could not immediately identify. After about a minute, I heard someone move behind me and then remove my blindfold.

It took me a few seconds to recover my sight. When I did, I saw three men wearing bandanas covering the lower part of their faces arrayed in a semi-circle around me. They were only a few feet away, sitting in identical wooden chairs that I presumed matched the one in which I was sitting. An image of facing a firing squad flashed through my mind but I tried to banish it. The only illumination came from a kerosene lamp placed on a table to my right. The weak light did not allow me to register many of the physical details of my captors. But from what I could tell, they were all of about the same height and weight, dressed in dark slacks and sweaters. What I had no difficulty in seeing was the revolver held by the man in the middle and pointed directly at my forehead.

There were a few moments of silence. Then the man with the gun said his voice still low and calm, "Well Señor Corbett, our first order of business is to make sure you are who you say you are."

I thanked my lucky stars I had thought to bring my passport. "My passport is in my shirt pocket underneath my sweater." I began to reach for it when I realized that my hands were still tied. I could see some amusement in my captors' eyes as I struggled for a few seconds to raise my arms.

Without a word, the man with the gun gestured to the comrade at his left to fetch the passport. Even though he knew my hands were bound, the man with the gun kept his weapon steadily aimed at my forehead while his colleague opened my jacket, lifted my sweater, and extracted my passport. He then took it over to the table with the lamp and opened it for inspection. I saw him studying the document carefully, glancing two or three times in my direction to make sure that my face matched my photo. Then he turned to the man with the gun and bobbed his head up and down. Getting a nod in return, he resumed his seat, leaving my passport on the table. I looked at it for a moment, hoping I would be able to recover it later.

"Well Señor Corbett. It looks as though you are who you say you are."

For a moment I thought about giving a sarcastic response. *Who else would have shown up in an isolated park at two-thirty in the morning? Hadn't it all been arranged beforehand?* But I held my tongue. And I began to appreciate the challenges facing the Argentine authorities in dealing with this bunch. They didn't take any chances. The ERP might have started out as an organization of idealistic young people with romantic notions in their head. But by now they were seasoned revolutionaries, with plenty of experience under their belt. They would not be easily subdued.

"Yes," I said, my voice steady now, "And all I want to do is ask you a few questions about…."

The man with the gun held up his free hand. "Before we get to your questions Señor…"

I interrupted him. "Please call me Frank." I thought that by having him use my first name we could lower the tension level a bit. Maybe he would even give me a name of his own, although I didn't expect it to be his real one. But he didn't bite.

"Before we get to your questions *Señor* Corbett," he repeated, "I have one for you. Just what were you doing at Roy Smallwood's office this… excuse me…yesterday afternoon?"

I could feel beads of sweat break out on my forehead and my heart began to pound heavily in my chest. "How did you…?"

He didn't let me finish. "We have kept a close watch on who goes in and out of Smallwood's office for several months now. We know that he works for the CIA and has been trying to infiltrate our organization for at least a year. So, to repeat," he said in a steely voice, "what were you doing in his office?"

I struggled to think of the right response. As I did so, I thought back on my feeling that I had been followed back to Alfredo's apartment after meeting with Smallwood. It provided cold comfort that my speculation concerning the ERP tracking me seemed to be on target. But then another thought it me. *What if Smallwood's notably unfriendly secretary was instead a plant? What if she was working with the ERP to keep tabs on what the agent was up to and who he met with?* From what I had seen so far of the organization's reach and abilities, it was a possibility I couldn't discount. At any rate, the best course – and probably the only one that would save my skin – was to stick to the truth.

"I'm a private investigator," I began, keeping my voice as calm and steady as I could, "And I've been hired to try to find an Argentine studying medicine at Duke University in the United States – Manuel Fernández – who has gone missing. Early on in my investigation, I spoke with a friend of mine in the State Department about the case" I could see the eyes of the man with the gun narrow at the words "State Department" and I tried not to look at his trigger finger. "He is on the Latin America desk and I thought he might have some helpful advice for me. When he heard that I was going to Buenos Aires to continue my search for Fernández, he gave me Smallwood's name as a person to contact. He didn't say anything about him being with the CIA." And, while that was the truth, I had my suspicions from the beginning, suspicions that were only confirmed when I met him. But I didn't think it would do me much good to reveal those suspicions. "So that's why I was at Smallwood's office yesterday."

An ominous silence followed. With most of the faces of my captors covered, I could only see their eyes and it was almost impossible to read their expressions. I tried to keep the look on my own face and my body language as relaxed as possible: the picture of a man telling the truth. But I couldn't control the drops of sweat that began to trickle down the side of my face. I hoped the men staring at me interpreted it as the natural reaction of anybody in my situation – my hands tied behind my back and staring at the business end of a pistol pointed directly at me.

Finally, the man with the gun said, "And why did you want to meet with us Señor Corbett?"

I breathed an inward sigh of relief. He seemed to have moved on from questions about Smallwood. Again, I stuck to the truth, but without revealing much in the way of details. "Well, I received information from several sources that suggested Manuel Fernández had left the United States voluntarily to join your organization. And the only way to confirm that was to arrange a meeting with you. And…."

My interrogator, in what was becoming a habit, held up a hand to stop me. Then, finally, he lowered the pistol. He still kept a grip on it as it rested in his lap, but it was no longer staring me in the face. I could see him shake his head a bit from side to side and even emit a low chuckle. I could imagine him thinking: *What a naïve idiot! To arrive in our country and think he could just waltz in and arrange a meeting with an organization dedicated to overthrowing that country's government and rightly suspicious of anybody connected with the 'Colossus of the North.' What a fool!*

And, I had to admit, if I were in his shoes, those would be my exact thoughts. But he surprised me. "Well Señor Corbett, I must say that I admire your courage - and your dedication to your job. But," he added, "before you get too comfortable, you are only here – and still in one piece – thanks to Alfredo Billinghurst. Without him assuring us that you are who you say you are and are not connected with your government your chances of living to see the dawn wouldn't be worth – how to you say it in your movies? – 'a plugged nickel.'"

I didn't know what to say, so I gave a brief nod of acknowledgement.

There was another long pause. Then he said, "Alfredo did tell us why you wanted to meet with us. But he didn't say anything about your meeting with Smallwood…."

I dared to interrupt. "He knew I was meeting with someone in the afternoon, but didn't know who."

He waved his hand dismissively. "I still have my suspicions about that Señor Corbett. But I am willing to give you the benefit of the doubt." He paused for a few seconds. Then, with absolute certainty in his voice, he said, "Let me assure you about one thing Señor Corbett. Manuel Fernández is *not* – and *never* has been – a member of the People's Revolutionary Army - or of any other revolutionary group."

I kept my expression blank, but I wondered if what I was hearing was the truth. *If Manuel actually had joined the ERP, would the man with the gun come right out and admit it? Wouldn't he want to hide that fact – especially from an American who had just that afternoon met with a CIA agent?* While I couldn't read the man with the gun's facial expression, the way he spoke when he denied Manuel's affiliation seemed genuine.

As if reading my mind, he said, "Members of our group have known Manuel Fernández for many years. And while he might share some of our goals, he has always made clear that he deplores and disapproves of our methods. Whoever suggested otherwise has been misleading you."

My thoughts turned to Dwight Whalen, who had first broached the possibility. *Why had he been so certain that Manuel had joined the ERP?* Not for the first time, I had to wonder what my old teammate was up to.

I didn't respond to the man with the gun's disclaimer. Maybe he was telling me the truth, maybe he wasn't. I really had no way to know except to go by my gut, which at the moment was leaning in his favor.

"But Señor Corbett," he continued, "what you should know is that a member of our group who had gone to school with Manuel Fernández saw him here in Argentina just last week." I let the surprise show on my face. "It was in Salta, in the north of the country, where he witnessed Manuel getting out of a car and going into a building in the downtown area of the city. He got only a quick glimpse, but he recognized him immediately, even though he had apparently lost a good deal of weight and was walking strangely – almost as though he had been drugged. But what is even more interesting was the identity of the person who was assisting him."

He paused for dramatic effect, obviously enjoying keeping me in suspense.

"Okay," I said. "I'll play along. Who was it?"

Even though I couldn't see the bottom of his face, I was sure he was grinning. "None other than our mutual acquaintance - Mister Roy Smallwood."

I sat back in my chair with a look of astonishment on my face. "So what do you make of that coincidence Señor Corbett? Intriguing, isn't it?"

For the moment, I was too flabbergasted to speculate, although I was beginning to think that there must be some connection that tied Smallwood and Dwight Whalen to Manuel Fernández's disappearance. But right now I couldn't figure out what it might be.

"I really don't know what to think. What do *you* suppose is going on?"

He shrugged. "It's hard to say specifically with regard to Manuel Fernández. What we do suspect, however, is that Mister Smallwood is engaged in something more than espionage in our country. We don't know just what, but it is more than likely something illegal. He makes frequent trips to the north of the country for reasons that seem to have little to do either with his cover as a businessman or his real profession as a secret agent. We just don't know what those reasons might be. We do not have sufficient resources to keep track of him when he makes these trips and…"

He stopped abruptly, realizing that he might be revealing more than he should. Instead, he just shrugged again.

I took some time to digest what he had told me. "Is there anything else you can tell me?" I asked.

"Not at the moment," he said. Then, after shifting his eyes right and left towards his companions, as if silently asking for their advice, he leaned forward and said, "But perhaps we can form an – how do you say it? – an alliance of convenience. We would dearly like to know what Smallwood is up to. If it is something illegal, then we can use that knowledge to our advantage. Moreover, Manuel Fernández has friends in our group and even if he disagrees with our methods, they are worried about him and don't want him to come to any harm. You, of course, want to find him and, I presume, rescue him from whatever difficulty he is in."

"Yes. Of course," I said, nodding in agreement.

"Well, here is what I propose. You go to Salta to see if you can find Manuel Fernández. We don't have many resources there, but we do have some." He paused and without even being told, the masked figure to his left handed him a small piece of paper and a pen. He scribbled something on it, looked at it for a few seconds, folded the paper and gave it back to the man on his left. That man, in turn, got up from the chair and went to the table where my passport still lay. Picking it up, he opened it and placed the piece of paper inside. Then he approached me and, again lifting my sweater, put the passport, now containing whatever was on the piece of paper, back into my shirt pocket. All the while, the man with the gun kept his eyes on me.

From one point of view, I thought to myself, this elaborate choreography seemed excessive. I still had my hands tied and had shown no inclination whatsoever to engage in any heroics. And we had begun the process of forming some kind of alliance. But, again I had to be impressed with the care and professionalism of this outfit. They still were not taking any chances.

Once the man who had replaced my passport had taken his seat, the man with the gun continued. "On that piece of paper is the phone number of a contact in Salta. We'll advise the contact that you will be calling in the next few days and will be looking for Fernández. When you make the call, ask for Sergio. If anyone else answers, hang up right away and don't call again. In that case, we'll contact you. Understood?"

I simply nodded, although I had some questions. *How would they know where to find me and who should I expect to contact me? Would it be the mysterious Sergio – or someone else?*

"And I expect you to commit the number to memory as soon as possible and destroy that piece of paper. We don't want any incriminating evidence to be found on your possession."

"Certainly. You have my word," I said.

I couldn't read his expression but I guessed from what I could see that he remained skeptical. Then he said some words that answered my questions but also caused my stomach to churn once more. "We are expecting you to keep your word Señor Corbett..." still no use of my first name "...*but* we are also going to keep a close watch on you. If we see you meeting again with Roy Smallwood – or perhaps going directly to the United States embassy – or doing anything that we suspect is out of line with what you profess to be doing to find Manuel Fernández...well that would be most unfortunate. Most unfortunate indeed." To punctuate the point, he raised the revolver that had been resting in his lap and waved it knowingly in my direction.

I took a big gulp and tried to keep my voice steady. "I assure you. No funny business. I only want to do my job and find out what happened to Manuel Fernández, nothing else."

Again I sensed skepticism, but he simply inclined his head slightly in my direction. Then he made a gesture to the man to his left, who again got up and approached me. As he did so, the man with the gun said, "We are going to blindfold you again Señor Corbett. Just follow our instructions and we'll get you back safely to where we picked you up."

I didn't know what the protocol was in such situations. Should I say *Thank you for not shooting me in the face?* I didn't think so. And with my hands still tied behind my back, I couldn't offer to shake on the agreement we had made. Instead, I kept silent once again only nodding in agreement as if to say, *Don't worry. There'll be no trouble from me.* And the fact was that even if I had some inclination to cause trouble, blindfolded, my hands secure, outnumbered three to one, and out-gunned one to nothing, there was little I could do. I was at their mercy until they let me go. I felt a little chill when I realized that even once they released me, I would still be under their observation. And I had no doubts about the sincerity of the man with the gun: If he and his comrades suspected I was deviating from the agreement we had made, they would do all they could to make me pay for it. I tried to push that thought aside as the blindfold sent me back into darkness and two sets of hands lifted me up off the chair and out the door, but it lingered nonetheless – one more complication in what was becoming an increasingly complicated set of circumstances.

Twenty Two

From what I could tell, my captors took a different route pack to the Parque Patricios. The return trip seemed shorter than the earlier one, although it might have been my imagination. My captors retained their silence throughout. When the car finally stopped, I was lifted out and placed on what I took to be a sidewalk. One of my captors began to loosen the rope that bound my hands while the man with the gun, whose voice was now burned into my brain, whispered into my ear to keep still and to remember that a weapon was still trained on the back of my neck. The same voice then whispered that I should wait at least thirty seconds before removing the blindfold. "Agreed," I said, keeping my head still.

Once my hands were free, I could feel the blood rush back into them. It would take some time for me to have full use of them — not that I was planning anything dramatic. I was tempted to make some show of independence after having been totally vulnerable ever since they had taken me from the park, but realized that was an irrational thought that would do much more harm than good.

With the blindfold still in place, the man with the gun told me that once I removed it, I could walk two blocks to my right where I would run into a main avenue. There I could find a taxi that would take me back to Alfredo's apartment.

I felt him squeeze my shoulder as he said, "Good luck to you Señor Corbett. I think you will need it. And remember…."

I interrupted: "Yes. The terms of our agreement. Yes. Don't worry. I won't forget."

He gave a low chuckle. "Make sure that you don't Señor Corbett. Make sure that you don't."

With those words still echoing in my ear, I heard the doors close and the car pull away. Just to be on the safe side, I counted to sixty in my head. Even though the car that carried my captors was probably well out of sight, I didn't put it past them to keep one or more of the trio nearby to make sure that I did as I was told. But when I finally took off the blindfold, I saw immediately that I was alone on the sidewalk that bordered the park with nary a soul in sight. I looked at my watch. It was almost five in the morning. That meant my whole captivity at the hands of the ERP had lasted only two hours from start to finish. Somehow it had seemed much longer.

Following the advice of the man with the gun, I turned right and started walking. In the distance, I could hear faint traffic sounds. After two blocks, I found myself at the corner of the avenue where Alfredo had dropped my off. I had to wait about fifteen minutes, but eventually I spotted a taxi and hailed it. Getting in, I gave the driver Alfredo's address and he took off with a lurch that hurled me back into the seat. I was tempted to tell him not to hurry, but decided that a quick ride through the still nearly-empty streets wasn't such a bad idea. I needed some rest and the quicker I got to a bed, the better.

Although it was still dark outside, the sky was getting lighter. It wasn't exactly the cold light of dawn, but as the taxi whisked me through the city, I began to contemplate the implications of the deal I had made with the ERP. Just an hour ago, it had seemed the logical thing to do. The revolutionaries had given me a solid lead in my efforts to find Manuel Fernández and had even offered to help me out once I reached Salta. But from the point of view of the U.S. government, what I was doing could also be easily described as "consorting with the enemy."

The main aim of the ERP, as I understood it, was to overthrow the Argentine government as part of a socialist revolution á la Cuba. The United States was a supporter of the Argentine government as well as of similar regimes throughout the continent. In the ERP's view, that made North American representatives such as businessmen, diplomats, AID officials, military advisors and others legitimate targets either for kidnapping or assassination or both. And while I hadn't kept abreast of all their activities, I knew that the ERP and the *Montoneros* had carried out actions against individual Americans as well as attacking American investments in banks and supermarkets. So from the U.S. point of view, the ERP and its like were clearly "enemies" and it wasn't too much of a stretch to conclude that my government considered itself involved in an undeclared war with these revolutionary organizations. It might be described as "low-level and low-intensity," but a war nevertheless.

To make matters worse for me, I could also be seen as cooperating in the group's efforts to unmask Smallwood as a CIA agent, effectively blowing his cover and presumably not only ending his effectiveness but also putting his life in danger. And the only evidence I had that he might be involved in something illegal came from the ERP. While I personally had some confidence that they were telling me the truth, I doubt if their word would carry any weight if I were to use that as a rationale for going along with them.

As I thought about it, the best and safest course was for me to head to the U.S. Embassy as soon as it opened for business and let officials there know that I had met with the ERP and tell all. I could ask them to protect me against any possible retaliation from the revolutionaries and get me on a plane back to the U.S. as soon as possible.

That, of course, would have been the sensible thing to do. But it would also mean that my search for Manuel Fernández would in essence be over. I could tell his sister what I had found and suggest that she hire somebody else to follow up the Salta lead. But my involvement would have to end.

Weighing my options, I thought about my brave words to Alfredo. How I had chosen a career that I thought suited me and for which I was well suited. That whatever the dangers involved, I intended to pursue the clues and the case wherever they might lead. And I didn't want those words to be hollow. So in spite of the risks involved – retaliation from the ERP if I deviated from our agreement or severe punishment from my own government – I determined to stick it out come what may.

By the time I had come to this conclusion, the taxi had deposited me at the front door of Alfredo's building. Dawn was beginning to break and there were streaks of pink and blue to the east. I paid my driver and turned to enter the building. The *portero*, wearing a pair of knee-high bright yellow rubber boots, was scrubbing down the sidewalk. I noticed others on the street doing the same. When the *portero* saw me get out of the taxi, he put down his mop and bucket and rushed to open the entrance door for me. *"Buenos días Señor Corbett. Cómo está?"* he said.

I gave him a wink and a smile and responded, *"Muy bien gracias. Muy bien."*

He gave me a smile back, closed the door behind me, and returned to his chores. If he was to report my early-morning arrival to his handlers, I hope I had left the impression that my night out had been with pleasurable female company and not with three masked men who had held me at gunpoint.

When I got to Alfredo's apartment, he opened the door before I had time to unlock it. He was disheveled and bleary-eyed and immediately wrapped me in a bear hug and pounded me on the back. "Frank. Frank, my good friend," he said, with relief in his voice. "You made it." Then, releasing me, he stepped back to give me a once over. "And in one piece too. Any bumps or bruises?"

"Nope, not really My wrists are a little sore from having my hands tied behind my back. But other than that, no lasting damage."

But just as I said that, I slumped against the wall and for a moment thought I was going to pass out. With a look of concern, Alfredo grabbed me by the arm and helped me onto the couch in the living room. As soon as I sat, the dizzy spell passed. But I still must have looked a bit woozy.

"Can I get you anything Frank?" Alfredo asked. "I have some coffee ready."

"No thanks *amigo*. I need to get some rest. It's been a long night. But I would appreciate some water. I suddenly have a powerful thirst."

"Right away pal. Right away." He went to the kitchen, opened the refrigerator, and extracted a bottle of mineral water. Removing the cap, he poured it into a glass and brought it to me. I took deep swallows and emptied the glass in about twenty seconds.

Alfredo took a chair across from me. "So tell me Frank. How did it go? What did you find out?"

At this stage, all I really wanted to do was hit the sack. The water had refreshed me, but I was still dead tired. But Alfredo deserved the full story. And I would need his help – and his advice – in what I was planning to do next. So I laid out everything in as much detail as I could muster. He listened carefully without interrupting, but I could see him file everything away in his mind. When I got to the part about the ERP source having seen Manuel Fernández in the company of Roy Smallwood in Salta, his eyebrows shot up in surprise but he said nothing.

After I had finished, he gave me a look that seemed to mix disbelief with grudging admiration. "Well Frank my friend that is quite a story. Quite a story indeed." For a moment, he looked down at his hands. When he looked up, he said with a quiver in his voice, "To tell you the truth *amigo*, I thought the odds were about fifty-fifty that I would see you alive this morning." Shaking his head, he continued, "But here you are safe and sound - and with a solid lead to follow. I can't quite believe it."

I grinned at him. "I can't quite believe it myself. And I'm not sure I would have survived if you hadn't vouched for me, especially after they had spotted me coming out of Smallwood's office. I must confess that when they hit me with that I thought I was a goner. But your reputation saved the day – and my skin."

"Well let's keep my 'reputation' with the ERP just between the two of us, okay? It's not the kind of thing I would want widely known. I'm skirting enough edges as it is."

"Don't worry Alfredo. Mum's the word."

He nodded. "Well I suppose you're planning to head up to Salta to see what you can find."

"Right you are; as soon as I can. I presume they have flights there. I'd like to book one right away. Not a moment to lose."

A frown crossed Alfredo's face. "Ordinarily yes Frank. But it so happens that the personnel of the local domestic line that services interior cities like Salta are on strike, with no quick resolution in sight."

"How about chartering a private plane?"

The frown remained in place. "That's a possibility. But it would be awfully expensive. Plus, we don't have that many available and with the strike I doubt if you could get one without some delay; probably a couple of days." Then, after a pause, he said, "How about if I drive you? We could leave right away. You could catch up on your sleep while I drove. If we drove straight through we could probably get there this time tomorrow."

I considered it, but then shook my head from side to side. "That's awfully generous of you my friend. But I've already imposed on you enough. You've got your responsibilities and you must be under some kind of pressure to get the López Rega story out by a deadline. And going to Salta would take at least three or four days out of your schedule. No. No. There must be another way. How about a train?"

Alfredo nodded. "Yes. I was thinking of that. It's not the best solution, but it might work. There is a train that will take you as far as Tucumán. If there are no delays, the trip takes about twelve hours. Then you grab a bus to Salta. Usually, that's another two or three hours. If all goes well, it is faster than going by car."

"How often do the trains to Tucumán run?"

"Once a day, leaving at six in the evening and arriving at about the same time in the morning of the next day."

"That sounds like it will work Alfredo. How do I make a reservation?"

He held up his hand, palm out. "Not so fast Frank. Because of the airline strike, the trains to the interior cities have been jam-packed. You might not be able to get a ticket for several days."

My shoulders slumped. I had gotten used to such complications during my previous travels to Latin America. But in the past the need to travel – and to travel fast – had not been so pressing and I hadn't minded hanging around until I caught whatever transportation I needed. But now was not one of those times.

"Listen Frank," Alfredo said. "Let's not despair. I have some connections with people in the railroads. Let me give them a call to see what I can do to get you a seat on tonight's train to Tucumán. What do you say that if that doesn't work out, we go to 'Plan B' and I drive you there?"

I was about to object when he said, "I appreciate the fact that you don't want to cause me further inconvenience. But the López Rega story is almost wrapped up and the people at *Chispa* can add the finishing touches without me." I'm not sure I believed him but kept my doubts to myself." Besides old friend," he went on, "this case you are on has all the makings of a hell of a story in its own right – the kidnapping of an important diplomat's son, the involvement of the ERP, and possible illegal activities by a CIA spook. That's front-cover news Frank." He rubbed his hands together and flashed a grin. "So it's not all that much of a sacrifice for me to tag along with you on your little adventure north. It could work to the advantage of both of us."

I remained skeptical. But I had to admit that he had a point. It would be a hell of a story, even if we failed to find Manuel Fernández. I thought hard for a few minutes and came up with what I hoped was a reasonable compromise. "Listen Alfredo, there are some complications in making all this public. First, there is the matter of the confidentiality I have to maintain with my client. Second, there is the matter of the agreement I have made with the ERP." I then laid out my concerns as how that might be seen by the U.S. government. And, added to that, I wasn't sure at this stage that I wanted Alfredo to reveal the true nature of Smallwood's role in Argentina with me as the source, even though it seemed to be known by more than a few. I could see him nod in agreement as I made my case.

As I spoke, my voice had gotten raspy and my eyelids were increasingly heavy. Seeing my fatigue, Alfredo said, "Listen Frank. You're about to pass out on me. You need some rest. Here's what we'll do. It's too early now to reach my contacts at the railroad, but they should be available around nine. I'll call then to see if I can get you a seat on the Tucumán train for this evening. If I can, you can proceed on your own as planned. If not, after you've gotten your sleep, we'll head up to Salta in my car. Is that a deal?"

I was too tired to argue. I just nodded wearily and headed for my bed. I undressed quickly and slid under the covers and after about fifteen seconds was fast asleep.

Twenty Three

I woke with somebody's hand shaking my shoulder. I must have been having some kind of nightmare and bolted upright, ready to defend myself against an unknown attacker. But it was only Alfredo, backing off momentarily when he saw my reaction.

"Easy Frank," he said, holding his hands out in a calming manner. "It's only me."

"Sorry *amigo*. A bit jumpy I guess. I didn't mean to startle you."

He smiled. "That's okay. You have a lot to be jumpy about."

Throwing off the covers, I asked, "Any news on the train?"

"Yes. I was able to get you a seat," he said, flourishing what looked to be a ticket in front of my face. "Here it is. All set for the six o'clock to Tucumán."

I had put my watch down on a side table and when I reached for it I saw it was almost four thirty. I had slept a good ten hours.

"Once you're ready Frank, I have some stuff for you that you might find useful."

"Thanks Alfredo. Do I have time for a shave and a shower?"

"Sure. But we should leave for the station around five thirty at the latest. Trains don't always leave on time, but you don't want to take any chances."

"I won't be long," I said as I headed for the bathroom.

Fifteen minutes later I was in Alfredo's living room, sitting next to him and sipping coffee. I had changed into a fresh set of clothes and was feeling like a new man. On the coffee table in front of me were the materials Alfredo had gathered. Handing them over to me, he said "Here are a couple of detailed maps of the city of Salta and the surrounding area.

And on this sheet I've listed the names and phone numbers of three friends of mine who live in Salta and who can help you out, especially if you get into some kind of jam. And here," he said, pointing to the bottom of the sheet with the contacts, "is a phone number that will get you in touch with me if I'm not at home." I was about to ask if it was his office number but then considered the possibility that it might be that of whoever wore the scent I had noticed when I first entered my friend's apartment and kept my mouth shut.

"One more thing Frank," he said, getting up from the couch and moving over to his desk. Taking out a key, he unlocked a bottom drawer and withdrew a revolver. It looked like a Smith and Wesson .38. "Do you want to take this with you?" he asked, showing it to me in the palm of his hand.

I thought about it. I was headed into unknown and dangerous territory and the probability that I would be dealing with some deadly characters was high. Being armed might help even the odds. But at the same time there were complications. *How would my ERP "allies," who promised to keep close tabs on me, react if they found out I was carrying a weapon? And what if the police, who seemed to be on high-alert everywhere in the country, discovered me with a gun? Would they shoot first and ask questions later?* I might be able to spin some kind of yarn that I had heard about the targeting of North Americans by the Argentine guerrillas and was only trying to defend myself, but I wasn't sure that would work. Finally, I decided that it wasn't worth the risk to carry the pistol.

"No thanks Alfredo. I've gotten along so far without a weapon. I'll just take my chances."

He gave me a skeptical look, shrugged, and replaced the gun from where he had gotten it. I wondered if he carried it himself on occasion, but decided that was a question for a later time.

Picking up what Alfredo had given me, I went to my room and packed for my trip. Alfredo had told me that Salta was a much more casual place than Buenos Aires and I would not need to take my suit. I decided to wear my blazer with a shirt and tie on the train and put my khakis, sweaters, and underwear into leather bag that Alfredo loaned me. It was smaller, lighter, and easier to manage than my suitcase but still had plenty of room for what I thought I needed. I even stuffed my jogging gear into it. Whether I would have time for running for recreational purposes was an open question, but better to have the necessary outfit than not if the occasion arose. I hoped that what I had packed would last me for however long it took to find out what had happened to Manuel Fernández in Salta, but of course had no way of knowing for sure. It might all be a wild goose chase that ended in a few days. Or it could go on for much longer. I would just have to play it by ear and whether I would have enough clean clothes to see me through was the least of my worries.

As I packed, I remembered that I had arranged to call Roy Smallwood's office at ten o'clock in the morning to see if he could arrange a meeting with the ERP. Now, of course, the call was unnecessary. And the last thing I wanted to do would be to reveal to Smallwood that his services in that regard were no longer required. But just to cover all the bases, I dialed his office, ready with some cock and bull story as to why I had failed to call earlier as promised. But there was no answer and I hung up.

We left Alfredo's building at five fifteen and arrived in front of Retiro Station twenty minutes later. The station, an impressive terminal that reminded me of some I had seen in Europe, was the main gateway for trains to the north of the country. There were also major commuter lines to the northern suburbs of Buenos Aires. There was a crush of taxis, buses, and private cars in front of the station, leaving some passengers off and picking up others. Alfredo offered to try to find a parking space and accompany me inside, but from what I could see, that would not be an easy task. Besides, I was already feeling guilty enough about having imposed on him as much as I had. So I declined the offer and told him I could manage on my own.

Once again I got that skeptical look. But he didn't put up a fight. Instead, he simply shrugged and pulled his car into a spot at the curb that had a sign reading "Reserved for Taxis." His maneuver set off a cacophony of car horns and several taxi drivers headed in our direction with scowls on their faces. Alfredo ignored them. He pointed to where I should enter the station and gave me instructions on how to locate the train to Tucumán. I reached over to shake his hand and he grabbed me in an *abrazo*. "Good luck *amigo*," he said with a somber look. "Take care. And keep in touch. If I don't hear from you in a couple of days, I'm going to worry. If it's three days, I'll send the cavalry."

"Thanks for everything my friend," I said, pasting a look of confidence on my face. "Don't worry. You'll hear from me."

With that, I got out of the car and closed the passenger door. Retrieving my bag from the back seat, I gave Alfredo a grin and a thumbs-up gesture and headed for the station entrance. As I reached it, I turned to give Alfredo a farewell wave and saw several irate taxi owners approach his Mercedes, angry scowls on their faces and their hands clenched into fists. He gave me one last wave of his own and then pulled from the curb before the mob could reach his vehicle, forcing several of the drivers to jump hurriedly out of the way to avoid being hit.

I chuckled at the scene. Alfredo had always seemed to me a larger than life character. He appeared to look for trouble and often enough he found it. But somehow – be it luck or ability or sheer guts – or a combination of all three – he managed to avoid the most serious consequences of his sometimes rash and impulsive actions. As I carried my bag onto the platform where the train to Tucumán was waiting, I hoped that a little of my friend's magic would somehow rub off on me.

Twenty Four

The crowd inside the Retiro terminal was an intriguing mixture. Alfredo had prepared me for what I would encounter there. During our ride, he had told me that at the station I would begin to get a taste of the "Real Argentina" that lay beyond the borders of Buenos Aires.

As I headed towards my train, I could see what he meant. Getting on the commuter trains were the well-dressed, European-looking members of the middle and upper classes heading to their comfortable suburban homes in the city's tonier suburbs. Getting off the long-distance trains from locations in the far-flung provinces of the north were people with darker-skin, many of them clearly *mestizos*. They were shabbily dressed and many of them had a dazed look as though momentarily lost.

These were, Alfredo had informed me, the internal migrants who had been flocking to Buenos Aires to find work and a better life ever since the 1930s and the beginnings of large-scale industrialization. Juan Perón had successfully cultivated the political support of this group and they had helped propel him to the presidency in the mid-1940s. Now that it looked as though he was about to resume power, the migratory flow had resumed, enriched now by Bolivians and Paraguayans fleeing the dreadful political and economic conditions in those neighboring countries.

Making my way through the crowd to platform number twelve, I saw that the Tucumán train was already filling up with passengers. Alfredo had booked me a seat in the Pullman car, which, in Argentina, did not, as in the U.S., mean that it had sleeping compartments. However, Alfredo assured me, it did have very comfortable reclining seats that would give me a chance to sleep as the train made its way through what Alfredo also assured me was exceptionally boring countryside.

The Pullman car was at the front of the train, right behind the engine. I boarded and located my seat about half-way down on the right-hand side. It was a window seat and for the moment the aisle seat was empty. After removing some reading material I had packed, I placed my bag along with my carefully-folded blazer in the overhead shelf. Alfredo had warned me that it might get cold at night and that I couldn't count on the car being heated. But I was pleased to see that like the airlines the train had provided each passenger with a small pillow and blanket.

As departure time approached, it appeared that every seat in the car except for the one next to mine was occupied. I could hear an excited buzz of conversation around me as the engine sounded its horn signaling that we were about to leave the platform exactly on time.

Just as I could feel the train moving, my seat-mate finally arrived. Before he sat down, he placed a small overnight bag next to mine on the overhead shelf. He was a little out of breath and, being the shrewd detective that I was, I guessed he had had to run to get on the train.

It took him a few seconds to get settled. Once he did, he turned towards me and asked in English, with an accent I couldn't quite place at first, "Excuse me. But are you North American?"

A little taken aback, I responded. "Why yes I am. How did you know?"

He smiled, showing perfect white teeth. "We Argentines learn to identify nationalities at an early age. And besides," he said pointing at my lap, "you are reading a mystery novel in English." I had brought a Ross Macdonald paperback with me, hoping that Lew Archer could teach me a few tricks of the detective trade. And then as if to show that he was no slouch in the field of detection, he added, "And your haircut and your clothes also suggest that you are from the United States."

I decided that two could play this game. I gave him a careful once-over. He was slim, about my age, with wavy blond hair parted on the side and cut carefully to curl fashionably over his collar. His eyes were gray-green, his skin very fair, and from the way he was dressed and from his accented English if I had to guess I would guess he was German. He was dressed casually but his clothes looked expensive; gray flannel slacks, light blue dress shirt, and a leather jacket. On his wrist was a gold watch and on the third finger of his left hand a large ring that looked like those you got from attending a university in the United States.

I gave him a smile and said, "If you don't mind me saying so, you don't look like the 'typical' Argentine. If I had to guess, I would say you were either German or Scandinavian."

He let out a low chuckle and nodded approvingly. "Well, I'm not sure there is such a thing as a 'typical' Argentine. We are like you in the United States; an immigrant country, a melting pot of different nationalities. But unlike you, our immigration was mostly from Italy and Spain – from southern not northern Europe." He said this in a tone that suggested it was not something necessarily to be proud of. "But we also have a substantial German and British community here and while we sometimes stay aloof and retain more of our customs than some of the other groups, we are as Argentine as anybody else." This time he sounded a bit defensive.

"I'm sorry. I usually try to avoid stereotyping people, but this time it looks as though…

He held up his right hand to interrupt. "It's perfectly all right. I experienced the same reaction when I studied in the United States." Pointing to the ring I had noticed, he explained, "Four years at Carnegie Mellon in Pittsburgh, getting my engineering degree."

Then, extending his hand, he said with a toothy grin, "Karl Schussler. As you guessed, of German descent but born and raised in Argentina."

I took his hand and returned the introduction. "Frank Corbett. Pleased to meet you."

"Likewise," he replied, holding my hand in his a bit longer than necessary to show me that despite his slim build he had a powerful grip.

"So what brings you to Argentina Frank? Business or pleasure?"

I wasn't about to reveal anything so I said, "Just pleasure. I've traveled around Latin America quite a bit but not to Argentina. So I had some free time and thought I'd add it to my list of countries visited."

"And why to Salta?" he asked.

That question put my radar on high alert. *How did he know I was going to Salta?* The train terminated in Tucumán and there were stops at major cities like Rosario and Córdoba along the way. He seemed to notice my reaction and tried to counteract it. "I mean, I presume you are going on to Salta. That's where most of the passengers, including me, are headed…."

He let it trail off and I nodded, pretending to accept his rather clumsy recovery. And perhaps he was telling the truth. But it certainly put me on guard. I didn't take him for an ERP sympathizer assigned to keep an eye on me, but you never know.

"Well I wanted to see more of the country than just Buenos Aires. And I've heard Salta is a beautiful city. So I decided to go."

He nodded back with a smile and said, "You are right. Salta is beautiful and well-worth seeing." But somehow I got the feeling that he knew that I was spinning a tale of my own and that my reasons for heading north had little to do with tourism.

As the train passed the far northern suburbs, it began to gather speed and we continued our conversation. Karl told me that he was a chemical engineer who had been an assistant manager in a plant just south of Buenos Aires. The company he worked for was sending him to Salta frequently to scout locations for a planned new operation in the north. Normally, he flew but with the strike was taking the train. It sounded plausible enough, but I still kept my guard up. I noticed, too, that he didn't ask me about my profession. Perhaps he was just being discreet – or perhaps he didn't care – but somewhere in the back of my mind I suspected that he already knew.

At about eight o'clock, we went to the dining car and shared a table. The choices were chicken and steak and we both chose the latter. As we were eating, I remarked on how impressed I was so far with the train and its service. The cars were new and comfortable, the porters attentive, and the food delicious. We had left on time and so far as I could tell were keeping to schedule.

He sniffed and looked scornful. "Yes Frank, this one is an exception. Since it is the only long-distance train to the north and serves many tourists the government has made sure that it is one of the few good ones. You should see the rest – out-of-date and totally unreliable." Then, leaning forward and lowering his voice, he said, "The British built our railways and did a fine job, constructing the most extensive and best system in Latin America. But in 1948 'Johnny Sunday' decided to take them over and have the government run them. And ever since..."

I interrupted: "'Johnny Sunday'"?

He laughed, but still kept his voice low. "Sorry Frank. Juan Domingo Perón. A little joke you know, Johnny for Juan and, Domingo is Spanish for Sunday."

I grinned at him. "Okay. I get it."

"Well as I said," he continued, "Perón took over the railroads in 1948 and they have never been the same since. Believe me."

What did I know? I just nodded in agreement and we switched to other topics. During our conversation, it came out that I had served in Vietnam. Karl perked up when he heard that. "I admire you for that Frank. If I had been a U.S. citizen I would have volunteered to go myself. Instead I had to watch my fellow students at Carnegie Mellon become radical anti-war protestors. They disgusted me. A bunch of spoiled brat cowards."

As he spoke, I wondered how much genuine protest there had been at Carnegie Mellon. Engineering students generally were either apolitical or conservative. I kept my expression neutral.

"And if you don't mind me saying so Frank," Karl continued, "your government should have done more to back you guys fighting in Vietnam. I'm afraid that pretty soon the North is going to conquer the South and kick the U.S. out of the country altogether. And once Vietnam goes communist so will the rest of Southeast Asia." Karl seemed to adhere to the questionable "Domino Theory." "And who knows. Maybe Latin America will be next. We almost had our own wave of leftist revolutions after Cuba and there are a few groups around who keep trying."

"You mean like the groups here in Argentina? The *Montoneros* and the People's Revolutionary Army?"

He seemed a little surprised by my knowledge but plunged ahead. "Yes. Nothing more than a bunch of juvenile gangsters. If you ask me, it is past time to crack down on them. And crack down hard. Close the universities, which are their breeding grounds, search every corner for them, and even execute a few in public. That would do the job," he said, banging both fists on the table enough to make the silverware jump.

Karl certainly did nothing to hide his reactionary views, but I had to wonder how genuine they were. His words were said with conviction, but I thought I saw something of a twinkle in his eyes as he said them. He reminded me of a couple of friends of mine who would make outrageous assertions just to see if they could get a rise out of the listener. If that was the case with Karl, I wasn't about to take the bait. Instead, I kept a neutral expression and again changed the conversation to less controversial matters like the weather and the food in Argentina.

By the time we had finished dinner and returned to our seats, it was almost ten o'clock. I took off my shoes, reclined my seat back as far as it would go, covered myself with the blanket that had been provided, and propped the pillow behind my neck, ready to go to sleep. We had separate overhead lights. I reached up and turned mine off. Karl told me that he had trouble sleeping on trains and if I didn't mind, he would keep his light on while he continued to read. "No problem," I told him. "I learned to sleep anywhere, anytime, and under any conditions in the Army."

We said our "good-nights." After about five minutes I was, to my surprise after my long nap earlier, fast asleep. When I woke about four hours later to go to the bathroom, Karl was, true to his word, still awake and ostensibly still reading. After returning from the bathroom, I resumed my position and tried to get back to sleep. But a few stray thoughts intruded. *Was Karl really unable to sleep – or was he under orders to keep an eye on me at all times? And was his diatribe against the guerrillas genuine – or was it merely a ploy to deflect any suspicions I might have that he was following the instructions of the ERP?* It was unlikely, but not impossible. *Or was there another explanation?* Whatever the reason, I was almost one hundred percent certain that him being my seatmate was not just a coincidence. Pushing those thoughts aside, and aided by rocking motion of the train, I managed to fall again into a deep slumber.

Twenty Five

I woke as I felt the train begin to slow. Opening my eyes, I raised the shade on the window and saw the first streaks of dawn beginning to light the skies. Turning to my left, I was greeted with a grin from my seatmate, who looked fresh as a daisy. "Good morning Frank," he said with a cheery tone. "We are about to pull into the Tucumán station. It looks as though you had a good night's sleep."

"Good morning to you Karl," I said, rubbing my eyes. "And how about you? Any luck in the sleep department?"

"I'm afraid not Frank. But I did almost finish my book," he said, showing me a paperback novel in Spanish for my inspection. "Mostly drivel, but it kept my occupied."

Around us, the other passengers began to stir, pulling their luggage down from the overhead racks and straightening their clothes, rumpled during the overnight ride. I joined the line at the bathroom and after about ten minutes was able to use the facilities. Just as I got back to my seat, the train came to a full stop and the conductor announced that we had arrived in Tucumán. I looked at my watch. It read six thirty; not precisely on time, but only half an hour off schedule.

There was a bit of pushing and shoving as the passengers in our car made their way out onto the platform. Karl and I took our time. We both had tickets for the same bus to Salta, which wasn't scheduled to leave for another hour. In the meantime, Karl invited me to join him for breakfast at the station bar. I didn't see any sense in turning him down. I had no good reason to do so and at this point, it would be a dead giveaway that I had my suspicions about him.

We had coffee, juice, and rolls and continued our idle conversation of the night before. Karl still hadn't asked me what I did for a living. I figured that at some point soon he would have to. Otherwise, the omission would be too glaring. It was such a natural question. And even though I was just about ninety-nine percent positive he already knew that I was a private detective, I had decided to come up with a cover story that would satisfy that one percent of doubt. And, just as we were finishing up, he gave me the opportunity, right on cue.

"So Frank," he said, "I haven't asked you. What do you do for a living?"

"I'm a free-lance writer. I do mostly feature stories for newspapers and magazines. In fact, I've been doing some pieces on my travels here in Argentina, hoping to sell them when I get back to the States."

I couldn't read his expression, but I sensed that he knew I was making this up. At any rate, he went along with the charade. "That's sounds pretty interesting. And you are able to support yourself that way?"

"Well, it does have its dry periods. But so long as I get something in print every once in a while it can pay pretty well. And, as a matter of fact, I got an advance from a travel magazine that helped defray my costs for this trip."

He gave me a thoughtful look and was about to say something. Instead, he looked at his watch. "Uh-oh," he said, "We'd better get going if we want to catch the eight o'clock bus."

Karl insisted on paying for the breakfast and I didn't argue. After the bill had been settled, we picked up our bags and made our way to the bus station which was only a few blocks away. It was a little before eight and there was a line forming to board what looked to be an Argentine version of a Greyhound touring bus. Many of those standing in line were familiar faces from the train. When we boarded, there was some more pushing and shoving even though we all had assigned seats. It came as little surprise when it turned out that Karl and I ended up sitting together, me at the window and him on the aisle. By now I knew it was more than coincidence. Someone had arranged to have him stick to me like glue. But who that someone might be was still a mystery.

The bus, like the train, left precisely on time. It went right through the heart of Tucumán, passing by the main square. As with any central plaza in Spanish America, it was flanked by a cathedral, the city hall, and an arcaded business block. The plaza itself was a mixture of gardens, statuary, and large swaths of brilliant green grass cut to golf-course standards. Ringing the whole area were orange trees ripe with fruit. Off in the distance I could see verdant hills, the first break in the flat monotony of the Argentine plains that I had glimpsed since my arrival.

Karl, seeming to go along with my cover story of being a travel writer, informed me that Tucumán was where Argentine independence was "officially" declared on July 9, 1816. Most evenings, he said, there was a light and sound show that sought to recreate that monumental event in the nation's history. Tucumán was also known as the "Garden of the Republic" for the wide variety of fruits and vegetables grown there, as well as the abundant vegetation and flowers to be found in and around the city. "But," he said with a grin, "it should really be called the 'Sweet Spot' of the Republic because Tucumán is the principal producer of sugar in the country, as you will soon see."

It didn't take long for me to discover what he meant. Beginning on the outskirts of the city, sugar cane plantations stretched out for miles on either side of the highway heading north to Salta. I could see workers, most of whom looked to be dark-skinned, swinging their machetes in rhythm as they cut and stacked the cane. It was still relatively cool and there was a ground mist that covered much of the area. But the sun was already out and I knew that as they day wore on, the heat would rise as would the discomfort of the workers. If it was like any place in the world where sugar was grown – and I had no reason to assume that it wasn't – field workers labored for ten or twelve hours a day, often six days a week, under brutal conditions and for little pay. The scene from our comfortable bus moving smoothly along the highway was picturesque, but I knew the reality was anything but.

"Hey Karl," I said, gesturing out the window. "I know that workers on sugar plantations in other parts of Latin America have provided fodder for revolutionary movements. Is anything like that happening here?"

He had a disdainful look. "Well, some have tried, but without much luck. Back in the early sixties, as I recall, there was a small group that tried to start something like the Cuban Revolution here in Tucumán. The military put them down pretty easily," he said with a smile of approval. "Why do you ask?"

'No reason. I was just curious." Then, thinking of my cover, I said "I thought there might be material for a story if there was something brewing out there."

He gave a sardonic laugh. "The only thing *brewing* out there is the *yerba mate* that they drink to keep up their energy."

I simply nodded. I knew that *yerba mate* was an herbal tea indigenous to the area and a popular drink throughout the Río de la Plata region. In Vietnam, Alfredo told me that he missed it when he was overseas. Sharing a *mate* with friends, he said, was a deeply-ingrained cultural practice. If I had the opportunity, I planned to try it myself before I left the country even though I wasn't much of a tea drinker.

For the next half hour or so, Karl kept up a steady flow of chatter. My comments on the sugar workers spurred him to repeat and elaborate on some of the reactionary political views he had expressed over dinner on the train. As he droned on, I began to tune him out and focus on the scenery.

About an hour after we had left Tucumán, the lush green landscape began to give way to something harsher. I could see various forms of cactus appear along the side of the road and the hills which had been distant in Tucumán started to close in on us. The texture of the soil now was sandier and rockier and the prominent colors now were reds, browns, and yellows, interspersed with the dull green of sagebrush and small trees which I could not identify and assumed needed little water in what was an obviously arid region. It began to remind me a great deal of the American southwest, particularly of Arizona and New Mexico.

When I mentioned this to Karl, he nodded in agreement. "Yes Frank. I know what you mean. You could probably film an American western movie in these surroundings and not know that you were in Argentina. It's even more bleak and barren farther to the north. Furthermore, the cities here, like Tucumán, Salta, Jujuy – were settled from the north by the Spaniards descending from Peru and Bolivia. And they still retain much of their Spanish colonial character. They are quite different from Buenos Aires. Not so many European immigrants. They are more provincial, less cosmopolitan." I couldn't tell from his tone whether he thought that was a good thing or a bad thing.

We lapsed into silence after that. Karl had purchased a newspaper in Tucumán and began to read it. I took out my Ross MacDonald paperback but couldn't really get into it, preferring to focus more on the scenery and to do a bit of daydreaming.

Just before noon, we began to descend into a valley and the city of Salta came into view. It was a spectacular sight. The mountain range to our east came right to the edge of the city while to the west and at a somewhat greater distance there was another range, serving as a natural frame, almost like a picture. "*Salta la Linda,*" "Salta the Beautiful," Karl remarked as I admired the view. As we entered into the city proper, I could see, just as Karl had told me, that Salta retained much of its Spanish colonial appearance —narrow cobble-stone streets, houses with red-tiled roofs and white stucco walls, numerous churches. And unlike Buenos Aires, there were few multi-story modern buildings to mar the effect.

When the bus pulled into the station, Karl asked me where I was staying. Alfredo had booked a room for me at the Hotel Salta, which he said was the best in town, right on the main plaza. When I told this to Karl, he clapped his hands and exclaimed, "What a happy coincidence. That's where I'm staying as well."

I was pretty sure that this was no "coincidence" but feigned enthusiasm that we would be staying in the same place. "That's great," I said.

The bus station wasn't that far from the main plaza so we decided to walk. Along the way, we passed some impressive colonial houses. Karl gave me a running commentary on the families who inhabited them, many of whom could trace their ancestry back to the earliest settlers. And, as was the case elsewhere in such colonial cities, the closer we got to the main plaza, the more distinguished the family.

After a walk of about ten minutes, we arrived at the hotel and checked in. I wouldn't have been surprised if Karl had the room adjoining mine but it turned out that I was on the third floor and he was on the fifth. While we waited for the elevator, Karl suggested that we have lunch as soon as we got settled in. I looked at my watch and saw it was a little after twelve thirty. I could use some food, but wasn't sure I wanted to eat with Karl. I put him off by saying that I needed about an hour to freshen up and suggested we meet in the lobby around one thirty. In the meantime, I planned to concoct a story that would allow me to shake him off my tail.

When the elevator got to the third floor and I got off, Karl said, "So one thirty in the lobby Frank. See you then."

"See you then Karl," I said. As the elevator door closed I saw a look on his face that seemed to indicate he was not happy to have me out of his sight. I considered the possibility that instead of going to his room Karl would double back and keep a watch on my room to make sure I didn't sneak out on him.

When I got to the door of my room and inserted my key, which was of the old-fashioned variety attached to a heavy piece of polished wood with the room number on it, I looked quickly over my shoulder, half-expecting to see Karl's head peeking around a corner. But he was nowhere in sight and I chastised myself for an over-active imagination.

My room was more spacious and comfortable than I had expected. It had high-beamed ceilings, heavy Spanish-style dark oak furniture, and a large bed. There were nice rugs on a polished wooden floor and French doors that led to a small balcony where I had a full view of the plaza below. Off in the distance, I could see the mountains to the east.

I opened my bag and pulled out some fresh clothes. After my long trip, I badly needed a shower and was pleased to see that while my room had colonial-style furnishings, the bathroom was modern. I shaved and then spent fifteen minutes luxuriating in a hot soapy shower. After drying off, I put on a new pair of pressed khakis, a blue button down shirt, and a dark blue sweater. But instead of the loafers I had been wearing, I decided to switch to my more comfortable running shoes. I figured they would be useful if I did a lot of walking and, if an emergency arose, I could move more quickly.

There was a phone in the room and after I had dressed, I picked it up and asked the hotel operator to call the number Alfredo had given me. I was not totally surprised when, after about ten rings, a female voice that was unfamiliar to me picked up on the other end. When I identified myself and asked for Alfredo, she said "Just a moment Señor Corbett," and a few seconds later I heard Alfredo say, "Frank my friend. So you made it to Salta. At least I presume that's where you're calling from."

"Yes I did Alfredo. No delays with either the train or the bus and I'm now enjoying this fine room you booked for me."

I could hear him chuckle. I was just about to tell him about Karl Schussler and my suspicions about him, when he said, "Since you've been gone Frank, I've done a little digging on this guy Roy Smallwood. And I've come up with some things that might interest you."

My ears perked up. "Sure thing Alfredo. What have you found?"

"Well, I talked to some of my contacts and it's no great secret that Smallwood is a CIA agent. One of my colleagues at another magazine is already preparing an exposé on him. He says that Smallwood has been with the agency for more than twenty years and has been posted around the globe – Saigon, Rome, Istanbul, you name it. From what he has been able to discover, despite Smallwood's years of experience and his many postings, he has not been able to advance beyond a kind of junior officer status. The impression he got was that he does his job competently enough but lacks the qualities that would move him up the career ladder. One of his sources told him that he also seems to spend more money than he could earn at his level in the CIA. Here in Buenos Aires he has a penthouse apartment in Palermo and drives a fancy car. He is also seen frequently out on the town with some high-priced 'escorts.'"

"Any idea where the 'extra' funds come from?"

"Well, it could be that the CIA adds to his salary so that he can keep up the cover of being a businessman. But my friend has no way of proving that. He suspects that Smallwood is engaged in something that is 'off the books,' but he doesn't know what. He plans to follow him closely for the next few weeks to see if he can find out."

I almost began to feel sorry for Smallwood. Not only was he being watched closely by the ERP but now an investigative reporter was hot on his heels. "Do you think there might be some connection between his free-spending and his frequent trips to the north?"

"Could be Frank. Could be. I thought of that myself, but damned if I can figure out what it might be."

At the moment, neither could I. *And what about the ERP guys I met with claiming that Smallwood was seen here in Salta with Manuel Fernández? What could that connection be?* Since Smallwood traveled to Salta on a regular basis, maybe I would have the chance to track him myself and find some answers. Given his taste for high living, he might even stay at the very same Hotel Salta. Now *that* would be a happy coincidence!

"Neither can I Alfredo," I said. "But thanks for the information. We'll see where it leads."

"No problem *amigo*."

"Listen Alfredo. I've got another favor to ask."

"Sure Frank. Ask away."

"I wondered if you have ever heard of a guy named Karl Schussler. He had the seat next to me on the train *and* the bus. He's been sticking to me like a leech. He's even booked into the same hotel and wants me to meet him for lunch. He says he's a chemical engineer who works for a company that is planning to open an operation in the north. It sounds legit, but I have my doubts. I'm pretty sure he's been assigned to keep tabs on me. But what I can't figure out is who he's working for. He doesn't seem the type to be part of the ERP, but you never know. They seem to be full of surprises."

"The name rings a distant bell," Alfredo said. "But not in association with the left. Can you give me a description?"

"Tall, blonde, fair-skinned, about my height and age. About ten to fifteen pounds lighter but in good shape. Oh, and he says he graduated from Carnegie Mellon and has the class ring to prove it. Although I imagine there are ways to get hold of a ring like that without actually having attended the school."

There were about fifteen seconds of silence and for a moment I thought the connection had been broken. In the background, though, I thought I heard Alfredo muttering something. Finally he came back on the line. "I'm not sure Frank, but it sounds a bit like a guy who has been mixed up with a right-wing political group called the *Tacuara*. They are a mirror image of the ERP and the *Montoneros*, using a virulent anti-communist position to try to counter the left. They profess a kind of ultra-nationalism that is not too far removed from fascism. And they have used pretty violent tactics in the past."

"That seems to fit Schussler. When we got into talking politics he had positions that would make William F. Buckley look like a New Dealer."

Alfredo laughed. "I know the type. But I need to do some more checking on this guy to confirm that he is who I think he is. It would help if I had a picture as the description you gave me is pretty generic for German-Argentines. And the name seems a little off from what I remember. But I'll look into it."

"Thanks Alfredo."

"One more thing Frank."

"Yes?"

"While the *Tacuara* claims to be an idealistic bunch fighting the good fight against the 'Red Menace,' some of its actions border on just plain criminality. In fact, some members not only cross that border but live on that side. I'm not sure that Schussler, if he is who I think he is, is part of that group. But it is a possibility. So keep your guard up."

"Don't worry my friend. I will."

Alfredo promised to get back to me as soon as he had anything definite on Karl. In the meantime, I would have to come up with some story to get him off my back. And the next item on my agenda made that a crucial priority.

Picking up the phone again, I dialed the contact number I had been given by the ERP and had memorized. After about a dozen rings, a male voice answered. In Spanish, it said, "Yes. Who is it?"

As instructed, I asked to speak to Sergio. The man on the other end responded in slightly-accented English, "Ah yes Mister Corbett. I have been expecting your call."

"That's good. Then you know why I am in Salta? When can we meet?"

"Quite soon actually," he responded. Then he asked, "Tell me Mister Corbett are you Catholic?"

I thought this a strange question but gave a straight answer. "No. I'm not. Why is that important?"

He gave a low laugh. "Well for the next hour, you will be." *What was going on here? Had I found a revolutionary with a sense of humor?* But the lighthearted tone immediately turned deadly serious. "Here is what I want you to do – and I hope I don't need to remind you that you should follow these instructions to the letter. If we suspect anything out of the usual, there will be severe consequences."

"I understand."

"Good. You should leave your hotel within the next ten to fifteen minutes." I looked at my watch. It was already one fifteen and I was scheduled to meet Karl in the lobby at one thirty. I didn't want to mention that particular complication at this time, so I kept my mouth shut and gave a grunt of acknowledgement. "When you exit, look to the right. About two blocks away you will see a large church tower, the tallest in South America. You can't miss it. It belongs to the *Iglesia San Francisco*. Go to the church, which is on the corner of Caseros and Córdoba. When you enter, on your right you will see two confessional boxes. Go to the one closest to the altar and seat yourself. The priest will already be in the box, expecting you. Just to make sure there are no misunderstandings, say to the priest, 'Forgive me father, for I have *not* sinned." The sense of humor had returned, at least for a moment. "That should serve to identify you. Then just follow the instructions he will give you. And don't worry. He won't make you say any 'Hail Marys.'"

Again the chuckle. I was tempted to tell him that maybe a few "Hail Marys" wouldn't be out of order but decided to keep it serious. I repeated the instructions and hung up, trying to think of a story that would get me rid of Karl Schussler, now a more pressing priority than ever.

Twenty Six

Karl Schussler was waiting for me in the hotel lobby when I arrived at one thirty on the button. He was leaning against a pillar from a position where he could scan the elevator door and all possible exits. He gave me a broad smile and looked relaxed enough, but I could see his foot tapping nervously as I approached him.

"How are you feeling Frank?" he asked. "Ready for some lunch?"

I had rehearsed my answer on the way down. "I'm sorry Karl. But something has come up and I'm afraid I won't be able to have lunch with you."

This seemed to catch him off guard and it took him a moment to regain his composure. I could see him struggling as to what to say next. I knew I couldn't leave him hanging without a further explanation, so I rolled out what I had concocted. "I just got off the phone with a person here in Salta who is something of a local expert on the city. He was recommended to me by a friend in Buenos Aires as a good source for any kind of article I might want to write. His schedule is pretty tight and the only time he can fit me in is right now," I said, looking at my watch, "in about fifteen minutes." Actually, there was some truth in all that.

Karl looked disappointed but rallied. "I understand Frank. Sounds like a good opportunity for you." Then after a pause, he said, "How about dinner tonight? Say about eight? I know a very good local restaurant."

I really didn't want to spend more time with him but figured turning him down would only heighten his suspicion that I was on to him. "That will be fine Karl. I'll see you here in the lobby – unless something comes up. If it does, I'll leave a message."

I could see that the possibility that I might back out of dinner as well bothered him but he simply nodded and wished me luck in my interview. However, just as I was about to pass him and head out the door, he grabbed my arm in a not too gentle manner. I gave him a look that showed my displeasure and he quickly released his grip. "I wondered if you needed directions on how to get to where you are going for your meeting. I know the layout of the city pretty well."

He probably did, but I knew his agenda and the trap he was trying to set. "No thanks Karl," I said. "My source gave me pretty clear instructions. I'm sure I can find my way on my own."

Karl was ready to argue but then seemed to realize that pressing the issue would be a red flag signaling that he was indeed intent on tracking my every move. He shrugged and again wished me luck. I thanked him and headed for the door. I could feel his eyes on the back of my neck as I exited the hotel.

Outside, I followed the instructions I had received over the phone. I easily spotted the church tower to my right. It was an unmistakable landmark. Before I headed for it, however, I wanted to make sure Karl – or anyone else – was not on my tail. So instead of turning right, as ordered, I turned left and walked a couple of blocks in that direction. Reaching an intersection, I stopped suddenly and slapped my forehead as though I had forgotten something. I made a quick turn back in the direction of the plaza, hoping to catch Karl – or whoever else might be following me – in the act. But there was no sign of my travel companion or anyone else that looked suspicious.

Reassured but still alert, I made a series of turns that took me back in the direction of the *Iglesia San Francisco*. I was glad that I had on my running shoes because I was almost at a jogging pace as I hurried to my meeting, afraid of being late.

Along the way, I began to wonder why the ERP had chosen a church and a priest for my rendezvous. It could be part of an elaborate scheme to throw anyone who might be following me off the scent. *Who would expect a radical revolutionary group to use the site of one of Latin America's most conservative institutions to arrange a meeting?* And I imagined the Catholic Church in the Argentine provinces was even more conservative than it was in Buenos Aires. *And what about the priest to whom I would be "confessing?* I figured he had to be the genuine article if he was, as I assumed from my phone conversation with the ERP contact, already to be in place when I arrived. On the other hand, maybe they were timing things so that they could sneak in one of their own number dressed as a priest to carry out the assignment. But if that were the case, I thought to myself, they seemed to be going to a lot of trouble – and running a considerable risk – just to arrange a clandestine meeting. It was more likely, as I had originally thought that the priest was the real deal. Many of the younger clergy in Latin America were caught up in the new trend of Liberation Theology. While with few exceptions they were not actually members of revolutionary groups, there were more than a few who sympathized and collaborated with them.

When I got to the church, I saw the usual scattering of beggars sitting on the steps in front of the main entrance, holding out their hands for alms. I reached into my pocket and distributed a few coins to grateful smiles and nods of thanks.

Entering the church, it took me a while to adjust from the bright sunlight outside to the dark interior. Pausing for a few seconds to get my bearings, I could see that there were about a dozen people seated in the pews. Most had their heads bowed in prayer or were staring ahead in contemplation. None paid me any attention as I headed for the confessional boxes on my right.

For a moment, I panicked as I tried to recall which one I was to enter. Then I remembered: The one closest to the altar. Seeing that the side for the confessor was unoccupied, I opened the door, seated myself, and then closed the door behind me. A few seconds later, the wooden panel that covered the meshed window that separated the confessor from the priest slid back and I could see a dim profile on the other side.

"Yes my son," he said in a deep voice, "How may I help you?"

Feeling a little foolish, I uttered the line I had been instructed to say. "Well that's a pleasant change," the priest said with a laugh. "It makes my day. How are you Mister Corbett?"

"I'm fine father," I said with a subdued laugh of my own. "Thank you for asking."

"That's all right. And I'm sorry for all the elaborate precautions we need to take, but I'm sure you can appreciate the fact that we cannot be too careful."

"I understand father."

"All right," the priest said. "Now here's what you need to do next. And it will require a bit of exercise. When you leave the church, turn left at the end of the block. Three blocks down you will run into a broad avenue named for our independence hero, Martín Güemes. Turn right and walk for about ten blocks. That will lead you to a small park at the base of a hill with a statue of a man on horseback in the middle." He paused to chuckle again. "I know what you are thinking. Hardly distinctive is it? But on closer inspection, you will see that it is a statue of the very same Martín Güemes. Around the statue are some benches. Take a seat and wait for fifteen minutes. If no one contacts you in that time, you can assume that the meeting is off and you need to return to your hotel for further instructions. Understood?"

"Yes father. And thank you."

"You are welcome my s…Mister Corbett. And good luck." With that he slid shut the panel that covered the opening through which we had been speaking.

I left the church and followed the route laid out for me. It was a beautiful day, the air crisp and cool and the sky a brilliant blue. When I reached Güemes, I turned right and could see the statue off in the distance. My route took me past some well-established homes, most of them walled in with broken glass fixed at the top to discourage any intruders.

It took me about fifteen minutes to reach my destination. There was a slight but constant incline along the way and by the time I arrived I my breathing was a bit labored. Salta was more than a mile above sea level and while the altitude was not a major problem, I could still feel its effects and gratefully took a seat on one of the benches around the equestrian statue as ordered.

The bench I occupied was on the east side of the statue and gave me a splendid view of the city sprawled out in front of me. Other than a few nannies with babies in tow, the park was virtually deserted except for a man dressed as a vendor of some sort who was sitting on a bench directly opposite me.

After I had cooled my heels for about five minutes, the vendor got up from his bench, turned around in a complete slow circle, and then headed in my direction. From the way he had scanned the horizon, I presumed he was my contact, making sure that I had not been followed. As he approached, I saw that he had a large thermos slung over his back along with another contraption that held small plastic cups. I had seen similarly equipped men – and occasionally women – in other places in Latin America, selling small cups of coffee at reasonable prices on the street. I doubted that this particular vendor was the real thing, but I supposed that it was not totally out of the realm of possibility.

By the time he was about three feet away, I had already risen from the bench. With one last look over his shoulder, he whispered in English, "Please sit down Mister Corbett." I did as I was told. Without another word, he took the thermos from his back, unscrewed the lid, and poured coffee into one of his plastic cups, added some sugar, and passed it to me. Going along with the charade, I reached into a pocket and passed him a few coins, which he counted carefully. To anyone watching, it would look like a perfectly normal transaction.

"As soon as you have finished your coffee," the "vendor" said, "walk six blocks north on Avenida Uruguay until you reach the intersection with Cornejo. There you will see a blue Ford Torino parked at the curb. It will be occupied by three persons, two in the front and one in the back. Get in the back."

I was about to ask him to tell me more, but he turned abruptly and walked away. He had delivered his instructions as crisply as he could. Now it was up to me to follow them.

It took about ten minutes for me to reach the designated location. The Torino was just where I had been told it would be. As soon as I got within five feet, the rear door behind the driver was flung open and hand gestured for me to get in. I had a moment of trepidation. *What if it were all a set-up? Once in the car, I would be at the mercy of whoever occupied it.* But the die had been cast. If I wanted to unravel the mystery of what had happened to Manuel Fernández, I had no choice but to do as I was told.

I closed the remaining distance quickly, slid into the back seat, and closed the door firmly. As soon as I did, the driver engaged the engine and pulled from the curb at a normal speed, quickly merging into the traffic that ran along the Avenida Uruguay.

Sitting in the back seat with me was a man who I judged to be my father's age. He was dressed in gray flannel slacks, a blue blazer with a white handkerchief neatly folded into the breast pocket, and a gray turtleneck sweater. He had pure white hair and the kind of tan that looked as though it might have been acquired on a tennis court or a golf course.

In the front were a young man and woman who looked to be in their twenties and in appearance and dress not much different from the young friends of Manuel that I had met in Buenos Aires. Somewhat to my surprise, the young woman was driving. And from what I could tell, quite expertly. The ERP, it seemed, believed in at least some gender equality.

Once we were in the flow of traffic, the older man sitting next to me said in English, "Good afternoon Mister Corbett. I hope you have enjoyed your little walk through part of our fair city." The voice was the same that I had heard over the phone in my hotel room.

"Yes indeed," I replied with a smile, "Very pleasant."

He returned my smile. "Excellent. Excellent." He almost sounded like the head of the local tourism bureau, gratified that I was finding Salta as advertised. Then, extending his hand, he said, "Let me introduce myself. My name is Fernando." As I took it, he nodded toward the front seat. The young man is Rafael and our driver is Monica." Rafael turned to give me a quick nod while Monica remained silent, concentrating on her driving.

I didn't for a second think that these were their real names. Later, if for some reason I was called on to identify them, I could give a physical description but would have no way of connecting their actual names to their faces. Unlike my previous experience with the ERP, they had not blindfolded me and no weapons were flourished, which I took as good signs. Maybe they had gotten instructions from their leadership that I could be trusted.

"Where are we going?" I asked Fernando.

He kept his smile in place. "Up into the hills Mister Corbett, where we can have a conversation without being disturbed. But first, we need to make sure we are not being followed."

As if on cue, Monica, who had been driving in the far right lane, suddenly cut across to the left lane and then made a sharp left turn that took us back in the direction of the downtown area. I thought her sudden maneuver might catch the attention of an alert traffic patrolman, but there were no sirens or flashing lights. She immediately slowed to a normal pace and spent about ten minutes in the city proper making left and right turns while Rafael checked the rearview mirror to see if anyone was on our tail.

Finally satisfied that we were not being followed, Rafael told Monica that the coast was clear. We were soon on the same broad avenue we had exited earlier. Monica gunned the engine and we picked up speed, heading now in the direction of the mountains to the east of the city.

Throughout all this maneuvering, I had resisted the temptation to ask more questions and maintained a discreet silence. I tried my best to relax, but some of the same unease I had felt getting into the car in the first place began to reappear. While it made perfect sense for my ERP hosts to get us to a place away from prying eyes and ears, it also meant that we would be going to an isolated area where, if they planned to do me harm there would be no witnesses. And just because they hadn't shown me any weapons didn't mean they didn't have them. *What if they had decided that I would make a useful captive, held for some kind of ransom? Or worse, had decided to get rid of me altogether? What if I was going along docilely and perhaps naively with an elaborate ruse that made it easier for them to end my life and dispose of my body in a remote location where my remains could be easily hidden?*

I tried to steady myself. It would do no good to panic. I had to play out the string and be prepared for whatever eventuality I might have to face.

It didn't take long for us to leave the city of Salta and begin our climb into the nearby hills. At first we followed a twisting but well-paved road that took us past scattered small towns and through stands of pine and eucalyptus trees. I could feel the pressure in my ears build as we ascended ever higher.

As soon as we were on the mountain road, Fernando had begun to ask me a series of questions about my background: Where had I been born? Where did I live? What was my family like? How had I decided to become a private investigator? It was the usual sort of "getting to know you" stuff.

After about twenty minutes, Rafael, who had been keeping his eyes glued to the road ahead, turned to look through the rear window at the road behind us. I turned to take a look myself, which earned a slight reproof from Fernando, who put his hand on my arm and said in a low voice and without a trace of a smile on his face, "Eyes straight ahead Mister Corbett if you please."

I felt like a schoolboy being reprimanded by the teacher. I didn't see what difference it made whether I looked through the rear window or not. Fernando, I thought to myself, was just reinforcing the idea that he was the boss and I had better do what he told me to do. I could feel the heat rise at the back of my neck and thought about showing some independence, but decided that at this stage it wasn't worth it. Instead, I kept my mouth shut and followed his instructions.

Apparently again satisfied that we were not being followed, Rafael told Monica to look for a turn to the left around the next bend. She nodded and sure enough, just past a sharp curve, I saw a road that seemed to lead deeper into the hills. Monica made the turn smoothly but we could all feel immediately that we had left the pavement. Pieces of gravel crunched under our tires and Monica slowed the car to a virtual crawl as we were bumped and jostled by the rough terrain.

After about a mile the gravel gave way to no more than dirt tracks. I imagined that when it rained the route we were on now would be impassible. Up to this point, the road had been covering generally level ground, but now it took a sharp upward grade. Going even more slowly than before, Monica expertly used the car's gears to keep us moving forward without stalling out. After about thirty minutes of slow but steady progress, Rafael pointed to a clearing among a group of eucalyptus trees and told her to back into it so that the car would be facing the track we had just followed.

It took a couple of tries, but Monica managed to complete the maneuver and then turned off the engine. I could see her shoulders slump in relief and when she removed her gloved hands from the steering wheel she wiggled her fingers to release the tension. She did all of this in silence. I had yet to hear her utter a word.

Fernando clapped me on the shoulder. "Come on Mister Corbett, time for another little walk."

Monica had gotten out from the driver's side and was holding the left rear door open for me to exit. I got out and quickly looked around. Once we had left the paved highway onto the gravel road, I had seen no signs of human activity. There had been no buildings along the way. Not even a farmhouse. No plowed fields, just bushes and trees. It seemed almost as though I had entered into some kind of national park. I could hear some song birds but otherwise there was total silence beyond the whistle of the wind. In the distance I could only see more hills.

Rafael joined Monica at my side. Fernando had gotten out on the right-hand side of the car and made his way around the back of the car to join us. Before he did so, however, he asked Monica to toss him the keys, which she did in a practiced and smooth manner. Fernando used the keys to unlock the trunk. His upper body disappeared for a moment as he bent into the trunk and when it reappeared I saw that he had a black canvas bag that seemed to have some heft to it. "Rafael," he said with a grunt, "Come give me a hand with this."

"Right away," Rafael said, hurrying to his aid. Without a word, Fernando turned the bag over to the younger man, whose knees buckled for a moment when he accepted the burden.

My imagination went into overdrive. *Why was the bag so heavy? What did it contain? Weapons? Instruments of torture?* Well, I figured, I would find out soon enough.

Twenty Seven

Fernando took me by the elbow. "This way Mister Corbett," he said, guiding me to the rear of the car. A few feet away there was the beginning of a path into a small forest.

"Just follow me Mister Corbett," Fernando said, disengaging his hand from my elbow. He assumed the lead position with me directly behind him as we proceeded along the path in single file. Monica was on my heels with Rafael taking up the rear.

It was neatly done. If I had any inclination to try to run for it, Fernando had me blocked from the front and Monica from behind. Rafael was encumbered with the heavy bag he was carrying, but could easily drop it and chase me down if he had to.

We followed the path through the woods in silence. We were, I estimated, now some two thousand feet above Salta and the altitude began to have a real effect. I felt light headed and short of breath. Tension and the lack of food also played a role. Behind me, I could hear Rafael laboring with the burden he was carrying and the wild thought entered my head to offer to take the load off his hands. But, if the bag contained what I suspected, I knew he would not let it out of his grasp.

After we had walked about a quarter of a mile, we came upon a small clearing in the middle of which sat a rough hut. Fernando opened the door and gestured for me to follow him in. Once inside, it was about as I expected. There was only one room. The walls were made of adobe, the floor was dirt, and the furnishings were spare – a cot in one corner and a plain wooden table in the center of the room surrounded by four unfinished wooden chairs. There was a fireplace of sorts in a far corner, but it looked as though it had not been used in some time.

As he saw me look around, Fernando said, "This used to be a shepherd's hut Mister Corbett, but it's been abandoned for several years. Not a place to spend too much time but perfect for our purposes." I wondered what he meant by "our purposes" and tried not to think the worst.

He sat down on one of the chairs with a sigh of relief and gestured for me to do the same. He looked to be in good shape physically, but the walk had been a strain for him and I could see a patina of perspiration on his brow. He took the carefully folded handkerchief from his blazer pocket and carefully dabbed at his forehead.

Rafael had followed us into the hut and expelled a deep breath as he placed the black bag onto the table. I couldn't be sure, but I thought I heard the clink of glass when he did so. Stretching his back and shaking his arms, he took a seat at the table.

Where was Monica? I asked myself. She had been right behind me the whole way until I had entered the hut. Now she was nowhere to be seen.

Fernando read my thoughts. "Monica is backtracking to make sure we were not followed," he explained. "She'll be joining us soon." Then, rubbing his hands together, he said, "And now, after all these precautions we have taken, I suppose you would like to – how do you North Americans say it? – 'get down to business.' Isn't that so?"

"Well, yes I would…"

He held a hand up. "Yes Mister Corbett. But before we do…Rafael, would you do the honors?"

Rafael rose from his chair and began to unzip the black bag that - to my mind – sat there like a ticking time bomb. As he reached into it, I half expected to see his hand emerge with some sort of weapon that would be pointed directly at me and prepared myself for evasive action. Instead, the first item he withdrew was a bottle of red wine, followed by two bottles of mineral water. I let out a small sigh of relief and sat back in my chair.

Fernando had been watching me closely and emitted a low chuckle. He had again divined my thoughts and had undoubtedly enjoyed keeping me off balance. Behind his smiling and sympathetic exterior lay a more ruthless and calculating mind. I had no doubts that if he determined I was some kind of threat to him and to the ERP he would have no compunctions about making sure that I be eliminated from the equation.

Rafael continued to unpack the bag. Almost like a magician's prop, it seemed to contain an endless quantity of supplies – plates, silverware, glasses, napkins, several loaves of bread, cold chicken wrapped in heavy paper, containers of potatoes and vegetables. As I saw the food being arrayed in front of me, I realized that I had not had anything substantial to eat since breakfast in Tucumán and was now ravenously hungry.

By the time Rafael had finished, Monica had returned to join us. Before sitting down to eat, she nodded to Fernando, a signal that no one was on our tail.

"Please help yourself Mister Corbett," Fernando said. "There is plenty for everybody."

"Thank you. I will," I said, reaching for the food and putting a generous portion on my plate. I was tempted to dig in immediately but remembered my manners and refrained until everyone else had a full plate in front of them. Rafael had opened the wine and filled our glasses up to the brim. I asked him for some water as well, mindful that at a high altitude even one glass of wine could do some damage to my mental alertness unless I could counterbalance it with some non-alcoholic liquid.

We ate mostly in silence. From time to time Fernando would ask me questions about my life and my career, continuing the line of conversation started in the car. Both Monica and Rafael remained mute, silently chewing on their food and taking judicious sips of wine. While the overall atmosphere was relaxed, they were still keeping alert for the unexpected.

Once we had finished our food and the bottle of wine was empty, Rafael reached into his magic bag and pulled out a thermos, not too different from the one the "vendor" had used to serve me coffee at the Güemes park. But instead of plastic cups, he also withdrew small ceramic mugs. When Rafael unscrewed the top, the aroma of coffee filled the room and, taking his time, he carefully poured each of us a portion that almost reached the top of our mugs. Making one last foray into the bag, he pulled out a container of sugar and some spoons. We each in turn helped ourselves to the sugar and after we had added it to our coffee, slowly stirred it in.

It made for a surreal scene. The only sound inside was that of our spoons lightly clanking against the side of our mugs. Outside, there was total silence except for occasional gusts of wind. To the casual observer who might have stumbled upon us, it would seem that we were four friends enjoying a leisurely lunch, not three hardened revolutionaries and one out-of-place North American - all with their own deadly-serious agendas. *And what kind of hardened revolutionary*, I asked myself, *takes the time and trouble to make sure that all of us have not just a basic meal – but a meal with all the trimmings?*

Yet again, Fernando seemed to read my mind. "Not what you expected Mister Corbett? A decent lunch here in the middle of nowhere? Not exactly the Vietcong with their sock full of rice is it?"

"No. It's not," I replied with a smile. "Not that I'm complaining. It was delicious."

He grinned and opened his arms wide. "Well, it was the least we could do after putting you through all your paces. And besides, we were hungry too."

Then, with the grin still in place, he put his hand into his inside blazer pocket and for a wild moment I thought he would draw out a gun and plug me on the spot. But instead, it was only a pipe. Taking a pouch from another pocket, he filled the pipe, lit it with a match and began to puff contentedly.

"All right," Fernando said after a few puffs had filled the air with the pleasant aroma of pipe tobacco, "*Now* we can get down to business. How can we help you Mister Corbett?"

"Please Fernando. Call me Frank."

"All right…Frank. How may we help you?"

"Well, as you know, I am a private investigator hired to locate a young Argentine who had been studying medicine in the United States. His name is…."

"Manuel Fernández," Fernando said his expression suddenly somber.

"Yes. Manuel Fernández. I could find no trace of him in the U.S. and various sources indicated that he might have secretly returned to Argentina to join your organization. But when I contacted your…uh…colleagues in Buenos Aires, they denied that Manuel had done that. But they also told me that he had been spotted in Salta by someone in your group. And in the company of a man named Smallwood, who poses as a businessman but who is in reality a CIA agent. So your colleagues suggested I go to Salta to track down that possible lead. And here I am, asking if you can tell me more; anything that will help me find Manuel."

"Yes Frank," he said, "We have been informed of the purpose of your visit and we are prepared to assist you in your mission." Then, holding the bowl of the pipe in the palm of his hand, he pointed the stem to Rafael. "And the person who caught a glimpse of young Fernández in the company of Smallwood is sitting right here." Then, switching from English to Spanish, he said, "Rafael, would you please tell Frank here what you can about this whole matter."

Before Rafael responded, the thought hit me that Fernando was handling the whole situation in a manner that led me to believe he might well be a college professor. The way he dressed, the gentle manner, the pipe – it was almost as though he were directing a seminar where the three of us were his students, expected to have done the reading and ready to report. Maybe that was literally true for Monica and Rafael. If so, I wouldn't have been surprised.

Rafael looked directly at me. "Well Señor Corbett," he began in a soft voice, "it was about a month ago. I just happened to be driving downtown when I saw Smallwood get out of a car parked at the curb. We have been trying to follow him every time he comes to Salta, but he must have eluded us on this occasion because seeing him caught me totally by surprise. I had no idea he was in the vicinity."

For a moment, he cast his eyes downward as though somehow he had been responsible for the failure to keep closer tabs on the CIA agent. I saw Fernando reach out to touch him on the arm as if to say, "*Don't worry. It wasn't your fault.*"

Looking up, he continued, "When I saw Smallwood, I pulled over a few spaces farther on and got out of my car so I could get a better look. He and another man I didn't recognize were busy helping someone out of the back seat of the car. I wasn't positive at the time because it was so unexpected, but my first thought was that the man being pulled from the back seat was Manuel Fernández. I had known Manuel at the University of Buenos Aires but I couldn't quite believe my eyes. What was he doing in Salta – and in the company of someone like Smallwood?"

He paused for a moment and took a sip of water. Putting down his glass, he continued. "Smallwood and the other man had a tight grip on both arms of the man I thought was Manuel and seemed to be almost dragging him from the car into a nearby building. I waited about five minutes and then approached the building. Along the side of the main door there were plaques with the names of doctors and lawyers. But I had no idea which office Smallwood and Manuel, if that's who it was, had gone into. I thought about entering the building myself, but then decided it might be too risky. I was worried that Smallwood might have allies within the building who would see me and I couldn't take the chance."

Rafael shot a sideways glance at Fernando, who nodded his assurance that he had done the right thing in exercising caution.

"So I waited outside, concealed in a nearby doorway. After about thirty minutes, Smallwood and the other man came out again holding on to arms of the man I thought was Manuel. I only saw them for a few seconds, but this time I was sure that it was Manuel. He looked much the same as when we had been at the university but he had a dazed look on his face almost as though he might have been drugged. Smallwood and the other man put Manuel into the back seat of the car and closed the rear door. Then they got into the front, the other man driving and Smallwood in the passenger's seat. Before he got in, Smallwood looked around to see if anyone was watching and I had to duck back inside the doorway. When I looked out again, they were pulling away from the curb. I waited until they reached the first intersection, where, luckily they had to wait for one of the few traffic lights we have in Salta. That gave me time to get to my own car so that I could follow them. I still had no idea why Manuel would be with Smallwood and was determined to try my best to find out. Besides, we wanted to keep track of Smallwood under any circumstances."

I was listening to all this intently. I had a few questions, but I didn't want to interrupt. I simply nodded from time to time to let Rafael know that I was absorbing every detail of his account.

"There were two cars between me and Smallwood's vehicle when the light turned green, so I don't think they knew I was behind them. As we passed through the city, I maintained my distance. Once we were on the outskirts, they then took the main road to the northwest, in the direction of Bolivia. There was enough traffic on that road to enable me to keep them in sight and still stay two or three vehicles behind."

Rafael paused for a moment in his account and I saw a look of frustration flicker across his face. "They kept on that road for about forty kilometers. But then they turned to the south onto a secondary route that leads into the mountains. It was much more isolated and after I made the turn to follow them, I had to stay further back so that I wouldn't be spotted." He took a deep breath and looked down at the table for a few moments. Raising his eyes I could see a mixture of pain and regret. "Then, after about fifteen kilometers, I ran out of petrol and lost them completely. I'm sorry Señor Corbett. But on that day I didn't know I would be following Smallwood out into the countryside. And I just didn't have enough fuel in my tank to follow him all the way to whatever his destination was. At any rate, that was the last I saw of the car carrying Manuel Fernández."

"I completely understand Rafael," I said. "And I appreciate your telling me what you saw." He gave me a small smile and a shrug.

I turned to Fernando. "Did you pursue this matter any further?"

He hesitated for a minute as though wrestling over how much he should reveal to me. Looking me in the eye, he finally said, "After Rafael reported what he had seen, we contacted our leadership in Buenos Aires and told them what had happened and asked for instructions. They said we should try to find out more if we could, but not to put ourselves at risk in doing so. The top priority had to be trying to keep an eye on Smallwood. Discovering the connection with Manuel Fernández was to be secondary."

Fernando paused to rub his cheeks. "And to tell you the truth Frank, we haven't been able to accomplish our main priority. Our sources in Buenos Aires tell us that Smallwood comes to Salta on a regular basis, usually on the weekends. But ever since Rafael spotted him with Fernández, we have not seen any trace of him."

I raised an inquisitive eyebrow. "It could be," Fernando said, "That he saw Rafael following him that day and since then has taken extra precautions to make sure he is not seen. We just don't know."

I turned to Rafael. "Did you ever try to find out which office Smallwood might have taken Manuel to? From what you tell me, it seems pretty likely that it was to a physician."

Rafael looked at Fernando, who gave him a "go-ahead" nod.

"We thought about that Señor Corbett. But we do not have enough manpower for that kind of investigation, especially for something that as Fernando told you our leadership said was not to be a top priority. Moreover," he added with a sober impression, "the authorities here have been increasing their pressure on us. Over the past few weeks, some of our comrades have been captured by the police. We are sure they are being tortured and at some point will reveal what they know about our group. And even though we have many safeguards, we have to be extra-cautious."

He looked downcast, as though he was sorry that he had to disappoint me. "But you are probably correct in assuming that Smallwood was taking Manuel to see a physician. There are six doctors in that building and perhaps you could do a little investigating on your own."

Taking a piece of paper and a pen from his shirt pocket, he wrote down the address of the building and passed it over to me.

"Thank you Rafael. I'm going to check this out first thing tomorrow."

He gave me a non-committal look. He was probably thinking as was I that I wouldn't have much success. I assumed that Argentines adhered to the same kind of doctor-patient confidentiality that we did. In addition, it seemed likely that if Smallwood had taken Manuel to see a doctor, he probably used a physician that he could influence one way or another to keep his mouth shut. But it was a lead, and I planned to follow up on it.

"One more thing Rafael," I said, pulling one of the maps of the area that Alfredo from my coat pocket. "Could you show me where you lost sight of Smallwood's car that day you followed him?"

Rising from his chair, he came over to my side and traced the route from Salta into the hills to the west. Tapping my map with his index figure, he said, "It was right about here Señor Corbett."

I nodded and taking out my own pen put an "X" on the spot he had indicated.

"I suppose I can rent a car in Salta," I said.

Rafael nodded, but there was a skeptical look on his face. "Yes you can. And if you are hoping to pick up the trail from where I last saw the vehicle carrying Manuel it had better be a sturdy one. The roads in that part of the mountains are pretty rough. Most of them are just hard-baked dirt with lots of bumps and ruts."

"And," Fernando interjected, "where Rafael lost the trail is pretty desolate territory Trying to locate Smallwood and Fernández will be like – how do you say it? – looking for a needle in a haystack."

"I understand," I said, "But it is a place to start. And I need to give it a try."

Both men nodded and I saw Monica, who had remained silent throughout, give me a look that seemed to be one of approval for my determination to follow any leads, no matter how slender they might be.

"All right Frank," Fernando said. "We can only wish you the best of luck with your efforts, but I'm afraid not much else. As Rafael explained, we are short on resources and trying to solve the mystery of why Manuel Fernández was seen in the company of Roy Smallwood is not something we can pursue at the moment."

"I appreciate that Fernando," I said. "And I also appreciate your providing me with the information you have. Without that I would have nowhere to go. Now, as we say, the ball is in my court."

I'm not sure they understood the idiom, but they all nodded in unison. They had taken the risk of meeting with me and providing whatever assistance they could. What happened next was up to me.

Twenty Eight

It was late afternoon when we left the cabin. Rafael and Fernando had gathered up the plates, glasses, and silverware along with the empty wine and water bottles and put them back into the black canvas bag. While they were removing traces of our visit, Monica had gone ahead to scout the area and make sure there were no unwelcome visitors in the vicinity.

We retraced our steps to the Ford Torino and again Monica took the wheel. The light was beginning to fade as we wound our way out of the mountains and into Salta. When they let me off at the Güemes statue, it was almost dark. As I prepared to get out of the car, I thanked my "hosts" once again. Fernando, who again had shared the back seat with me, extended his hand for me to take. As I took it in mine, he put his other hand over mine and wished me luck. Both Monica and Rafael turned their heads and quietly echoed that sentiment. When I got out of the car and quietly closed the door, they all gave me a wave as the car slowly pulled from the curb and entered the flow of traffic.

Walking back to the hotel, I felt a mixture of emotions. One was of excitement and exhilaration. I now had what I took to be a reliable confirmation that Manuel Fernández was indeed in Argentina – and perhaps not too far from where Rafael had last seen him. And despite what my old buddy Dwight Whalen had implied, there was no indication that Manuel had joined the revolutionaries. Instead, somehow Roy Smallwood and presumably the CIA had something to do with Manuel's disappearance. Just what the connection might be was unclear but I was beginning to develop some theories as to a plausible explanation.

But along with the excitement of what I had discovered returned the nagging question of getting assistance from the ERP. *And talk about "consorting with the enemy"*! Not only had I met with them to get information, they had laid on an elaborate spread for me to share with them. I had literally broken bread with dedicated Marxist revolutionaries who saw my country as the major oppressor of Third World nations around the globe. When we had approached the Güemes statue, Fernando had made a point of telling me that just as the local hero and others had freed Argentina from Spanish imperialism, the ERP now fought to liberate their country from the claws of *Yanquí* imperialism. And while he might not blame me personally for my country's alleged misdeeds, I was still a representative of that nation and as such at least partly responsible for its policies.

Furthermore, while my "hosts" had given me solid leads in my search for Manuel Fernández, I knew they had not done so simply out of their desire to help a Yankee private investigator do his job. If somehow in my pursuit I should run across Roy Smallwood and find out what he was up to, that could prove useful to them. They had not said anything about reporting back to them about whatever I might uncover. But I presumed that despite their claims of a lack of manpower, they still had ways to keep track of me; and if that should lead to Smallwood, so much the better for them. So once again I had to consider the possibility that by using the ERP for my own reasons, they were using me for theirs. And in the process it could lead to the public "outing" of a CIA agent – if not worse. And I would be seen by my own government as complicit in that outcome. In fact, if that were the result, I might come uncomfortably close to being charged with treason.

To complicate my ethical dilemma, there was something about the members of the ERP that I had met – especially in Salta – that I found personally appealing. I couldn't help but admire their efficiency and their dedication to what, in some ways, was a noble cause. And it wasn't just the lunch and the information that they had provided. Perhaps I was being naïve, but I found a certain humanity underneath their rigid ideological exterior. I could imagine that under different circumstances, we might all have been friends. As this thought crossed my mind, I uttered a sardonic chuckle and said to myself: *Don't get carried away! They could just have easily put a bullet in your brain and buried you out in the woods as provide you with lunch and information.*

With that cheery thought still stuck in my brain, I got back to the Hotel Salta around seven thirty. There was no sign of Karl Shussler in the lobby and I headed straight for my room, taking the stairs instead of the elevator. Once inside, I immediately called Alfredo to see if he had any additional information for me but was told by the hotel operator that the long distance lines were not functioning due to some kind of technical problem. He apologized and promised to contact me as soon as the problem was resolved. I thanked him and hung up the phone.

After my large and late lunch, I was not particularly hungry but decided that it was best to keep my date with Karl Shussler. I was positive that he had been assigned to keep an eye on me and report to whomever had assigned him to do so. Aware of that, I could, I hoped, somehow turn that knowledge against him. And if his surveillance of me had anything to do with Manuel Fernández's disappearance, as I strongly suspected it did, he could be another lead for me to follow.

I cleaned up as best I could. I thought about changing my clothes, but decided that I might as well keep to the casual and comfortable gear I had on. But, given that it was cooling off considerably, I added a sweater to my ensemble.

It was a few minutes before eight when I descended to the lobby, again taking the stairs. Karl was waiting for me in a chair that faced both the elevators and the stairs. *No getting by him!*

As soon as he saw me, he got up and approached with his hand extended and a smile pasted on his face. "How are you Frank? Did you have a good day? Did you get the information you needed?"

These questions came in rapid fire. At the same time, he gave my hand a pretty tight squeeze, which I did my best to return. Realizing after a few seconds that perhaps he had gone too far, he released his grip and gave me an apologetic look.

I didn't know quite how to respond to his last query: *"Did you get the information you needed?" Was there a hidden meaning in that question?* I had indeed, but I wasn't about to let him know that.

I answered his questions in sequence. "I'm fine Karl. Thanks for asking. And I had a great day. I learned an awful lot about Salta. My source was quite informative. Very, very helpful."

I wondered if Karl would pursue the matter further, asking me for details as to just who "my source" might be and in what ways "helpful," but he left it alone. I was sure that he didn't for a minute believe my cover story about being a writer and meeting someone who would provide background for a travel article. But whether he suspected me of meeting with the ERP was another matter altogether – and I wasn't about to enlighten him.

He gave me a look that I couldn't quite read and then asked, "Do you mind doing a little walking Frank? The restaurant I have in mind is about a mile away. We could take a taxi, but I've been cooped up in my room most of the afternoon and could use the exercise. Besides, it would help you get to know more of the city. What do you say?"

I had already done my share of walking, but I wasn't about to let Karl know that. Besides, another mile would be no problem. Despite the rigors of the day, I was pumped up and still feeling pretty good about my prospects for tracking down Manuel Fernández.

"Fine with me Karl," I said. "I usually do a morning jog and since I missed out today, a bit of walking would do me good. Let's go."

Karl grinned again and I thought I saw a gleam of satisfaction in his eyes. Grabbing my elbow as if to assure himself that I would not escape his grasp he escorted me through the hotel's main door. Once outside, he steered me to the left and we headed west.

After we had walked to the first intersection, I gently but firmly disengaged my elbow from his hand. It was not unusual for men in Latin America to hold on to one another as they walked, but I had no desire to do so with Karl Schussler. He didn't say anything but kept close enough so that our shoulders were no more than an inch or two apart.

As we walked, Karl began a line of chatter about his time as a student in the United States. After about five minutes, I tuned him out, simply nodding and grunting to show that I was paying some attention. As he yammered away, I tried to concentrate on the route we were taking.

Once we left the main plaza, we passed through a commercial district with most of the shops closing down for the night. After about four blocks, there were fewer lights and fewer people on the streets. It was quite a contrast with the lively night-time atmosphere of Buenos Aires but I presumed the common scene in the provinces. Overhead the night sky was bright and clear and I could see what looked to be millions of stars.

The temperature had dropped by about ten or fifteen degrees from what it had been during the day and I was glad I had decided to wear a sweater along with my jacket.

As we continued to head generally due west, Karl took some twists and turns that led us through small parks and plazas. I didn't know if he was doing this because it was the fastest way to get to our destination or if he was trying to disorient me. Whatever the case, I took careful note of my surroundings, confident that I could retrace my steps to the hotel if it became necessary.

After about fifteen minutes of walking, we reached what seemed to be the outskirts of the city. We passed by open stretches of land which, from what I could see in the darkness, appeared to be truck farms and orchards. The sidewalks we had been following suddenly gave way to nothing more than a rough dirt road. We were virtually alone except for the occasional stray dog. For the second time that day I wondered if I wasn't being led into some kind of ambush.

I decided to interrupt Karl's monologue. "Say Karl. Are you sure this is the way to the restaurant? It looks like we are in the middle of nowhere."

He stopped and laughed. "Sorry Frank. I should have warned you that we would be passing through a rather desolate stretch. But don't worry. The restaurant is less than a quarter of a mile further on. We'll soon see the lights. And believe me it is well worth the walk"

I wasn't reassured and I thought about turning back. I was reasonably confident that I could handle Karl if he were suddenly to jump me. But he might also have some henchmen hiding in the shadows to assist him - and I wasn't sure what my chances would be if I was outnumbered. Nonetheless, I decided to keep walking with him, staying alert to any dangers.

After about five minutes had passed, my fears were momentarily laid to rest when I spotted the lights of what Karl told me was the restaurant we were headed for. As we got closer, I saw that the restaurant's exterior was done in typical Spanish style – white stucco walls and a red tile roof. There was a wooden sign in the front garden that said *El Cabrito Asado*, the Roasted Goat, and off to the side were about a dozen parked cars. As we got even closer, I could smell roasted meat and hear the voices of the patrons.

Again taking me by the elbow, Karl led me to the entrance. "I know it's a little off the beaten path Frank," he said. "But it's a local favorite and a place that not every tourist gets to visit. I'm sure you'll find it to your liking."

Once inside, we were greeted by a waiter decked out in a gaucho costume of flared black trousers tucked into shiny knee-high black boots, a long-sleeved white shirt, and a bright red scarf. Most of the tables were occupied but he escorted us to one at the back that was free. As we took our seats, he handed over menus covered with thick brown leather and promised to return in a few minutes to take our orders. Before leaving us to ponder our choices, Karl asked him to bring us some red wine and two bottles of mineral water.

"The local wine is not the greatest," Karl informed me, "But it is passable."

I didn't tell him, of course, that I had already sampled the local variety earlier that day. I simply nodded, deferring to his greater knowledge.

Looking around, I saw that the other customers were mostly male. I presumed that they were likely local businessmen and professionals. Some were dressed casually but the majority wore suits and probably had come straight from their offices without stopping at home to change. From what I could tell, they all looked to be Argentine. We appeared to be the only non-Salteños in the place and Karl the only one with blonde hair. We had attracted a few looks as we had been led to our table, but nothing out of the ordinary. Once we had been seated, nobody paid us any undue attention.

It didn't take our waiter more than a minute to return with our drinks. After showing the label on the wine bottle to Karl, who nodded in approval, he deftly uncorked it and poured him a sample to sip. Karl went through the ritual and declared the wine acceptable, much to the delight of the waiter, who poured us both a generous portion. The glasses into which he decanted the wine were not the traditional globe with a stem but instead were squat and heavy in tune with the rustic décor that surrounded us. The walls were covered with gaucho gear, notably the famous *bolas*, three heavy stones covered in leather and attached to three strands. The gaucho used them to hurl at fleeing animals, who were brought down when their legs became entangled.

Karl had not bothered to look at the menu. "I know what I want Frank," he said. "The specialty of the house is, not surprisingly, the roasted goat. I highly recommend it. It's really something; the best I've ever had."

"That sounds good to me Karl. I'll follow your lead."

"Excellent Frank," he said, waving the waiter over so he could place our orders. "I'm positive that you won't be disappointed." Then, giving me a sly look, he added, "And it's more local color for you to put in your article."

I was pretty sure he was baiting me, pretending to go along with my cover story to see how I would react. But I stuck to my guns. "Yes indeed Karl, Great material. Thanks a lot for bringing me here."

He grinned and nodded. "You're welcome Frank. Glad to be of assistance."

We drank our wine, which was nothing to write home about. I measured my intake, knowing that I needed to keep my wits about me. Karl continued to dominate the conversation and I began to wonder if he would ever run out of things to say. Finally, our meal arrived and for a moment Karl was silent as he cut and chewed. As advertised, the goat was delicious and even though I had not been particularly hungry when we had left the hotel, the walk had piqued my appetite. I devoured every bit of meat that was on my plate along with a hefty portion of potatoes and some salad.

When we had finished the main course, we both ordered coffee and dessert. Before it arrived, I took advantage of the momentary lull in Karl's monologue to ask him how his day had been. He looked a bit startled by the innocuous question but quickly recovered. "Oh, you know how it is in the business world Frank. I met with some potential clients at the hotel and we discussed the opportunities that my company could offer them in opening up provincial markets; not very exciting but a necessary part of the job."

Karl said this smoothly enough. And of course it was completely plausible. But I didn't believe him. I was sure that he had spent most of the day just hanging around the hotel so he could keep tabs on me. I thought about pressing him for details about his alleged meetings with clients, but decided it wouldn't lead anywhere.

By the time we had finished and Karl had paid the bill, which he insisted on doing, the restaurant crowd had thinned out considerably. We were among only a few patrons remaining. As we made our way out the door, I could see only two or three cars still parked outside. All of a sudden I felt a shiver run up my spine as I contemplated the walk back to the hotel.

The streets would be even more deserted and the opportunities for some kind of ambush that much greater.

As we stood on the veranda outside the restaurant, I said to Karl, "Shouldn't we call a taxi to take us back to the hotel? It's going to be quite a hike after a heavy meal and a long day. And I'm not sure how safe it is."

I knew that I sounded like a wimp. In reality, I wasn't concerned about the walk or the safety. I just wanted to see how Karl responded.

His first reaction was one of scorn. But he quickly replaced it with one of reasonableness. "Salta isn't Buenos Aires Frank," he explained, stating the obvious. "The restaurant would have to call a taxi for us. And there aren't that many here who operate late at night. By the time we got one to come for us, we could already have walked back to the hotel and be in our rooms. It makes much more sense to go back the way we came. Unless, of course," he said in a challenging tone, "you're not up to it."

I shrugged. "No Karl. That makes sense. Let's get going."

He gave me a satisfied smile and we set off towards the center of town. But all my senses were now on high alert. Karl had made it obvious that he wanted us to walk back. I was sure the reason had less to do with the time it would take to get a taxi to carry us and more to do with something he had planned for me along the way. Just what that might be I didn't know but I suspected that it would be some kind of ambush.

Despite my heightened awareness, Karl managed to catch me by surprise. We were about ten minutes into our walk, passing by the same desolate area we had traversed on our way to the restaurant, when Karl suddenly stumbled and fell to the ground.

Without thinking, I instinctively bent over to help him back on his feet. As I did so, someone whose presence I had not detected grabbed me from behind and wrapped his arms across my chest, clasping powerful hands in a tight grip at my sternum. With this maneuver my unseen attacker had immobilized my arms and was simultaneously pulling back in such a way as to lift me several inches off the ground. Quick as the proverbial cat, Karl leapt to his feet and with a wicked grin on his face delivered a right hook to my breadbasket. With my arms trapped, I was powerless to avoid the blow. Even though I had clenched my stomach muscles in anticipation, it still caused enough damage for me to vomit my recently-consumed meal onto the street. Part of my discharge landed on

Karl and he responded with a vicious kick to my right shin, producing a howl of agony.

Even outnumbered two to one, I wasn't about to give up without a fight. Bringing my head back swiftly, I caught whoever was holding me from behind unawares and had the satisfaction of hearing the bone of his nose break. I could feel the warmth of his blood on the back of my neck. But he was tough and still held on tight.

My next maneuver was to try to stomp on the toes of the man holding me, but before I could, Karl landed a haymaker to my jaw and for a moment I saw stars.

"Stop struggling Frank," Karl hissed, all pretense of friendship now long gone. "It's no use. Just do what we say and you won't suffer any more damage."

By this time, a large black sedan had pulled to the curb and I heard a door open. I didn't need to be told that the next move would be to get me into the car. I didn't think that would necessarily be a bad outcome. In fact, it might even work to my advantage. If my attackers had wanted to get rid of me, they could have done the job right there and then. Instead, I thought, they wanted me alive, at least for the time being. And if, as I strongly suspected, all of this had something to do with the disappearance of Manuel Fernández, maybe getting into the car would somehow help me find out what had happened to him.

My suspicions were confirmed when I heard the voice of a third man, who apparently had been driving the car. "Come on you guys. Pick him up and put him in the back seat. Somebody might come along at any minute."

I recognized the voice immediately. Turning my head to the left, even though there wasn't much light, I saw the unmistakable figure of Roy Smallwood standing at the rear door of the sedan.

If I had been thinking clearly, the smartest move at that point would have been to submit and let them hustle me into the waiting car without sustaining additional damage. But some sort of perverse instinct kicked in. I had recovered enough from Karl's blow to the head to carry through on my original plan to stomp my heel down on the toes on the right foot of the man holding me from behind. When I did so, I was rewarded by a sharp cry of pain and a momentary loosening of the vise around my chest.

But it wasn't enough. Before I had time to wriggle free, he had regained his hold. This time, he moved his arms upward, one across my throat and another to the side of my head. He began squeezing on my throat, applying enough pressure to cut off my breathing. I could see Karl ready to hurl another punch to my jaw if needed, but just then my eyes clouded over and I felt my mind go blank As I descended into darkness, my last thought was that I had been treated much better and more gently by the ERP.

Twenty Nine

When I regained consciousness, the first sound I heard was the chirping of early-morning birds greeting the sunrise. I was stretched out on a cot a little too short for me, my legs bent at the knees. As soon as I tried to rise, I felt a sharp pain in my stomach where Karl had pounded me the night before, giving me a reminder of a score to settle. My jaw was sore and swollen, also thanks to Karl. Grimacing, I swung my legs over to the floor and sat upright, trying to get my bearings. The effort produced a brief dizzy spell and some nausea, but it passed.

I wasn't alone. Directly across from me, not six feet away, sitting on a cot exactly like mine was a very thin young man, with a shock of black hair and dark eyes.

"How do you feel?" he asked in a soft voice.

It took me a few seconds to recognize him. And when I did, I felt a glow of satisfaction. I had not exactly covered myself in glory in doing it, but after traveling thousands of miles, playing tag with some pretty dangerous characters, and overcoming various obstacles, I had accomplished what I had set out to do. *I had found Manuel Fernández!* Although given the circumstances, that fact did not seem to offer much promise that it would do either of us much good.

"I'll live," I said, my voice harsh from the effects of the arm across the throat that had rendered my unconscious. "And how about you? How are you doing Manuel?"

His eyes grew wide with surprise. "How do you know who I am?" he said, with a tone of suspicion.

"Good question. I'm a private investigator. Your sister...."

"Elena?"

219

"Yes. Elena. She hired me to find you - and now I have."

He looked upset. "But I don't understand. She wasn't supposed to... How did you...?"

"It's a long story," I said. "And I don't know how much time we have before someone comes to check on us. The most important thing at the moment is getting out of this place. And to do that, you need to trust me. I'm on your side."

I could see doubt on his face. And I couldn't blame him. I must seem to him to be some kind of apparition, suddenly appearing out of nowhere claiming to be his rescuer. I could also see that he was wan and undernourished, adding to his sense of confusion.

"First Manuel, do you have any idea where we are?"

I followed his eyes as they wandered around our room. It was not large but big enough to hold the two of us comfortably. The walls were bare, the only furniture the two cots. There was only one window at about eye-level, through which the dawn light began to filter. There was no glass in the window, only iron bars. Opposite the window was a heavy oak door on solid metal hinges.

"I'm not really sure Mister..." He halted in mid-sentence. "I'm sorry. You know my name, but what is yours?"

"My apologies Manuel. It's Frank. Frank Corbett. Please call me Frank."

He gave me a slight smile. "Okay Frank. I don't know exactly where we are. I was unconscious when they brought me here and I've only been outside once in the weeks that I've been here. And that was when I was taken to a doctor in what I think was Salta."

I nodded. "Yes. It was."

A look of surprise crossed his face. "How did you know?"

I waved a hand. "That's not important right now."

Again he looked doubtful, but continued. "Yes. I was pretty sick, running a high fever and unable to keep anything down. So my captors took me to see a doctor who gave me an injection and some medicine to take. But I was drugged most of the time and that, combined with whatever I was suffering from, made everything kind of fuzzy. I do remember that after we left the doctor's office, we headed westward. However, I passed out along the way and the next thing I knew I was back here," he concluded sadly, his head hanging down. "I'm sorry Frank, but that's the best I can do."

"That's all right Manuel. Don't worry. I arrived here in the same condition. But if I had to guess, I would say we are somewhere in the hills to the west of Salta, maybe thirty or forty miles from the city."

He was about to ask me again how I knew that, but instead simply shrugged.

Before I continued questioning him, I decided to do a bit of exploring. I had been sitting on the cot facing Manuel. I got up slowly, still feeling a bit woozy, and walked to the door. Giving a tug on the large brass handle, it was, as I expected, firmly locked. There was a peephole and I looked through it onto an empty corridor.

Turning around, I went to the window and peered out. The first thing I saw was a cobble-stone courtyard below, interspersed with small garden plots of flowers and cactus. Surrounding the courtyard on three sides was a thick adobe wall that looked to be about twelve to fifteen feet high. It was topped with a row of embedded broken glass, glittering in the early morning light like dangerous diamonds. Beyond the wall I could see a very rugged countryside, the features of which were just emerging in the dawn light. It looked very much like what I had seen on the road from Tucumán to Salta, mostly bare, arid terrain with the occasional desert-like vegetation. In the distance I could see the shapes of mountains bathed in rosy hues. I saw no sign of human or animal life beyond the wall; not even the distant smoke of some rural hut or campfire. The only sounds were made by the birds that had awakened me.

Still staring out the window, I tried to make some plans for escape. If somehow we could make it out the window, there was a drop of about twenty feet to the courtyard below. Then we would have to climb the outer wall and get over it somehow without cutting ourselves on the jagged glass. Once outside the wall we faced the daunting challenge of navigating some difficult terrain until we reached safety. And looking at Manuel, I wondered if he would be physically able to withstand all of those rigors or if I would have to carry him a good bit of the way. But I was getting ahead of myself. One step at a time.

I turned back to Manuel. "It looks as though we are in some sort of hacienda – and one that seems completely isolated."

He nodded a confirmation, a discouraged look on his face.

I went back to my cot and sat down again, facing Manuel "What about our captors Manuel? Any idea as to how many?" I already knew there were at least three.

"I've seen five men. There is a red-headed North American who seems to be in charge and a blonde-headed Argentine of German extraction who is some kind of chemist." He had described Smallwood and Schussler, no surprises there. "Then there are three big guys who provide the muscle. I think they are Argentines, but one or two of them might be from some other Latin American country. They don't say much and I can't really get a handle on their accents. And there is one more. I haven't seen him but I have heard his voice. He's another American and I think he arrived here recently."

That was interesting, I thought to myself. I wasn't yet positive, but I was beginning to form a pretty good idea as to who the new arrival might be.

"How often do they check up on you?" I asked.

"Usually four or five times a day. They bring me meals and take me to the bathroom." Looking at the light coming through the window, he said, "Breakfast is usually about an hour after sunrise."

I instinctively looked at my wrist to check the time but saw that they had taken my watch. Manuel gave a doleful smile and said, "They took mine too. But I've gotten pretty good at telling the time by the sun and shadows. I think they'll probably bring us our breakfast in about thirty minutes."

"Okay. Then we have a little time before they show up. Can you tell me what happened to you? I think I know most of the story, but it would help if you could fill in the gaps so I can get an idea of how much time we have to get out of here."

He paused for a moment and I saw him struggle to control his emotions. "I'm sorry Frank. The whole thing has been such a nightmare and I…"

I gave him a moment to compose himself. "That's okay Manuel. Just take your time," I said, even though I wasn't sure that was a luxury we could afford.

He took a deep breath and looked me in the eye. "There is a lot I don't remember Frank. They have kept me pretty doped up most of the time and many things are hazy. But what I do remember is that a few weeks ago I was in my apartment in Durham…You know that I was a med student at Duke, right?" I nodded. "My roommate had gone home and I was alone, studying when there was a knock on the door. When I opened it, there was the red-haired man…."

"His name is Roy Smallwood," I said.

"Okay. It was this guy Smallwood and another man with blonde hair and blue eyes about your age." I suspected I knew who this was as well, but didn't interrupt.

"They showed me identification that said they were government agents. I think they were from the State Department, but they flashed them so quickly I didn't have time to check. I guess I should have," he said with a look of embarrassment. I simply shrugged and gestured for him to continue.

"They told me that they were there on a matter concerning my father and asked to come in. The way they said it seemed to imply that my father was in some kind of trouble so I let them in - a big mistake. Once they were inside, they began to ask questions about me and my father that really didn't make a lot of sense. I was just about to tell them I had no idea what they were talking about when the man you say is Smallwood asked if he could have a glass of water. I told him to go to the kitchen and help himself. But just as he was passing me, supposedly on the way to get his water, he turned and grabbed me around the neck. I tried to struggle, but the other man was on me too, grabbing my arm and sticking me with a needle. Whatever he put in my body, it must have been very powerful, because I went out like a light." He closed his eyes for a few seconds, reliving the painful moment.

"I can remember that part pretty clearly, but afterwards it's all bits and pieces. I have a vague recollection of being on an airplane and then in some kind of van. I don't know how they got me out of the States and into Argentina. They must have used some kind of drug that kept me functioning but totally under their control – maybe something that produces a sort of hypnotic effect. At any rate, I ended up here." He gave a little laugh. "It's almost like an episode of *Star Trek*, you know. One minute I'm in Durham and the next I've been transported by magic to somewhere in northern Argentina. Really weird."

I was pleased to see that he had regained something of a sense of humor. I suppose too that it helped to share the details of his ordeal with a sympathetic listener. Whatever it took to lift his spirits was all to the good.

"So what's the deal?" I asked, although I already thought I knew the answer. "They're holding you for ransom, right?"

He gave me a baleful look. "Well yes, sort of. But it's not the usual kind. No outright demands for money from my parents. Nothing like that. It's more complicated."

"Let me guess," I said. "Something to do with your father."

"That's right Frank. That's it exactly." He again paused, looking down at his hands. Then he raised his head and continued. "My captors haven't given me the full story but I've been able to pick up enough to piece together what's going on. It all has to do with drug smuggling, mostly cocaine but some heroin as well. Up to now, Chile has been the main South American center of distribution for both drugs. But the situation there is unstable and these guys expect a military coup later in the year." I flashed back to Dwight's lecture on the state of affairs in South America and his suggestion that something might be in the works to end the Allende regime. "They think the military will crack down on trafficking so they need to find a new distribution center."

"And they think it will be in Argentina."

"Yes. Right now, most of the drugs go north out of Chile to the U.S. market. But Argentina is already in the picture with some drugs crossing over the Andes for eventual shipment to Europe. If the military takes over in Chile, then the base of operations will shift here. And that's where my father and I come in." He looked down at the floor for a moment, then back up to me.

"I guess you know that my father is a high-ranking official in the Argentine embassy in Washington." I nodded in the affirmative. "Well, what these guys want is for him to agree to use his influence to help them get their drugs into the U.S., probably using the diplomatic pouch. I'm not sure of all the details, but I am the bargaining chip. They plan on holding me captive for as long as it takes for my father to comply. In the meantime, they have concocted a story that I have joined the guerrillas here, something that they will make public if he doesn't do what they want."

It all sounded rather elaborate and convoluted, but I guess it made a certain amount of sense. It certainly explained why the elder Fernández had been reluctant to pursue any serious investigation into his son's disappearance. He was probably playing for time until he could figure out what to do. And it also explained why he had tried to discourage Elena from hiring someone like me to dig deeper.

"Do you know if your father has responded to their demands?" I asked.

"No. Not really. As I said, they don't tell me much."

I now had most of the pieces of the puzzle connected. And the picture was not a pretty one for either one of us. From what I knew of kidnap situations in general, if Manuel's father held out, further pressures would be applied, probably by sending him one of his son's ears or fingers. And even if he did go along, I didn't see the plan as a long-term arrangement. There were too many risks. My guess was that Smallwood and company were looking to use the elder Fernández to help them make a big score. Then they would either retire or think of some other way to get the drugs into the U.S.

For the plan to work, it was important to keep Manuel alive. I was sure that his father would demand proof of life before he made any decision. But once the plan had run its course, I was not optimistic about Manuel's chances for survival. This was not the traditional "We exchange our prisoner for a cash payment" deal. This was one where the perpetrators needed to cover their tracks and tie up all the loose ends.

And I, of course, was also a pretty prominent "loose end." *Why was I still alive?* I couldn't imagine they were going to hold me for ransom. Perhaps there was another use for me – a fall guy perhaps? No way to know at the moment.

Before Manuel and I had a chance to resume our conversation, we heard the key turn in the lock and the door to our room open. Two burly guys entered. I was heartened to see that one of them had adhesive tape over his nose and was sporting two black eyes. He was obviously the one I had head-butted the night before. I was about to make a wiseass remark when I saw that he had an automatic pistol in his fist pointed directly at my chest and a look on his face that indicated he would love any excuse to pull the trigger. I sat as still as I could, focusing on the pistol that never wavered. It was not the first time during my visit to Argentina that I had

had the business end of a weapon aimed at me, but that didn't make it any more pleasant.

While the guy with the broken nose covered me, the other one put a tray with our breakfast down on the floor. He was careful never to come between me and the gun. Both men paid little attention to Manuel, judging, I assumed, that in his weakened condition he did not pose any threat.

Once the man who had carried the tray rose, I said, "Listen. I need to talk to Smallwood. Tell him I have something he'll want to hear." I was just making it up. I had no real idea what I would say to him, but if given the chance I would try to come up with something.

Neither man responded. They had been silent throughout and they stayed that way. The guy with the gun kept me covered as the one who had carried the tray went out the door and into the corridor beyond. As the door closed, the man whose nose I had broken gave me a look that said, *"You are going to pay dearly for what you did to me. And I am going to enjoy every minute of it."* He then locked us in again and we could hear the pair's footsteps echoing down the corridor.

Once the door closed, I let out a deep breath and realized that my fists had been clenched and my shoulders and back stiff as a board. I could feel sweat trickling down the inside of my shirt despite the chill wind that was blowing through the open window. Facing the business end of a gun in the hand of someone who had a grudge will do that to you.

Manuel was grinning at me. "Did you do that Frank? Break that guy's nose?"

"Yeah. And I wish I could have done more," I added with a bit of bravado, hoping that he didn't see how tense I had been just a few seconds before. "Maybe later."

Manuel laughed. "Well good for you Frank. You can't believe how many times I dreamed of punching one of those guys." Then he turned somber. "But of course in my condition it probably would be like a flea trying to down an elephant."

I tried to lift his spirits. "Well let's do what we can to get you into condition. How's your appetite?"

"To be honest Frank," he said. "Up until now, it hasn't been too good. They provide me with plenty of food, but I usually leave most of it untouched. I must have lost fifteen or twenty pounds since I've been here. Look," he said, raising his shirt. I could count his ribs. "It might have something to do with the drugs. Or maybe it's depression. Or maybe I know that these guys want to keep my in good shape and I'm resisting. I don't know, but food just doesn't appeal to me."

"Well Manuel," I said, "At the moment we cannot do much about our situation but make the best of it. And if we are going to get out of here, we are going to need all the strength we can muster."

Reaching over, I lifted the cover off the breakfast tray. On it were a variety of fruits, some pastries, and even half a dozen hard boiled eggs. There was also some juice in small cardboard containers and a pot of coffee. All in all, pretty substantial.

I picked up the tray and handed it to Manuel, who put it gingerly on his lap. I picked out some fruit, pastries, and a couple of eggs for myself and poured us both some coffee into the mugs that had been provided. "Okay Manuel, this is for me," I said, "and the rest is for you. And I want to see you eat every bite."

He gave me another grin. "Yes mother," he said, picking up a pastry, taking a healthy chunk in his teeth, and beginning to chew.

I gave him a grin back and began to eat some of the food myself. The punch Karl had landed on my jaw made chewing painful, but I knew I had to follow the advice I had given Manuel. I would need all my strength if we were to have any hope of getting out of our current predicament in one piece.

Thirty

After I had swallowed the last drop of coffee and chewed the last of my fruit and pastries, I immediately felt better. Getting some food in my belly – a belly that I had emptied the night before on a street in Salta – did wonders.

While Manuel still worked on his breakfast, I made a closer inspection of our room. Lifting the mattress off the cot, I saw something that might be of help. Letting the mattress back into place, I went to the windows and checked the bars that kept us in. I pulled on one to test it and it seemed pretty solid. But I noticed some rust at the bottom of one of them and a bit of deterioration in the plaster and stucco in which it was anchored.

I was just beginning to form an escape plan when the key in the door turned and it slowly opened. It was the same two muscle-men who had brought us breakfast. But instead of coming straight through into the room, as they had before, the one whose nose I had broken pushed the door open with his foot, waiting until it had swung inwardly enough so that he could see both of us. He had the same pistol in his hand and it was again pointed straight at me.

These guys are pros, I thought to myself. They had made sure that one of us was not hiding behind the door, ready to jump them as they entered.

The guy with the gun kept me covered while the other one gathered our breakfast dishes and placed them on the tray. Again, he was careful not to get between me and the gun. I wasn't about to make any quick moves and sat stoically on the edge of my cot, staring without expression into the swollen eyes of the guy with the broken nose. I wasn't about to give him any excuse to fire but at the same time I wanted to show him that I wasn't intimidated either.

The guy with the tray went out the door first while the other one kept me covered. He didn't seem to pay much attention to Manuel, probably figuring he was too weak to provide much of a threat. I was still staring at him when he finally spoke. "You," he said in Spanish, wiggling the gun in my direction, "Come with me." The voice was a little distorted due to the broken nose, but the message was clear.

I got up from the cot slowly and made my way to the door. The man with the gun kept it leveled at me the whole time, maintaining his distance in case I might lunge at him. When I got to the door, I turned and gave Manuel an encouraging nod which belied the trepidation I felt.

As I stepped into the corridor, I saw that the guy with the tray was standing next to another bruiser who also had a weapon – it looked like an Uzi – also pointed in my direction. They were taking no chances. Manuel had told me that he had seen three muscle men and I wondered if there might be even more somewhere in the vicinity.

The guy whose nose I had broken took a position behind me while the one with the Uzi stayed at my side, the barrel of his weapon only inches from my head. The one with the tray took the lead. I thought about slamming into the guy at my side and grabbing his weapon, then turning on the guy following me. But the odds were against me and I decided to wait for a better opportunity.

At the end of the corridor was a broad staircase that led to the floor below. We descended into a spacious entrance hall and I could see large double doors that led to the courtyard. The man with the tray moved to the left and we entered another corridor that took us, after about twenty steps, to yet another door. Our guide put the tray down on a nearby table and, after knocking briefly, pushed it open. Stepping aside, he gestured for me to enter.

When I crossed the threshold, it took me a few seconds to take in the scene. The bright morning sun was pouring through an east window and reflecting off the tile floor and into my face. The room seemed to be some kind of library with bookshelves to my right, stocked floor to ceiling with leather-bound volumes. In the center of the room was a large oak table at the far end of which sat three men, whose features at first, with the sun in my eyes, I had trouble making out.

I heard the door close behind me and the barrel of a gun briefly pressed into my back. At least one of my "escorts" was still behind me. Then I heard the familiar voice of Roy Smallwood say with a sneer, "Take a seat Corbett. Make yourself comfortable."

I did as I was told, sitting down on a dark wooden chair with leather-covered seat and high back in the Spanish style. Idly I wondered if the leather were thick enough to stop a bullet. I didn't think so and I wasn't about to find out.

As my eyes adjusted, I now had no trouble recognizing the three men at the other end of the table about ten feet away. It was no surprise that two of them were Roy Smallwood and Karl Schussler. But the sight of the third man did jar me, even though I had begun to have my suspicions as I had followed the twisted trail that had led me to Manuel Fernández, especially after Manuel told me that one of the two men who had kidnapped him was about my age with blond hair and blue eyes.

"Well, well," I said, "Fancy meeting you here Dwight. And I can't say that it is a pleasure."

"Always the wise guy huh Frank," Dwight Whalen said with a sardonic smile. "I figured from the moment you came into my office to ask about Manuel Fernández that somehow we'd end up like this. You always were a persistent son of a bitch."

"So what's the deal Dwight?" I shot back, "I thought you were the ambitious career officer on the rise, playing it safe. Now what? You're up to your neck in kidnapping, extortion, and drug smuggling. How's that going to look on your resumé?"

He gave me condescending look. "Well if all goes as we plan, none of this will come to light."

"I still don't get it Dwight," I said. "I mean I can guess why your pals are involved. It must be the money. Karl here," I said, nodding in his direction, "was probably spinning me a tale about his position in a promising business. And even if it's true, he wouldn't mind making more on the side dealing in cocaine and heroin. And our spook," I said, nodding at Smallwood, "probably thinks he's owed something for all the years he's spent serving his country in faraway places without moving up the career ladder. Now it is payback time, building up a nice nest egg for a cushy retirement in some exotic locale. Right *Roy.*"

Smallwood clenched his fists and his face turned red. He was about to say something when Dwight held up his hand to stop him. It was clear who was in charge here.

"But you Dwight," I continued. "I just don't get it. Why take the risk? What's in it for you?"

He looked at me with some amusement. "You mean *besides* the money?"

"Yeah. Besides that."

"It's really pretty simple Dwight. I'm just doing my job. Following orders."

"You mean your job now is to kidnap a foreign ambassador's son so that his father will let you and your gang smuggle drugs into the U.S.," I said sarcastically. "Since when has this become State Department policy? Help me out here buddy. I'm a little lost."

"Come on Frank," he said, "You know how things work. What does the State Department actually *do* these days? Most of the major foreign policy decisions are made and carried out in the White House, especially with Nixon and Kissinger in charge. We've become errand boys, assigned the small and boring jobs while the real action takes place elsewhere."

Dwight took a breath and I prepared for him to break into his lecture mode again. He didn't disappoint.

"Look Frank. You know our foreign-policy history. We are supposedly spreading democracy around the world. But in reality we are protecting and promoting the interests of Wall Street and the big corporations looking to make a buck overseas, especially in Latin America. The United Fruit Company, Standard Oil, Anaconda and Kennicott Copper, IT&T – you name it. They've been calling the shots and we've been following their orders; maybe not directly, but pretty close."

Despite my best efforts to stay still as he spoke, I gave a couple of involuntary nods of the head in agreement. While it was oversimplified, Dwight had a point.

"And now, in the year of Our Lord Nineteen Hundred and Seventy Three, there are other interests to serve. Do you have any idea of the size of the profit margin from selling drugs Frank?" It was a rhetorical question. "Currently it's in the tens of millions – and it's just beginning to take off. Demand in the U.S. is insatiable and Europe is not far behind. A few years down the road we'll be talking about billions and billions of dollars. And powerful interests are already formed to maximize those profits."

"You mean like the Mafia?"

Dwight nodded. "Yes. They're players. But there are others as well. Mostly legitimate businesses that have added drug trafficking to their portfolio. You'd be surprised at some of the names."

Dwight had a smug look on his face as he gave his little spiel. I desperately wanted to wipe that look off with my fist but at the moment was in no position to do so. Instead, I said, "Yes, I suppose I would."

"So you wanted to know how I got involved in all this," he said, waving his hand in a circle. "Well, about a year ago a pretty important guy – I won't name names but you'd probably recognize it if I told you – came into my office and laid out my future for me. If I wanted a swift ride up the bureaucratic ladder – and make some significant additions to my measly salary – all I had to do was to help him and the organization he represented find ways to get drugs from South America into the U.S. using the privileges of diplomatic immunity as a conduit."

"And you agreed," I said with a tone of disgust.

He shrugged. "Sure, why not? After all, my predecessors had done essentially the same thing for years at the behest of big banks and big companies. How was this any different?"

"Well for one thing," I said, "I doubt that many took outright bribes. And for another, they weren't involved in an illegal trade that could cause widespread pain and suffering for the citizenry they were supposed to serve."

Dwight waved away my arguments. "Semantics Dwight. Most of the old-timers came from money themselves. Besides, you know there is a revolving door between the government and the big moneyed interests. In fact, some of my predecessors came from the corporate and financial world, served their time in State defending those interests, and then returned to their cushy jobs. Just look at the top guys in the Eisenhower administration who had ties to United Fruit and who helped organize the coup in Guatemala in 1954 that overthrew Arbenz."

I resisted the temptation to nod in agreement again and just stared at Dwight has he continued to make his case.

"And so far as 'pain and suffering' goes, you could argue that what I and others are doing to promote the drug trade is a kind of payback for the abuses of our banks and multinationals who have taken obscene profits out of Latin America and helped keep most of the population in misery. Now, small coca farmers get greater profits from their crop as drug use in the U.S. increases, providing more benefits for the *campesinos* than any Alliance for Progress agrarian reform program ever could."

I had to wonder how much of this claptrap Dwight really believed. It sounded more like the kind of discussion you might have in a late-night bull session than a serious argument. But maybe he had convinced himself that what he was doing was justified by his own crazy and self-serving logic. And then another thought hit me. *Why was Dwight telling me all this? Was he really concerned with justifying his actions to me or, more likely, was he revealing the depth of his involvement in this business because he knew that I wouldn't be passing the story on to anyone else?* I feared that the latter explanation was the correct one.

"All very noble of you Dwight," I said dryly. "Righting the wrongs of the past. But I still don't get why you took the risk of kidnapping Manuel to put pressure on his father to help you and your buddies feather their nests. It smacks of desperation to me."

I saw Roy Smallwood begin to rise from his chair and head in my direction, but Dwight put a hand on his arm and he resumed his seat. Karl, however, sat stoically and said nothing. I wondered if he agreed with my assessment.

"You have a point Frank," Dwight said. "You have a point. But as they say, no risk no rewards. If we can get Fernández Senior to go along, we anticipate some substantial profits. Argentina is already a major transit point for drugs and we are confident the traffic will increase dramatically in the months ahead." This jibed with what Manuel had told me. "It might be a short-term arrangement, but a highly profitable one."

As Dwight was waxing enthusiastic over the profits that would come rolling in from his little scheme, I latched on to the fact that Manuel's father had yet to concede to their demands. However, I imagined that the patience of Dwight and his partners was wearing thin and I could foresee the all-too-likely scenario of them increasing the pressure in some rather nasty ways. But I held on to the hope that if I could somehow get

Manuel out of our make-shift prison, their plan would blow up in their faces. How to achieve our escape, however, was another matter altogether. What I desperately needed was time – and I wasn't sure how much I had. I decided to try to find out.

"That all sounds peachy keen Dwight," I said with a smirk, "And what plans to you have for me? I guess I'm a kind of – what's the right word? – an *inconvenience*."

"That you are Frank," he said, shaking his head from side to side, "That you are indeed. In fact, I'd say that *pain in the ass* would be more accurate." He leaned forward, placing his palms flat down on the table. "We've had some lively discussions about your fate. My colleagues here," he said, nodding towards Schussler and Smallwood, "wanted to cut your throat and leave you to die in the desert. But I thought we'd better get in touch with some higher ups before we made any hasty decisions. Plus, we don't know who you might have told about what you had learned before we snatched you. Perhaps you left a trail that somehow could lead to us. And we certainly wouldn't want that, would we?"

I kept my mouth shut. "Well I don't want to leave you hanging Frank," Dwight said. "I owe you that much. We have contacted the people who give the orders and told them about the *inconvenience* you pose. They told us to hold onto you until they could come to a decision. So far, we haven't heard from them – but we expect a call fairly soon. If, as I suspect, they want us to wring some information from you, well then we'll do it of course. *We always follow orders*." Dwight was clearly enjoying himself. "And Juan here, the one with the patch over his nose, is really looking forward to that assignment."

I threw a glance over my shoulder and saw *Juan* giving me an evil glare while he pounded his fist into his palm with a loud smack.

Turning back towards Dwight, I said, "And after that?"

He shrugged. "It all depends on what I'm told Frank. What happens to you ultimately is really out of my hands."

I was getting a little tired of his Adolf Eichmann routine – "Just following orders."

"Let's cut to the chase Dwight. If the orders come to 'cut my throat and leave me in the desert' I want you to be the one to do it. Not one of your hired help."

Dwight shifted uneasily in his chair and I could see a look of indecision on his face. I added a little pressure. "A doomed man's last request Dwight. A favor for a friend. What do you say? Are you up to it? Getting your hands dirty – or in this case, bloody?"

I got some measure of satisfaction in seeing his discomfort. I had put him on the spot. If I knew Dwight, I doubted that he had ever been the one to mete out punishment personally. It just wasn't his style. That was something for those he bossed. But now I had issued a direct challenge in front of the men he commanded. I was sure they were anxious to see how he responded.

He looked a little pale and there was a slight stammer in his voice as he responded. "We'll see about that Frank. We'll see. I have to get my orders first."

I had shaken him for a moment, but then he recovered. "Until then," he said, his voice steadied, "You'll have some time to consider whether you want to provide us with the information we need from you the easy way or," gesturing over my shoulder to Juan behind me, "the hard way."

I gave him a grin as one of the muscle men grabbed me by the upper arm and hauled me out of my chair. "See you later Dwight," I said in parting. He gave no response, but I could see looks of disappointment on the faces of Schussler and Smallwood. They undoubtedly did not to wait for orders from higher-ups to begin punishing me.

While I was escorted back to my room by the same trio that had taken me to meet with Dwight and his two co-conspirators, I tried to absorb what I had just heard. The fact that Manuel's father had yet to yield to his son's kidnappers' demands and that Dwight was awaiting orders from above before determining my fate meant that we had at least some time to try to escape. The question that brought a frown to my face, however, was: *Would it be enough?*

Thirty One

My "escorts" deposited me none too gently through the door of the room in which Manuel and I were being held. After they slammed the door shut, Manuel rose from his cot with a look of deep concern on his face.

"Frank, are you all right?" he asked, inspecting me for damage

"I'm fine Manuel," I responded in a reassuring tone. "At least for now. But we need to get out of here - and the sooner the better."

I motioned for him to go back to the cot while I went to the peephole to make sure that no-one was outside listening in on our conversation. The corridor was clear. I then sat down next to Manuel and in a low voice told him what had transpired at my meeting with Dwight and his henchmen. His eyes glistened when I told him that his father had not yet acquiesced to their ransom demands but he blanched when I told him what I expected would happen next – one of his body parts sent to the U.S. as an inducement. I didn't add to his concerns by informing him of what they had in store for me, but he was undoubtedly smart enough to figure it out on his own.

"So how do we get out of here Frank?"

I told him what I had in mind. "And I need your help Manuel."

"I'm ready Frank. Whatever you say. Whatever I can do"

Considering his frail condition, I knew I couldn't expect too much from him. Plus, he had to save his strength for the rigors we would face later if my plan proceeded as I hoped it would.

"Okay Manuel," I said. "What I want you to do now is keep watch at the peephole and let me know the minute you hear or see anybody coming." He nodded his understanding.

"What time do they usually bring lunch?" I asked.

"It's hard to say exactly without a watch Frank. But I think around one o'clock."

"Okay Manuel. That should give me plenty of time to get started."

Manuel took up his position at the door while I went to my cot and lifted a corner of the mattress. In my previous inspection, I had noticed that under the mattress was a metal frame connected to the four corners by tightly-wound springs. With some tugging and pulling, I yanked out two of the springs and got to work.

My idea was to fashion a tool out of the springs, straightening one of the ends while keeping enough of the body of the spring to serve as a handle. As with many things what seemed simple in theory proved more difficult in practice. A pair of pliers and a vise to hold the spring would have made the job a lot easier but of course there were none to be had. Instead, I had to improvise by placing the spring on the floor and using my foot to try to straighten out one end. Without anything to hold the round spring securely, it took my several tries and a fair number of muffled curses before I began to enjoy some success.

After about an hour, I had managed to get the two springs into the shape I needed. While I worked, Manuel kept one eye on the peephole and one on my efforts. Luckily, there were no interruptions.

The next step would be trickier.

I went to the window and again inspected the vertical bars that stood between us and freedom. There were four of them set about eight inches apart. I thought that if I could somehow remove two of them, we could squeeze through and make our way to the courtyard below.

I grabbed the two in the middle with both hands and gave an experimental tug. As expected, there was no give. They seemed to be solidly in place. But I had also noted before that the plaster at the base of each one was cracked and beginning to flake away. My plan was to use my newly-fashioned tool to scrape away the plaster and see what lay at the base. My guess was that I would soon find adobe brick, into which the bottom of the bars rested. Given the age of the building, I thought I might have a chance to chip away at the mortar between the bricks and loosen the bars.

The question now was when to begin. I had no idea how much time I had before Dwight heard from his superiors and our fates were sealed. Chipping away at the plaster now was risky because what I was doing would be obvious to whoever brought us our meals. Waiting until after dinner would be the wisest course, *but did we have the time?*

I decided to talk it over with Manuel. He listened carefully and we eventually decided to risk the delay.

It made for a long and tense day. When we heard the key turn in the door at what we guessed was around one in the afternoon, we didn't know if it would be lunch or a more chilling prospect that included dismemberment and death. But it was just the usual pair of thugs with a tray of food.

As with the breakfast, the lunch was abundant. I presumed that his captors were worried about Manuel's state of health. They wanted to make sure he had enough strength to respond to a phone call from his father seeking definite proof that he was still alive before he submitted to their demands.

After about an hour, the two guys returned to take the tray and to escort us to the bathroom. Once we returned and the door was locked, I suggested we try to get some sleep. We would need it.

I lay down carefully on my cot, not entirely sure that it would hold me after I had removed the two connecting springs. I had taken them from opposite corners and as I stretched out, the frame groaned but held.

I wasn't sure I could sleep under the circumstances. But I closed my eyes and took deep breaths. The next thing I knew, Manuel was shaking my shoulder to wake me. He had heard footsteps coming down the corridor and wanted me prepared to face whatever might come next.

Swinging my legs over the side of the cot, I sat upright and rubbed the sleep out of my eyes. The light through the window was already beginning to fade and the only illumination in our room was from a single flickering light bulb over the door.

As the key turned in the lock, I clenched my fists, ready to put up a fight if necessary. The odds might have been stacked against me, but I would go down swinging.

When the door opened, I unclenched my fists. It looked as though we had caught a lucky break. It was the same two guys as before, one carrying a tray and the other one, the man whose nose I had broken, covering us with a gun. For some reason, which they didn't bother to explain, they were serving us dinner early. That was fine with me. It gave us more time to work on our escape.

We followed the usual routine. Neither of us was particularly hungry but we knew we would need all the sustenance we could get to endure the rigors ahead and we swallowed every bite.

This time, our two guardians came back after only about half an hour to pick up the tray and escort us to the bathroom. I wondered why the rush. *Was something in the works?* But I knew I wouldn't get an answer if I asked. I kept silent and thanked my lucky stars that at least for now it seemed we would have the time we needed to try to get out of our cell.

Once we were returned to our room, we waited for about fifteen minutes before we went into action. I again had Manuel take up his position at the door while I removed the two "tools" I had fashioned from the bed-springs and began to work.

At first, it went well. Using both hands and both tools, I attacked the plaster and mortar at the base of the two inner bars. As I suspected, it was old and crumbly and fell away quickly, making a pile on the floor at my feet.

It took me about twenty minutes to get rid of the surface matter. I thought about trying to push the debris under my cot in case our captors returned as it would be a dead giveaway as to what I was trying to do. But Manuel kept giving me a thumbs' up "all clear" sign as I worked and I decided to leave it where it lay.

Once I got to the adobe brick, the going got harder. The mortar between the bricks *was* aged, but there was a lot of it and it was tightly packed. As I chipped away at it, my hands began to cramp, forcing me to alternate between the right and the left. I was reasonably ambidextrous, but it still slowed me down.

After about an hour of laborious work, I was able to remove the bricks that held one of the bars and felt a sense of exultation. *This thing might work!*

My exhilaration was dampened, however, when I tugged at the bottom of the bar. I had hoped that with the leverage I could apply, I could pull it completely free. But it was still held firmly at the top and barely moved even when I exerted all my strength to try to wrench it out.

I saw Manuel give me a look of concern as I swore under my breath in frustration. I decided at this point to have him join me at the window. If someone were to come in, at this point there was no way to hide what we were up to. I figured it was more important to combine our efforts rather than for him to stay at the door.

I handed him the other bent spring and instructed him to begin work at the base of the other inner bar. I was concerned that he might not have the strength to make much of a dent, but he gave me a nod and a tight smile and began to chip away.

I lost track of time as we worked, our shoulders touching and both of us perspiring from the effort. We scraped our knuckles more than once as our improvised tools became slippery in our sweaty palms. And while we focused on our tasks, we also kept our ears open for any footsteps in the corridor, which undoubtedly would seal our fates. But our luck held and there were no unexpected visits.

Finally, our combined efforts were rewarded and the bars were loose enough to be removed. But just in case, I decided to keep them where they were for the time being. I didn't want somebody walking around the courtyard to spot the empty space before we were ready to wriggle out the window.

Manuel was exhausted by the effort he had made and I told him to sit on the cot and rest while I worked on our preparations. He seemed reluctant not to be doing his part, but I told him that he would need all his strength for what lay ahead.

Before he went to his cot, I removed his sheets and blankets as well as my own. We had at least a twenty foot drop from our window to the courtyard below. While I might be able to jump down without serious injury I doubted if Manuel, in his frail condition, could do the same. So I took a clue from the dozens of escape movies I had seen and began to twist our sheets into a rope that we could use to descend out the window without breaking any bones. I used some of the rope I fashioned to tie our blankets into bundles that we could carry on our backs. Fortunately, the blankets our captors had provided us were of heavy wool, designed to keep out the northern night chill. I speculated that this wasn't out of any special consideration on the part of our captors but rather because they didn't want to complicate further their situation by having Manuel come down with pneumonia.

Once I had the blankets rolled, I went to the window and attached the end of my makeshift rope to one of the bars to the side still anchored in the window. I was reasonably confident that it would hold our weight without coming loose although there was the chance that the excavation we had done on the other bars might have loosened the two remaining ones as well. It was a chance we would have to take.

"Okay Manuel," I said. "I think we're about ready."

While I had been working, Manuel had lain down on the cot and had tried unsuccessfully to doze off. When I spoke, he pulled himself upright and I could see a gleam in his eyes as he straightened his shoulders. I hoped the gleam was from anticipation and not, as I was afraid it might be, from a fever. He was trembling slightly, but that could have been due to the cold wind that was coming through the window; or perhaps from a fear of the unknown that lay ahead of us.

"Okay Frank," he said, his voice low. Then with a grin, he added, "Let's get the hell out of here."

I returned his grin. Reassured by the gumption he was showing, I moved to the door and looked out the peephole. There was no sign of anybody in the corridor and no sounds reached me. I didn't know exactly what time it was, but guessed that it was after midnight. I hoped that all of our captors were fast asleep and had not placed any guards on night duty.

Reaching up and using my handkerchief as a buffer, I unscrewed the light bulb above our door. Taking a few seconds to adjust my eyes to the dark, I then went to the window and looked outside. There was a full moon that bathed everything in a ghostly light. It was one of those "good news, bad news" things. It helped me to see clearly if anyone was keeping watch to make sure we didn't escape. But the moonlight also would expose us as we made our way out the window and onto the courtyard. We could only hope that it would work in our favor. I didn't see anyone outside nor could I hear any voices. The only sounds were the chirping of insects and the occasional cry of some animal in the distance.

I removed the two bars, putting them softly onto the floor. Then, I picked up the rolled sheets and dropped them out the window. Leaning over, I was pleased to see that they almost reached the ground.

Manuel and I had agreed beforehand that I would go out the window first. Once on the courtyard, I could help him break a fall if, in his weakened condition, he slipped from the rope.

Pulling my cot over to where it was directly under the window, I used it as a stepping-stone to boost myself up onto the ledge. Grabbing the two remaining bars in both hands, I scrambled up the wall and managed to get my legs out the window. It was a maneuver that would have made an acrobat proud.

Halfway out the window, I let go of the bar on my left and grabbed the twisted sheets. Holding on to them with a death grip, I released my right hand from the bar and then switched it over to join my left, praying that the sheets wouldn't rip. They held and I slowly made my way hand over hand down to the courtyard.

At any moment I expected to hear a cry of alarm – or perhaps the crack of a rifle shot. But there was only silence as my feet touched the ground.

I looked up and could see Manuel holding one of the bundles I had made. Without a word, he dropped the first one into my waiting arms. The second bundle soon followed. I put both of them on the ground next to me and waited for Manuel to make his descent.

Thanks to the moonlight, I could see his face clearly above me, looking down at where I stood waiting for him. His face disappeared for a moment and then I saw his feet dangling over the window ledge. I don't know if he copied my maneuver or not but the next thing I saw was him grabbing the twisted sheets with both hands and, like a gymnast, wrapping his feet around them as well.

A few seconds later he was on the courtyard floor beside me, a look of excitement on his face. I gave him a silent nod and a wink. We had agreed to keep silent until we were well away from the hacienda.

Our next step was to get beyond the external wall. I had thought about trying to find the principal doorway, which was out of view from our room. But I figured it would be well secured and impossible to budge. Moreover, there might be a guard posted there.

Our best option was to try to scale the wall. The quickest way to the wall from where we were was directly across the courtyard. But the moonlight illuminated that path as though it were a stage in a theater.

So instead, we hugged the interior walls and headed to a place where the shadows would help cover our escape.

It took us about five minutes of moving in a stop-and-go fashion, half the time crouched over so we would not be seen, to get where we were going. Now came the tricky part. The wall was only about ten feet high, but the broken glass on top could rip us to shreds. However, we were ready. With my back to the wall, I put my hands together and Manuel, facing me, grabbed my shoulders and put his right foot into my improvised stirrup. On his back, held by some extra rope that I had fashioned from the sheets, were the two bundles made from our blankets.

When I gave him the signal by bobbing my head, he hoisted himself up towards the top of the wall. In this instance, his weight loss worked to our advantage. While I wouldn't describe him as light as a feather, I was able to absorb the burden of his weight without buckling.

My hands were at chest level when he put his feet on my shoulders, straddling me. We were both breathing heavily from the exertion but that was the only sound we made.

I held Manuel's ankles to my shoulders while he placed the blanket bundles over the broken glass. Then I felt his feet leave my shoulders as he pulled himself on top of the blankets. I half expected to hear him cry out in pain if the cushion of the blankets was not sufficient to keep his flesh from the glass. But all I heard was his labored breathing.

Looking up I could only see the lower half of his body as he lay prone on top of the wall. Then I saw the extra rope I had fashioned curling down towards my face. I grabbed it in both hands and gave a gentle tug. That was the signal for Manuel to use the other end of the rope to drop down to the other side while I held on to support him.

At that signal, his legs disappeared and I held on tightly to my end as he descended down the other side. The plan was for him to try to find something solid to tie the twisted sheets to so that I could use them to make my own climb over the wall. Manuel insisted that he could provide enough ballast to support me. But after considerable argument, he reluctantly agreed that if nothing was available on the other side, he was to leave me to my own devices. And if I wasn't over the wall in five minutes, he was to take off on his own. If it came to that, I told him, the most important thing was for him to get free and clear. I didn't mention that I thought, given his condition, the chances of him getting away alone were slim indeed.

The only thing I could do now was to wait. I could hear Manuel's footsteps outside the wall and kept a firm grip on my end of the twisted sheets as I counted the seconds. In less than a minute I felt two tugs on my end, our prearranged signal that Manuel had succeeded in securing the other end to something solid.

As I began to pull myself up, I had a moment of panic. The thought crossed my mind that if – contrary to our agreement - it *was* only Manuel on the other end or if the improvised rope should somehow tear. Then I might soon find myself flat on my back on the courtyard floor with some broken bones. But the twisted sheets held and in a few seconds I was at the top of the wall. Getting my feet under me, but remaining crouched over so that I would not make a visible target, I stepped carefully over the broken glass and picked up the two blanket bundles and tossed them down to Manuel. Then I turned around and slowly put my legs over the side of the wall, grabbing onto the top with both hands. I looked down and saw that the earth below me was smooth and that only a drop of about five feet awaited me. I let go and hit the ground with a soft thud, none the worse for wear. Manuel was at my side to steady me just in case.

He had found a hardy shrub close to the wall and had attached the other end of our twisted sheets to it. I went to the shrub and untied the makeshift rope and wrapped it around my waist. Removing the evidence of how we escaped probably wouldn't do us much good once our captors found out we were gone. But I didn't see any reason to make things easy for them. Besides, the sheets might come in handy if we had to navigate steep terrain.

Rejoining Manuel, who was waiting in the shadows of the wall, he and I shared a brief congratulatory *abrazo. We were out!* Everything so far had gone exactly as planned. We had carried out each step quickly and smoothly and without uttering a sound. But these were just the first steps. Equal if not greater challenges lay ahead. We had gotten out of our prison but we were still a long way from being free.

Thirty Two

In the shelter of the wall, Manuel and I made preparations for the next stage of our escape. I had kept one of the tools I had fashioned from the bed spring and used it to cut a slit in each blanket. We both had sweaters and jackets, but the makeshift ponchos provided extra protection against the cold. Mine fit reasonably well but Manuel's hung loose on his bony frame.

Our main concern now was to put as much distance between ourselves and the hacienda as we could. *But which way to go?* Neither of us had a precise idea of just where we were and how to get to a place where we would be safe. I had made a rough estimate of the compass points by the direction of the sun during the day and what I could make out of the southern constellations at night. As best I could tell, we were presently facing north and Salta lay somewhere to our east. If those calculations were correct, then the most direct route would be to turn right and start walking.

That had been my plan during the day when I looked out the window. But now that I was on the outside with a better view, I saw that there was nothing but open and relatively flat ground to our right, with little in the way of shelter. It was the easier route but also the most dangerous. If we were spotted in the open terrain, we would be sitting ducks.

The safest route would be to head for a ridge outlined directly in front of us. It meant going down a slight incline for what I judged to be about half a mile and then ascending a rather steep grade for a distance I couldn't adequately measure from where we stood. It would be tough going, but it would have the advantage of providing more cover. And, hopefully, once we crested the ridge, we would find a path that would lead us eastward towards Salta.

I explained my reasoning to Manuel in a whisper. He nodded in agreement and we headed off towards the distant ridge.

At first, things went smoothly. The path we took was on a slight downhill incline and the footing underneath was firm. The moonlight illuminated our way and helped us avoid the rocks and desert-like vegetation in our path. I took some comfort in the fact that as we passed through stands of cactus that were at our height or higher, anyone who might be looking from the hacienda would have a hard time distinguishing us from the surrounding plants.

From time to time, I threw a glance over my shoulder to keep an eye on Manuel, who was following carefully in my footsteps. So far he seemed to be holding up okay. I was also encouraged by the fact that there was no sign from the hacienda, the outlines of which were becoming increasingly distant, that our escape had yet been discovered.

It took us about forty minutes to get to the bottom of the incline. We had reached a dry arroyo and I decided to take a little break before we began our ascent.

"How are you doing Manuel?" I asked.

He flashed a grin. "Fine Frank. Just fine."

Manuel looked all right, but I suspected that he was still feeling the effects of the surge of excitement we both had experienced during our successful escape from the hacienda and our first taste of freedom. Stiffer challenges lay ahead and I was worried about his condition once the adrenaline high wore off.

We sat down on the ground to rest, facing the hacienda. There were still no signs of alarm. "Let's get going Manuel," I said after about five minutes had passed. "We have to get to the top of the ridge before Dwight and his friends discover we are missing."

"Right behind you Frank," Manuel replied.

There was no clear path to the top, so I blazed a trail through small trees, rock outcroppings, and the occasional cactus. The incline was not exceptionally steep, but it was steady and there were places where we had to grab hold of rocks and tree trunks to keep ourselves upright and move forward.

We were about a third of the way to the crest when I heard Manuel give a cry of pain. When I turned, I saw him fall to the ground and grab his right ankle.

"Easy Manuel," I said, rushing to his side. "What happened?" I asked, even though I had a pretty good idea.

"I'm sorry Frank," he whispered through clenched teeth, "I must have tripped over something and hurt my ankle."

"Let me have a look."

I took off his shoe and pulled down his sock. There was a nasty bruise on the inside of his ankle where the bone protruded and I thought I detected some swelling.

"Can you wiggle your toes?" I asked.

He did, stifling a cry of anguish. "I don't think it's broken," he said. "It's just a sprain."

I hoped he was right. He was a medical student after all. But perhaps the desperation of the moment also had something to do with his self-diagnosis. Whatever it was I had to do something to get him moving again.

The twisted sheets I had brought with me came in handy sooner than I had expected. Unwinding a section from around my waist, I used the sharpened spring to cut off about a yard of the material. Then I used the cloth to wrap up Manuel's ankle as best I could. He was in considerable pain, but kept his cries muffled as I went about my task.

"It looks as though you've had some practice at this Frank," he said with a note of approval.

"I used to tape my ankles religiously every time I went onto the basketball court."

"Did you ever have any injuries?"

"Not to my ankles. But my nose took more than a few blows from flying elbows," I said with a smile.

Once I had finished wrapping Manuel's ankle, I helped him put his sock and his shoe back on, making sure the laces were tight and tucking them in so that he wouldn't trip over them. Then I helped him to his feet and asked him to try walking. He stepped gingerly forward and I saw him grimace in pain.

"Let's take it nice and easy Manuel," I said. Moving to his side, I told him to put his right arm over my shoulder for support while I put my left hand around his waist.

"Thanks Frank," he said. "Once we get moving again, my ankle should feel better and I can manage on my own."

I had serious doubts on that score. Maybe if we were walking on flat terrain he could manage. But we were climbing over rocks and roots in a steady ascent, demanding enough under the best of circumstances.

"Okay Manuel," I said, trying my best to sound encouraging.

It didn't take long to figure out that we weren't going to be able to make it to the top with our version of a three-legged race. It was just too awkward. Manuel did his best to help out, putting his right foot down as often as he could to relieve the burden. But each time he did I could hear him grunt with pain at the effort. He obviously had a serious sprain and he wasn't going to feel any better as time progressed. If anything, it would get worse.

After about fifteen minutes of practically dragging him over the ground, I told him to stop and lean against a large rock.

"Look Manuel," I said. "This isn't working. What I want to do is…."

He interrupted. "I know Frank. I know. The best thing is for you to leave me here. You can get away and come back with help. I'll try to find a place to hide and…"

I cut him off. "No way Manuel. We've already discussed this. I'm not leaving you here and that's that. No arguments, okay."

"That was what we agreed to Frank," he said with a pained expression on his face. "But that was before I hurt my ankle. I'm just too much of a burden. I'm slowing you down. And if those guys in the hacienda track us down, what can we do with me unable to move? Please, just get going. I'll be all right."

He had a point. But I wasn't ready to concede it. "Here's what we're going to do Manuel. I'm going to carry you to the top of the ridge. Once we get over, we'll be out of sight of the hacienda. And it should be easier for both of us going down on the other side. Now let's get going. We're just wasting time here."

He was about to protest. Before he could I grabbed him by the arms and slung him over my shoulders. My sudden maneuver caught him off guard. He gave a little cry that mixed surprise and pain. At first he tried to struggle, but I told him to keep quiet and stop wriggling. "Okay Frank," he said resignedly, "Whatever you say."

As I moved on up the hill, I felt confident that I had done the right thing. I guessed that Manuel only weighed about one hundred and thirty pounds at the most. And over the first fifty yards or so, we went about twice as fast as we had when I had been supporting him on the ground. But then reality began to set in. The incline grew steeper, the trail I was trying to blaze rockier and rougher, and the burden I was carrying even heavier. A couple of times I tripped over some unseen obstacle and almost tumbled to the ground, barely able to regain my balance to avert disaster. Manuel uttered muffled gasps as I stumbled but otherwise maintained a stoic silence.

The moonlight helped, but there were shadows that obscured obstacles along the way. So I kept my eyes peeled to the ground as I kept heading upwards.

I had been carrying Manuel for about twenty minutes when the effort and the altitude began to have a noticeable effect. My breathing became more and more labored and I could feel my heart pounding in my chest. The muscles of my leg began to register the pain and discomfort of the climb and I started to feel dizzy and light-headed.

I stopped for a moment to rest, putting Manuel down carefully so as not to jar his ankle. He could see that I was in some distress but didn't say anything, instead giving me a look of sympathy. I tried to reassure him. "It's okay Manuel. We're going to make it. I just need a breather."

He simply nodded his face expressionless. By now, I hoped, he realized that arguing with me was useless. We either would make it my way or we wouldn't.

I took advantage of the break to look back at the hacienda. Again, there were no signs of life. Then I shifted my gaze upward. It was hard to tell, but I thought the top of the ridge was about half a mile away. I gave Manuel a grin and said, "Just a little bit longer and we'll be at the top."

He had been looking in the same direction and I could see the skepticism etched in his face. But he didn't resist when I bent down and lifted him over my shoulders, carrying him as a fireman would if we were exiting a burning building, holding his head and shoulders with my right hand and his legs with my left. The thought that passed through my mind was that playing the role of a fireman carrying an incapacitated resident from a blaze was not a bad metaphor for the current situation we were in.

The rest had helped, but soon I was feeling the pain return and breathing becoming more difficult. There was nothing to be done but resolutely put one foot in front of the other and try to ignore the pain. It helped to think back on basketball games that had gone into overtime, when it felt as though my body wouldn't let me continue to drive for the basket or to guard my man. But somehow I found the resources to do so. Mind over matter, I suppose.

I lost track of time as I plugged ahead. Just as spots began to appear in front of my eyes and I was afraid I was going to pass out, I heard Manuel, who had remained silent, whisper in my ear. "Look Frank. Look ahead." There was a note of excitement in his voice.

I stopped in my tracks and lifted my head. *We had made it!* Just a few feet more and we would be at the top of the ridge. I managed to summon enough energy to shuffle the remaining distance. Then with a deep sigh of relief came to a halt and bent over to let Manuel down as gently as I could. As soon as he was on his feet, gingerly favoring his twisted ankle, I sank to the ground and lay prone on my back. There were rocks underneath me, but I didn't care. I looked up at the clear night sky, filled with stars, and took in deep gulps of the crisp night air.

After about thirty seconds, I realized with a shock that while I was lying on the ground, Manuel was still standing. If anyone was looking for us, his profile could be seen from miles away. "Manuel," I almost shouted, "Get down. Get down."

He immediately caught on to my concern. As quickly as he could he lay down flat next to me. "Sorry Frank," he said. "I wasn't thinking."

"That's all right Manuel," I said. "I wasn't either."

Turning over, I crept forward on my belly to take a look at the hacienda. Even though we were now what I estimated to be three miles away, I could see the building clearly. And what I saw sent a shiver down my spine. There were lights on now in the main house and outside the wall were floodlights. Thank goodness they had not been on when we made our escape.

Even from a distance, I could see the outlines of figures near a jeep that also had its lights on. It was too far away to tell exactly who they were, but I counted five figures. My guess was that the group included Smallwood, Schussler, and my old friend Dwight Whalen along with two of the three musclemen. They had undoubtedly discovered our escape and were probably leaving one of the men behind in case we decided to double back while they took after us.

We had some advantages. We had gotten a good head start and were now in a position to move beyond the ridge to where it would be more difficult to spot us. Moreover, while our pursuers knew that we had somehow gotten over the wall, I hoped they had no clear idea in which direction we had gone. And unless they had the kind of tracker you saw in the western movies, I doubted they could pick up our trail in the dark and over the rough terrain we had traversed.

I tried to guess what their plan of action would be. The smart thing would be to wait until daylight. Trying to track us down at night was akin to the needle-in-the- haystack approach. But maybe they weren't thinking too clearly, caught off guard by our escape and desperate to find us. If we got away, not only would their plan to use Manuel to exert pressure on his father fall apart but also there was a strong likelihood they would end up in prison. So why waste time waiting for dawn to break when they might get lucky and locate us before we had put too much distance between them and us?

And that seemed to be what was happening. I saw two figures get in the jeep. The sound of the doors closing reached me several seconds later. The jeep then began to move away from the hacienda, its lights casting long shadows on the ground. I breathed a sigh of relief when I saw the lights turn away from us and head south. That took two of the five out of the equation. *What about the other three?*

With the jeep and its lights now gone, I could barely make out the profiles of the three men. They were clustered together and I imagined they were discussing what to do next. I decided that whatever the result of their discussion, we had to get moving. There were still several hours until daybreak and we needed to take advantage of the cover of darkness. Once the sun was up, it would be more difficult to hide. And I didn't know exactly what resources our pursuers could call on. Perhaps there were more in their employ who could join the hunt. And maybe that was where the jeep was headed – to round up more men. And I couldn't discount the possibility that they could get hold of a small airplane to try and locate us.

There were other possibilities, but I figured there was no sense dwelling on them. I told Manuel what I had seen and he bobbed his head as I sketched out the likely scenarios. We both agreed that whatever our pursuer might decide, the only real choice we had was to stick to our plan to keep moving and put as much distance between us and them as we could.

Thirty Three

The walk down the other side of the ridge was only marginally easier than the ascent. While the incline was at a gentler angle, the footing underneath was still very rough and we had to watch every step.

Before we had left the crest, I had found a fallen tree branch that served as a crutch for Manuel. Nonetheless, he still had to lean on me from time to time.

Our progress was steady but slow. If either one of us happened to trip and fall it could mean big trouble. I did my best to stay patient, but had to fight an image of one or more of our pursuers appearing at the crest of the ridge and sending rifle bullets into our backs. Every once in a while, I looked over my shoulder towards the top of the hill behind us, but could see no one on the horizon.

We had been walking for what I guessed to be about two hours, when the incline began to level off and we could hear the sound of running water ahead of us. The first hint of dawn was making the sky lighter with pale streaks of pink and blue when we got to the banks of a sizeable stream.

If my calculations were correct, it ran from west to east. Our best bet, then, was to turn right and follow it in what I hoped was the direction to Salta.

"Let's rest here for a minute Manuel," I said, sitting down next to the stream. "Do you think the water is safe to drink?"

We had no water with us and we both had perspired heavily despite the night chill. And while having an early dinner had helped facilitate our escape from the hacienda it also meant that we were beginning to feel the effects of empty stomachs. I didn't see much prospect of any food coming our way in the next hours, but having a steady supply of water at hand would be a help and was another reason for us to stay close to the stream.

Manuel shrugged. "It should be. We are in an isolated area and the current is pretty strong, so there shouldn't be any contamination. Ordinarily, I wouldn't take the risk. But under these circumstances, what choice do we have?"

I gave him a smile. "Not much," I answered. Then I bent over the rushing water, cupped my hands, and began to take some generous gulps. The water was ice cold and I had to slow down my intake despite my thirst.

Manuel followed my example. After slurping up about a quart each, we sat back on the creek bank.

"I don't know about you Manuel," I said. "But I feel a lot better."

"Me too Frank," he replied." Let's hope we can say that about an hour from now."

"Ready to get going?" I asked.

"Whenever you are Frank," he replied.

I got on my feet first. Then I put a hand under Manuel's right armpit and helped hoist him up. He winced with pain but choked back any cry. Grabbing his make-shift crutch, he prepared to follow me alongside the creek.

By now, the sun had begun to rise directly in our faces, confirming we were indeed headed east. The morning light also revealed a rough path that ran parallel to the stream we were following. As we set out, we still encountered the occasional rock or root, but now we had the advantage of seeing them clearly so as to avoid tripping over them. Moreover, we were now more or less on level ground.

But it was another one of those "good news, bad news" situations. The going was easier and we could make better time. But the fact that we were following what appeared to be a well-worn path worried me. Trying to put myself in the mind of our pursuers, they might easily come to the conclusion that we were taking what was literally the "path of least resistance" and react accordingly by looking for us along the most likely route of our escape. I tried to put this "bad news" interpretation to one side, but it nagged at me nonetheless.

We had walked for about an hour when we stopped to rest. The sun was now well above the horizon and the day had begun to warm. The sky was cloudless and there was only a gentle breeze blowing, so we no longer needed our "ponchos," which we removed. I thought about discarding them altogether, but figured we should hold on to them just in case. I used the leftover rope to fashion a kind of backpack that would allow us to carry the blankets but keep our hands free, something that was especially important for Manuel. Even though his ankle seemed to be improving and he was making reasonably good time, he still needed his tree-branch crutch for support.

So far, we had felt no ill effects from drinking water from the stream. So, after relieving ourselves into the shrubs to our right, we swallowed more handfuls before taking off again.

The water helped, but the lack of food and our exertions were beginning to take their toll on both of us. We were beginning to run out of gas and our pace slowed significantly even though the going was easier. After about half an hour from our last break, Manuel, who was about ten feet behind me, called out, "Frank. I'm sorry, but I need to stop."

I turned and went to help him sit down on some cleared ground a few feet from the path.

"I'm sorry Frank," he said again. "But I'm just beat. Can we rest here? Maybe get a little sleep? Then we can go on."

I considered our options. There was no doubt that Manuel was running on empty. His face was haggard and his eyes drooped with fatigue. Given his weakened condition to begin with along with his sprained ankle, it was a minor miracle he had made it as far as he had. I thought about hoisting him onto my back again, but had to face the fact that I wasn't in much better shape than Manuel. I doubted I could get very far with the added burden. For a moment, I entertained the fanciful notion of fashioning some kind of raft so that we could sail down the stream to safety. But there was nothing nearby to use for such a purpose and the swift current over what looked to be a shallow and rock-filled stream made me quickly abandon that idea.

The only reasonable alternative, I finally decided, was to take the time to rest. We both needed it.

Looking around, I spied a small grove of what looked like willow trees. They would provide us some cover and were far enough from the path so that anyone following in our footsteps would likely pass by without seeing us.

Pointing in the direction of the grove, I helped Manuel up and said, "That's where we can try to get some rest."

"I'm sorry to be such a burden…."

I cut him off: "None of that Manuel. I'm as tired as you are. Let's see if we can get some rest."

We made our way into the grove and laid our blankets onto the bare ground. I was glad I had kept them. Manuel stretched out and almost immediately fell asleep, a sign of how close he was to the point of total collapse. I lay down on my blanket, not as confident that sleep would find me so quickly. I wondered whether I was making the right choice, but rationalized it with the thought that there was no sense in doing our pursuers a favor by succumbing to exhaustion as we tried to escape. The rationalization worked because before I knew it, I too was fast asleep.

Thirty Four

I woke with the sun shining directly in my eyes through the trees. Turning to my left, I saw Manuel a few feet away dead to the world. Then, for a few seconds, I wondered if that might be literally true. Perhaps everything he had gone through had finally taken its toll on his weakened and fragile body. But I could see the gentle rise and fall of his chest as he slept.

Sitting up, I tried to remember some of the dreams I had had, but couldn't. It took me a moment to orient myself and to remember just exactly where we were and what we were doing.

Getting to my feet, I took stock of my physical condition. The rest had done me good. I felt refreshed and some of my aches and pains had diminished. I decided to let Manuel sleep. I walked quietly to the stream and splashed water onto my face. Again I cupped my hands and took some healthy swallows.

As I turned back to where Manuel was sleeping, I was feeling pretty chipper. Even though we had seen no signs of the kind of human life that would help us complete our escape, I was confident that it we kept plugging along the path by the stream, eventually we would end up somewhere safe.

But at that very moment I was entertaining those cheery thoughts, I looked up to the crest of the ridge we had crossed and momentarily froze in my tracks. Quickly I ducked into the cover of the willow trees, praying that I had not been spotted. Peering up to the ridge line to make sure I wasn't imagining things, I saw three figures outlined against the clear blue sky. I couldn't make out their features, but could see that all three had rifles slung over their backs. They might have been hunters and even our salvation. But I didn't think so. I was probably half-right – they *were* hunters – *and we were the prey*!

Even though they were at least half a mile away, we were in an enclosed valley and sound carried. I tried to block out the noises of nature – the gurgling stream, the occasional squawk of a bird, the rustling of leaves – and pick up any human voices. Straining to hear, I was almost startled when I heard one of the three figures shout out: *"We know you're down there Corbett and we're coming to get you. Why don't you give up now and save us all a lot of trouble? We just want you and the boy back with us – no harm, no foul."*

Well that solved one mystery. The voice was unmistakably that of Roy Smallwood. How he had tracked us down was more of a mystery, but I presumed that my reasoning had been correct. They had figured out that we had gone north over the ridge and were following the easiest path east.

Solving those mysteries didn't do us a lot of good. I wasn't sure that Smallwood or the others had actually seen us. He was probably just trying to draw us out. And I didn't put any stock in his offer of surrender. I doubted they would shoot Manuel. They still needed him. But I was now clearly excess baggage and expendable.

I guessed that Smallwood would give his ploy some time to work. But when it didn't, he and his two companions would be heading down the ridge and on our tail. I estimated that in daylight and in better shape than we had been when we made the descent, they would reach the trail in half an hour at the most.

Smallwood's yell had awakened Manuel, who rubbed his eyes and sat up. I put my finger over my mouth in a signal to be quiet and while he looked confused, he got the message. I moved over to his side and in a low voice told him what I had seen.

At first, he looked scared and confused. But then, as I explained what we were going to do next, that look was replaced with one of grim determination. We had come too far, it seemed to say, to give up now.

I told Manuel to stay where he was while I moved further into the grove of trees to a spot where I could see Smallwood and company but was sure they could not see me. As soon as I spied them leave the ridge and begin their descent, I signaled to Manuel that it was time for us to get going. But before we headed for the path, I instructed him to head for the stream and to drink as much water as he could.

I helped him stand up, giving him his makeshift crutch, and walked with him to the stream. As I had done a few minutes earlier, he splashed some on his face and then took some healthy swallows. We were running a risk in delaying our departure, but we needed the water badly. The sun was still shining brightly overhead and despite the occasional breeze it was getting warmer by the minute. We still had our blanket rolls and I debated leaving them behind. But for what I had in mind, they still might come in handy so we hoisted them onto our backs and headed down the path.

There wasn't much cover to protect us as we made our way. My hope – and it was only that – a hope – was that our pursuers would be focusing on blazing their own trail down the ridge, just as we had done last night and would be so occupied that they would not spot us on the trail. I also had to hope that when Smallwood had shouted out, he still hadn't seen us and was just playing the odds. I kept my fingers crossed that when he and his two companions had crested the ridge at the particular location where I had seen them, it had just been a lucky chance and that they still had no definitive proof that we had taken the route they had presumed we had. Still, I couldn't shake the fear that any second I would hear the boom of a rifle and a millisecond later feel a bullet enter my body.

Pushing on ahead, I looked for a place that would serve the purpose I had in mind. As I had explained to Manuel, unless I was sorely mistaken, it was only a matter of time before Smallwood and his friends caught up with us. We couldn't outrun them. When I told him this, he protested: "Maybe *we* can't outrun them Frank," he said, pointing to his ankle, "But *you* could. Why don't you…"

"Look Manuel. I'm getting tired of this. You need to get it through that thick head of yours that I'm just not going to leave you, no matter what. Besides, who knows if the three men I saw are the only ones in the vicinity who are after us. There might be more down the path and Smallwood is just trying to lead us into a trap, kind of like the beaters in an African safari. So if I leave you behind, they get both of us, one way or the other."

I don't think he bought my reasoning, but simply shrugged: "Whatever you say Frank."

Then I laid out the plan. It was really pretty straightforward. We would set up an ambush and use the element of surprise to our advantage. If all went well, we would put our pursuers out of commission and take their weapons, which would prepare us for other pursuers who might show up along the way.

In theory, of course, it sounded simple. But the practice would be another matter. And while I had a few thoughts whirring around in my head as to how we might accomplish this minor miracle, some of the details had yet to be worked out. I consoled myself with the thought that we really didn't have any viable options. This wasn't a Hollywood Western and we couldn't expect the cavalry to come to our rescue. If we were to get out of the jam we were in, we would have to do it ourselves.

Thirty Five

We had walked for about forty-five minutes and I was beginning to get discouraged. While there were the occasional trees and rocks on either side of us, there was nothing that would sufficiently hide us from our pursuers for my plan to work. I had no idea how close Smallwood and his companions might be behind us. But I knew that time was running short. I was still feeling pretty good and kept up a steady pace, but every ten minutes or so I had to stop either to give Manuel a breather or help him navigate a rough patch of ground.

Just as I was about to give up my original idea and try to come up with another plan, my prayers were answered. As we turned a bend, I saw no more than twenty feet in front of us that a rockslide had blocked much of the path. Ordinarily, I would have cursed the fates for the obstacle in our way. But in this instance, it was heaven-sent.

As we got closer, I saw that someone had removed some of the smaller rocks to create a continuation of the path we were following. It was barely wide enough for one man to pass through the pile of boulders on either side, which were at about eye-level. I had to turn and go through sideways while the skinnier Manuel was able to scrape through without turning. The footing underneath was all rocks and we both had to be careful as we navigated the gap, which ran about fifteen feet, before we managed to clear the slide.

Once we were on the other side, I told Manuel that this was where we were going to make our stand. "And the first thing we need to do is to gather some rocks."

The look on his face seemed to say that the best place to look for rocks would be inside my head. But he knew what I had in mind and headed towards the stream to find what we needed – and also, as I advised, to drink some more water.

While he was doing that, I took off my blanket pack and loosed the length of rope that I had made with twisted sheets. Disentangling it, I laid it on the ground, untwisting one of the ends so that it formed a pocket about twelve inches in length and eight inches across. Then I scoured the ground around me for a suitable rock. There were plenty around and it didn't take long for me to find one that was perfect for what I had in mind. It was smooth and round, a little bigger than a baseball. I fitted it into the open end of my rope and re-tied it so that the rock was now firmly secured at one end. I picked it up and tested it, swinging it back and forth until I was sure that it would do what I wanted it to do when the time came, taking care not to hit myself with the business end as I did so.

I was taking a page from the Argentine *gauchos*, fashioning a kind of *bolas* for my own use. It would only have one heavy rock rather than the traditional three and I was planning to use it on a human, not an animal, but the principle was the same.

Just as I finished fashioning my *bolas*, Manuel returned from his expedition. He had used his blanket to carry about a dozen smooth rocks, which he displayed with a certain amount of pride.

"That's great Manuel," I said, patting him on the shoulder. "Now let's find a place for you to hide where you won't be seen."

I walked with him towards the stream until I found a place that would serve our purposes. Up to that point, the accumulated boulders were at eye level, but about ten feet from the water they were only about waist high. Manuel could crouch down behind them and still be out of sight. They also would allow him to cause the distraction that was vital for my plan to work.

After I left Manuel with his pile of rocks and instructions, I returned to where I had left my gear. The outcropping of boulders where I was located was taller than I was and provided a perfect cover for the ambush I hoped to spring. I didn't know how many armed men I would be dealing with, but had to assume that it would include at least Smallwood and the two I had seen with him on the ridge. Outnumbered and outgunned, I had to count on the element of surprise. And I had to hope that my pursuers would assume that we were trying to outrun them and were not prepared to stand and fight.

The place we were in was perfect for what I had in mind. The way the rockslide had occurred allowed for few options to get to the other side except to follow the path we had taken. Any detours would be difficult and time consuming. My only fear was that Smallwood, or someone else, would see immediately, as I had, that this was a perfect place for an ambush and take extra precautions. The idea crossed my mind that maybe they would decide not to take the risk and simply stay on the other side from where I was hiding until reinforcements arrived, perhaps coming up behind us. If so, there was little I could do about it. I had no choice but to prepare as best I could and hope for the best.

I hunkered down behind the large boulders and tried to make myself comfortable. The sky was still cloudless and the sun was making the day ever warmer. I could feel sweat break out on my brow and attributed it to one part the sun and one part nerves. Sitting quietly, I made a tempting target for some of the biggest horse-flies I had ever seen who seemed hell-bent on tormenting me. I brushed them away as best I could.

I was in the middle of defending myself from another onslaught, when I heard the distinctive sound of someone's booted foot disturbing the smaller rocks that lined the path. Moving carefully, I slowly stood up and took a careful peek around the boulders, praying that I would not be seen.

It was what I had expected. About twenty feet from where I was hiding was one of the musclemen who had been at the hacienda. Fortunately, at that moment I peeked out, he had stopped and was looking over his shoulder, apparently receiving instructions from someone I couldn't see. My guess was that the person giving the orders was Smallwood, who, sensing the possibility of an ambush, was letting one of his charges go through first. If there were to be any surprises, he didn't want to be the one to suffer the consequences. Before I ducked back down, I saw that the muscleman had moved the rifle slung on his back to his hands. He held it pointed straight ahead, ready to fire.

I reached down and grabbed the end of my *bolas*, getting ready to spring into action. I couldn't risk another look, so I tried to block out the buzz of the flies, the gurgle of the nearby stream, and the occasional bird call and focus on the sound of leather against rock.

It took only a few seconds for me to hear the muscleman resume moving in my direction. His pace was slow and I tried to develop a mental image of just how long it would take him to reach the spot where I would attack him. As his footsteps got nearer, I resisted the temptation to lunge out prematurely. Instead, I took deep breaths and told myself to be patient.

I got lucky. Even though he had been moving slowly and quietly, his foot slipped on a rock and he couldn't help but give a brief cry that told me he was just where I wanted him. Of course, he still had the advantage of being armed and prepared for the possibility of an ambush. But I was ready. I gave out a sound that I hoped imitated one of the local birds. As soon as Manuel heard our pre-arranged signal, he began to hurl the rocks he had collected in the general direction of where our pursuer now stood. I wasn't expecting any of the rocks to find their mark, but did expect them to distract him sufficiently for me to use my *bolas*.

It worked to perfection. Stepping out from where I was hiding, I saw the muscle-man turned in Manuel's direction, raising his rifle. Swinging my makeshift weapon with all the force and velocity I could muster, I hit him directly on the right side of his forehead. The sound was sickening, like taking a baseball bat to an overripe pumpkin. The muscleman fell to the ground without uttering a sound, his skull cracked

Almost simultaneously, rifle shots began to ping off the boulders around me. From the volume, I couldn't tell if they came from more than one shooter. Luckily, the rifle that the guy I had knocked out had fallen onto the path and I was able to reach its barrel and pull it towards me during a brief lull in the firing.

By prearrangement, Manuel and I had agreed that we would maintain silence unless verbal communication became absolutely necessary. I was sure that he must be desperate to know if our plan had worked. But I didn't dare shout out anything to him with one or more of our pursuers firing in our direction. I could only hope that he stayed down and out of sight.

The rifle I finally had in my hands was a familiar one – a standard army-issue M-16. Even though I had not had the occasion to fire it in live action in Vietnam, I had trained with it and still remembered how to disassemble and reassemble it with my eyes closed.

I saw that it was fully loaded, with twenty rounds in the magazine. I switched it to semi-automatic, planning to use short bursts. I knew that

I had to conserve ammunition. While I now had the advantage of being armed, I had lost the advantage of surprise. And I had to presume that whoever was firing at me – probably Smallwood and perhaps the other man I had seen – were at least equally equipped and undoubtedly with more ammunition and fire-power in reserve.

After about a minute of rather constant fire, all of sudden there was dead silence. I guessed that whoever was on the other side had decided that it was a waste of ammunition to keep sending bullets into the heavy boulders that provided our cover.

My pursuers and I were now in a standoff. I couldn't move without being cut down by rifle fire and they couldn't advance knowing that I was now armed. I suspected they might try to buy some time by either waiting for reinforcements or trying somehow to encircle us. That meant I would have to make some kind of move before too long. But for the moment, I just stayed silent and held my ground.

Five or so minutes passed before the silence was broken with the sound of Roy Smallwood's voice. "Hey Corbett," he shouted. "What do you say we make a deal? You give us the kid and we let you go. How about it?"

What did he think I was? A total moron? There was no way he and Dwight were going to let me get away. I knew too much. Besides, there was also no way I was going to abandon Manuel. But just as I was about to tell him to take a flying leap, I heard Manuel yell out, "Okay Mister Smallwood. You've got a deal. Just spare Frank."

If I had been next to Manuel, I would have punched him. *What was he doing?* From where I was, I couldn't see him. But I had to presume that he was about to show himself to Smallwood. They still needed him, so I didn't think he would be harmed. But once they had him under their control again, we would be back to square one – and that wasn't something I was about to let happen.

I decided to take the risk and again peek around from the boulder that hid me. Once again, I was incredibly lucky. Some thirty feet away was Smallwood, his own M-16 at his shoulder. But instead of it being pointed in my direction, he was looking to his left where he had heard Manuel's voice. I didn't hesitate. In one continuous motion, I raised the rifle I had captured and sent three deadly rounds in Smallwood's direction. My scores on the army rifle range had been about average. Moreover, it had been some years since I had held a rifle in my hands. But it didn't matter. All three rounds found their mark and Smallwood fell to the ground, blood spurting from the three holes in his chest.

My adrenaline was racing. I had never shot at anyone before and now, in the space of a few minutes, I was pretty sure I had killed two men. I took deep breaths and tried to think clearly. Two of our pursuers were down, *but what about the third?* He must still be out there, waiting for us to show our heads and then trying to finish us off. Suddenly, I thought of Manuel. I didn't know if his offer to surrender had been genuine or a ploy to catch Smallwood off guard. Moreover, he might have concluded that the three shots he had heard had been intended for me.

By now, there was no sense hiding our presence. I cried out, "Manuel. It's me Frank. I'm okay. Our plan worked and I got Smallwood and the other man. But we're not out of the woods yet. Stay down. There is a third man somewhere out there and…"

He shouted back. "Frank. Frank. Thank God you're okay. I heard all those shots and I was afraid you had been hit."

"No. I'm still in one piece. And I've got a weapon. So just sit tight."

"Sure thing Frank. Sure thing," he yelled back.

I kept under cover, crouching behind my protective boulders, the M-16 in my hands. From time to time, I took a look around the edge. I could see the man I had hit in the face with my improvised *bolas*, flat on his back, blood seeping from his mouth and ears and his eyes staring sightlessly up at the blue sky. The flies that had bedeviled me were beginning to buzz around him. Looking up I saw some carrion birds begin to circle. Farther on, although I couldn't see his body as clearly, Smallwood lay in the same position.

I thought about venturing out to retrieve Smallwood's weapon but decided it wasn't worth the risk. If the third man was out there and I broke cover, I would be an easy target. Besides, Smallwood had fired so many bullets at me there might not be enough ammunition left in his weapon to make the risk worth the gamble.

So I followed my own advice to Manuel and just sat tight. After all the noise of the exchange of fire, the ensuing silence was almost surreal. I kept my ears attuned for anything unusual – another boot scraping on rocks, the splash of somebody fording the creek, the snick of a rifle bolt - but there was nothing.

It would have been tempting to stay put. We were in as good a defensive position as we could have hoped for and were likely to find. And maybe someone not connected with our pursuers had heard the shots, would come to investigate what had happened, and would help us escape.

But these were idle thoughts. We had to keep moving. The buzzards floating overhead were descending ever closer to the two exposed bodies and for anybody looking for us, were a clear signal as to our location.

Ten minutes had passed and there was no sign of the third man. Maybe he had been left behind, maybe he had taken a different route to try to head us off – and maybe he was hidden just out of sight ready to pick us off. We would just have to take our chances. So far, our gambles and our plans had worked out just as we had hoped. I could only hope that our luck would continue to hold.

Thirty Six

"Manuel," I shouted. "I'm coming to you. Hold on. I'll be there in just a minute."

I figured that by this point, after all the yelling and gunfire, if anybody was listening to us it didn't make much difference if he knew whether I was with Manuel or not. And I didn't want Manuel to be surprised when I suddenly appeared from around the bend of rocks to his location.

I carefully stood up with the M-16 pointed through the gap in the boulders, ready to fire. There was no sign of the third man. Taking one last look at the area beyond where Smallwood's body lay, I moved quickly over the opening between the boulders. Within ten seconds I was crouching down with Manuel in his hiding place.

He greeted me with a broad grin and an *abrazo*. "You did it Frank. Just as you planned."

"*We* did it Manuel. Without your distractions, it never would have worked. We make a pretty good team." I decided not to ask him if his offer to surrender had been genuine. Whatever the intent, it had done the trick and had helped me bring Smallwood down.

"Listen, "I told him. "We can't stay here forever. We need to get moving. How are you feeling? Are you up to it?"

He didn't look all that great. His face was haggard and his skin had an unhealthy pallor. But there was a look of determination in his eyes and his voice was steady. "You bet I am Frank. We've come too far to stop now. But what about the third man you mentioned?"

"He may still be out there - perhaps behind us or maybe ahead of us. But we have to press on." Pointing to the birds overhead that were now beginning to descend, I said, "Those vultures are going to attract attention and we need to put as much distance between ourselves and this place as fast as we can. And if the third man is on our trail," I said, brandishing the M-16, "at least we have something on our side we didn't have before."

I told Manuel to go ahead of me back to the path while I followed with my back to him and my gun aimed to the west where I figured the "third man" would be. I also told him to keep low and continue to take advantage of the protection the rockslide had provided. Once we got on the path and resumed our journey eastward, we still stayed crouched for about twenty yards. No shots rang out and after we had passed a bend and were moving through a small grove of trees, we assumed our normal upright posture and began to proceed more quickly.

The sun was now at our back and I estimated that it was sometime in the mid-afternoon, maybe around three o'clock. I took the lead again, my head on a swivel, my eyes scanning the terrain ahead and behind, ready to fire my M-16 at a moment's notice.

After about thirty minutes, we took a break. Manuel was doing his best to keep up but was still hampered by his damaged ankle. I sat him down on a rock and took off his shoe. Carefully unraveling the support bandage I had applied, I saw that the swelling had gone down a bit. I rewrapped it and then searched around for a sturdy branch that could serve as a cane and help take some of the pressure off. The one Manuel had used during the night had gotten misplaced in the confusion of the ambush. It only took me a few minutes of looking around to find a suitable replacement.

Before resuming, we took a minute to go to the stream and drink more water. It helped, but we both were beginning to feel the effects of no food. I wasn't sure how long either of us would be able to keep up the pace we were maintaining. But desperation and necessity had taken us this far and we had to hope that it would continue to carry us forward.

We had walked for about an hour longer when we saw a welcome sight. Just ahead of us, there were some twenty sheep grazing on both sides of the path. I hoped their presence meant that somewhere not too far away was a shepherd or a farmer who could offer us some assistance. For a moment, too, I entertained shooting one of the sheep and carrying its carcass with us for dinner that night. But I had no knife and no matches to make a fire. Plus, carrying it would slow me down. I discarded the idea as impractical. But the image of roasting lamb caused my mouth to water.

I kept in reserve the idea that there would be more sheep further on. If we had to bed down for the night, perhaps I could improvise enough to provide us with much-needed food.

Manuel heard me utter a low chuckle as I spun this fantasy. "What is it Frank?" he asked.

When I told him, he laughed too. But he also gave me a look that said: *Is Frank beginning to lose it?* And maybe he was right. The accumulation of all we had been through was undoubtedly taking its toll, both physically and mentally. I shook my head from side to clear the cobwebs and did my best to bring myself back to reality.

We passed through the grazing sheep and continued to forge ahead. About half a mile farther down the trail, I decided it was time to take another break. We again headed to the stream and drank as much water as we could. We sat down on adjoining rocks, both of us by now pretty beat. Manuel was holding up as best he could, but I wondered for how much longer. If he couldn't go on, I could carry him only so far and I began to consider the possibility that pretty soon we should try to find shelter off the trail where we could hide from any pursuer and get some rest.

Just as I was about to suggest this to Manuel, I heard what sounded like a curse in English.

"Manuel," I said. "Did you hear that? Or am I just imagining things?"

There was a look of alarm on his face. "No Frank. I heard it too."

Since sound carried easily through the canyon we were navigating, I had no precise idea of just how close or how far away whoever uttered the curse might be. "You stay here Manuel," I said, handing him the rifle. "I'm going to take a look."

Keeping low, I made my way to the other side of the trail where there was a slight rise in the ground along with some trees. I chose a tree that looked sturdy enough to hold me and carefully began to climb. When I was about fifteen feet above the ground, I stopped and looked in the direction where I thought the shouted curse had come from. If my calculations were correct, it had come from somebody who had been following us on the trail.

It would have helped if I had had binoculars. And the sun was in my eyes. But holding on to the tree with my left hand and using my right as a shade, I began to scour the path we had just traversed. There were shadows and I had trouble seeing everything clearly. As my eyes moved down the path, I couldn't spot anything that resembled a human form over the first two hundred yards or so. But just then, the westerly breeze brought me the unmistakable sound of boots on loose rock. I shifted my gaze a bit farther down the path and I saw a man outlined against the sky. Even from that distance, I had no trouble identifying him. It was Dwight Whalen.

I kept my eyes on him for a few more seconds. He was moving slowly, and with a noticeable limp. I guessed that he had suffered the same fate as Manuel and had turned his ankle. That probably explained the curse we heard. But he still was moving in our direction and he was undoubtedly driven by the same desperation that drove us. He might be slowed, but he wasn't going to stop until something – or someone – stopped him. And whatever his weakened condition, I could see that he carried an M-16 slung over his shoulder.

I hurried down the tree and back to Manuel, who was waiting anxiously where I had left him.

"What is it Frank? Did you see anything?"

"Yeah. Kind of like I figured. It's Dwight Whalen, following us on the trail. It looks as though he's twisted his ankle too. But he's armed and he's coming our way."

He took it calmly, which encouraged me. After all that he had been through, it would have been perfectly understandable if he had simply given up the ghost - Dwight's presence being one obstacle too many to overcome. But I could see a glint in his eyes that said he was ready to deal with Dwight no matter what. Perhaps, too, he was beginning to have some confidence that I would be able to pull another rabbit out of the hat and get us out of yet another tight spot. I hoped, for both our sakes, that I would not disappoint him.

"So what are we going to do Frank?" he asked. "Another ambush?"

I gave him a tight grin. "Exactly. But this time it will be different," I said, taking the M-16 from his hands. "This time it's one-on-one with both of us armed. And this time, I want you out of the action."

He was about to argue, but I cut him off. "Look Manuel. All that we've accomplished so far goes down the drain if you are recaptured. I'm pretty sure I can handle Dwight. But if for some reason I can't, I want you to have a fighting chance to get away. You have to keep moving down the trail. Get as far away as you can. After I deal with Dwight, I'll catch up, I promise."

I could see that he wasn't happy. We had been together through thick and thin. Now for the first time since we had escaped, I was forcing us to go our separate ways. He was stubborn and tough. For a minute I thought he was going to defy me and stay put. But after about fifteen seconds of silence, he shrugged and said, "All right Frank. All Right. I don't like it. But it makes sense."

"Okay then Manuel. You better get moving. Dwight is moving slowly, but he is still covering ground and heading in our direction."

He picked up the branch I had found for him, hoisted one of the blanket packs onto his back, and gave me a quick *abrazo* before heading for the trail. "Good luck Frank." he said his voice cracking, "I'll be waiting for you."

We both had more to say to each other, but didn't have the time.

"See you soon Manuel. See you soon," I said, pushing him gently towards the trail.

As I touched his back, I could feel his frail bones under my palm and wondered again how far he would be able to get on his own. And what would happen to him if I failed to do as I promised – *deal with Dwight Whalen?* So far, he had proved remarkably resourceful and resilient. I could only hope that those qualities would see him through if the encounter between me and my old teammate didn't turn out the way I had promised.

Thirty Seven

I watched Manuel move slowly down the trail, favoring his right leg. I kept my eye on him until he rounded a bend and was out of sight. Now, I had to determine my next moves. Should I stay where I was and wait for Dwight? Or should I move in his direction and try to stop him in his tracks before he closed more distance between himself and me – and Manuel?

There wasn't a lot of cover between me and where I figured Dwight would be. But there was enough and I decided to head in his direction. As I backtracked, ducking behind trees and rocks every ten paces or so, I tried to put myself in Dwight's frame of mind.

If I were Dwight, I would have waited for help to arrive before resuming the hunt for us. I had removed the advantage he had enjoyed in manpower by taking out Smallwood and the muscleman. And now I was armed. Plus, I already had used an ambush successfully so why not another one? And it wouldn't be with makeshift *bolas* this time, but a high-powered automatic weapon. I could be hiding behind any tree or any rock, ready to rain down some deadly fire as he proceeded along the path. That concern, along with his recently-twisted ankle, probably explained why he was moving so slowly.

But even though he was moving slowly, he was moving. So, as I had speculated earlier, he was as desperate to catch us as we were to escape.

I had found shelter behind a tree after covering about one hundred and fifty yards when I heard footsteps on the trail ahead of me. I stole a glance around the tree trunk and saw Dwight about thirty yards away. At this distance, I could see clearly that he was struggling. He was grimacing in pain with every step as he limped along on his injured ankle. His head was up and he was turning it like a metronome right and left, looking for

273

any trouble ahead. His rifle, however, was loose in his arms and pointed to the ground.

Slowly, I raised my own rifle until I had Dwight in my sights. He made the perfect target. All I had to do was release the safety and pull the trigger and he would be done. And that would have been the smart thing to do. Even though he was hurt, he still posed a danger. He was armed and I had no doubt that he would not hesitate to fire at me if our situations were reversed. Besides, I owed it to Manuel – and to my client, his sister – to do whatever it took to assure his safety.

I felt my finger tighten on the trigger. *But I just couldn't do it.* I hadn't hesitated to shot Smallwood. But I had barely known him. Besides, he fired at me first. With Smallwood, it was simply a matter of self-defense and self-preservation. The same with the muscleman I had dispatched with a rock. But Dwight was different. We had been teammates and friends of a sort for years. I had memories of him feeding me perfect passes for easy layups that helped pad my scoring statistics and setting screens so I could get off jump shots. There was too much history between us. I couldn't make myself take the final step and blow him away without warning.

"Dwight," I shouted. "Don't move. I've got you in my sights. Just put down the rifle."

My voice startled him and he looked to both sides of the trail, ready to dive for cover. To discourage him, I fired two warning shots, one to his right and one to his left and he froze in position.

I moved out from behind the tree and faced him straight on, my rifle barrel pointed directly at him.

"Come on Dwight," I said. "Just do as I say. Don't make any foolish moves. Put down the gun."

He just stared at me for a few seconds. I could imagine the gears moving in his head, calculating the odds. Finally, with a shrug, he put the rifle down and raised his hands.

"Okay Frank. Okay. Take it easy. You've got me. What's next?"

That was a good question. What exactly was I going to do now that Dwight was my prisoner? Tie him up and take him along with us to deliver to the authorities was my first thought.

"Just stay still Dwight," I said. "I'm coming for you."

There was a flicker of a grin on his face as I began to move towards him, keeping my rifle trained on him as I did so. But that proved to be a near fatal mistake. As I moved closer to him, I could see that Dwight's face was covered in sweat and his eyes were bloodshot. He's had a rough day, I thought to myself, and must be close to exhaustion. But by focusing so intently on Dwight, I neglected to be careful where I stepped. I was about ten feet from Dwight when I felt my right foot slip on some loose rock and I momentarily lost my balance. As soon as Dwight saw me stumble, he lowered his right arm and pulled a revolver from behind his back and began to fire.

It all happened in a matter of seconds. As soon as I saw him pull the gun, I dropped to the ground and rolled to my right. Again some boulders provided me with cover. I still held my rifle and once I had settled myself behind the boulders, I poked my head above them and began to send bullets in Dwight's direction. But he, too, had found cover, and my shots glanced harmlessly off another group of boulders about fifteen feet away.

I cursed myself for my ambivalence and my carelessness. I should have finished Dwight when I had the chance. Now I had lost the advantage.

I checked the magazine of the M-16. I still had ten rounds left. I hoped that would be enough. In the excitement, I had lost track of how many shots Dwight had fired. Maybe he had emptied his gun. But then again, maybe he hadn't – or had a spare. At any rate, I couldn't risk a frontal assault. On the other hand, I couldn't stay pinned down forever. I had to make some kind of move, but for the moment wasn't sure what that would be.

Dwight helped me make up my mind. After about thirty seconds of silence, he yelled out: "Frank, Frank old friend. You still there?"

"Yes 'old friend,' no thanks to you."

He laughed. "Well my friend, I should have known better. You always were stubborn - and resourceful. I should have had our men keep a closer watch on you. Getting out of the hacienda with Fernández and making it this far Frank, that was unexpected. But I guess, knowing you, not surprising. But killing Smallwood and the other guy Frank. *That* did surprise me. I didn't think you had it in you. And now here we are."

"Yes Dwight. Here we are."

"I don't suppose I could convince you to join up with us Frank could I? Suppose we just let bygones be bygones, go round up young Mister Fernández, and pretend this whole unpleasantness never happened. We go back to the hacienda, Manuel's father agrees to our terms, and we both get to make a lot of money. What do you say Frank? How does that sound?"

I didn't think Dwight was serious. He was just trying to buy time. But what was his game? Was he waiting for help to arrive? That seemed the most likely scenario. And if he was expecting help, that meant I couldn't waste much more time. I had to move.

"That sounds intriguing Dwight. Tell me more."

I wasn't really interested in what Dwight had to say. But I wanted to keep him talking.

There was a different tone in his voice as he began to explain how everything might work out for the best if I went along with his scheme. I let him blather on, not paying much attention to the words. Looking at the terrain, I debated my best course of action. I had to get to Dwight and disarm him. Going straight at him, firing as I went, might work, but it would expose me to his return fire, presuming he still had ammunition. Heading back to the path and taking advantage of whatever cover I could find seemed the safest course. But I wasn't sure I could navigate the ground without making some noise. And I suspected, too, that Dwight would be thinking along the same lines and would be prepared.

The best course, I determined, would be to slip down into the stream, only about five feet to my right, and try to sneak up on Dwight from that direction. The sound of the rushing water would hide the noise of my own advance and coming in from that direction would hopefully catch Dwight by surprise.

"What do you think Frank?" Dwight shouted, apparently having ended his spiel.

Even though I hadn't been paying much attention, part of what he had been saying stuck in my mind. "Tell me again how it will work once we get Manuel's father to go along."

That got him started up again. As soon as I heard his voice, I headed straight for the steam and stepped in. Almost immediately I began to think that I had made a serious mistake. The current was strong, the water was freezing, and the footing underneath was slippery. One misstep could be fatal. Either Dwight would hear me and finish me off or I would be carried downstream like a piece of driftwood. Luckily, there were plenty of small trees and bushes along the bank of the stream to give me firm handholds as I made my way against the current towards where Dwight was hiding. I had slung my rifle over my right shoulder so that I had both hands free to pull myself along. And, as I had hoped, the sound of the current seemed to drown out the noise I was making as I pulled my legs through the freezing water.

It didn't take me as long as I had thought to get to where I wanted to be. After only a few minutes, I could hear Dwight's voice to my immediate left and almost simultaneously caught sight of him. He was crouched on his knees, his back to me, watching the path and the terrain above it. I could see the pistol in his right hand, ready to blast away as soon as he caught sight of me.

Grabbing hold of two branches that jutted over the stream, I slowly pulled myself up onto the bank just a few feet away from where Dwight was hunkered down. Just as I did so, Dwight, who had gone momentarily silent, shouted out: "Hey Frank. Are you listening? What do you say friend? Is it a deal?"

He was still turned away from me as I got my footing and began to remove the M-16 from my shoulder. But the strap caught on my clothing and before I could get ready to fire, Dwight whirled around and pointed his pistol in my face and pulled the trigger. I dove to the ground just in time as the bullet grazed my side. But I was totally at his mercy, lying prone on the ground with my weapon pinned under me.

I looked up and saw Dwight limp towards me, his gun centered on my forehead. "Well, well Frank," he said with a sneer. "Looks like the tables have turned haven't they. Just stay where you are. Don't move a muscle."

I was in no position to do anything else. My only hope was that Dwight would get close enough so I could make a desperate lunge and maybe, just maybe, knock him off balance.

But he was too smart for that. He advanced to a spot about three feet away, just out of my reach. Looking up at him, I saw a look in his eyes that seemed to border on madness. But the hand that held the gun was rock steady. "I suppose it's too late to accept your offer," I said.

He gave a short laugh. "You bet it is Frank. You bet it is."

"Not that it was genuine to begin with," I said.

He didn't say anything. Again I tried to read what was going through his mind. Now that he had me securely in his sights, was he having some of the same reservations I had had a few minutes earlier? Was he willing to pull the trigger on his friend and former teammate? I wasn't about to beg for mercy. I desperately tried to think of something to say that would convince him not to fire.

But I was thinking too rationally, putting Dwight into my own frame of mind. He was angry and frustrated. "God Damn It Frank," he sputtered, spittle flying out of the corners of his mouth. "You've ruined everything, everything. Why did you have to be so damn stubborn? Why couldn't you have…"

I wanted to keep him talking. "Why couldn't I have what Dwight?"

But he was done talking. I saw his eyes narrow and his finger tighter on the trigger. He had made up his mind. From this distance, he couldn't miss, but I rolled over to my right just as he fired, hoping that at least he would miss a vital area and give me a fighting chance. But instead of the roar of the pistol, all I heard was an empty click.

He either had run out of ammunition or his gun had misfired. I didn't take the time to find out. Instead, I got up on my hands and knees and launched myself at him. He was looking down at his gun in disbelief when I hit him waist-high and we both went crashing to the ground. I could hear the breath go out of him as I landed on top and raised my right fist for a swing at his jaw. But Dwight, despite his obvious exhaustion, was still driven by desperation and still had the reflexes of the college athlete he had once been.

Before I could land my punch, he managed to raise his left arm to block my effort and then with his right delivered a blow of his own to the left side of my head. I was momentarily stunned. Dwight wriggled free, crawling on all fours towards where my rifle lay between us and the stream. I shook off the effects of his blow and threw myself onto his back before he could reach the M-16.

Soon the weapon was forgotten as we wrestled on the ground, neither one of us letting go of the other. I was on his back, trying to get my arm around his throat so I could choke the life out of him, but he was able to slip my grasp and in a lightening move reverse our positions. Now I was the one fighting to keep him from shutting off my flow of oxygen. Just as he was about to succeed, I made a supreme effort and was able to grab him in a bear hug. We were now face to face, lying on the ground, almost like lovers in a passionate embrace. Dwight's face was only inches from mine and I could see him move his head backward about to give me a vicious head butt, when I turned us both over to avoid the blow. The maneuver worked, but we were on an incline that led to the stream and before we knew it, we both were plunged into the icy water.

In the stream, we remained locked together. I knew that if I let Dwight go, he would try his best to hold my head under water until all the life had gone out of me. And I planned to do the same to him. But nature had other ideas. Unable to gain any footing when we were close to the bank, we were soon swept into the middle of the stream where the current was stronger and the water was well over our heads even if we had been standing.

We both were struggling to keep our mouths above water while at the same time clinging to one another. But as the current caught us, I felt Dwight being ripped from my grasp and we both were carried at an increasingly rapid rate downstream. I remembered that Dwight had been a champion swimmer in high school. But that didn't do him any good in these circumstances. Both of us were helpless, fighting simply to stay afloat.

After about fifteen seconds of struggling, I decided that the best course was simply to let the current carry me and try to maneuver myself as close to the bank of the stream as I could. That was easier said than done. I was about at the end of my rope physically. The current showed no signs of letting up, and the freezing water was beginning to numb my whole body. I guessed that my lips were already blue.

As I struggled to get closer to solid ground, I almost lost sight of Dwight. He was now about twenty feet ahead of me, caught fully in the middle of the current. I could see his arms flailing as he tried to gain control, but he was making no progress. It might have been my imagination, but my last glimpse of him was with his face turned in my direction with a look of anguish and his mouth forming the words, "Please help me Frank." Then he disappeared from view, swallowed up by the relentless current.

I didn't have time to worry about Dwight. I was being swept downstream and making little progress in getting closer to dry land. It was all I could do to keep my head above water. Fortunately, the water was deep enough so that I wasn't running into any obstructions. But the stream was narrowing, the current was getting even stronger, and in the distance I could hear the roar of what sounded like a waterfall.

As I rounded a bend, I was still afloat, but just barely. If there were rapids and a waterfall ahead, I didn't like my chances of making it through alive. But my good luck held. Ahead, jutting out from the bank on my right was a fallen tree, its roots still connected to the ground. It extended about fifteen feet or so directly into the stream, about a foot above the water.

I exerted whatever strength I had left and paddled my way as close to the bank as I could get. Suddenly, the fallen tree was right in front of me and as I passed under it I reached up with both arms and embraced it like a long-lost friend. But the lower half of my body was still in the water and I didn't know how long I could maintain my grip. I tried my best to lift my legs out of the water to wrap them around the fallen tree as well, but my efforts were futile.

Just as I was about to give up the ghost and take my chances in the water, I heard Manuel shout out, "Hold on Frank. Hold on. Help is on the way."

I hoped that Manuel wasn't trying any heroics. I didn't think he would have the strength needed to haul me up and if he tried to do so we might both end up in the raging water. But within seconds, I saw a figure clad in a red poncho with a black stripe crawl onto the fallen tree and make his way carefully to where I was holding on for dear life. Behind him was a similarly-clad man, who was holding on to his companion's feet.

The first man took hold of my right wrist in a powerful grip. In Spanish, he said, "I have you señor. Don't worry. I have you." Then he began to pull me up towards him, grunting with effort. Gradually, he lifted me from the water. I still had enough strength left to use my left arm to hoist myself up onto the tree and to safety.

We must have made a strange sight. I was stretched out prone on the tree, gasping for breath, my feet extended towards the stream and my head facing the bank. My rescuer was also prone on the tree, facing me while keeping a tight grip on my wrists. And his companion was behind him, still holding on firmly to his feet. We made a kind of human chain.

My rescuer gave me an encouraging grin. "Let me know when you are ready to move señor. We need to get off this tree as soon as we can."

I knew he was right. Our combined weight had lowered the tree to the point where it nearly touched the water. At any moment the roots that held it in place might give way and sweep us all away.

"Okay," I said, returning his grin. "Let's get moving." Slowly, with his companion taking the lead, we began to inch ourselves back towards the shore, the two strangers crawling backwards on their bellies while I moved forwards on mine. We could have moved faster if we had stood or even been on our hands and knees. But the risks would have been greater as well. Retaining our balance on the fallen tree, which was slick with water from the stream, would have been near impossible. So we took it slow and easy. And while I expected to hear the tree tear from its roots at any moment and was prepared to be plunged back into the stream, the roots held and we finally made it to solid ground, where Manuel was anxiously awaiting us.

"You made it Frank. You made it. Thank God, you made it," he said, tears in his eyes, his voice caught in his throat. While the two men who had saved my life looked on, Manuel wrapped the blanket he had been carrying since we had fled the hacienda around me. I needed it. The combination of my exertions and immersion in the stream produced uncontrollable shivering. I felt light-headed and disoriented. Just as Manuel was about to tell me how he had met the two strangers who had saved my life, I felt myself fall to the ground. Suddenly everything went dark as I slipped into unconsciousness.

Thirty Eight

I woke to the smell of wood smoke. When I opened my eyes, I felt disoriented and for a few seconds the thought crossed my mind that I had somehow been magically transported to the cabin in the mountains where I had shared a meal with the ERP. The place I was in now was eerily similar - one-room with adobe walls, a thatched roof, a plain wooden table surrounded by several rough-hewn chairs in the center. I was lying on a bed that had no springs or mattress. Putting my hand down, I felt a pile of sheepskins that served the same purpose. Through the windows, I saw it was dark outside. I wondered how long I had been asleep. Was it still the same day when I had killed two men and been responsible for the death of a person who had once been my friend? Or had I slept through the night and the next day?

Raising myself to a sitting position, I saw a stone fireplace with a crackling fire only a few feet away. I also saw two large dogs curled up in front of the fire.

My movement caught the attention of the dogs. They sat up and looked at me with curiosity. It also stirred someone else in the room, which was dimly lit by a kerosene lantern on the wooden table. "Señor Fernández," I heard a low-pitched voice whisper in Spanish. "Señor Fernández, your friend is awake."

Looking in the direction of the voice, I could make out the form of a man bending over someone lying in a bed. As the shapes became clearer, I recognized the man who had grabbed my wrists and fished me out of the water. He was gently shaking the shoulder of someone who had to be Manuel.

"Thanks Martín," Manuel said, getting up and moving to stand in front of me, rubbing the sleep from his eyes.

Grinning down at me, he said, "Welcome back to the land of the living Frank."

"Thanks Manuel. Good to be back," I said, returning his grin. "Where am I?"

I got ready to swing my feet on to the dirt floor and remove the blankets that covered me when I realized that I was naked. "And where are my clothes?"

"Right over there," Manuel said, pointing to a length of rope suspended in front of the fire, where my pants, shirt, jacket, sweater, underwear, and socks were hanging. "The first thing we did when we got here," he said, "was get you out of your wet clothes. We had to warm you up. After all you've been through we didn't want you to catch pneumonia. So how are you feeling?"

I made a quick check. I had a few bumps and bruises from my struggle with Dwight and the wild ride in the stream. My right side was a bit sore where Dwight's bullet had grazed me, but there was only a small line of pink to show its passage. Overall, I felt pretty good. There were no signs of a fever and I was ravenously hungry and had a powerful thirst. "I'm fine Manuel - but I could sure use something to eat and drink."

Manuel turned to the other man in the room. "Martín, could you bring us some water?"

"Right away Señor Fernández," he replied, bringing over a cup filled to the brim with ice-cold water. I drained it in seconds and held it out empty for a refill.

"Better take it easy Frank," Manuel said, as Martín returned with another cupful. "Don't overdo it."

He was right. The shock of the cold water had caused my belly to cramp and I could feel some pain behind my eyes. I sipped the next cup more slowly.

"And we better get you covered up Frank," Manuel said. In the process of sitting up, I had let the blankets slip down to my waist and my upper torso was bare. Even though the fire was keeping me warm, Manuel was right. Leaving me for a moment, he went to where my clothes were hanging and brought me my undershirt and sweater. "These are dry Frank," he said, handing them to me. I dutifully slipped them on. "Now how about something to eat?" he asked.

"Sure thing Manuel. But you need to put me into the picture. First, what day is it? Second, where are we and who are our hosts?" I asked, nodding in the direction of Martín, whose back was turned to us as he tended to the fire.

Putting his hand toward me palm out in a gesture that said *be patient*, Manuel turned to retrieve a chair that he pulled over next to me. Keeping his voice low and speaking in English, he said "It's still the same day Frank. We arrived here about mid-afternoon. I'm not sure of the exact time now, but it probably is about nine o'clock at night." I remembered that Manuel had developed a good sense of the time of day during his captivity and assumed he was more or less correct as to the present time.

"As to where we are, we are in the cabin of two local shepherds," he continued. "They look after various flocks scattered along the hillsides, including the one we saw on the trail. This cabin is only about a mile away from where you and I parted company. When they heard the gunshots, they mounted their horses to investigate. They thought somebody might be poaching their herds. I ran into them along the trail about ten minutes after we split up."

"What did you tell them?" I asked.

"I said that a North American friend and I had been on a hiking and camping expedition and had run into some trouble. We had lost most of our gear, including our food and water, and were looking for help. I told them that you had instructed me to keep on the trail while you tried to determine what the shooting was all about. Maybe if hunters were in the vicinity, they could help us. We were headed back up the trail to where we had parted when we saw you struggling in the water. Our only thought was to rescue you. After we pulled you out, I told them that in your search for the 'hunters' you must have somehow slipped and fallen into the sream." He gave an apologetic little shrug. "It was the best I could come up with. I don't know if they believed me, but they didn't hesitate to help."

His voice chocked when he added, "And it was a near thing Frank. If we hadn't gotten to you, there are rapids farther down that would have ripped you to shreds."

A mental picture formed of the fate that Dwight undoubtedly had suffered once he had entered that deadly stretch of the stream. Perhaps he was already unconscious by that time. At any rate, I had survived and he had not in what had been a struggle where both of us might have ended up dead. Nonetheless, I couldn't escape a nagging sense of regret at Dwight's fate. A better outcome would have been for me to prevail somehow in subduing my old classmate, turning him over to the authorities, and revealing the details of his scheme. If that were the choice, I rationalized perhaps Dwight would have preferred death to dishonor.

I kept these thoughts to myself. "It looks as though we caught another lucky break Mnuel. Who knows where we'd be if these two men hadn't showed up."

A somber look crossed his face and he nodded. "Yes indeed. And after you collapsed, they helped me get you on a horse and here to the cabin. The one who is with us now tending the fire is Martín, the older of the two. The other is his nephew, Carlos."

"And where is he?" I asked.

"I'm not sure Frank. I went to sleep as soon as we got you taken care of. And the next thing I knew, Martín was shaking me to tell me that you were awake. Do you want me to ask him about Carlos?"

I was probably being paranoid again. But I always held to the belief that if things were too good to be true – then they *were* too good to be true. Maybe the missing Carlos had figured out that we were not who we professed to be. Perhaps we might even be involved in some sort of criminal activity and his uncle had sent him to locate the nearest authorities to turn us in. Or maybe these innocent-seeming shepherds were somehow in cahoots with the people at the hacienda who still might be trying to track us down. I knew I was letting my imagination run wild, but I couldn't convince myself we were out of danger yet.

I didn't share my concerns with Manuel. Instead, I said, "Yes, perhaps you should. But try to make it sound like an innocent inquiry."

His face showed his curiosity, but he seemed to pick up on what was bothering me. Turning towards our host, he asked, "By the way Martín. Where is Carlos?"

Martín, who had finished working on the fire said, "He's right outside Señor Fernñndez, gathering more wood for the fire." As if on cue, the door to the cabin swung open and the younger shepherd, who I had last seen helping me get safely onto solid ground, came in, his arms full of logs for the fire. Placing them down next to the fireplace, he looked over at me and gave me a shy smile. I nodded an acknowledgement and felt a flush of embarrassment for my exaggerated fears. Another cliché came to mind – *Don't look a gift horse in the mouth.* The two shepherds had saved our lives. Without them, I would have suffered the same fate as Dwight Whalen and Manuel would not have survived much longer on his own. I decided to push my suspicions to the back of my mind and accept the fact that our two rescuers were exactly as they seemed to be – simple folk who were helping out two strangers in need.

After Manuel brought me the rest of my clothes, I joined him and our two hosts at the wooden table for something to eat. Carlos ladled out generous portions of a hearty lamb stew. Martín produced a bottle of red wine that was the perfect accompaniment. Manuel and I gobbled down every bit, much to the approval of our hosts, who thankfully did not besiege us with questions as we ate. I had anticipated that living the kind of isolated lives they did, they would be anxious for conversation. But perhaps appreciating the shape Manuel and I were in and the need for us to recuperate – or perhaps being not very communicative by nature – they mostly maintained a stoic silence while we finished our meal. What conversation did take place occurred between Manuel and Martín and basically involved Manuel asking our host questions about what life was like for him and his nephew.

Once we had cleaned our plates and polished off the last or our wine, Carlos told us to bundle up and then led us outside to use the facilities. Just as with the night before, the sky was crystal clear and resplendent with stars and a full moon. But on this night, thankfully, we were not running for our lives over unfamiliar terrain. Instead we were enjoying the comfort of a full meal and a warm – and I hoped safe – place to sleep.

Without speaking, Carlos pointed to a small structure that sat about twenty feet to our right and uphill. I let Manuel go first and then followed him after he had finished.

When we returned to the cabin, we found that Martín had added more wood to the fire and the bare room was now almost uncomfortably warm. Manuel and I thanked our hosts for their hospitality and then retired to our respective beds. I felt a pang of guilt when I saw Martín and Carlos lay out some blankets directly on the bare floor and settle down for the night. While the "beds" Manuel and I occupied were bare-bones, they were the only ones available and the shepherds had surrendered them to us without a word.

I stripped to my underwear before slipping under the covers, keeping my pants and shoes close at hand in case I might need them. There was always the possibility that I might have to answer nature's call in the middle of the night. And, still nagging me was the thought that we were not yet out of danger. By now, I was more or less convinced that Martín and Carlos posed no danger - but what about the others from the hacienda? Karl Schusller and at least two more musclemen were still out there. *Were they on our trail, a trail that might lead them directly to this cabin? And if they did come upon us, how would we defend ourselves?* I had seen an old shotgun propped up in one corner of the cabin and presumed that it was loaded. But even so, would it be enough to fend off an attack by three men equipped with modern automatic weapons?

The presence of the two dogs provided some assurance. I had been introduced to them during our meal. They had generic names that corresponded to something along the lines of "Ranger" and "Scout." They were of an indeterminate breed but appeared to have some of the features of a collie. They were used primarily to help with the sheep but Carlos had informed me that they were also trained as guard dogs and were quick to pick up the scent of any wild animal that might pose a threat. I hoped that also meant they would provide some warning if that threat walked on two legs rather than four. After having been fed from the scraps of our meal, they had resumed their positions in front of the fire.

Along with the presence of the dogs and the shotgun, I also consoled myself with the thought that with their leaders missing in action, the rest of the crew at the hacienda would most likely either stay put or head for greener pastures. After mulling over these and other favorable possibilities, I began to relax. Soon the warmth of the fire and the food and the wine began to have their effect and I drifted off to sleep.

Thirty Nine

I awoke suddenly when I heard one of the dogs barking outside the cabin. Flinging off my blanket, I reached for my pants and my shoes. The fire was out and the kerosene lamp extinguished, but morning sunshine was streaming through a window behind me. While I struggled into my pants, I cast my eyes towards the corner where I had seen the shotgun. To my dismay, I saw that it was missing. Also missing were Martín and Carlos - along with the two dogs.

The noise I was making awakened Manuel. "What is it Frank?" he said, his voice groggy. "What's the matter?"

He threw off his covers and sat up facing me, a worried expression on his face. "I don't know Manuel," I answered. "I heard one of the dogs bark and…"

"And what Frank?"

I didn't have a good answer. I was imagining the worst. The dog was barking because we were about to be attacked by Karl Schussler and others from the hacienda. *And we didn't have a weapon with which to defend ourselves!*

I could feel the sweat break out on my forehead and saw panic on Manuel's face. His thoughts probably mirrored mine: *Had all we gone through been for nothing? Were we about to be recaptured – or suffer an even worse fate? Had we been betrayed by the two shepherds?*

I was just about to tell Manuel to put on his shoes and get ready to make a run for it, when the cabin door opened and the two dogs bounded in, their tails wagging. Right behind them were Martín and Carlos, the older man carrying the shotgun and the younger swinging two dead rabbits in each hand. "*Buenos Días Señores*" Martín said with a broad smile on his face. "How are you this morning?" he asked cheerily.

Apparently, he had not noticed the look of near-desperation on my face, which I quickly replaced with a broad smile of my own. "We are just fine Martín," I said, breathing a silent sigh of relief, "Just fine."

Putting his shotgun in the corner, Martín explained that he and Carlos had gotten up at the crack of dawn to check the traps they had set for the rabbits. They had left quietly so as not to disturb us, knowing that we needed all the rest we could get. I didn't ask, but I assumed that he had taken the shotgun with him as a matter of course. And I didn't say anything to him about my imagined fears. There was still the possibility that there were men from the hacienda in the vicinity looking for us. But now awake and alert, I felt better prepared to face any challenge that might arise.

Manuel and I made our excuses and headed for the outhouse. "How are you feeling Manuel?" I asked. His limp was less pronounced and his color had improved.

"A lot better Frank," he said. "A solid meal and a good night's sleep have done wonders."

After we had finished using the facilities, such as they were, and were walking back to the cabin, I said to Manuel, "Listen. We aren't home free just yet. There may be other men from the hacienda out looking for us. So we need to keep alert."

"I understand Frank. I don't think I'll feel completely safe until I'm back in Durham," he said with a wry look on his face.

"I know what you mean Manuel, but one step at a time."

"Sure Frank. Sure."

When we got back to the cabin, our hosts had prepared for us some *yerba mate* along with bread and eggs. We gulped down everything in front of us, fortified for whatever might lay ahead. After we had finished, Martín offered to let us stay as long as we wanted – or needed – but I told him that it was important for us to get in touch with our parents as soon as possible. They hadn't heard from us in several days, I explained, which was close to the truth, and were undoubtedly beginning to worry. The quicker we could reassure them that we were all right, the better.

Martín nodded his head in understanding. "Very well Señor Corbett. We can help you. Just as soon as you are ready to go, let me know."

I looked at Manuel, who bobbed his head, indicating he was set to leave. But before we did so, I thought it only fair that I tell Martín and Carlos the truth about what had happened to us. They probably already suspected that Manuel's cover story had a few holes in it. But I wanted to come clean with them so they would be fully aware of the possible risks involved in helping us out. Both men listened without expression as I sketched out the details of Manuel's kidnapping, his being held hostage at the hacienda over the ridge, my own abduction, our escape, and the fact that some bad men were out looking for us. I also explained how I had killed the muscleman and Roy Smallwood, whose bodies presumably were decomposing on the trail as we spoke. At some point, unless they were discovered and disposed of by others from the hacienda, there was the possibility that the birds of prey circling over them would attract attention. If so, I didn't want them to come under suspicion. I also described my fight with Dwight and the fact that he must have perished in the stream. His body, or what was left of it, might also be found and cause them complications.

When I finished, the two shepherds exchanged glances with each other. After a few seconds of silent communication, they inclined their heads toward one another in a way that was almost imperceptible. "Thank you for telling us what you have Señor Corbett," Martín said. "We know something about the hacienda you mentioned. We have heard rumors about what goes on there. And as for the two men you had to kill, Carlos will take care of their bodies. Do not worry."

Carlos, with a stoic look on his face said, "Yes Señor Corbett. Don't worry. I can take care of the bodies so that nobody will find them."

"Look Martín, Carlos," I said. "You have done enough already. And we are extremely grateful for your kindness. But we…" I looked at Manuel, who nodded in agreement… "But we don't want to put you in any more danger. We can go back and dispose of the bodies ourselves. Then we can keep going on our own…"

"No. No Señor Corbett. It is too much for you. It is too far – at least twenty kilometers to the nearest road. I'll take you. We have horses. It's all right. We want to help."

I was about to argue when I saw Manuel give me a look that said, *I know these people Frank. They really do want to help us – and would be offended if we didn't let them.* Or maybe that's what I wanted to read in his expression.

I shrugged and said, "Okay Martín. Okay. But maybe you should bring your shotgun along just in case."

He gave me a smile and retrieved the shotgun from the corner, slinging it over his shoulder. I told him that we were ready to leave now and he went to fetch the horses that would carry us down the trail towards Salta.

After Manuel and I had put on our jackets we met Martín in front of the cabin. He held the reins of two sturdy looking horses. Since there were only two mounts, Martín suggested that I ride alone on one while he and Manuel shared the other. Carlos would stay behind and attend to the gruesome chore of burying Smallwood and the muscleman. In the distance, I could see vultures circling where we had left the bodies. I did not envy Carlos his task.

Before mounting up, we both gave Carlos a warm *abrazo* and thanked him profusely for his help. He mumbled a few *de nadas* and scuffed the ground in front of him shyly. Then we got onto our horses and, waving goodbye to Carlos, headed onto the by now familiar trail. Martín and Manuel took the lead while I followed behind.

It was another cool, clear day. The morning sun was in our eyes and warmed our faces as we headed eastward. We moved at a steady pace and I enjoyed having my horse do the work while I scanned the trail ahead for any signs of an ambush. But our luck held. After about two hours, we reached the secondary road that led to the main highway to Salta. Along the way, we had not seen another living soul.

We dismounted and waited by the side of the road. Martín informed us that there were many trucks that used the road to bring products from nearby farms and ranches for the markets in Salta. And sure enough, after about ten minutes, we saw a truck heading toward us from the south. Martín told us to wait while he walked to the middle of the road and began waving his arms. The truck slowed and then came to a complete stop, kicking up a cloud of dust as it did so. Martín moved around to the driver's side and asked him if he could give Manuel and me a lift into Salta. Apparently, they knew one another and the driver grinned and waved us aboard. We scrambled around to the passenger side and prepared to step up into the cab. Before we did so, however, we gave Martín the same treatment as Carlos, each of us embracing him, patting him on the back, and thanking him for all he had done.

He was a little less diffident than his nephew, but was still reserved in his response. "*De nada señores. De nada.*" Then, as we climbed up and took our seats, he shut the door behind us and wished us luck. Even before the door had closed, the driver, who was carrying a load of fruit and vegetables, had engaged the gears and resumed his journey.

Manuel, who was between me and the driver, introduced us. The driver said his name was Miguel and that he was indeed heading to the markets of Salta and would be happy to take us into the center of the city.

Just before we crested a hill, I turned around to catch a last glimpse of Martín. He was almost out of sight, heading back to Carlos and their cabin. He was astride the horse I had ridden, leading the other by the reins. As he disappeared from view, I uttered a silent plea that he and his nephew would not suffer any retribution for the assistance they had provided us. There was little doubt that we owed our lives to them.

Forty

Miguel, as promised, let us off at the main plaza directly in front of the Hotel Salta. Manuel and I had discussed what we should do when we arrived in the city. I had suggested that we contact the police, tell them that Manuel had escaped from kidnappers, and ask them to help us contact Manuel's father at once. But Manuel vetoed that idea. First, he said, the police would ask too many questions and might not accept our story, delaying any communication with the U.S. Second, there was always the possibility that among the local police were members who were in the pay of Smallwood and Whalen. By bad luck we might end up with officials who were in the pay of the very men who had held us. I thought that was unlikely, but I deferred to Manuel, who knew his country and his countrymen a lot better than I did.

We decided that the best course was to go directly to the Hotel Salta and call Manuel's father from there. I had booked my room for a week in advance and presumably, even though I had been missing for two nights it was still being held for me. Regardless, I presumed the desk clerk would allow us to use the phone. I had to hope that whoever was on duty would recognize me because both Manuel and I were without any identity papers or any money. After our harrowing journey, we also were unshaven, our clothes were torn and filthy, and we badly needed a shower.

As we approached the hotel's entrance, the doorman moved as though to block our way. But then a light or recognition appeared on his face and he broke into a broad smile. "Right this way Señores," he said, opening the door for us. "Your friends have been waiting for you."

His news about "friends" caught me by surprise. For a few seconds I thought we might be walking into some kind of a trap and considered grabbing Manuel by the arm and beating a hasty retreat. But then, as the door opened, I saw Alfredo Billinghurst rushing to greet me, his arms extended wide and an ear-splitting grin on his face.

"Frank. Frank," he shouted, enveloping me in his arms and giving me a bear hug and slaps on the back. "You made it. You made it."

It took me a moment to catch my breath from his enthusiastic greeting. "Yes Alfredo. But how did you…?"

"I'll explain later," he said. Then, releasing me from his grip, he turned his attention to Manuel, who had been at my side as we had entered the hotel lobby and who looked stunned by Alfredo's boisterous reception.

"And this must be Manuel Fernández," Alfredo said. Manuel nodded in acknowledgement and gave him a smile, receiving from Alfredo a somewhat more restrained version of the greeting I received.

"Listen Alfredo," I said. "We have to get to a phone right away. Manuel needs to contact his father to let him know he is all right."

Before Alfredo had a chance to respond, we were suddenly surrounded by about half a dozen men dressed in dark suits. They didn't look particularly threatening, but they weren't smiling either. Four of them, who I identified immediately as my fellow countrymen, wore identical dark suits, white shirts, and ties. Two had blonde hair and two had light brown hair cut to regulation and all looked fit. Right away I assumed they were from the FBI or some such agency. Two others, also dressed in dark suits, had darker complexions and black hair and I guessed they were Argentines. One of the light-brown haired men stepped forward and introduced himself.

"Mister Corbett," he said, "My name is Clint Brubaker." Then he fished into his inside coat pocket and showed me a leather-clad photo ID along with a gold badge. "I'm part of a special interagency task force of the U.S. government."

"Let me have a closer look at your credentials," I said.

"Sure. Here they are," he said, extending them out for me to take. I checked them over and they looked genuine, although there was no specific agency listed. I let Manuel have a look and then handed them back to Brubaker. The credentials looked legitimate but I still harbored my doubts. Too much recent betrayal had made me edgy and suspicious.

Turning to Manuel, Brubaker said, "We are overjoyed to see you alive and well Manuel, and extended his hand for a shake. Manuel hesitated for a moment and then clasped the extended hand. He probably shared some of my wariness. "We can help you make that phone call Manuel," Brubaker said, "Just head this way," pointing to a doorway that was to the left of the hotel's main desk.

Sensing my reluctance, Alfredo sought to reassure me. "It's okay Frank," he said. "These are the good guys."

"Okay Mister Brubaker," I said, putting my arm around Manuel's shoulders in a protective manner, "Let's go."

Brubaker signaled for me to follow him across the lobby. For the guests watching us, we must have made a strange sight: two scruffy young men, dressed in casual clothes that had taken a beating following in the wake of the suit-clad Brubaker with the five others who were similarly dressed and Alfredo, who was attired in a sport coat and slacks, trailing behind. But I suppose that given the many bizarre things that had gone on in Argentina in recent years, perhaps it was not that unusual a sight. We attracted a few curious looks, but for the most part the dozen or so guests in the lobby paid us little attention.

When we got to the doorway, Brubaker opened it and ushered Alfredo, Manuel, and one of his entourage inside. He told the others to wait outside and then closed the door. "This is the hotel manager's office," he explained. "He is letting us use it for the time being." Then, pointing to a telephone that rested on the manager's desk, he said to Manuel, "You can use that phone to call your father son. Just pick it up and ask for the hotel operator. He will place the call for you."

Manuel moved quickly to the desk, sat in the manager's chair, picked up the phone and asked the operator to connect him to the number in the United States that he gave him. While he waited for the call to go through, Brubaker suggested that the rest of us sit down and make ourselves comfortable. Alfredo and I sank into a couch against the wall while Brubaker and the other man occupied chairs in front of the desk.

Holding the phone against his ear, Manuel flashed me a grin. "I can hear it ringing," he said. "I'm calling the embassy and..." The call must have gone through. We heard him say in Spanish, "Yes señorita. I would like to speak to Guillermo Fernánandez. Please tell him that it is his son, Manuel. Yes. That's right. His *son* - Manuel."

About ten seconds passed and I could see the emotion on Manuel's face as he waited to speak with his father. "Yes father. Yes. It's me. Yes…I'm all right." We couldn't hear the other end of the conversation but we could see the tears begin to trickle down Manuel's cheeks. "Yes father. It's a long story. But a very brave man named Frank Corbett rescued me." I could feel my own eyes get a bit moist. "Yes. We are in Salta. In the Hotel Salta. There are some men here from the United States government who are helping us and….Yes father. Yes…"

Manuel held the phone out to Brubaker. "My father would like to speak with you."

Brubanker took the phone. In passable Spanish he identified himself and mentioned some names that were unfamiliar to me but presumably helped to verify his bona fides. "Yes Señor. Your son is now in our care and we promise to deliver him back to you safe and sound. You have my word." There was then a pause while he listened to whatever the elder Fernández was saying. Then he repeated his assurances and added. "If all goes well, we should have him back to you by tomorrow at around this time." There was another pause while he listened. Then he said, "Yes sir. You have nothing to worry about it. We'll take care of all the details. Now here is your son," he said, handing the phone back to Manuel. As Manuel put the receiver to his ear, Brubaker said, "He wants a private word with Manuel. Perhaps we should leave him alone."

We nodded in agreement and followed him out of the room and into the lobby, where the rest of the entourage was standing around with expectant looks on their faces. Brubaker and his colleague left Alfredo and me by the main desk while they went to confer with the others, presumably to inform them that Manuel had been able to contact his father. Alone for the moment with my friend, I got ready to pepper him with questions. But he read my mind. "I know Frank. I know. It all must seem pretty strange at the moment. But you can trust Brubaker and the others. They are who they say they are."

"Well *amigo*, after all I've been through, my level of trust in officials working for the U.S. government is pretty low. But I *do* trust you. And if you say that these guys are legit, then that's good enough for me."

Alfredo put his hand on my shoulder and was about to say something when Brubaker approached us. "Hey Corbett," he said brusquely, "We have a lot of questions to ask you and we need to…"

I resisted the temptation to tell him to shove it. "Look Brubaker. Manuel and I have been through a lot. Once he finishes talking with his father, we both need to get cleaned up and have something to eat. After that, I'll be more than happy to chat."

He was about to object, but must have seen something in my face that dissuaded him. "Okay Corbett. Okay. But we can't wait too long. We need to get you and young Fernández back to the States as soon as possible. And before we do, we need to tie up whatever loose ends there are."

Just then, Manuel came out of the office and joined us. I explained to him what I had told Brubaker, and he nodded his agreement.

"Hey Frank," Alfredo said, "I checked and the hotel still has your room waiting for you. I booked another for Manuel right next to yours."

"Thanks my friend. I assume that my clothes are still there. But while we get cleaned up, how about seeing if you can buy something for Manuel to wear?"

I automatically reached for my wallet to dig out some pesos, but then remembered that it and my passport were back at the hacienda. "Sorry buddy, but I don't have any cash."

Alfredo waved aside my concern. "Don't worry about it Frank." Then with a wink, he added, "I can charge it as a business expense."

Alfredo and Brubaker accompanied us to the main desk, where the clerk gave Manuel and me our room keys. Turning to Brubaker, who seemed reluctant to let us out of his sight, I said, "Give us half an hour to get cleaned up and into fresh clothes Brubaker. Then we can answer all your questions while we have lunch. Okay?"

He didn't seem happy, and his foot was tapping nervously. It reminded me of Karl Schussler who had shown the same impatience in the same lobby just two days ago. And that got me to thinking about what had happened to the German-Argentine. *Had he fled the hacienda when it had become clear that his partners in crime were not returning, or was he still there?* I promised to include that item on my agenda when we finally got down to talking with Brubaker. But for the moment, the only thing I could think of was to get out of my odorous clothes, shave off several days of stubble, and have a hot shower.

Forty One

Once in the shower, I was tempted to take my time. The needles of hot water removed the accumulated grime and dried sweat and helped relieve some of the pain from the various sore spots on my body. But I knew that it was important to fill Brubaker in on what had happened in case there might be some way to round up the rest of Dwight's crew. I also didn't want to cause any delays in getting Manuel and me out of Argentina and back to the U.S.

Finishing my shower, I dried off and dressed quickly. When I opened my room door and stepped into the corridor, I saw Brubaker and one of his colleagues sitting in adjoining chairs. I didn't know if they were there to protect us or to make sure that we didn't somehow slip out of their sight. Maybe it was a little of both.

I gave them a quick nod and then banged on Manuel's door. "Manuel. It's Frank. You ready?"

"Coming Frank," he said through the door. "Just give me a minute." About thirty seconds later, he joined me in the corridor. The clothes that Alfredo had bought him – brown corduroy pants, a plaid shirt, and a tan sweater – hung a little loose on his bony frame, but served their purpose. "I had to put another hole in the belt so that my pants wouldn't fall to my ankles Frank. That's what caused the delay," Manuel said.

"No problem Manuel," I said. "And you are looking better." And he was. He had washed his hair, which had been tangled and greasy, and after shaving and showering, he looked almost like a new man. There was a shine in his eyes, his skin color looked better, and there was a spring to his step.

"Thanks Frank. I feel a lot better, especially now that I've had a chance to talk with my father and put his mind to rest."

Manuel was about to say something else when Brubaker interrupted him, in what was becoming an annoying habit. "Look gentlemen," he said in a businesslike manner, "we have chartered a plane that leaves at four p.m. for Buenos Aires. Then we're booked on the seven o'clock Pan Am flight to New York." He looked at his watch. "It's now a little after two. So if there are things for me to know before we leave Salta, we don't have much time to spare. What do you say we head downstairs for lunch and kill two birds with one stone – get something to eat and have an exchange of information?"

I wasn't about to argue. "Sure thing Brubaker," I said. "Let's go."

We walked down the stairs to the main lobby. Waiting for us were Alfredo and the others who had been with Brubaker earlier. Brubaker had reserved two tables in the hotel dining room and led the way in. There wasn't much of a crowd, but Brubaker nonetheless had chosen two tables in a distant corner where our conversation had fewer chances of being overheard.

Each table had room for five. I insisted that Alfredo be seated with us. "Look Corbett, Brubaker said, "We appreciate the help your friend has provided us, but he *is* a journalist. And what we'll be talking about is pretty sensitive stuff."

He had a point. But I owed Alfredo. And I trusted his judgment – and his discretion. If there was a story to be told, no matter how "sensitive" and he thought it should be told, then I was okay with that no matter how much Brubaker might object. "Listen Brubaker. If Alfredo doesn't sit with us, then we'll just have a nice *quiet* lunch and be on our way."

Brubaker had the same intense blue eyes as Dwight Whalen. He gave me an icy stare and for a moment I thought he even might take a swing at me. But his colleague put a hand on his arm and whispered something in his ear. Whatever he said, it seemed to work in my favor. Brubaker shrugged his shoulders and said, "All right Corbett. All right." Then, turning to Alfredo, he said, "But what we talk about is strictly *off the record*. Understood? If you write something, no names. Agreed?"

Alfredo gave him a broad smile. "Of course Mister Brubaker. Of course."

With that out of the way, the five of us took our seats. We occupied the table in the corner while the other four men took the one next to us closer to the center of the room, forming an extra buffer between us and others who were dining.

A waiter came to take our order and we all asked for the standard steak, potatoes, and a salad. When he asked if we wanted wine to accompany our meal, Brubaker spoke for all of us and said only water. Alfredo gave me a look that said, *What do you expect from an up-tight bureaucrat?* I gave him a quick grin but also had to admit that Brubaker had a point. While Manuel and I were refreshed, we were still feeling the effects of our ordeal. And wine, while welcome, might not have the right effect under the circumstances. There would be time for relaxation and celebration once we were safely on our way home.

As soon as the waiter left our table, Brubaker, who was sitting to my right, said in a low voice, "Okay Corbett. It's time to start talking. How did you manage to rescue Fernández here?" he asked, pointing a thumb in the direction of Manuel, who was to my left.

Before I answered, I thought about telling Brubaker to call me Frank. But then decided I didn't have any reason to put our relationship on a friendly basis. If he wanted to keep things formal and businesslike, I would play by his rules.

"Well sir that is a long story." I then took him through all that had happened, from the time Elena Fernández hired me to find her brother to when Manuel and I walked into the Hotel Salta. Brubaker was a good listener. He let me lay out the story with only occasional interruptions. I saw his eyes widen when I told him about contacting the ERP and the help they had provided, without which, I observed, I probably never would have found Manuel. He didn't comment but I saw him shift in his chair. When I got to the part about killing Smallwood and the muscleman, my voice wavered, but I said I was acting in self-defense and Brubaker gave me a small nod of agreement. While he listened intently, his colleague had taken out a small notebook and was scribbling in it as I spoke.

When I got to the part about my fight with Dwight, Brubaker asked, "So you don't know whether or not he survived?"

I shrugged. "I doubt that he did. The current was powerful and he was right in the middle of it. And I did see him go under. In addition, I was closer to solid ground than he was and I wouldn't have made it if I hadn't been rescued." I then explained how Martín and Carlos had fished me out of the raging water.

Brubaker considered my argument. "You're probably right Corbett, but…" He let it trail off.

Our food had arrived while I was briefing Brubaker. We took a break to eat, mostly in silence. After the plates were cleared I finished my story. As I had spun my tale, I looked directly at Brubaker, but out of the corner of my eye I could see Alfredo hanging on every word. Once in a while he shook his head in what I took to be amazement. On several occasions I heard him let out a loud exhalation. Manuel remained silent.

I couldn't read Brubaker's expression when I finished. He maintained his businesslike approach, but I thought I saw a glint of admiration for what I had accomplished peeking through the stolid exterior.

"Now that you've heard our story," I said, nodding towards Manuel, "How about telling us yours? How did you end up here in Salta?"

He gave me a tight smile. "Fair enough Corbett. Fair enough" He took a few sips of the coffee he had ordered, taking time to gather his thoughts. I guessed he was trying to decide what to tell us and what to leave out. "The truth is, we've had our suspicions about Dwight Whalen – and Smallwood - for some time. I can't go into the details, but six months ago we got information that the two were involved in some 'off the books activity' that merited looking into. Since then, we've had both men under surveillance. Again, I can't tell you how, but we also received word about their plan to kidnap young Fernández here," he said, nodding in Manuel's direction, "and use him as a pawn to force his father to help them in their drug smuggling operation. Unfortunately, we weren't notified in time to stop the kidnapping from taking place. But…"

I interrupted. "And after Manuel disappeared, you sent men to Durham to try to find out where he might have been taken." That explained the two mysterious government agents who had interrogated Manuel's roommate. "And then you found out that I was on the case and you had them – or another pair – follow me to Durham to see if I might turn up something."

A flicker of amusement crossed Brubaker's face. "I can neither confirm nor deny your speculations Corbett," he said. "But you're correct in assuming that we knew you had been hired to try to find Manuel Fernández."

"So you were following me to see what I might turn up," I said. "But if that were the case, how did it work out that you arrived in Salta after I had been taken as well?"

"That's a good question Corbett," Brubaker said. I noticed that now his colleague was no longer taking notes but instead was just listening with his hands folded while his superior had the floor. "It was essentially a question of manpower. We could keep a watch on you in D.C., but when you flew to Argentina we didn't have the resources available to shadow you. One of our agents did spot you when you arrived at Ezeiza and saw you meet with Billinghurst here," he said, nodding in Alfredo's direction, "who is a pretty well-known personality. When we got that information in Washington, we figured it wouldn't be too hard to locate you through your connection with your Argentine friend. We also were beginning to put two and two together and suspect that Dwight Whalen was in Argentina overseeing the whole kidnapping scheme. But by the time we could assemble our team, clear everything with the Argentine officials, and fly to Buenos Aires, you already had left for Salta. Luckily, we were able to convince Billinghurst that we were on your side and he told us where you were. We got here yesterday afternoon and of course when we checked the hotel and they told us you hadn't been seen for a couple of days, well naturally we thought the worst. If you hadn't shown up when you did, we were planning a search – but without any clues as to your whereabouts…" He shrugged and raised his eyebrows.

I let all that he had told me sink in. What he had left out of his account was exactly *how* he had gotten the information about Manuel's kidnapping and my being hired to try to find him. The only explanation I could come up with was that Fred Matthews had somehow gotten the word to somebody – or to Brubaker himself. I couldn't imagine my father having been the source, although he might have done it to try to protect me. For a moment I was angry. But then realized that whoever had passed the word had done me a favor. Without Brubaker's promised help, I didn't like my chances of getting out of Argentina without -at the least - having to answer a lot of questions.

"What can you tell me about this task force of yours Brubaker?"

He looked down at his hands and took a deep breath. I could tell he was reluctant to answer. "Why do you want to know?" he asked.

"Look Brubaker. The only reason I'm sitting here talking to you is because Alfredo vouched for you." He was about to interrupt but I cut him off before he could. "I know. I know," I said, waving my hand dismissively. "You showed me your credentials and they looked genuine enough. But they didn't say what agency you work for. And after my recent experience with Smallwood and Whalen, I'm not all that confident that U.S. government officials are telling me the truth. So a little more information about you and your friends here," I said, pointing to the guys at the other table," would help to set my mind at ease that we are indeed in good hands."

I was gilding the lily a bit. I was pretty confident that Brubaker and his crew were who they said they were. But I was curious and wanted as much information as I could get about everything connected to the case.

Brubaker looked annoyed, but after exchanging glances with his note-taking colleague, said in a low voice. "Okay Corbett. I guess you've earned it. But listen. And you too Billinghurst. This *really* has to be off the record. If word gets out about who we are and what our assignment is then a lot of time and tax-payer money will have been wasted. Not to mention the fact that a serious threat to national security will become even more dangerous. So are we agreed?" he asked. "Not a word to anyone?"

We all nodded in unison. Speaking for the three of us, I said. "Don't worry Brubaker. We'll keep whatever you tell us confidential."

He looked skeptical but leaned forward and began to talk. "The problem of drugs like cocaine, heroin, and marijuana being introduced into the United States has not been a top governmental priority until recently. Over the past several years, however, there has been a dramatic uptick in supply, most of which comes from Latin America, and demand, which, unfortunately, is growing by leaps and bounds in our country. Of course, the current administration has been busy with things like ending the Vietnam War, trying to establish détente with the Soviet Union, improving relations with Communist China, and working for peace in the Middle East. But now the president has decided that the drug problem represents an increasing national security threat and needs to be addressed forcefully."

Brubaker paused for a minute and I had a mental image of Dwight Whalen lecturing me on the current political situation in Latin America. He took a sip of water and continued. "Last year, the White House decided to create a special inter-agency task force to confront the issue of drug trafficking and do what it could to curtail it. At the moment, there is no single agency dedicated to drug enforcement although word is that one will soon be created. Until that happens, we have the assignment."

"Why inter-agency?" I asked, although I thought I knew the answer.

"The problem has too many components to be handled by any single existing department. The FBI is supposed to stick to the domestic side of things, the CIA and the State Department the foreign angle. Customs and Immigration should be a major player, but it is often outmanned and out-resourced – and besides, most of the drugs are smuggled in where we have no border controls. Treasury has a role, but it's mostly in trying to prevent the laundering of dirty money. The Pentagon is involved, but they have a lot on their plate. So the only solution is to bring together elements of all these departments to unite in a common effort. And so here we are," he said with the hint of a smile.

"And that's why your ID is generic," I said.

"Exactly," Brubaker responded.

I thought back to what Fred Matthews had told me about the rivalries and tensions between the FBI and the CIA. "And how is the inter-agency idea working out?" I said, my tone probably a bit more provocative than I had intended and with a touch of sarcasm in it.

Brubaker didn't take the bait. "Actually it's going pretty well, especially when you consider the fact we were formed less than a year ago."

I figured Brubaker had told us as much as he was going to and decided not to press it further. I saw him look at his watch. "It's three thirty," he said. "We need to wrap things up here and get you to the airport. But before we go, what can you tell us about the hacienda where you were held hostage? We sure would like to check it out."

"Well I was unconscious when I was taken there and Manuel was heavily sedated. But if you give me a map, I think I can give you a general idea of where it might be."

Brubaker motioned to one of the dark-haired men at the next table, who apparently had overheard us. He reached down into a briefcase at his side and pulled out a map of the area, which he brought to me. I unfolded it and took a minute to orient myself. It was a good map, with lots of detail. I located the road into the western hills that the ERP had pointed me to and traced it with my right index finger. I found what I thought was the stream we had followed where it intersected with that road, which must have been the one we had taken that morning back to Salta. The map also showed the line of hills that ran parallel to the stream and again tracing with my finger, I estimated the distance we had traveled to the point where we had crossed the ridge.

The map, for all its detail, did not show any secondary road that led from the one we had been on this morning to where I thought the hacienda was located. But it was the best I could do. Jabbing the map with my index finger, I said, "I can't be one hundred percent positive Brubaker, but I think the hacienda must be about here," indicating a spot to the south of the line of hills we had crossed.

I also gave him a description of Karl Schussler. I hoped they could nab him, but chances were he was long gone. I resisted the temptation to volunteer to stay on to hunt him down. I owed him a punch in the jaw. But at least I had the satisfaction of knowing that he would be a marked man from now on.

As Brubaker called the waiter over and paid the bill, I began to consider what he and his crew were up against. He had it right. The demand for hard drugs was growing and so was the supply. Inadvertently, I had helped put the finish to Dwight Whalen and his scheme. *But how many others were out there?* There were probably hundreds if not thousands, planning to cash in on an increasingly lucrative business. And they could be anywhere – in big cities, small towns, jungle hideaways, or remote haciendas in the north of Argentina. I hoped there were not too many like Smallwood and Dwight, supposedly on the side of truth, justice, and the American way, but easily corrupted by the dream of easy money. Brubaker and his agency had their hands full and I didn't envy them the challenges that lay ahead.

Forty Two

Brubaker kept his word. The three of us – Manuel, Alfredo, and I – were taken to the Salta airport, where we boarded a small jet that got us to Ezeiza in plenty of time to catch the Pan Am flight to New York. He had left two of his agents behind to work in Salta with the two dark-haired men, who were, as I suspected, Argentines, to try to locate the hacienda and follow whatever leads might develop. He and his note-taking pal, who was a guy named Ellison, would accompany us all the way to Washington.

Before Brubaker escorted us through immigration, I had a moment alone with Alfredo in a corner of the main hall. "Thanks *amigo*," I said, "I owe you big time."

He gave me his big smile. "Not at all Frank. Nothing like a little excitement to break up the monotony."

"Yeah. Some monotony!" Then I remembered. "Say, is the story on López Rega out yet?"

"It appears tomorrow - and it's going to be a bombshell." He saw the look of concern on my face. "Nothing I can't handle Frank. There's no need to worry."

I wasn't at all sure about that, but let it pass. "What about my little adventure? Am I going to see my face on the cover of *Chispa*?"

He paused for a moment. "It's a hell of a story Frank. And you *are* a hero. Just think of it, taking out a bent CIA man and a corrupt State Department official while rescuing the son of an Argentine diplomat. You'd become an instant celebrity."

I could feel the color rise in my cheeks. "Listen Alfredo, I appreciate the sentiments, but…"

He interrupted me. "Put your mind at rest Frank. Although it goes against all my journalistic instincts, I'm going to put a lid on the story for the moment. There are too many complications. Besides, the full story would have to include your contacts with the ERP, which, given my role, could prove – how should I put it? – a little dicey for me if it were to appear in print. And I *did* promise Brubaker I would keep what he had to say off the record. Ordinarily, that kind of a promise can be a bit flexible, but in this case I think I'll stick to it."

"Thanks Alfredo," I said, breathing a sigh of relief. "I just wouldn't feel comfortable if I became some kind of press sensation. And while knocking off two U.S. government employees might play well in Argentina, I'm not so sure how it would go over back home. But I do feel bad that, given all you've done for me, you don't get something out of it."

He gave me a grin and a wink. "Don't forget Frank. I said I was going to hold off *for the moment*. That doesn't mean that I won't write something about all this in the future – provided, of course, I get the go ahead from you. I mean, this is a story that will make a splash whenever it appears."

I grinned back. "It's a deal Alfredo. Maybe after the dust has settled. In the meantime," I said, "let's keep in touch."

"Sure thing Frank, sure thing," he said, enveloping me in his powerful *abrazo* as we exchanged hearty pats on the back. "And *buena suerte*. I think you have found your calling."

"I think you are right. And good luck to you. And once again, thanks for everything."

Just then, Brubaker came over and took me by the arm. "Come on Corbett. We need to get moving."

The last I saw of Alfredo as Brubaker pulled me towards a door behind the Pan Am ticket counter, he was waving his arms in farewell and I could see his eyes glistening. Tears were forming in my own eyes and I quickly brushed them away.

Still holding my arm as if afraid I might somehow decide to stay in Argentina, Brubaker opened the door behind the counter and we stepped into a small office that reminded me of the one we had used in the Hotel Salta. Manuel was already there as was Ellison, who was talking to a couple of Argentines dressed in blue blazers and had the look of officialdom stamped all over them. Brubaker took over and explained who we were and the special circumstances surrounding our departure. The wheels must have been greased previously because with little discussion the two officials whisked us out of the room and down a corridor that led to the gate area, in the process bypassing immigration and passport control. They accompanied the four of us to the departure gate, where they flashed some credentials to the crew overseeing the boarding process, who then waved us through. Before they let us go, Brubaker shook their hands and thanked them for their assistance. It was all done efficiently and discreetly and I had to admire how Brubaker had handled everything.

We were able to board before most of the other passengers. When we had climbed the steps and reached the plane's door, Brubaker, who was holding our boarding passes, showed them to the stewardess. She gave us the standard smile and welcomed us aboard.

"This way gentlemen," Brubaker said, turning towards the front of the plane and giving us what for him passed as a smile. "Thanks to Señor Fernández we are flying first class. Otherwise, government policy would require that it be strictly coach."

We made our way into the first-class cabin and settled into our seats. Manuel took one next to the window and I sat down next to him. Brubaker and Elllison took the seats opposite us on the other side of the aisle.

In a matter of seconds, a stewardess appeared at my side and asked if we would like something to drink. I looked at Manuel. "What do you say Manuel? Time to celebrate?"

He gave me a smile. "Absolutely Frank. Absolutely."

"Two glasses of champagne please," I told the stewardess. She returned with them in record time. Manuel and I clinked glasses and exchanged toasts to our health, which seemed entirely appropriate. I turned to Brubaker and Ellison to see if they wanted to share in the festivities but they declined mumbling something about agency policy against the public consumption of alcohol. I didn't feel too sorry for them. After all, we *were* in first class.

Once we were airborne, we were served more drinks and then dinner, which, not surprisingly, featured Argentine beef. Manuel and I kept up a steady flow of chatter before, during, and after dinner. We talked mostly about our families. Gradually I steered the conversation in the direction of his sister. He picked up immediately on my interest and as he told me about Elena, I could see a mischievous twinkle in his eye. *Was I that obvious?* I guess I was.

About an hour after dinner, we both ran out of gas simultaneously. It had been a long day and we had been through a lot. Up to this point, we had been operating on adrenaline and nervous energy. Now we could relax. When the stewardess brought us blankets and pillows, we turned off our overhead lights and within seconds Manuel was fast asleep.

I took a few minutes longer. I thought about our arrival in New York. Brubaker had told us the whole Fernández clan would be there to greet us. I think I was looking forward to it as much as Manuel was. I was happy that I would have the pleasure of seeing him reunited with his family and proud that I was going to deliver him back in one piece. And let's admit it - I was especially looking forward to seeing Elena Fernández. As I closed my eyes and drifted off to sleep, I knew that Alfredo was right. I *had* found my calling.

Printed in the United States
By Bookmasters